L.A. CONFIDENTIAL

L.A. CONFIDENTIAL

James Ellroy

ARROW BOOKS

Arrow Books Limited
20 Vauxhall Bridge Road, London SW1V 2SA

An imprint of the Random Century Group

London Melbourne Sydney Auckland
Johannesburg and agencies throughout
the world

First published in Great Britain by Mysterious Press 1990
Arrow edition 1991

Printed and bound in Great Britain by
Cox & Wyman Ltd, Reading, Berks

ISBN 0 09 964930 6

To Mary Doherty Ellroy

A glory that costs everything and means nothing –
Steve Erickson

Prologue

February 21, 1950

An abandoned auto court in the San Berdoo foothills; Buzz Meeks checked in with ninety-four thousand dollars, eighteen pounds of high-grade heroin, a 10-gauge pump, a .38 special, a .45 automatic and a switchblade he'd bought off a pachuco at the border – right before he spotted the car parked across the line: Mickey Cohen goons in an LAPD unmarked, Tijuana cops standing by to bootjack a piece of his goodies, dump his body in the San Ysidro River.

He'd been running a week; he'd spent fifty-six grand staying alive: cars, hideouts at four and five thousand a night – risk rates – the innkeepers knew Mickey C. was after him for heisting his dope summit and his woman, the L.A. Police wanted him for killing one of their own. The Cohen contract kiboshed an outright dope sale – nobody could move the shit for fear of reprisals; the best he could do was lay it off with Doc Englekling's sons – Doc would freeze it, package it, sell it later and get him his percentage. Doc used to work with Mickey and had the smarts to be afraid of the prick; the brothers, charging fifteen grand, sent him to the El Serrano Motel and were setting up his escape. Tonight at dusk, two men – wetback runners – would drive him to a beanfield, shoot him to Guatemala City via white powder airlines. He'd have twenty-odd pounds of Big H working for him stateside – if *he* could trust Doc's boys and *they* could trust the runners.

Meeks ditched his car in a pine grove, hauled his suitcase out, scoped the setup:

The motel was horseshoe-shaped, a dozen rooms, foothills against the back of them – no rear approach possible.

The courtyard was loose gravel covered with twigs,

paper debris, empty wine bottles – footsteps would crunch, tires would crack wood and glass.

There was only one access – the road he drove in on – reconnoiterers would have to trek thick timber to take a potshot.

Or they could be waiting in one of the rooms.

Meeks grabbed the 10-gauge, started kicking in doors. One, two, three, four – cobwebs, rats, bathrooms with plugged-up toilets, rotted food, magazines in Spanish – the runners probably used the place to house their spics en route to the slave farms up in Kern County. Five, six, seven, bingo on that – Mex families huddled on mattresses, scared of a white man with a gun, 'There, there' to keep them pacified. The last string of rooms stood empty; Meeks got his satchel, plopped it down just inside unit 12: front/courtyard view, a mattress on box springs spilling kapok, not bad for a last American flop.

A cheesecake calendar tacked to the wall; Meeks turned to April and looked for his birthday. A Thursday – the model had bad teeth, looked good anyway, made him think of Audrey: ex-stripper, ex-Mickey inamorata; the reason he killed a cop, took down the Cohen/Dragna 'H' deal. He flipped through to December, cut odds on whether he'd survive the year and got scared: gut flutters, a vein on his forehead going tap, tap, tap, making him sweat.

It got worse – the heebie-jeebies. Meeks laid his arsenal on a window ledge, stuffed his pockets with ammo: shells for the .38, spare clips for the automatic. He tucked the switchblade into his belt, covered the back window with the mattress, cracked the front window for air. A breeze cooled his sweat; he looked out at spic kids chucking a baseball.

He stuck there. Wetbacks congregated outside: pointing at the sun like they were telling time by it, hot for the truck to arrive – stoop labor for three hots and a cot. Dusk came on; the beaners started jabbering. Meeks saw two white men – one fat, one skinny – walk into the courtyard. They waved glad-hander style; the spics waved back. They didn't look like cops or Cohen goons. Meeks stepped outside, his 10-gauge right behind him.

The men waved: big smiles, no harm meant. Meeks checked the road – a green sedan parked crossways, blocking something light blue, too shiny to be sky through fir trees. He caught light off a metallic paint job, snapped: Bakersfield, the meet with the guys who needed time to get the money. *The robin's-egg coupe that tried to broadside him a minute later.*

Meeks smiled: friendly guy, no harm meant. A finger on the trigger; a make on the skinny guy: Mal Lunceford, a Hollywood Station harness bull – he used to ogle the carhops at Scrivener's Drive-in, puff out his chest to show off his pistol medals. The fat man, closer, said, 'We got that airplane waiting.'

Meeks swung the shotgun around, triggered a spread. Fat Man caught buckshot and flew, covering Lunceford – knocking him backward. The wetbacks tore helter-skelter; Meeks ran into the room, heard the back window breaking, yanked the mattress. Sitting ducks: two men, three triple-aught rounds close in.

The two blew up; glass and blood covered three more men inching along the wall. Meeks leaped, hit the ground, fired at three sets of legs pressed together; his free hand flailed, caught a revolver off a dead man's waistband.

Shrieks from the courtyard; running feet on gravel. Meeks dropped the shotgun, stumbled to the wall. Over to the men, tasting blood – point-blank head shots.

Thumps in the room; two rifles in grabbing range. Meeks yelled, 'We got him!', heard answering whoops, saw arms and legs coming out the window. He picked up the closest piece and let fly, full automatic: trapped targets, plaster chips exploding, dry wood igniting.

Over the bodies, into the room. The front door stood open; his pistols were still on the ledge. A strange thump sounded; Meeks saw a man spread prone – aiming from behind the mattress box.

He threw himself to the floor, kicked, missed. The man got off a shot – close; Meeks grabbed his switchblade,

5

leaped, stabbed: the neck, the face, the man screaming, shooting – wide ricochets. Meeks slit his throat, crawled over and toed the door shut, grabbed the pistols and just plain breathed.

The fire spreading: cooking up bodies, fir pines; the front door his only way out. *How many more men standing trigger?*

Shots.

From the courtyard: heavy rounds knocking out wall chunks. Meeks caught one in the leg; a shot grazed his back. He hit the floor, the shots kept coming, the door went down – he was smack in the crossfire.

No more shots.

Meeks tucked his guns under his chest, spread himself dead-man style. Seconds dragged; four men walked in holding rifles. Whispers: 'Dead meat' – 'Let's be reeel careful' – 'Crazy Okie fuck.' Through the doorway, Mal Lunceford not one of them, footsteps.

Kicks in his side, hard breathing, sneers. A foot went under him. A voice said, 'Fat fucker.'

Meeks jerked the foot; the foot man tripped backward. Meeks spun around shooting – close range, all hits. Four men went down; Meeks got a topsy-turvy view: the courtyard, Mal Lunceford turning tail. Then, behind him, 'Hello, lad.'

Dudley Smith stepped through flames, dressed in a fire department greatcoat. Meeks saw his suitcase – ninety-four grand, dope – over by the mattress. 'Dud, you came prepared.'

'Like the Boy Scouts, lad. And have you a valediction?'

Suicide: heisting a deal Dudley S. watchdogged. Meeks raised his guns; Smith shot first. Meeks died – thinking the El Serrano Motel looked just like the Alamo.

Part One

Bloody Christmas

Chapter One

Bud White in an unmarked, watching the '1951' on the City Hall Christmas tree blink. The back seat was packed with liquor for the station party; he'd scrounged merchants all day, avoiding Parker's dictate: married men had the 24th and Christmas off, all duty rosters were bachelors only, the Central detective squad was detached to round up vagrants: the chief wanted local stumblebums chilled so they wouldn't crash Mayor Bowron's lawn party for under-privileged kids and snarf up all the cookies. Last Christmas, some crazy nigger whipped out his wang, pissed in a pitcher of lemonade earmarked for some orphanage brats and ordered Mrs. Bowron to 'Strap on, bitch.' William H. Parker's first yuletide as chief of the Los Angeles Police Department was spent transporting the mayor's wife to Central Receiving for sedation, and now, a year later, *he* was paying the price.

The back seat, booze-packed, had his spine jammed to Jell-O. Ed Exley, the assistant watch commander, was a straight arrow who might get uppity over a hundred cops juicing in the muster room. And Johnny Stompanato was twenty minutes late.

Bud turned on his two-way. A hum settled: shopliftings, a liquor store heist in Chinatown. The passenger door opened; Johnny Stompanato slid in.

Bud turned on the dash light. Stompanato said, 'Holiday cheers. And where's Stensland? I've got stuff for both of you.'

Bud sized him up. Mickey Cohen's bodyguard was a month out of work – Mickey went up on a tax beef, Fed time, three to seven at McNeil Island. Johnny Stomp was back to home manicures and pressing his own pants. 'It's *Sergeant* Stensland. He's rousting vags and the payoff's the same anyway.'

'Too bad. I like Dick's style. You know that, *Wendell*.'

Cute Johnny: guinea handsome, curls in a tight pompadour. Bud heard he was hung like a horse and padded his basket on top of it. 'Spill what you got.'

'Dick's better at the amenities than you, *Officer White*.'

'You got a hard-on for me, or you just want small talk?'

'I've got a hard-on for Lana Turner, you've got a hard-on for wife beaters. I also heard you're a real sweetheart with the ladies and you're not too selective as far as looks are concerned.'

Bud cracked his knuckles. 'And you fuck people up for a living, and all the money Mickey gives to charity won't make him no better than a dope pusher and a pimp. So my fucking complaints for hardnosing wife beaters don't make me you. *Capisce*, shitbird?'

Stompanato smiled – nervous; Bud looked out the window. A Salvation Army Santa palmed coins from his kettle, an eye on the liquor store across the street. Stomp said, 'Look, you want information and I need money. Mickey and Davey Goldman are doing time, and Mo Jahelka's looking after things while they're gone. Mo's diving for scraps, and he's got no work for me. Jack Whalen wouldn't hire me on a bet and there was no goddamn envelope from Mickey.'

'No envelope? Mickey went up flush. I heard he got back the junk that got clouted off his deal with Jack D.'

Stompanato shook his head. 'You heard wrong. Mickey got the heister, but that junk is nowhere and the guy got away with a hundred and fifty grand of Mickey's money. So, Officer White, *I* need money. And if your snitch fund's still green, I'll get you some fucking-A collars.'

'Go legit, Johnny. Be a white man like me and Dick Stensland.'

Stomp snickered – it came off weak. 'A key thief for twenty or a shoplifter who beats his wife for thirty. Go for the quick thrill, I saw the guy boosting Ohrbach's on the way over.'

Bud took out a twenty and a ten; Stompanato grabbed them. 'Ralphie Kinnard. He's blond and fat, about forty.

10

He's wearing a suede loafer jacket and gray flannels. I heard he's been beating up his wife and pimping her to cover his poker losses.'

Bud wrote it down. Stompanato said, 'Yuletide cheer, Wendell.'

Bud grabbed necktie and yanked; Stomp banged his head on the dashboard.

'Happy New Year, greaseball.'

Ohrbach's was packed – shoppers swarmed counters and garment racks. Bud elbowed up to floor 3, prime shoplifter turf: jewelry, decanter liquor.

Countertops strewn with watches; cash register lines thirty deep. Bud trawled for blond males, got sideswiped by housewives and kids. Then – a flash view – a blond guy in a suede loafer ducking into the men's room.

Bud shoved over and in. Two geezers stood at urinals; gray flannels hit the toilet stall floor. Bud squatted, looked in – bingo on hands fondling jewelry. The oldsters zipped up and walked out. Bud rapped on the stall. 'Come on, it's St. Nick.'

The door flew open; a fist flew out. Bud caught it flush, hit a sink, tripped. Cufflinks in his face, Kinnard speed-balling. Bud got up and chased.

Through the door, shoppers blocking him; Kinnard ducking out a side exit. Bud chased – over, down the fire escape. The lot was clean: no cars hauling, no Ralphie. Bud ran to his prowler, hit the two-way. '4A31 to dispatcher, requesting.'

Static, then: 'Roger, 4A31.'

'Last known address. White male, first name Ralph, last name Kinnard. I guess that's K-I-N-N-A-R-D. Move it, huh?'

The man rogered; Bud threw jabs: bam-bam-bam-bam-bam. The radio crackled: '4A31, roger your request.'

'4A31, roger.'

'Positive on Kinnard, Ralph Thomas, white male, DOB – '

'Just the goddamn address, I told you – '

11

The dispatcher blew a raspberry. 'For your Christmas stocking, shitbird. The address is 1486 Evergreen, and I hope you – '

Bud flipped off the box, headed east to City Terrace. Up to forty, hard on the horn, Evergreen in five minutes flat. The 12, 1300 blocks whizzed by; 1400 – vet's prefabs – leaped out.

He parked, followed curb plates to 1486 – a stucco job with a neon Santa sled on the roof. Lights inside; a prewar Ford in the driveway. Through a plate-glass window: Ralphie Kinnard browbeating a woman in a bathrobe.

The woman was puff-faced, thirty-fivish. She backed away from Kinnard; her robe fell open. Her breasts were bruised, her ribs lacerated.

Bud walked back for his cuffs, saw the two-way light blinking and rogered. '4A31 responding.'

'Roger, 4A31, on an APO. Two patrolmen assaulted outside a tavern at 1990 Riverside, six suspects at large. They've been ID'd from their license plates and other units have been alerted.'

Bud got tingles. 'Bad for ours?'

'That's a roger. Go to 5314 Avenue 53, Lincoln Heights. Apprehend Dinardo, D-I-N-A-R-D-O, Sanchez, age twenty-one, male Mexican.'

'Roger, and you send a prowler to 1486 Evergreen. White male suspect in custody. I won't be there, but they'll see him. Tell them I'll write it up.'

'Book at Hollenbeck Station?'

Bud rogered, grabbed his cuffs. Back to the house and an outside circuit box – switches tapped until the lights popped off. Santa's sled stayed lit; Bud grabbed an outlet cord and yanked. The display hit the ground: exploding reindeer.

Kinnard ran out, tripped over Rudolph. Bud cuffed his wrists, bounced his face on the pavement. Ralphie yelped and chewed gravel; Bud launched his wife beater spiel. 'You'll be out in a year and a half, and I'll know when. I'll find out who your parole officer is and get cozy with him. I'll visit you and say hi. You touch her again I'm

12

gonna know, and I'm gonna get you violated on a kiddie raper beef. You know what they do to kiddie rapers up at Quentin? Huh? The Pope a fuckin' guinea?'

Lights went on – Kinnard's wife was futzing with the fuse box. She said, 'Can I go to my mother's?'

Bud emptied Ralphie's pockets – keys, a cash roll. 'Take the car and get yourself fixed up.'

Kinnard spat teeth. Mrs. Ralphie grabbed the keys and peeled a ten-spot. Bud said, 'Merry Christmas, huh?'

Mrs. Ralphie blew a kiss and backed the car out, wheels over blinking reindeer.

Avenue 53 – Code 2 no siren. A black-and-white just beat him; two blues and Dick Stensland got out and huddled.

Bud tapped his horn; Stensland came over. 'Who's there, partner?'

Stensland pointed to a shack. 'The one guy on the air, maybe more. It was maybe four spics, two white guys did our guys in. Brownell and Helenowski. Brownell's maybe got brain damage, Helenowski maybe lost an eye.'

'Big maybes.'

Stens reeked: Listerine, gin. 'You want to quibble?'

Bud got out of the car. 'No quibble. How many in custody?'

'Goose. We get the first collar.'

'Then tell the blues to stay put.'

Stens shook his head. 'They're pals with Brownell. They want a piece.'

'Nix, this is ours. We get them booked, we write it up and make the party by watch change. I got three cases: Walker Black, Jim Beam and Cutty.'

'Exley's assistant watch commander. He's a nosebleed, and you can bet he don't approve of on-duty imbibing.'

'Yeah, and Frieling's *the* watch boss, and he's a fucking drunk like you. So don't worry about Exley. And I got a report to write up first – so let's just do it.'

Stens laughed. 'Aggravated assault on a woman? What's that – six twenty-three point one in the California Penal

13

Code? So I'm a fucking drunk and you're a fucking do-gooder.'

'Yeah, and you're ranking. So now?'

Stens winked; Bud walked flank – up to the porch, gun out. The shack was curtained dark; Bud caught a radio ad: Felix the Cat Chevrolet. Dick kicked the door in.

Yells, a Mex man and woman hauling. Stens aimed head high; Bud blocked his shot. Down a hallway, Bud close in, Stens wheezing, knocking over furniture. The kitchen – the spics dead-ended at a window.

They turned, raised their hands: a pachuco punk, a pretty girl maybe six months pregnant.

The boy kissed the wall – a pro friskee. Bud searched him: Dinardo Sanchez ID, chump change. The girl boo-hooed; sirens scree'd outside. Bud turned Sanchez around, kicked him in the balls. 'For ours, Pancho. And you got off easy.'

Stens grabbed the girl. Bud said, 'Go somewhere, sweetheart. Before my friend checks your green card.'

'Green card' spooked her – *madre mia! Madre mia!* Stens shoved her to the door; Sanchez moaned. Bud saw blues swarm the driveway. 'We'll let them take Pancho in.'

Stens caught some breath. 'We'll give him to Brownell's pals.'

Two rookie types walked in – Bud saw his out. 'Cuff him and book him. APO and resisting arrest.'

The rookies dragged Sanchez out. Stens said, 'You and women. What's next? Kids and dogs?'

Mrs. Ralphie – all bruised up for Christmas. 'I'm working on it. Come on, let's move that booze. Be nice and I'll let you have your own bottle.'

Chapter Two

Preston Exley yanked the dropcloth. His guests oohed and ahhed; a city councilman clapped, spilled eggnog on a society matron. Ed Exley thought: this is not a typical policeman's Christmas Eve.

He checked his watch – 8:46 – he had to be at the station by midnight. Preston Exley pointed to the model.

It took up half his den: an amusement park filled with papier-mâché mountains, rocket ships, Wild West towns. Cartoon creatures at the gate: Moochie Mouse, Scooter Squirrel, Danny Duck – Raymond Dieterling's brood – featured in the *Dream-a-Dream Hour* and scores of cartoons.

'Ladies and gentlemen, presenting Dream-a-Dreamland. Exley Construction will build it, in Pomona, California, and the opening date will be April 1953. It will be the most sophisticated amusement park in history, a self-contained universe where children of all ages can enjoy the message of fun and goodwill that is the hallmark of Raymond Dieterling, the father of modern animation. Dream-a-Dreamland will feature all your favorite Dieterling characters, and it will be a haven for the young and young at heart.'

Ed stared at his father: fifty-seven coming off forty-five, a cop from a long line of cops holding forth in a Hancock Park mansion, politicos giving up their Christmas Eve at a snap of his fingers. The guests applauded; Preston pointed to a snow-capped mountain. 'Paul's World, ladies and gentlemen. An exact-scale replica of a mountain in the Sierra Nevada. Paul's World will feature a thrilling toboggan ride and a ski lodge where Moochie, Scooter and Danny will perform skits for the whole family. And who is the Paul of Paul's World? Paul was Raymond Dieterling's son, lost tragically as a teenager in 1936, lost

15

in an avalanche on a camping trip – lost on a mountain just like this one here. So, out of tragedy, an affirmation of innocence. And, ladies and gentlemen, every nickel out of every dollar spent at Paul's World will go to the Children's Polio Foundation.'

Wild applause. Preston nodded at Timmy Valburn – the actor who played Moochie Mouse on the *Dream-a-Dream Hour* – always nibbling cheese with his big buck teeth. Valburn nudged the man beside him; the man nudged back.

Art De Spain caught Ed's eye; Valburn kicked off a Moochie routine. Ed steered De Spain to the hallway. 'This is a hell of a surprise, Art.'

'Dieterling's announcing it on the *Dream Hour*. Didn't your dad tell you?'

'No, and I didn't know he knew Dieterling. Did he meet him back during the Atherton case? Wasn't Wee Willie Wennerholm one of Dieterling's kid stars?'

De Spain smiled. 'I was your dad's lowly adjutant then, and I don't think the two great men ever crossed paths. Preston just *knows* people. And by the way, did you spot the mouse man and his pal?'

Ed nodded. 'Who is he?'

Laughter from the den; De Spain steered Ed to the study. 'He's Billy Dieterling, Ray's son. He's a cameraman on *Badge of Honor*, which lauds our beloved LAPD to millions of television viewers each week. Maybe Timmy spreads some cheese on his whatsis before he blows him.'

Ed laughed. 'Art, you're a pisser.'

De Spain sprawled in a chair. 'Eddie, ex-cop to cop, you say words like "pisser" and you sound like a college professor. And you're not really an "Eddie", you're an "Edmund." '

Ed squared his glasses. 'I see avuncular advice coming. Stick in Patrol, because Parker made chief that way. Administrate my way up because I have no command presence.'

'You've got no sense of humor. And can't you get rid

of those specs? Squint or something. Outside of Thad Green, I can't think of one Bureau guy who wears glasses.'

'God, you miss the Department. I think that if you could give up Exley Construction and fifty thousand a year for a spot as an LAPD rookie, you would.'

De Spain lit a cigar. 'Only if your dad came with me.'

'Just like that?'

'Just like that. I was a lieutenant to Preston's inspector, and I'm still a number two man. It'd be nice to be even with him.'

'If you didn't know lumber, Exley Construction wouldn't exist.'

'Thanks. And get rid of those glasses.'

Ed picked up a framed photo: his brother Thomas in uniform – taken the day before he died. 'If you were a rookie, I'd break you for insubordination.'

'You would, too. What did you place on the lieutenant's exam?'

'First out of twenty-three applicants. I was the youngest applicant by eight years, with the shortest time in grade as a sergeant and the shortest amount of time on the Department.'

'And you want the Detective Bureau.'

Ed put the photo down. 'Yes.'

'Then, first you have to figure a year minimum for an opening to come up, then you have to realize that it will probably be a Patrol opening, then you have to realize that a transfer to the Bureau will take years and lots of ass kissing. You're twenty-nine now?'

'Yes.'

'Then you'll be a lieutenant at thirty or thirty-one. Brass that young create resentment. Ed, all kidding aside. You're not one of the guys. You're not a strongarm type. *You're not Bureau*. And Parker as Chief has set a precedent for Patrol officers to go all the way. Think about that.'

Ed said, 'Art, I want to work cases. I'm connected and I won the Distinguished Service Cross, which some people might construe as strongarm. And I will *have* a Bureau appointment.'

De Spain brushed ash off his cummerbund. 'Can we talk turkey, Sunny Jim?'

The endearment rankled. 'Of course.'

'Well . . . you're good, and in time you might be really good. And I don't doubt your killer instinct for a second. But your father was ruthless and likable. And you're not, so . . .'

Ed made fists. 'So, Uncle Arthur? Cop who left the Department for money to cop who never would – what's your advice?'

De Spain flinched. 'So be a sycophant and suck up to the right men. Kiss William H. Parker's ass and pray to be in the right place at the right time.'

'Like you and my father?'

'*Touché*, Sunny Jim.'

Ed looked at his uniform: custom blues on a hanger. Razor-creased, sergeant's stripes, a single hashmark. De Spain said, 'Gold bars soon, Eddie. And braid on your cap. And I wouldn't jerk your chain if I didn't care.'

'I know.'

'And you *are* a goddamned war hero.'

Ed changed the subject. 'It's Christmas. You're thinking about Thomas.'

'I keep thinking I could have told him something. He didn't even have his holster flap open.'

'A purse snatcher with a gun? He couldn't have known.'

De Spain put out his cigar. 'Thomas was a natural, and I always thought he should be telling me things. That's why I tend to spell things out for you.'

'He's twelve years dead and I'll bury him as a policeman.'

'I'll forget you said that.'

'No, remember it. Remember it when I make the Bureau. And when Father offers toasts to Thomas and Mother, don't get maudlin. It ruins him for days.'

De Spain stood up, flushing; Preston Exley walked in with snifters and a bottle.

Ed said, 'Merry Christmas, Father. And congratulations.'

18

Preston poured drinks. 'Thank you. Exley Construction tops the Arroyo Seco Freeway job with a kingdom for a glorified rodent, and I'll never eat another piece of cheese. A toast, gentlemen. To the eternal rest of my son Thomas and my wife Marguerite, to the three of us assembled here.'

The men drank; De Spain fixed refills. Ed offered his father's favorite toast: 'To the solving of crimes that require absolute justice.'

Three more shots downed. Ed said, 'Father, I didn't know you knew Raymond Dieterling.'

Preston smiled. 'I've known him in a business sense for years. Art and I have kept the contract secret at Raymond's request – he wants to announce it on that infantile television program of his.'

'Did you meet him during the Atherton case?'

'No, and of course I wasn't in the construction business then. Arthur, do you have a toast to propose?'

De Spain poured short ones. 'To a Bureau assignment for our soon-to-be lieutenant.'

Laughter, hear-hears. Preston said, 'Joan Morrow was inquiring about your love life, Edmund. I think she's smitten.'

'Do you see a debutante as a cop's wife?'

'No, but I could picture her married to a ranking policeman.'

'Chief of Detectives?'

'No, I was thinking more along the lines of commander of the Patrol Division.'

'Father, Thomas was going to be your chief of detectives, but he's dead. Don't deny me my opportunity. Don't make me live an old dream of yours.'

Preston stared at his son. 'Point taken, and I commend you for speaking up. And granted, that was my original dream. But the truth is that I don't think you have the eye for human weakness that makes a good detective.'

His brother: a math brain crazed for pretty girls. 'And Thomas did?'

'Yes.'

'Father, I would have shot that purse snatcher the second he went for his pocket.'

De Spain said, 'Goddammit'; Preston shushed him. 'That's all right. Edmund, a few questions before I return to my guests. One, would you be willing to plant corroborative evidence on a suspect you knew was guilty in order to ensure an indictment?'

'I'd have to – '

'Answer yes or no.'

'I . . . no.'

'Would you be willing to shoot hardened armed robbers in the back to offset the chance that they might utilize flaws in the legal system and go free?'

'I . . . '

'Yes or no, Edmund.'

'No.'

'And would you be willing to beat confessions out of suspects you knew to be guilty?'

'No.'

'Would you be willing to rig crime scene evidence to support a prosecuting attorney's working hypothesis?'

'No.'

Preston sighed. 'Then for God's sake, stick to assignments where you won't have to make those choices. Use the superior intelligence the good Lord gave you.'

Ed looked at his uniform. 'I'll use that intelligence as a detective.'

Preston smiled. 'Detective or not, you have qualities of persistence that Thomas lacked. You'll excel, my war hero.'

The phone rang; De Spain picked it up. Ed thought of rigged Jap trenches – and couldn't meet Preston's eyes. De Spain said, 'It's Lieutenant Frieling at the station. He said the jail's almost full, and two officers were assaulted earlier in the evening. Two suspects are in custody, with four more outstanding. He said you should clock in early.'

Ed turned back to his father. Preston was down the hall, swapping jokes with Mayor Bowron in a Moochie Mouse hat.

Chapter Three

Press clippings on his corkboard: 'Dope Crusader Wounded in Shootout'; 'Actor Mitchum Seized in Marijuana Shack Raid.' *Hush-Hush* articles, framed on his desk: 'Hopheads Quake When Dope Scourge Cop Walks Tall'; 'Actors Agree: *Badge of Honor* Owes Authenticity to Hard-hitting Technical Advisor.' The *Badge* piece featured a photo: Sergeant Jack Vincennes with the show's star, Brett Chase. The piece did not feature dirt from the editor's private file: Brett Chase as a pedophile with three quashed sodomy beefs.

Jack Vincennes glanced around the Narco pen – deserted, dark – just the light in his cubicle. Ten minutes short of midnight; he'd promised Dudley Smith he'd type up an organized crime report for Intelligence Division; he'd promised Lieutenant Frieling a case of booze for the station party – Hush-Hush Sid Hudgens was supposed to come across with rum but hadn't called. Dudley's report: a favor shot his way because he typed a hundred words a minute; a favor returned tomorrow: a meet with Dud and Ellis Loew, Pacific Dining Car lunch – work on the line, work to earn him juice with the D.A.'s Office. Jack lit a cigarette, read.

Some report: eleven pages long, very verbal, very Dudley. The topic: L.A. mob activity with Mickey Cohen in stir. Jack edited, typed.

Cohen was at McNeil Island Federal Prison: three to seven, income tax evasion. Davey Goldman, Mickey's money man, was there: three to seven, down on six counts of federal tax fraud. Smith predicted possible skirmishing between Cohen minion Morris Jahelka and Jack 'The Enforcer' Whalen; with Mafia overlord Jack Dragna deported, they loomed as the two men most likely to control loansharking, bookmaking, prostitution and the

race wire racket. Smith stated that Jahelka was too ineffec-
tual to require police surveillance; that John Stompanato
and Abe Teitlebaum, key Cohen strongarms, seemed to
have gone legitimate. Lee Vachss, contract trigger
employed by Cohen, was working a religious racket –
selling patent medicines guaranteed to induce mystical
experiences.

Jack kept typing. Dud's take hit wrong: Johnny Stomp
and Kikey Teitlebaum were pure bent – they could never
go pure straight. He fed in a fresh sheet.

A new topic: the February '50 Cohen/Dragna truce
meeting – twenty-five pounds of heroin and a hundred
and fifty grand allegedly stolen. Jack heard rumors: an ex-
cop named Buzz Meeks heisted the summit, took off and
was gunned down near San Bernardino – Cohen goons
and rogue L.A. cops killed him, a Mickey contract: Meeks
stole the Mick blind and fucked his woman. The horse was
supposedly long gone unfound. Dudley's theory: Meeks
buried the money and shit someplace unknown and was
later killed by 'person or persons unknown' – probably a
Cohen gunman. Jack smiled: if LAPD was in on a Meeks
hit, Dud would never implicate the Department – even
in an interdepartmental report.

Next, Smith's summary: with Mickey C. gone, mob
action was at a lull; the LAPD should stay alert for new
faces looking to crash Cohen's old rackets; prostitution
was sticking over the county line – with Sheriff's Department sanction. Jack signed the last page 'Respectfully,
Lieutenant D. L. Smith.'

The phone rang. 'Narcotics, Vincennes.'

'It's me. You hungry?'

Jack kiboshed a temper fit – easy – what Hudgens just
might have on him. 'Sid, you're late. And the party's
already on.'

'I got better than booze. I got cash.'

'Talk.'

'Talk this: Tammy Reynolds, co-star of *Hope's Harvest*,
opens tomorrow citywide. A guy I know just sold her
some reefer, a guaranteed felony pinch. She's tripping the

light fantastic at 2245 Maravilla, Hollywood Hills. You pinch, I do you up feature in the next issue. Because it's Christmas, I leak my notes to Morty Bendish at the *Mirror*, so you make the dailies, too. Plus fifty cash and your rum. Am I fucking Santa Claus?'

'Pictures?'

'In spades. Wear the blue blazer, it goes with your eyes.'

'A hundred, Sid. I need two patrolmen at twenty apiece and a dime for the watch commander at Hollywood Station. And *you* set it up.'

'Jack! It's Christmas!'

'No, it's felony possession of marijuana.'

'Shit. Half an hour?'

'Twenty-five minutes.'

'I'm there, you fucking extortionist.'

Jack hung up, made an X mark on his calendar. Another day, no booze, no hop – four years, two months running.

His stage was waiting – Maravilla cordoned off, two bluesuits by Sid Hudgens' Packard, their black-and-white up on the sidewalk. The street was dark and still; Sid had an arclight set up. They had a view of the Boulevard – Grauman's Chinese included – great for an establishing shot. Jack parked, walked over.

Sid greeted him with cash. 'She's sitting in the dark, goofing on the Christmas tree. The door looks flimsy.'

Jack drew his .38. 'Have the boys put the booze in my trunk. You want Grauman's in the background?'

'I like it! Jackie, you're the best in the West!'

Jack scoped him: scarecrow skinny, somewhere between thirty-five and fifty – keeper of inside dirt supreme. He either knew about 10/24/47 or he didn't; *if* he did, their arrangement was lifetime stuff. 'Sid, when I bring her out the door, I do not want that goddamned baby spot in my eyes. Tell your camera guy that.'

'Consider him told.'

'Good, now count twenty on down.'

Hudgens ticked numbers; Jack walked up and kicked the door in. The arclight snapped on, a living room caught flush: Christmas tree, two kids necking in their undies. Jack shouted 'Police!'; the lovebirds froze; light on a fat bag of weed on the couch.

The girl started bawling; the boy reached for his trousers. Jack put a foot on his chest. 'The hands, slow.'

The boy pressed his wrists together; Jack cuffed him one-handed. The blues stormed in and gathered up evidence; Jack matched a name to the punk: Rock Rockwell, RKO ingenue. The girl ran; Jack grabbed her. Two suspects by the neck – out the door, down the steps.

Hudgens yelled, 'Grauman's while we've still got the light!'

Jack framed them: half-naked pretties in their BVDs. Flashbulbs popped; Hudgens yelled, 'Cut! Wrap it!'

The blues took over: Rockwell and the girl hauled bawling to their prowler. Window lights popped on; rubberneckers opened doors. Jack went back to the house.

A maryjane haze – four years later the shit still smelled good. Hudgens was opening drawers, pulling out dildoes, spiked dog collars. Jack found the phone, checked the address book for pushers – goose egg. A calling card fell out: 'Fleur-de-Lis. Twenty-four Hours a Day – Whatever You Desire.'

Sid started muttering. Jack put the card back. 'Let's hear how it sounds.'

Hudgens cleared his throat. 'It's Christmas morning in the City of the Angels, and while decent citizens sleep the sleep of the righteous, hopheads prowl for marijuana, the weed with roots in Hell. Tammy Reynolds and Rock Rockwell, movie stars with one foot in Hades, toke sweet tea in Tammy's swank Hollywood digs, not knowing they are playing with fire without asbestos gloves, not knowing that a man is coming to put out that fire: the free-wheeling, big-time Big V, celebrity crimestopper Jack Vincennes, the scourge of grasshoppers and junk fiends everywhere. Acting on the tip of an unnamed informant, Sergeant Vincennes, blah, blah, blah. You like it, Jackie?'

'Yeah, it's subtle.'

'No, it's circulation nine hundred thousand and climbing. I think I'll work in you're divorced twice 'cause your wives couldn't stand your crusade and you got your name from an orphanage in Vincennes, Indiana. The Biggg Veeeee.'

His Narco tag: Trashcan Jack – a nod to the time he popped Charlie 'Yardbird' Parker and tossed him into a garbage bin outside the Klub Zamboanga. 'You should beat the drum on *Badge of Honor*. Miller Stanton's my buddy, how I taught Brett Chase to play a cop. Technical advisor kingpin, that kind of thing.'

Hudgens laughed. 'Brett still like them prepubescent?'

'Can niggers dance?'

'South of Jefferson Boulevard only. Thanks for the story, Jack.'

'Sure.'

'I mean it. It's always nice seeing you.'

You fucking cockroach, you're going to wink because you know you can nail me to that moralistic shitbird William H. Parker anytime you want – cash rousts going back to '48, you've probably got documentation worked around to let you off clean and crucify me –

Hudgens winked.

Jack wondered if he had it *all* down on paper.

25

Chapter Four

The party in full swing, the muster room SRO.

An open bar: scotch, bourbon, a case of rum Trashcan Jack Vincennes brought in. Dick Stensland's brew in the water cooler: Old Crow, eggnog mix. A phonograph spewed dirty Christmas carols: Santa and his reindeer fucking and sucking. The floor was packed: nightwatch blues, the Central squad – thirsty from chasing vagrants.

Bud watched the crowd. Fred Turentine tossed darts at Wanted posters; Mike Krugman and Walt Dukeshearer played 'Name That Nigger,' trying to ID Negro mugshots at a quarter a bet. Jack Vincennes was drinking club soda; Lieutenant Frieling was passed out at his desk. Ed Exley tried to quiet the men down, gave up, stuck to the lock-up: logging in prisoners, filing arrest reports.

Almost every man was drunk or working on it.

Almost every man was talking up Helenowski and Brownell, the cop beaters in custody, the two still at large.

Bud stood by the window. Garbled rumors tweaked him: Brownie Brownell had his lip split up through his nose, one of the taco benders chewed off Helenowski's left ear. Dick Stens grabbed a shotgun, went spic hunting. He credited that one: he'd seen Dick carrying an Ithaca pump out to the parking lot.

The noise was getting brutal – Bud walked out to the lot, lounged against a prowler.

A drizzle started up. A ruckus by the jail door – Dick Stens shoving two men inside. A scream; Bud cut odds on Stens finishing out his twenty: with him watchdogging, even money; without him, two to one against. From the muster room: Frank Doherty's tenor, a weepy 'Silver Bells.'

Bud moved away from the music – it made him think of his mother. He lit a cigarette, thought of her anyway.

He'd seen the killing: sixteen years old, helpless to stop it. The old man came home; he must have believed his son's warning: you touch Mother again and I will kill you. Asleep – cuffs on his wrists and ankles, awake – he saw the fuck beat Mother dead with a tire iron. He screamed his throat raw; he stayed cuffed in the room with the body: a week, no water, delirious – he watched his mother rot. A truant officer found him; the L.A. Sheriff's found the old man. The trial, a diminished capacity defense, a plea bargain down to Manslaughter Two. Life imprisonment, the old man paroled in twelve years. His son – Officer Wendell White, LAPD – decided to kill him.

The old man was nowhere.

He'd jumped parole; prowling his L.A. haunts turned up nothing. Bud kept looking, kept waking to the sound of women screaming. He always investigated; it was always just wisps of noise. Once he kicked in a door and found a woman who'd burned her hand. Once he crashed in on a husband and wife making love.

The old man was nowhere.

He made the Bureau, partnered up with Dick Stens. Dick showed him the ropes, heard out his story, told him to pick his shots to get even. Pops would stay nowhere, but thumping wife beaters might drive the nightmares out of his system. Bud picked a great first shot: a domestic squawk, the complainant a longtime punching bag, the arrestee a three-time loser. He detoured on the way to the station, asked the guy if he'd like to tango with a man for a change: no cuffs, a walk on the charge if he won. The guy agreed: Bud broke his nose, his jaw, ruptured his spleen with a dropkick. Dick was right: his bad dreams stopped.

His rep as *the* toughest man in the LAPD grew.

He kept it up; he followed up: intimidation calls if the fuckers got acquitted, welcome home strongarms if they did time and got parole. He forced himself not to take gratitude lays and found women elsewhere. He kept a list of court and parole dates and sent the fuckers postcards at the honor farm; he got hit with excessive-force com-

plaints and toughed them out. Dick Stens made him a
decent detective; now he played nursemaid to his teacher:
keeping him half sober on duty, holding him back when
he got a hard-on to shoot for kicks. He'd learned to keep
himself in check; Stens was now all bad habits: scrounging
at bars, letting stick-up men slide for snitch dope.

The music inside went off key – wrong, not really
music. Bud caught screeches – screams from the jail.

The noise doubled, tripled. Bud saw a stampede:
muster room to cellblock. A flash: Stens going crazy,
booze, a jamboree – bash the cop bashers. He ran over,
hit the door at a sprint.

The catwalk packed tight, cell doors open, lines forming. Exley shouting for order, pressing into the swarm,
getting nowhere. Bud found the prisoner list; checkmarks
after 'Sanchez, Dinardo,' 'Carbijal, Juan,' 'Garcia, Ezekiel,' 'Chasco, Reyes,' 'Rice, Dennis,' 'Valupeyk, Clinton'
– all six cop beaters in custody.

The bums in the drunk cage egged the men on.

Sten hit the #4 cell – waving brass knucks.

Willie Tristano pinned Exley to the wall; Crum Crumley grabbed his keys.

Cops shoved cell to cell. Elmer Lentz, blood splattered,
grinning. Jack Vincennes by the watch commander's office
– Lieutenant Frieling snoring at his desk.

Bud stormed into it.

He caught elbows going in; the men saw who it was
and cleared a path. Stens slid into 3; Bud pushed in. Dick
was working a skinny pachuco – head saps – the kid on
his knees, catching teeth. Bud grabbed Stensland; the
Mex spat blood. 'Heey, Mister White. I knowww you,
puto. You beat up my frien' Caldo 'cause he whipped his
puto wife. She was a fuckin' hooer, *pendejo*. Ain' you got
no fuckin' brains?'

Bud let Stens go; the Mex gave him the finger. Bud
kicked him prone, picked him up by the neck. Cheers,
attaboys, holy fucks. Bud banged the punk's head on the
ceiling; a bluesuit moved in hard. Ed Exley's rich-kid
voice: 'Stop it, Officer – that's an order!'

28

The Mex kicked him in the balls – a dangling shot. Bud keeled into the bars; the kid stumbled out of the cell, smack into Vincennes. Trashcan, aghast – blood on his cashmere blazer. He put the punk down with a left-right; Exley ran out of the cellblock.

Yells, shouts, shrieks: louder than a thousand Code 3 sirens.

Stens whipped out a pint of gin. Bud saw every man there skunked to niggertown forever. Up on his tiptoes, a prime view – Exley dumping booze in the storeroom.

Voices: attaboy, Big Bud. Faces to the voices – skewed, wrong. Exley still dumping, Mr. Teetotaler Witness. Bud ran down the catwalk, locked him in tight.

Chapter Five

Shut into a room eight feet square. No windows, no tele-phone, no intercom. Shelves spilling forms, mops, brooms, a clogged-up sink filled with vodka and rum. The door was steel-reinforced; the liquor stew smelled like vomit. Shouts and thudding sounds boomed through a heat vent.

Ed banged on the door – no response. He yelled into the vent – hot air hit his face. He saw himself pinioned and pick-pocketed, Bureau guys who figured he'd never squeal. He wondered what his father would do.

Time dragged; the jail noise stopped, fired up, stopped, started. Ed banged on the door – no luck. The room went hot; booze stench smothered the air. Ed felt Guadalcanal: hiding from the Japs, bodies piled over him. His uniform was sopping wet; if he shot the lock the bullets could ricochet off the plating and kill him. The beatings had to go wide: an I.A. investigation, civil suits, the grand jury. Police brutality charges; careers flushed down the toilet. Sergeant Edmund J. Exley crucified because he could not maintain order. Ed made a decision: fight back with his brains.

He wrote on the back of official departmental forms – version one, the truth:

A rumor started it: John Helenowski lost an eye. Serge-ant Richard Stensland logged in Rice, Dennis, and Valu-peyk, Clinton – he spread the word. It ignited all at once; Lieutenant Frieling, the watch commander, was asleep, unconscious from drinking alcohol on duty in violation of interdepartmental regulation 4319. Now in charge, Serge-ant E. J. Exley found his office keys misplaced. The bulk of the men attending the station Christmas party stormed the cellblock. The cells containing the six alleged assaulters were opened with the misplaced keys. Sergeant

Exley attempted to relock those cells, but the beatings had already commenced and Sergeant Willis Tristano held Sergeant Exley while Sergeant Walter Crumley stole the spare keys attached to his belt.

Sergeant Exley did not use force to get the spare keys back.

More details:

Stensland going crazy, policemen beating helpless prisoners. Bud White: lifting a squirming man, one hand on his neck.

Sergeant Exley ordering Officer White to stop: Officer White ignoring the order; Sergeant Exley relieved when the prisoner freed himself and eliminated the need for a further confrontation.

Ed winced, kept writing – 12/25/51, the Central Jail assaults in detail. Probable grand jury indictments, interdepartmental trial boards – Chief Parker's prestige ruined. Fresh paper, thoughts of inmate witnesses – mostly drunks – and the fact that virtually every officer had been drinking heavily. *They* were compromised witnesses; *he* was sober, uncompromised, and had made attempts to control the situation. *He* needed a graceful out; the Department needed to save face; the high brass would be grateful to a man who tried to circumvent bad press – who had the foresight to see it coming and plan ahead. He wrote down version two.

A digression on number one, the action shifted to limit the blame to fewer officers: Stensland, Johnny Brownell, Bud White and a handful of other men who'd already earned or were close to their pensions – Krugman, Tucker, Heineke, Huff, Disbrow, Doherty – older fish to throw the D.A.'s Office if indictment fever ran high. A subjective viewpoint, tailored to fit what the drunk tank prisoners saw, the assaulters trying to flee the cellblock and liberate other inmates. The truth twisted a few turns – impossible for other witnesses to disprove. Ed signed it, listened through the vent for version three.

It came slowly. Voices urged 'Stens' to 'wake up for a piece'; White left the cellblock, muttering what a waste it

31

all was. Krugman and Tucker yelled insults; whimpers answered them. No further sound of White or Johnny Brownell; Lentz, Huff, Doherty prowling the catwalk. Sobs, *Madre mia* over and over.

6:14 A.M.

Ed wrote out number three: no whimpers, no *madre mia*, the cop beaters inciting other inmates. He wondered how his father would rate the crimes: brother officers assaulted, the assaulters ravaged. Which required absolute justice?

The vent noise dwindled; Ed tried to sleep and couldn't; a key went in the door.

Lieutenant Frieling – pale, trembling. Ed nudged him aside, walked down the corridor.

Six cells wide open – the walls slick with blood. Juan Carbijal on his bunk, a shirt under his head soaked red. Clinton Valupeyk washing blood off his face with toilet water. Reyes Chasco one giant contusion; Dennis Rice working his fingers – swollen blue, broken. Dinardo Sanchez and Ezekiel Garcia curled up together by the drunk cage.

Ed called for ambulances. The words 'Prison Ward, County General' almost made him retch.

Chapter Six

Dudley Smith said, 'You're not eating, lad. Did a late night with your chums spoil your appetite?'

Jack looked at his plate: T-bone, baked potato, asparagus. 'I always order large when the D.A.'s Office picks up the tab. Where's Loew? I want him to see what he's buying.'

Smith laughed; Jack eyed the cut of his suit: baggy, good camouflage – make me a stage Irishman, cover my .45 automatic, knuckle dusters and sap. 'What's Loew have in mind?'

Dudley checked his watch. 'Yes, thirty-odd minutes of amenities should be a sufficient prelude to business on our grand savior's birthday. Lad, what Ellis wants is to be district attorney of our fair city, then governor of California. He's been a deputy D.A. for eight years, he ran for D.A. in '48 and lost, there's an off-year election coming up in March of '53, and Ellis thinks he can win. He's a vigorous prosecutor of criminal scum, he's a grand friend to the Department, and despite his Hebraic genealogy I'm fond of him and think he'll make a splendid district attorney. And, lad, you can help elect him. And make yourself a very valuable friend.'

The Mex he'd duked out – the whole deal might go wide. 'I might need a favor pretty soon.'

'One which he'll supply willingly, lad.'

'He wants me to run bag?'

' "Bagman" is a colloquialism I find offensive, lad. "Reciprocity of friendship" is a more suitable phrase, especially given the splendid connections you have. But money is at the root of Mr. Loew's request, and I'd be remiss in not stating that at the outset.'

Jack pushed his plate aside. 'Loew wants me to shake down the *Badge of Honor* guys. Campaign contributions.'

'Yes, and to keep that damnable *Hush-Hush* scandal rag off his back. And since reciprocity is our watchword here, he has specific favors to grant in return.'

'Such as?'

Smith lit a cigarette. 'Max Peltz, the producer of the show, has had tax trouble for years, and Loew will see to it that he never stands another audit. Brett Chase, whom you have so brilliantly taught to portray a policeman, is a degenerate pederast, and Loew will never prosecute him. Loew will contribute D.A.'s Bureau files to the show's story editor and you will be rewarded thusly: Sergeant Bob Gallaudet, the D.A.'s Bureau whip, is going to law school, doing well and will be joining the D.A.'s Office as a prosecutor once he passes the bar. You will then be given the chance to assume his old position – along with a lieutenancy. Lad, does my proposal impress you?'

Jack took a smoke from Dudley's pack. 'Boss, you know I'd never leave Narco and you know I'm gonna say yes. And I just figured out that Loew's gonna show up, give me a thank-you and not stay for dessert. So yes.'

Dudley winked; Ellis Loew slid into the booth. 'Gentlemen, I'm sorry I'm so late.'

Jack said, 'I'll do it.'

'Oh? Lieutenant Smith has explained the situation to you?'

Dudley said, 'Some lads don't require detailed explanations.'

Loew fingered his Phi Beta chain. 'Thank you then, Sergeant. And if I can help you in any way, *any way at all*, don't hesitate to call me.'

'I won't. Dessert, sir?'

'I would like to stay, but I have depositions waiting for me. We'll break bread another time, I'm sure.'

'Whatever you need, Mr. Loew.'

Loew dropped a twenty on the table. 'Again, thank you. Lieutenant, I'll talk to you soon. And gentlemen – Merry Christmas.'

Jack nodded; Loew walked off. Dudley said, 'There's more, lad.'

'More work?'

'Of sorts. Are you providing security at Welton Morrow's Christmas party this year?'

His annual gig – a C-note to mingle. 'Yeah, it's tonight. Does Loew want an invitation?'

'Not quite. You did a large favor for Mr. Morrow once, did you not?'

October '47 – too large. 'Yeah, I did.'

'And you're still friendly with the Morrows?'

'In a hired-hand sort of way, sure. Why?'

Dudley laughed. 'Lad, Ellis Loew wants a wife. Preferably a Gentile with a social pedigree. He's seen Joan Morrow at various civic functions and fancies her. Will you play Cupid and ask fair Joan what she thinks of the idea?'

'Dud, are you asking me to get the future L.A. D.A. a fucking date?'

'I am indeed. Do you think Miss Morrow will be amenable?'

'It's worth a try. She's a social climber and she's always wanted to marry well. I don't know about a hebe, though.'

'Yes, lad, there is that. But you'll broach the subject?'

'Sure.'

'Then it's out of our hands. And along those lines – was it bad at the station last night?'

Now he gets to it. 'It was very bad.'

'Do you think it will blow over?'

'I don't know. What about Brownell and Helenowski? How bad did they get it?'

'Superficial contusions, lad. I'd say the payback went a bit further. Did you partake?'

'I got hit, hit back and got out. Is Loew afraid of prosecuting?'

'Only of losing friends if he does.'

'He made a friend today. Tell him he's ahead of the game.'

Jack drove home, fell asleep on the couch. He slept through the afternoon, woke up to the *Mirror* on his porch.

On page four: 'Yuletide Surprise for *Hope's Harvest* co-stars.'

No pix, but Morty Bendish got in the 'Big V' shtick; 'One of his many informants' made it sound like Jack Vincennes had minions prowling, their pockets stuffed with *his* money – it was well known that the Big V financed his dope crusade with his own salary. Jack clipped the article, thumbed the rest of the paper for Helenowski, Brownell and the cop beaters.

Nothing.

Predictable: two cops with minor contusions was small potatoes, the punks hadn't had time to glom a shyster. Jack got out his ledger.

Pages divided into three columns: date, cashier's check number, amount of money. The amounts ranged from a C-note to two grand; the checks were made out to Donald and Marsha Scoggins of Cedar Rapids, Iowa. The bottom of the third column held a running total: $32,350. Jack got out his bank-book, checked the balance, decided his next payment would be five hundred flat. Five yards for Christmas. Big money until your Uncle Jack drops dead – and it'll never be enough.

Every Christmas he ran it through – it started with the Morrows and he saw them at Christmastime; he was an orphan, he'd made the Scoggins kids orphans, Christmas was a notoriously shitty time for orphans. He forced himself through the story.

Late September 1947.

Old Chief Worton called him in. Welton Morrow's daughter Karen was running with a high school crowd experimenting with dope – they got the shit from a sax player named Les Weiskopf. Morrow was a filthy-rich lawyer, a heavy contributor to LAPD fund drives; he wanted Weiskopf leaned on – with no publicity.

Jack knew Weiskopf: he sold Dilaudid, wore his hair in a jig conk, liked young gash. Worton told him a sergeantcy came with the job.

He found Weiskopf – in bed with a fifteen-year-old redhead. The girl skedaddled; Jack pistol-whipped Weiskopf, tossed his pad, found a trunk full of goofballs and bennies. He took it with him – he figured he'd sell the shit to Mickey Cohen. Welton Morrow offered him the security man gig; Jack accepted; Karen Morrow was hustled off to boarding school. The sergeantcy came through; Mickey C. wasn't interested in the dope – only Big H flipped his switch. Jack kept the trunk – and dipped into it for bennies to keep him juiced on all-night stake-outs. Linda, wife number two, took off with one of his snitches: a trombone player who sold maryjane on the side. Jack hit the trunk for real, mixing goofballs, bennies, scotch, taking down half the names on the *down beat* poll: THE MAN, jazzster's public enemy number one. Then it was 10/24/47 –

He was cramped in his car, staking the Malibu Rendez-vous parking lot: eyes on two 'H' pushers in a Packard sedan. Near midnight: he'd been drinking scotch, he blew a reefer on the way over, the bennies he'd been swallowing weren't catching up with the booze. A tip on a midnight buy: the 'H' men and a skinny shine, seven feet tall, a real geek.

The boogie showed at a quarter past twelve, walked to the Packard, palmed a package. Jack tripped getting out of the car; the geek started running; the 'H' men got out with guns drawn. Jack stumbled up and drew his piece; the geek wheeled and fired; he saw two shapes closer in, tagged them as the nigger's backup, squeezed off a clip. The shapes went down; the 'H' men shot at the spook and at him; the spook nosedived a '46 Studebaker.

Jack ate cement, prayed the rosary. A shot ripped his shoulder; a shot grazed his legs. He crawled under the car; a shitload of tires squealed; a shitload of people screamed. An ambulance showed up; a bull dyke Sheriff's deputy loaded him on a gurney. Sirens, a hospital bed, a doctor and the dyke whispering about the dope in his system – blood test validated. Lots of drugged sleep, a newspaper on his lap: 'Three Dead in Malibu Shootout – Heroic Cop Survives.'

The 'H' guys escaped clean – the deaths pinned on them.

The spook was dead at the scene.

The shapes weren't the nigger's backup – they were Mr. and Mrs. Harold J. Scoggins, tourists from Cedar Rapids, Iowa, the proud parents of Donald, seventeen, and Marsha, sixteen.

The doctors kept looking at him funny; the dyke turned out to be Dot Rothstein, Kikey Teitlebaum's cousin, known associate of the legendary Dudley Smith.

A routine autopsy would show that the pills taken out of Mr. and Mrs. Scoggins came from Sergeant Jack Vincennes' gun.

The kids saved him.

He sweated out a week at the hospital. Thad Green and Chief Worton visited; the Narco guys came by. Dudley Smith offered his patronage; he wondered just how much he knew. Sid Hudgens, chief writer for *Hush-Hush* magazine, stopped in with an offer: Jack to roust celebrated hopheads, *Hush-Hush* to be in on the arrests – cash to discreetly change hands. He accepted – and wondered just how much Hudgens knew.

The kids demanded no autopsy: the family was Seventh-Day Adventist, autopsies were a sacrilege. Since the county coroner knew damn well who the shooters were, he shipped Mr. and Mrs. Harold J. Scoggins back to Iowa to be cremated.

Sergeant Jack Vincennes skated – with newspaper honors.

His wounds healed.

He quit drinking.

He quit taking dope, dumped the trunk. He marked abstinent days on his calendar, worked his deal with Sid Hudgens, built his name as a local celebrity. He did favors for Dudley Smith; Mr. and Mrs. Harold J. Scoggins torched his dreams; he figured booze and hop would put out the flames but get him killed in the process. Sid got him the 'technical advisor' job with *Badge of Honor* – then just a radio show. Money started rolling in; spending it on clothes and women wasn't the kick he thought it would be. Bars and dope shakedowns were awful temptations. Terrorizing hopheads helped a little – but not enough. He decided to pay the kids back.

His first check ran two hundred; he included a letter: 'Anonymous Friend,' a spiel on the Scoggins tragedy. He called the bank a week later: the check had been cashed. He'd been financing his free ride ever since; unless Hudgens had 10/24/47 on paper he was safe.

Jack laid out his party clothes. The blazer was London Shop – he'd bought it with Sid's payoff for the Bob Mitchum roust. The tassel loafers and gray flannels were proceeds from a *Hush-Hush* exposé linking jazz musicians to the Communist Conspiracy – he squeezed some pinko stuff out of a bass player he popped for needle marks. He dressed, spritzed on Lucky Tiger, drove to Beverly Hills.

A backyard bash: a full acre covered by awnings. College kids parked cars; a buffet featured prime rib, smoked ham, turkey. Waiters carried hors d'oeuvres; a giant Christmas tree stood out in the open, getting drizzled on. Guests ate off paper plates; gas torches lit the lawn. Jack arrived on time and worked the crowd.

Welton Morrow showed him to his first audience: a group of Superior Court judges. Jack spun yarns: Charlie Parker trying to buy him off with a high-yellow hooker, how he cracked the Shapiro case: a queer Mickey Cohen stooge pushing amyl nitrite – his customers transvestite strippers at a fruit bar. The Big V to the rescue: Jack Vincennes single-handedly arresting a roomful of bruisers auditioning for a Rita Hayworth lookalike contest. A round of applause; Jack bowed, saw Joan Morrow by the Christmas tree – alone, maybe bored.

He walked over. Joan said, 'Happy holidays, Jack.'

Pretty, built, thirty-one or two. No job and no husband taking its toll: she came off pouty most of the time. 'Hi, Joan.'

'Hi, yourself. I read about you in the paper today. Those people you arrested.'

'It was nothing.'

Joan laughed. 'Sooo modest. What's going to happen to them? Rock what's-his-name and the girl, I mean.'

'Ninety days for the girl, maybe a year honor farm for Rockwell. They should hire your dad – he'd get them off.'

'You don't really care, do you?'

'I hope they cop a plea and save me a court date. And I hope they do some time and learn their lesson.'

'I smoked marijuana once, in college. It made me hungry and I ate a whole box of cookies and got sick. You wouldn't have arrested me, would you?'

'No, you're too nice.'

'I'm *bored* enough to try it again, I'll tell you that.'

His opening. 'How's your love life, Joanie?'

'It isn't. Do you know a policeman named Edmund Exley? He's tall and he wears those cute glasses. He's Preston Exley's son.'

Straight-arrow Eddie: war hero with a poker up his ass. 'I know who he is, but I don't really know him.'

'Isn't he cute? I saw him at his father's house last night.'

'Rich-kid cops are from hunger, but I know a nice fellow who's interested in you.'

'You do? Who?'

'A man named Ellis Loew. He's a deputy district attorney.'

Joan smiled, frowned. 'I heard him address the Rotary Club once. Isn't he Jewish?'

'Yeah, but look to the bright side. He's a Republican and a comer.'

'Is he nice?'

'Sure, he's a sweetheart.'

Joan flicked the tree, fake snow swirled. 'Well, tell him to call me. Tell him I'm booked up for a while, but he can stand in line.'

'Thanks, Joanie.'

'Thank *you*, Miles Standish. Look, I think I see Daddy giving me the come-hither. Bye, Jackie!'

Joan skipped off; Jack geared up for more shtick –

maybe the Mitchum job, a soft version. A soft voice: 'Mr. Vincennes. Hello.'

Jack turned around. Karen Morrow in a green cocktail dress, her shoulders beaded with rain. The last time he'd seen her she was a too-tall, too-gawky kid forced to say thank you to a cop who'd strongarmed a hop pusher. Four years later just the too-tall stuck – the rest was a girl-to-woman changeover. 'Karen, I almost didn't recognize you.'

Karen smiled. Jack said, 'I'd tell you you've gotten beautiful, but you've heard it before.'

'Not from you.'

Jack laughed. 'How was college?'

'An epic, and not a story to tell you while I'm freezing. I told my parents to hold the party indoors, that England did not inure me to the cold. I have a speech prepared. Do you want to help me feed the neighbor's cats?'

'I'm on the job.'

'Talking to my sister?'

'A guy I know has a crush on her.'

'Poor guy. No, poor Joanie. Shit, this is not going the way I planned.'

'Shit, then let's go feed those cats.'

Karen smiled and led the way, wobbling, high heels on grass. Thunder, lightning, rain – Karen kicked off her shoes and ran barefoot. Jack caught up at the next-door porch – wet, close to laughing.

Karen opened the door. A foyer light was on; Jack looked at her – shivering, goose bumps. Karen shook water from her hair. 'The cats are upstairs.'

Jack took off his blazer. 'No, I want to hear your speech.'

'I'm sure you know what it is. I'm sure lots of people have thanked you.'

'You haven't.'

Karen shivered. 'Shit, I'm sorry, but this is not going the way I planned.'

Jack draped his coat around her shoulders. 'You got the L.A. papers over in England?'

41

'Yes.'

'And you read about me?'

'Yes. You – '

'Karen, they exaggerate sometimes. They build things up.'

'Are you telling me those things I've read are lies?'

'Not ex – no, they're not.'

Karen turned away. 'Good, I knew they were true, so here's your speech, and don't look at me, because I'm flustered. One, you got me away from taking pills. Two, you convinced my father to send me abroad, where I got a damn good education and met nice people. Three, you arrested that terrible man who sold me the pills.'

Jack touched her; Karen flinched away. 'No, let me tell it! Four, what I wasn't going to mention, is that Les Weiskopf gave girls pills for free if they slept with him. Father was stingy with my allowance and sooner or later I would have done it. So there – you kept my goddamned virtue intact.'

Jack laughed. 'Am I your goddamned hero?'

'Yes, and I'm twenty-two years old and not the school-girl-crush type.'

'Good, because I'd like to take you to dinner sometime.'

Karen swung around. Her mascara was ruined; she'd chewed off most of her lipstick. 'Yes. Mother and Father will have coronaries, but yes.'

Jack said, 'This is the first stupid move I've made in years.'

Chapter Seven

A month of shit.

Bud ripped January 1952 off his calendar, counted felony arrests. January 1 through January 11: zero – he'd worked crowd control at a movie location – Parker wanted a muscle guy there to shoo away autograph hounds. January 14: the cop beaters acquitted on assault charges, Helenowski and Brownell chewed up – the spics' lawyer made it look like they instigated the whole thing. Civil suits threatened; 'get a lawyer?' scribbled by the date.

January 16, 19, 22: wife thumpers paroled, welcome home visits. January 23–25: stakeouts on a burglary ring, him and Stens acting on a tip from Johnny Stomp, who just seemed to know things, per a rumor: he used to run a blackmail racket. Gangland activity at a weird lull, Stomp scuffling to stay solvent, Mo Jahelka – looking after Mickey C.'s interests – probably afraid to push too much muscle. Seven arrests total, good for his quota, but the papers were working the station brouhaha, dubbing it 'Bloody Christmas,' and a rumor hit: the D.A.'s Office had contacted Parker, IAD was going to question the men partying on Christmas Eve, the county grand jury was drooling for a presentation. More notes: 'talk to Dick,' '*lawyer???*', '*lawyer when??*'

The last week of the month – comic relief. Dick off duty, drying out at a health ranch in Twenty-nine Palms; the squad boss thought he was attending his father's funeral in Nebraska – the guys took up a collection to send flowers to a mortuary that didn't exist. Two felony notches on the 29th: parole violators he'd glommed off another Stomp snitch – but he'd had to beat the shit out of them, kidnap them, haul them from county turf to city so the Sheriff's couldn't claim the roust. The 31st: a dance with Chick Nadel, a barkeep who ran hot appliances out of the Moonglow Lounge. An impromptu raid; Chick with a stash of hot radios; a snitch on the guys who boosted the truck, holed up in San Diego, no way to make it an LAPD caper. He busted Chick instead: receiving stolen goods with a prior, ten felony arrests for the month – at least a double-digit tally.

Pure shit – straight into February.

Back to uniform, six days of directing traffic – Parker's idea, Detective Division personnel rotating to Patrol for a week a year. Alphabetically: as a 'W' he stood at the rear of the pack. The late bird loses the worm – it rained all six of those days.

Floods on the job, a drought with the women.

Bud thumbed his address book. Lorene from the Silver Star, Jane from the Zimba Room, Nancy from the Orbit Lounge – late-breaking numbers. They had the look: late thirties, hungry – grateful for a younger guy who treated them nice and gave them a taste all men weren't shitheels. Lorene was heavyset – the mattress springs always banged the floor. Jane played opera records to set the mood – they sounded like cats fucking. Nancy was a lush, par for bar-prowl course. The jaded type – the type to break things off even quicker than he usually did.

'White, check this.'

Bud looked up. Elmer Lentz held out the *Herald* front page.

The headline: 'Police Beating Victims to File Suit.'

Subheadings: 'Grand Jury Ready to Hear Evidence,' 'Parker Vows Full LAPD Cooperation.'

Lentz said, 'This could be trouble.'

Bud said, 'No shit, Sherlock.'

Chapter Eight

Preston Exley finished reading. 'Edmund, all three versions are brilliant, but you should have gone to Parker immediately. Now, with all the publicity, your coming forth smacks of panic. Are you prepared to be an informant?'

Ed squared his glasses. 'Yes.'

'Are you prepared to be despised within the Department?'

'Yes, and I'm prepared for whatever displays of gratitude Parker has to offer.'

Preston skimmed pages. 'Interesting. Shifting most of the guilt to men with their pensions already secured is salutary, and this Officer White sounds a bit fearsome.'

Ed got chills. 'He is. Internal Affairs is interviewing me tomorrow, and I don't relish telling them about his stunt with the Mexican.'

'Afraid of reprisals?'

'Not really.'

'Don't ignore your fear, Edmund. That's weakness. White and his friend Stensland behaved with despicable disregard for departmental bylaws, and they're both obvious thugs. Are you prepared for your interview?'

'Yes.'

'They'll be brutal.'

'I know, Father.'

'They'll stress your inability to keep order and the fact that you let those officers steal your keys.'

Ed flushed. 'It was getting chaotic, and fighting those men would have created more chaos.'

'Don't raise your voice and don't justify yourself. Not with me, not with the I.A. men. It makes you appear – '

A breaking voice. 'Don't say "weak," Father. Don't

draw any sort of parallel with Thomas. And don't assume that I can't handle this situation.'

Preston picked up the phone. 'I know you're capable of holding your own. But are you capable of seizing Bill Parker's gratitude before he displays it?'

'Father, you told me once that Thomas was your heir as a natural and I was your heir as an opportunist. What does that tell you?'

Preston smiled, dialed a number. 'Bill? Hello, it's Preston Exley . . . Yes, fine, thank you . . . No, I wouldn't have called your personal line for that . . . No, Bill, it's about my son Edmund. He was on duty at Central Station Christmas Eve, and I think he has valuable information for you . . . Yes, tonight? Certainly, he'll be there . . . Yes, and my regards to Helen . . . Yes, goodbye, Bill.'

Ed felt his heart slamming. Preston said, 'Meet Chief Parker at the Pacific Dining Car tonight at eight. He'll arrange for a private room where you can talk.'

'Which one of the depositions do I show him?'

Preston handed the paperwork back. 'Opportunities like this don't come very often. I had the Atherton case, you had a little taste with Guadalcanal. Read the family scrapbook and *remember those precedents*.'

'Yes, but which deposition?'

'You figure it out. And have a good meal at the Dining Car. The supper invitation is a good sign, and Bill doesn't like finicky eaters.'

Ed drove to his apartment, read, remembered. The scrapbook held clippings arranged in chronological order; what the newspapers didn't tell him he'd burned into his memory.

1934 – the Atherton case.

Children: Mexican, Negro, Oriental – three male, two female – are found dismembered, the trunks of their bodies discovered in L.A. area storm drains. The arms and legs have been severed; the internal organs removed.

The press dubs the killer 'Dr. Frankenstein.' Inspector Preston Exley heads the investigation.

He deems the Frankenstein tag appropriate: tennis racket strings were found at all five crime scenes, the third victim had darning-needle holes in his armpits. Exley concludes that the fiend is recreating children with stitching and a knife; he begins hauling in deviates, cranks, loony bin parolees. He wonders what the killer will do for a face – and learns a week later.

Wee Willie Wennerholm, child star in Raymond Dieterling's stable, is kidnapped from a studio tutorial school. The following day his body is found on the Glendale railroad tracks – decapitated.

Then a break: administrators from the Glenhaven State Mental Hospital call the LAPD – Loren Atherton, a child molester with a vampire fixation, was paroled to Los Angeles two months before – and has not yet reported to his parole officer.

Exley locates Atherton on skid row: he has a job washing bottles at a blood bank. Surveillance reveals that he steals blood, mixes it with cheap wine and drinks it. Exley's men arrest Atherton at a downtown theater – masturbating during a horror movie. Exley raids his hotel room, finds a set of keys – the keys to an abandoned storage garage. He goes there – and finds Hell.

A prototype child packed in dry ice: male Negro arms, male Mexican legs, a male Chinese torso with spliced-in female genitalia and Wee Willie Wennerholm's head. Wings cut from birds stitched to the child's back. Accoutrements rest nearby: horror movie reels, gutted tennis rackets, diagrams for creating hybrid children. Photographs of children in various stages of dismemberment, a closet/darkroom filled with developing supplies.

Hell.

Atherton confesses to the killings; he is tried, convicted, hanged at San Quentin. Preston Exley keeps copies of the death photos; he shows them to his policemen sons – so that they will know the brutality of crimes that require absolute justice.

Ed flipped pages: past his mother's obit, Thomas' death. Outside of his father's triumphs, the only time the Exleys made the papers was when somebody died. He made the *Examiner*: an article on the sons of famous men fighting World War II. Like Bloody Christmas, there was more than one version.

The *Examiner* ran the version that won him his DSC: Corporal Ed Exley, sole survivor of a platoon wiped out in hand-to-hand combat, takes down three trenches filled with Jap infantry, twenty-nine dead total, if there were an officer present to witness the act he would have won the Congressional Medal of Honor. Version two: Ed Exley seizes the opportunity to make a scout run when a Jap bayonet charge is imminent, dawdles, comes back to find his platoon obliterated and a Jap patrol approaching. He hides under Sergeant Peters and Pfc Wasnicki, feels them buckle when the Japs strafe bodies; he bites into Wasnicki's arm, chews his wristwatch strap clean off. He waits for dusk, sobbing, covered by dead men, a tiny passage between bodies feeding him air. Then a terror run for battalion HQ – halted when he sees another slaughter scene.

A little Shinto shrine, tucked into a clearing covered with camouflage netting. Dead Japs on pallets, jaundice green, emaciated. Every man ripped stomach to ribcage; ornately carved swords, blood-caked, stacked neatly. Mass suicide – soldiers too proud to risk capture or die from malaria.

Three trenches cut into the ground behind the temple; weaponry nearby – rifles and pistols rusted out from heavy rain. A flamethrower wrapped in camouflage cloth – in working order.

He held it, knowing just one thing: he would not survive Guadalcanal. He'd be assigned to a new platoon; his scout run dawdlings wouldn't wash. He could not request an HQ assignment – his father would deem the act cowardice. He would have to live with contempt – fellow LAPD men wounded, awarded medals.

'Medals' led to 'Bond Tours' led to crime scene reconstructions. He saw his opportunity.

He found a Jap machine gun. He hauled the hara-kiri men to the trenches, put useless weapons in their hands, arranged them facing an opening in the clearing. He dropped the machine gun there, pointed toward the opening, three rounds left in the feeder belt. He got the flamethrower, torched the Japs and the shrine past forensic recognition. He got his story straight, made it back to battalion HQ.

Recon patrols confirmed the story: fighting Ed Exley, armed with Jap ordnance, french-fried twenty-nine of the little fuckers.

The Distinguished Service Cross – the second highest medal his country could bestow. A stateside bond tour, a hero's welcome, back to the LAPD a champion.

Some kind of wary respect from Preston Exley.

'Read the family scrapbook. Remember those precedents.'

Ed put the book away, still not sure how he'd play Bloody Christmas – but certain what the man meant.

Opportunities fall easy – you pay for them later.

Father, I've known it since I picked up that flamethrower.

Chapter Nine

'If it goes to the grand jury, you won't swing. And the D.A. and I will try to keep it from going there.'

Jack counted favors on deposit. Sixteen G's to Loew's slush fund – Miller Stanton helped him lube the *Badge of Honor* gang. He tweaked Brett Chase himself, a concise little threat – a *Hush-Hush* exposé on his queerness. Max Peltz coughed up large – Loew frosted out a tax audit. A Cupid favor – tonight the man meets pouty Joan Morrow.

'Ellis, I don't even want to testify. I'm talking to some IAD goons tomorrow, and it *is* going to the grand jury. So fix it.'

Loew played with his Phi Beta chain. 'Jack, a prisoner assaulted you, and you responded in kind. You're clean. You're also somewhat of a public figure and the preliminary depositions that we've received from the plaintiff's attorneys state that four of the beating victims recognized you. You'll testify, Jack. But you won't swing.'

'I just thought I'd run it by you. But if you ask me to squeal on my brother officers, I'll plead fucking amnesia. *Comprende*, Counselor?'

Loew leaned across his desk. 'We shouldn't argue – we're doing too well together. Officer Wendell White and Sergeant Richard Stensland are the ones who should be worrying, not you. Besides, the grapevine tells me you have a new lady in your life.'

'You mean Joan Morrow told you.'

'Yes, and frankly she and her parents disapprove. You are fifteen years older than the girl, and you've had a checkered past.'

Caddy, ski instructor – an orphanage kid good at servicing rich folks. 'Joanie offer details?'

'Just that the girl has a mad crush on you and believes your press clippings. I assured Joan that those clippings are true. Karen tells Joan that so far you've behaved like a gentleman, which I find hard to believe.'

'That ends tonight, I hope. After our little double date, it's the *Badge of Honor* wrap party and an intimate interlude somewhere.'

Loew twisted his vest chain. 'Jack, has Joan been playing hard to get or does she really have that many men chasing her?'

Jack twisted the knife. 'She's a popular kid, but all those movie star guys are just fluff. Stick to your guns.'

'Movie stars?'

'Fluff, Ellis. Cute, but fluff.'

'Jack, I want to thank you for coming along tonight. I'm sure you and Karen will be superb icebreakers.'

'Then let's hit it.'

Don the Beachcomber's – the women waiting in a wraparound booth. Jack made introductions. 'Ellis Loew, Karen Morrow and Joan Morrow. Karen, don't they make a lovely couple?'

Karen said, 'Hello,' no hand squeeze – six dates and all she put out were bland good-night kisses. Loew sat next to Joan; Joanie checked him out – probably sniffing for signs of Jewishness. 'Ellis and I are good phone chums already. Aren't we?'

'We are indeed' – Loew working his courtroom voice.

Joan finished her drink. 'How do you two know each other? Do the police work closely with the District Attorney's Office?'

Jack kiboshed a laugh: I'm Jewboy's bagman. 'We build cases together. I get the evidence, Ellis prosecutes the bad guys.'

A waiter hovered. Joan ordered an Islander Punch; Jack asked for coffee. Loew said, 'Beefeater martini.' Karen put a hand over her glass. 'Then this Bloody Christmas thing will strain relations between the police and Mr. Loew's office. Isn't that likely?'

Loew hit quick. 'No, because the LAPD rank and file

51

wish to see the wrongdoers dealt with severely. Right, Jack?'

'Sure. Things like that give all policemen a black eye.'

The drinks arrived – Joan took hers down in three gulps. 'You were there, weren't you, Jack? Daddy said you always go to that station party, at least since your second wife left you.'

Karen: '*Joanie!*'

Jack said, 'I was there.'

'Did you take a few licks for justice?'

'It wasn't worth it to me.'

'You mean there weren't any headlines to be had?'

'Joanie, be quiet. You're drunk.'

Loew fingered his tie; Karen fingered an ashtray. Joan slurped the rest of her drink. 'Teetotalers are always so judgmental. You used to attend that party after your *first* wife left you, didn't you, Sergeant?'

Karen gripped the ashtray. 'You goddamn bitch.'

Joan laughed. 'If you want a hero policeman, I know a man named Exley who at least risked his life for his country. Granted, Jack's smooth, but can't you see what he is?'

Karen threw the ashtray – it hit the wall, then Ellis Loew's lap. Loew stuck his head in a menu; Joanie bitch glowered. Jack led Karen out of the restaurant.

Over to Variety International Pictures – Karen bad-mouthing Joanie non-stop. Jack parked by the *Badge of Honor* set; hillbilly music drifted out. Karen sighed. 'My parents will get used to the idea.'

Jack turned on the dash light. The girl had dark brown hair done in waves, freckles, a touch of an overbite. 'What idea?'

'Well . . . the idea of us seeing each other.'

'Which is going pretty slow.'

'That's partly my fault. One minute you're telling me these wonderful stories and the next minute you just stop. I keep wondering what you're thinking about and thinking

52

that there's so many things you can't tell me. It makes me think you think I'm too young, so I pull away.'

Jack opened the door. 'Keep getting my number and you won't be too young. And tell me some of your stories, because sometimes I get tired of mine.'

'Deal? My stories after the party?'

'Deal. And by the way, what do you think of your sister and Ellis Loew?'

Karen didn't blink. 'She'll marry him. My parents will overlook the fact that he's Jewish because he's ambitious and a Republican. He'll tolerate Joanie's scenes in public and hit her in private. Their kids will be a mess.'

Jack laughed. 'Let's dance. And don't get star-struck, people will think you're a hick.'

They entered arm in arm. Karen went in starry-eyed; Jack scoped his biggest wrap bash yet.

Spade Cooley and his boys on a bandstand, Spade at the mike with Burt Arthur 'Deuce' Perkins, his bass player, called 'Deuce' for his two-spot on a chain gang: unnatural acts against dogs. Spade smoked opium; Deuce popped 'H' – a *Hush-Hush* roust just looking to happen. Max Peltz glad-handing the camera crew; Brett Chase beside him, talking to Billy Dieterling, the head camera-man. Billy's eyes on his twist, Timmy Valburn, Moochie Mouse on the *Dream-a-Dream Hour*. Tables up against the back wall – covered with liquor bottles, cold cuts. Kikey Teitlebaum there with the food – Peltz probably had his deli cater the party. Johnny Stompanato with Kikey, ex-Mickey Cohen boys huddling. Every *Badge of Honor* actor, crew member and general hanger-on eating, drinking, dancing.

Jack swept Karen onto the floor: swirls through a fast-tune medley, grinds when Spade switched to ballads. Karen kept her eyes closed; Jack kept his open – the better to dig the shmaltz. He felt a tap on the shoulder.

Miller Stanton cutting in. Karen opened her eyes and gasped: a TV star wanted to dance with her. Jack bowed. 'Karen Morrow, Miller Stanton.'

Karen yelled over the music. 'Hi! I saw all those old Raymond Dieterling movies you made. You were great!'

Stanton hoisted her hands square-dance style. 'I was a brat! Jack, go see Max – he wants to talk to you.'

Jack walked to the rear of the set – quiet, the music lulled. Max Peltz handed him two envelopes. 'Your season bonus and a boost for Mr. Loew. It's from Spade Cooley.'

Loew's bag was fat. 'What's Cooley want?'

'I'd say insurance you won't mess with his habit.'

Jack lit a cigarette. 'Spade doesn't interest me.'

'Not a big enough name?'

'Be nice, Max.'

Peltz leaned in close. 'Jack, *you* try to be nicer, 'cause you're getting a bad rep in the Industry. People say you're a hard-on, you don't play the game. You shook down Brett for Mr. Loew, fine, he's a goddamn faigeleh, he's got it coming. But you can't bite the hand that feeds you, not when half the people in the Industry blow tea from time to time. Stick with the shvartzes – those jazz guys make good copy.'

Jack eyeballed the set. Brett Chase in a hobnob: Billy Dieterling, Timmy Valburn – a regular fruit convention. Kikey T. and Johnny Stomp shmoozing – Deuce Perkins, Lee Vachss joining in. Peltz said, 'Seriously, Jack. Play the game.'

Jack pointed to the hard boys. 'Max, the game is my life. You see those guys over there?'

'Sure. What's that – '

'Max, that's what the Department calls a known criminal assembly. Perkins is an ex-con wheelman who fucks dogs, and Abe Teitlebaum's on parole. The tall guy with the mustache is Lee Vachss, and he's made for at least a dozen snuffs for Mickey C. The good-looking wop is Johnny Stompanato. I doubt if he's thirty years old, and he's got a racket sheet as long as your arm. I am empowered by the Los Angeles Police Department to roust those cocksuckers on general suspicion, and I'm derelict in my duty for not doing it. Because I'm *playing the game*.'

Peltz waved a cigar. 'So keep playing it – but pianissimo

on the tough-guy stuff. And look, Miller's bird-dogging your quail. Jesus, you like them young.'

Rumors: Max and high school trim. 'Not as young as you.'

'Ha! Go, you fucking gonif. Your girl's looking for you.'

Karen by a wall poster: Brett Chase as Lieutenant Vance Vincent. Jack walked over; Karen's eyes lit up. 'God, this is so wonderful! Tell me who everyone is!'

Full-blast music – Cooley yodeling, Deuce Perkins banging his bass. Jack danced Karen across the floor – over to a corner crammed with arclights. A perfect spot – quiet, a scope on the whole gang.

Jack pointed out the players. 'Brett Chase you already know about. He's not dancing because he's queer. The old guy with the cigar is Max Peltz. He's the producer, and he directs most of the episodes. You danced with Miller, so you know him. The two guys in skivvies are Augie Luger and Hank Kraft – they're grips. The girl with the clipboard is Penny Fulweider, she couldn't quit working even if she wanted to – she's the script supervisor. You know how the sets on the show are so modernistic? Well, the blond guy across from the bandstand is David Mertens, the set designer. Sometimes you'd think he was drunk, but he's not – he's got some rare kind of epilepsy, and he takes medicine for it. I heard he was in an accident and hit his head, that that started it. He's got these scars on his neck, so maybe that's it. Next to him there's Phil Shenkel, the assistant director, and the guy next to him is Jerry Marsalas, the male nurse who looks after Mertens. Terry Riegert, the actor who plays Captain Jeffries, is dancing with that tall redhead. The guys by the water cooler are Billy Dieterling, Chuck Maxwell and Dick Harwell, the camera crew, and the rest of the people are dates.'

Karen looked straight at him. 'It's your milieu, and you love it. And you care about those people.'

'I like them – and Miller's a good friend.'

'Jack, you can't fool me.'

'Karen, this is Hollywood. And ninety percent of Hollywood is moonshine.'

'Spoilsport. I'm gearing myself up to be reckless, so don't put a damper on it.'

Daring him.

Jack tumbled; Karen leaned into the kiss. They probed, tasted, pulled back the same instant – Jack broke off the clinch dizzy.

Karen let her hands linger. 'The neighbors are still on vacation. We could go feed the cats.'

'Yeah . . . sure.'

'Will you get me a brandy before we go?'

Jack walked to the food table. Deuce Perkins said, 'Nice stuff, Vincennes. You got the same taste as me.'

A skinny cracker in a black cowboy shirt with pink piping. Boots put him close to six-six; his hands were enormous. 'Perkins, your stuff sniffs fire hydrants.'

'Spade might not like you talkin' to me that way. Not with that envelope you got in your pocket.'

Lee Vachss, Abe Teitlebaum watching them. 'Not another word, Perkins.'

Deuce chewed a toothpick. 'Your quiff know you get your jollies shakin' down niggers?'

Jack pointed to the wall. 'Roll up your sleeves, spread your legs.'

Perkins spat out his toothpick. 'You ain't that crazy.'

Johnny Stomp, Vachss, Teitlebaum – all in earshot. Jack said, 'Kiss the wall, shitbird.'

Perkins leaned over the table, palms on the wall. Jack pulled up his sleeves – fresh tracks – emptied his pockets. Paydirt – a hypo syringe. A crowd forming up – Jack played to it. 'Needle marks and that outfit are good for three years State. Hand up the guy who sold you the hypo and you skate.'

Deuce oozed sweat. Jack said, 'Squeal in front of your friends and you stroll.'

Perkins licked his lips. 'Barney Stinson. Orderly at Queen of Angels.'

Jack kicked his legs out from under him.

Perkins landed face first in the cold cuts; the table crashed to the floor.

The room let out one big breath.

Jack walked outside, groups breaking up to let him through. Karen by the car, shivering. 'Did you have to do that?'

He'd sweated his shirt clean through. 'Yeah, I did.'

'I wish I hadn't seen it.'

'So do I.'

'I guess reading about things like that are one thing and seeing them is another. Would you try to – '

Jack put his arms around her. 'I'll keep that stuff separate from you.'

'But you'll still tell me your stories?'

'No . . . yeah, sure.'

'I wish we could turn back the clock on tonight.'

'So do I. Look, do you want some dinner?'

'No. Do you still want to go see the cats?'

There were three cats – friendly guys who tried to take over the bed while they made love. Karen called the gray one Pavement, the tabby Tiger, the skinny one Ellis Loew. Jack resigned himself to the entourage – they made Karen giggle, he figured every laugh put Deuce Perkins further behind them. They made love, talked, played with the cats; Karen tried a cigarette – and coughed her lungs out. She begged for stories; Jack borrowed from the exploits of Officer Wendell White and spun gentler versions of his own cases: minimum strongarm, lots of sugar daddy – the bighearted Big V, protecting kids from the scourge of dope. At first the lies were hard – but Karen's warmth made them easier and easier. Near dawn, the girl dozed off; he stayed wide awake, the cats driving him crazy. He kept wishing she'd wake up so he could tell her more stories; he got little jolts of worry: that he'd never remember all the phony parts, she'd catch him in whoppers, it would blow their deal sky high. Karen's body grew warmer as she slept; Jack pressed closer to her. He fell asleep getting his stories straight.

Chapter Ten

A corridor forty feet long, both sides lined with benches:
scuffed, dusty, just hauled up from some storage hole.
Packed: men in plainclothes and uniform, most of them
reading – newspapers screaming *Bloody Christmas*. Bud
thought of him and Stens front page smeared: nailed by
the spics and their lawyers. He'd gotten his call to appear
at 4:00 A.M., pure I.A. scare tactics. Dick across the hall
– back from the dry-out farm, into the jug. Six Internal
Affairs interviews apiece – neither of them had snitched.
A regular Christmas reunion, the gang's all here – except
Ed Exley.

Time dragged, traffic flowed: interrogation room grill-
ings. Elmer Lentz dropped a bomb: the radio said the
grand jury requested a presentation – all the officers at
Central Station 12/25/51 were to stand a show-up tomorrow, prisoners would be there to ID the roughnecks.
Chief Parker's door opened; Thad Green stepped outside.
'Officer White, please.'

Bud walked over; Green pointed him in. A small room:
Parker's desk, chairs facing it. No wall mementoes, a
gray-tinted mirror – maybe a two-way. The chief behind
his desk, in uniform, four gold stars on his shoulders.
Dudley Smith in the middle chair; Green back in the chair
nearest Parker. Bud took the hot seat – a spot where all
three men could see him. Parker said, 'Officer, you know
Deputy Chief Green, and I'm sure you know of Lieutenant Smith. The lieutenant has been serving me as an
advisor during this crisis we've been having.'

Green lit a cigarette. 'Officer, you're being given a last
chance to cooperate. You've been questioned repeatedly
by Internal Affairs, and you've repeatedly refused to cooperate. Normally, you would have been suspended from
duty. But you're a fine detective, and Chief Parker and I

58

are convinced that your actions at the party were relatively blameless. You were provoked, Officer. You were not wantonly violent like most of the men accused.'

Bud started to talk; Smith cut him off. 'Lad, I'm sure that I speak for Chief Parker in this, so I will take the liberty of stating it without ellipses. It's a damn pity that the six scum who assaulted our brother officers weren't shot on the spot, and the violence visited upon them I deem mild. But, parenthetically, police officers who cannot control their impulses have no business being police officers, and the shenanigans perpetrated by the men outside have made the Los Angeles Police Department a laughingstock. This cannot be tolerated. Heads must roll. We must have cooperative policemen witnesses to offset the damage done to the Department's image – an image that has vastly improved under the leadership of Chief Parker. We have one major policeman witness already, and Deputy D.A. Ellis Loew stands firm in his desire not to prosecute LAPD officers – even if the grand jury hands down true bills. Lad, will you testify? For the Department, not the prosecution.'

Bud checked the mirror – two-way for sure – make D.A.'s Bureau goons taking notes. 'No, sir. I won't.'

Parker scanned a sheet of paper. 'Officer, you picked a man up by the neck and tried to bash his brains out. That looks very bad, and even though you were verbally provoked, the action stands out more than most of the abuse heaped on the prisoners. That goes against you. But you were heard muttering "This is a goddamned disgrace" when you left the cellblock, which is in your favor. Now, do you see how appearing as a voluntary witness could offset the disadvantages caused by your . . . imaginative show of force?'

A snap: Exley's their boy, *he* heard me, locked in the storeroom. 'Sir, I won't testify.'

Parker flushed bright red. Smith said, 'Lad, let's talk turkey. I admire your refusal to betray fellow officers, and I sense that loyalty to your partner is what stands behind it. I admire that especially, and Chief Parker has authorized me to offer you a deal. If you testify as to Dick Stensland's actions and the grand jury hands down a bill against him, Stensland will serve no time in jail if convicted. We have Ellis Loew's word on that. Stensland will be dismissed from the Department without pension, but his pension will be paid to him sub rosa, through monies diverted from the Widows and Orphans Fund. Lad, will you testify?'

Bud stared at the mirror. 'Sir, I won't testify.'

Thad Green pointed to the door. 'Be at Division 43 grand jury chambers tomorrow at 9:00. Be prepared to stand in a show-up and be called to testify. If you refuse to testify, you'll receive a subpoena and be suspended from duty pending a trial board. Get out of here, White.'

Dudley Smith smiled – very slightly. Bud shot the mirror a stiff middle finger.

Chapter Eleven

Streaks and smudges on the two-way – expressions came off blurred. Thad Green tough to read; Parker simple – he turned ugly colors. Dudley Smith – lexophile with a brogue – too calculated to figure. Bud White too *too* easy: the chief quoted, 'This is a goddamned disgrace'; a big thought balloon popped up: 'Ed Exley is the stool pigeon.' The middle finger salute was just icing.

Ed tapped the speaker; static crackled. The closet was hot – but not stifling like the Central Jail storeroom. He thought of his last two weeks.

He'd played it brass balls with Parker, presenting all three depositions, agreeing to testify as the Department's key witness. Parker considered his assessment of the situation brilliant, the mark of an exemplary officer. He gave the least damaging of the three statements to Ellis Loew and his favorite D.A.'s investigator, a young law school graduate – Bob Gallaudet. The blame was shifted, more than deservedly, to Sergeant Richard Stensland and Officer Wendell White; less deservedly to three men with their pensions already secured. The chief's reward to his exemplary witness: a transfer to a detective squadroom – a huge promotion. With the lieutenant's exam aced, within a year he would stand as Detective Lieutenant E. J. Exley.

Green left the office; Ellis Loew and Gallaudet walked in. Loew and Parker conferred; Gallaudet opened the door. 'Sergeant Vincennes, please' – static out of the speaker.

Trashcan Jack: sleek in a chalk-striped suit. No amenities – he took the middle seat checking his watch. A look passed – Trash, Ellis Loew. Parker eyed the new fish, an easy read – pure contempt. Gallaudet stood by the door, smoking.

Loew said, 'Sergeant, we'll get right to it. You've been very cooperative with I.A., which is to your credit. But nine witnesses have identified you as hitting Juan Carbijal, and four drunk tank prisoners saw you carrying in a case of rum. You see, your notoriety preceded you. Even drunks read the scandal sheets.'

Dudley Smith took over. 'Lad, we need your notoriety. We have a stellar witness who will tell the grand jury that you hit back only after being hit, and since that is probably the truth, further prisoner testimony will vindicate you. But we need you to admit bringing the liquor the men got drunk on. Admit to that interdepartmental infraction and you'll get off with a trial board. Mr. Loew guarantees a quashed criminal indictment should one arise.'

Trashcan kept still. Ed read in: Bud White brought most of the booze, he's afraid to inform on him. Parker said, 'There will have to be a large shake-up within the Department. Testify, and you'll receive a minor trial board, no suspension, no demotion. I'll guarantee you a light slap on the wrist – a transfer to Administrative Vice for a year or so.'

Vincennes to Loew. 'Ellis, have I got any more truck with you on this? You know what working Narco means to me.'

Loew flinched. Parker said, 'None, and there's more. You'll have to stand in the show-up tomorrow, and we want you to testify against Officer Krugman, Sergeant Tucker and Officer Pratt. All three men have already earned their pensions. Our key witness will testify roundly, but you can plead ignorance to questions directed at the other men. Frankly, we must sate the public's clamor for blood by giving up some of our own.'

Dudley Smith: 'I doubt if you've ever drawn a stupid breath, lad. Don't do it now.'

Trashcan Jack: 'I'll do it.'

Smiles all around. Gallaudet said, 'I'll go over your testimony with you, Sergeant. Dining Car lunch on Mr. Loew.' Vincennes stood up; Loew walked him to the door.

Whispers out the speaker: ' . . . and I told Cooley you wouldn't do it again' – 'Okay, boss.' Parker nodded at the mirror.

Ed walked in, straight to the hot seat. Smith said, 'Lad, you're very much the man of the hour.'

Parker smiled. 'Ed, I had you watch because your assessment of this situation has been very astute. Any last thoughts before you testify?'

'Sir, am I correct in assuming that whatever criminal bills the grand jury hands down will be stalled or quashed during Mr. Loew's postindictment process?'

Loew grimaced. He'd hit a nerve – just like his father said he would. 'Sir, am I correct in that?'

Loew, patronizing. 'Have you attended law school, Sergeant?'

'No, sir. I haven't.'

'Then your esteemed father has given you good counsel.'

Voice steady. 'No, sir. He hasn't.'

Smith said, 'Let's assume you're correct. Let's assume that we are bending our efforts toward what all loyal policemen want: no brother officers tried publicly. Assuming that, what do you advise?'

The pitched he'd rehearsed – verbatim. 'The public will demand more than true bills, stalling tactics and dismissed indictments. Interdepartmental trial boards, suspensions and a big transfer shake-up won't be enough. You told Officer White that heads must roll. I agree, and for the sake of the chief's prestige and the prestige of the Department, I think we need criminal convictions and jail sentences.'

'Lad, I am shocked at the relish with which you just said that.'

Ed to Parker. 'Sir, you've brought the Department back from Horrall and Worton. Your reputation is exemplary and the Department's has greatly improved. You can assure that it stays that way.'

Loew said, 'Spill it, Exley. Exactly what does our junior officer informant think we should do?'

Ed, eyes on Parker. 'Dismiss the indictments on the men with their twenty in. Publicize the transfer shake-up and give the bulk of the men trial boards and suspensions. Indict Johnny Brownell, tell him to request a no-jury venue and have the judge let him off with a suspended sentence – his brother was one of the officers initially assaulted. And indict, try and convict Dick Stensland and Bud White. Secure them jail time. Boot them off the Department. Stensland's a drunken thug, White almost killed a man and supplied more liquor than Vincennes. Feed them to the goddamn sharks. Protect yourself, protect the Department.'

Silence, stretching. Smith broke it. 'Gentlemen, I think our young sergeant's advice is rash and hypocritical. Stensland has his rough edges, but Wendell White is a valuable officer.'

'Sir, White is a homicidal thug.'

Smith started to speak; Parker raised a hand. 'I think Ed's advice is worth considering. Ace them at the grand jury tomorrow, son. Wear a smart-looking suit and ace them.'

Ed said, 'Yes, sir.' He forced himself not to shout his joy to the rafters.

Chapter Twelve

Spotlights, height strips: Jack at 5'11"; Frank Doherty, Dick Stens, John Brownell the short guys, Wilbert Huff, Bud White topping six. Central Jail punks across the glass, couched with D.A.'s cops taking names.

A speaker squawked, 'Left profile'; six men turned. 'Right profile,' 'Face the wall,' 'Face the mirror'; 'At ease, gentlemen.' Silence; then: 'Fourteen IDs apiece on Doherty, Stensland, Vincennes, White and Brownell, four for Huff. Oh shit, the P.A.'s on!'

Stens cracked up. Frank Doherty said, 'Eat shit, cocksucker.' White stayed expressionless – like he was already at the honor farm protecting Stens from niggers. The speaker: 'Sergeant Vincennes to room 114, Officer White report to Chief Green's office. The rest of you men are dismissed.'

114 – the grand jury witness room.

Jack walked ahead, through curtains down to 114. A crowded room: Bloody Christmas plaintiffs, Ed Exley in a too-new suit, loose threads at the sleeves. The Xmas boys sneered; Jack braced Exley. 'You're the key witness?'

'That's right.'

'I should've known it was you. What's Parker throwing you?'

'Throwing me?'

'Yeah, Exley. *Throwing you.* The deal, the payoff. You think *I'm* testifying for free?'

Exley futzed with his glasses. 'I'm just doing my duty.'

Jack laughed. 'You're playing an angle, college boy. You're getting something out of this, so you won't have to hobnob with the fucking rank-and-file cops who are going to hate your fucking guts for snitching. And if Parker promised you the Bureau, watch out. Some Bureau

65

guys are gonna burn in this thing and you're gonna have to work with friends of theirs.'

Exley flinched; Jack laughed. 'Good payoff, I'll admit that.'

'You're the payoff expert. Not me.'

'You'll be outranking me pretty soon, so I should be nice. Did you know Ellis Loew's new girlfriend has the hots for you?'

A clerk called, 'Edmund J. Exley to chambers.'

Jack winked. 'Go. And clip those threads on your coat or you'll look like a rube.'

Exley walked across the hall – primping, pulling threads.

Jack killed time – thinking about Karen. Ten days since the party; life was mostly aces. He had to apologize to Spade Cooley; Welton Morrow was pissed over him and Karen – but the lukewarm Joanie/Ellis Loew deal almost made it up for him. Hotel shacks were a strain – Karen lived at home, his place was a dive, he'd been neglecting his payments to the Scoggins kids to make the freight at the Ambassador. Karen loved the illicit romance; he loved her loving it. Aces. But Sid Hudgens hadn't called and L.A. was heroin dry – no Narco jollies. A year at Ad Vice loomed like the gas chamber.

He felt like a fighter ready to dive. The Christmas geeks kept staring; the punk he'd thumped had on a nose splint – probably a phony some Jew lawyer told him to wear. The grand jury room door stood ajar; Jack walked over, looked in.

Six jurors at a table facing the witness stand; Ellis Loew hurling questions – Ed Exley in the box.

He didn't play with his glasses; he didn't hem and haw. His voice went an octave lower than normal – and stayed even. Skinny, not a cop type, he still had authority – and his timing was perfect. Loew pitched perfect outside sliders; Exley knew they were coming, but acted surprised. Whoever coached him did a fucking-A bang-up job.

Jack picked out details, sensed Exley reaching, a war hero – not a weak sister in a cellblock full of rowdies. Loew glossed over that; Exley's answers hit smart: he was outnumbered, his keys were snatched, he was locked in a storeroom – and that was that. He was a man who knew who he was, knew the futility of cheap heroics.

Exley spieled: rat-offs on Brownell, Huff, Doherty. He called Dick Stensland the worst of the worst, didn't blink snitching Bud White. Jack smiled when it hit him: everything is skewed toward our side. Krugman, Pratt, Tucker, pension safe – were set up – for *his* testimony. Stensland and White – heading for indictment city. What a fucking performance.

Loew called for a summation. Exley obliged: pap about justice. Loew excused him; the jurors almost swooned. Exley left the box limping – he'd probably jammed his legs asleep.

Jack met him outside. 'You were good. Parker would've loved it.'

Exley stretched his legs. 'You think he'll read the transcript?'

'He'll have it inside ten minutes, and Bud White'll fuck you for this if it takes the rest of his life. He was called in to Thad Green after the show-up, and you can bet Green suspended him. You had better pray he cops a deal and stays on the Department, because that is one civilian you do not want on your case.'

'Is that why you didn't tell Loew he brought most of the liquor?'

A clerk called, 'John Vincennes, five minutes.'

Jack got up some nerve. 'I'm snitching three old-timers who'll be fishing in Oregon next week. Next to you, I'm clean. *And smart.*'

'We're both doing the right thing. Only you hate yourself for it, and that's not smart.'

Jack saw Ellis Loew and Karen down the hall. Loew walked up. 'I told Joan you were testifying today, and she told Karen. I'm sorry, and I told Joan in confidence. *Jack, I'm sorry.* I told Karen she couldn't watch in chambers, that she'll have to listen over the speaker in my office. *Jack, I'm sorry.*'

'Jewboy, you sure know how to guarantee a witness.'

Chapter Thirteen

Bud nursed a highball.

Jukebox noise pounded him; he had the worst seat in the bar – a sofa back by the pay phones. His old football wounds throbbed – like his hard-on for Exley. No badge, no gun, indictments shooting his way – the fortyish red-head looked like the best thing he'd ever seen. He carried his drink over.

She smiled at him. The red looked fake – but she had a kind face. Bud smiled. 'That an old-fashioned you're drinking?'

'Yes, and my name's Angela.'

'My name's Bud.'

'Nobody was born with the name "Bud." '

'They stick you with a name like "Wendell," you look for an alias.'

Angela laughed. 'What do you do, *Bud*?'

'I'm sorta between jobs right now.'

'Oh? Well, what *did* you do?'

SUSPENDED! YOU DUMB FUCK LOOKING A GIFT HORSE IN THE MOUTH! 'I wouldn't play ball with my boss. Angela, what do you say – '

'You mean like a union dispute or something? I'm in the United Federation of Teachers, and my ex-husband was a shop steward with the Teamsters. Is that what you – '

Bud felt a hand on his shoulder. 'Lad, might I have a word with you?'

Dudley Smith. CALL IT I.A. RUNNING TAILS.

'This business, Lieutenant?'

'It is indeed. Say good night to your new friend and join me by those back tables. I've told the bartender to turn the music down so we can talk.'

A jump tune went soft; Smith walked off. A sailor had his hooks into Angela. Bud eased over to the lounges.

Cozy: Smith, two chairs, a table – a newspaper covering the top, a little mound underneath. Bud sat down. 'Is I.A. tailing me?'

'Yes, and other likely indictees. It was your chum Exley's idea. The lad has a piece of Chief Parker's ear, and he told him that you and Stensland might be driven to commit rash acts. Exley vilified you and many other fine men on the witness stand, lad. I've read the transcript. His testimony was high treason and a despicable affront to all honorable policemen.'

Stens – holed up on a bender. 'Don't that paper say we been indicted?'

'Don't be precipitous, lad. I've used my piece of the chief's ear to have your tail called off, so you're with a friend.'

'Lieutenant, what do you want?'

Smith said, 'Call me Dudley.'

'*Dudley*, what do you want?'

Ho, ho, ho – a beautiful tenor. 'Lad, you impress me. I admire your refusal to testify and your loyalty to your partner, however unfounded. I admire you as a policeman, particularly your adherence to violence where needed as a necessary adjunct to the job, and I am most impressed by your punishment of woman beaters. Do you hate them, lad?'

Big words – his head spun. 'Yeah, I hate them.'

'And for good reason, judging from what I know of your background. Do you hate anything else quite so much?'

Fists so tight his hands ached. 'Exley. Fucking Exley. Trashcan Jack, he's gotta be up there, too. Dick Stens is giving himself cirrhosis 'cause those two squealed us off.'

Smith shook his head. 'Not Vincennes, lad. He was the stalking horse for the Department, and we needed him to give the D.A.'s Office some bodies. He only snitched twenty-year men, and he took the blame for the liquor you brought to the party. No, lad, Jack does not deserve your hatred.'

Bud leaned over the table. 'Dudley, what do you want?'

'I want you to avoid an indictment and return to duty, and I have a way for you to do it.'

Bud looked at the newspaper. 'How?'

'Work for me.'

'Doing what?'

'No, more questions first. Lad, do you recognize the need to contain crime, to keep it south of Jefferson with the dark element?'

'Sure.'

'And do you think a certain organized crime element should be allowed to exist and perpetuate acceptable vices that hurt no one?'

'Sure, pork barrel. The game's gotta be played that way a little. What's this got to do – '

Smith yanked the paper – a badge and .38 special gleamed up. Bud, scalp prickles. 'I knew you had juice. You squared it with Green?'

'Yes, lad, I squared it – with Parker. With the part of his ear that Exley hasn't poisoned. He said if the grand jury didn't hand down a bill against you, your refusal to testify would not be punished. Now pick up your things before the proprietor calls the police.'

GLEAMING – Bud grabbed his goodies. 'There's no goddamn bill on me?'

Ho, ho, ho – mocking. 'Lad, the chief knew he was giving me a long shot, and I'm glad you haven't read the Four Star *Herald*.'

Bud said, '*How?*'

'Not yet, lad.'

'What about Dick?'

'He's through, lad. And don't protest, because it's unavoidable. He's been billed, he'll be indicted and he'll swing. He's the Department's scapegoat, on Parker's orders. And it was Exley who convinced him to hand Dick over. Criminal charges and jail time.'

71

A broiling hot room – Bud pulled his necktie loose, closed his eyes.

'Lad, I'll get Dick a nice berth at the honor farm. I know a woman deputy there who can fix things, and when he gets out I'll guarantee him a shot at Exley.'

Bud opened his eyes; Smith had the *Herald* spread full. The headline: 'Policemen Indicted in Bloody Christmas Scandal.' Below, a column circled: Sergeant Richard Stensland flagged on four charges, three old-timer cops billed, Lentz, Brownell, Huff swinging on two bills apiece. Underlined: 'Officer Wendell White, 33, received no true bills, although several sources within the District Attorney's Bureau had stated that first-degree assault bills seemed imminent. The grand jury's foreman stated that four police-beating victims recanted their previous testimony, which had Officer White attempting to strangle Juan Carbijal, age 19. The recanted testimony directly contradicted the testimony of LAPD Sergeant Edmund J. Exley, who had sworn under oath that White had, in fact, attempted to grievously injure Carbijal. Sergeant Exley's testimony is not considered tainted, since it resulted in probable indictments against seven other officers; however, although the grand jurors doubted the credibility of the recantings, they deemed them sufficient to deny the D.A.'s Office true bills against Officer White. Deputy D.A. Ellis Loew told reporters: "Something suspicious happened, but I don't know what it was. Four retractions have to supersede the testimony of one witness, even as splendid a witness as Sergeant Exley, a decorated war hero." '

Newsprint swirling. Bud said, 'Why? Why'd you do that for me? And how?'

Smith crumpled the paper. 'Lad, I need you for a new assignment Parker has given me the go-ahead on. It's a containment measure, an adjunct to Homicide. We're going to call it the Surveillance Detail, an innocuous name for a duty that few men are fit for, but you were born for. It's a muscle job and a shooting job and a job that entails asking very few questions. Lad, do you follow my drift?'

'In Technicolor.'

'You'll be transferred out of Central dicks when Parker announces his shake-up. Will you work for me?'

'I'd be crazy not to. Why, Dudley?'

'Why what, lad?'

'You shivved Ellis Loew to help me out, and everyone in the Bureau knows you and him are tight. Why?'

'Because I like your style, lad. Will that answer suffice?'

'I guess it'll have to. Now let's try "how?" '

'How what, lad?'

'How you got the spics to retract.'

Smith laid brass knucks on the table: chipped, caked with blood.

CALENDAR

1952

EXTRACT: L.A. *Mirror-News*, March 19:

POLICE BEATING SCANDAL:
COPS DISCIPLINE THEIR OWN
BEFORE WORST CULPRITS STAND TRIAL

LAPD Chief William H. Parker promised that he would seek justice – 'wherever the search takes me' – in the tangled web of police brutality and civilian lawsuits that has come to be known as the 'Bloody Christmas' scandal.

Seven officers have received criminal assault indictments stemming from their actions at the Central Division Jail on Christmas morning of last year. Those officers are:

Sergeant Ward Tucker, indicted for Second Degree Assault.

Officer Michael Krugman, Second Degree Assault and Battery.

Officer Henry Pratt, Second Degree Assault.

73

Sergeant Elmer Lentz, First Degree Assault with Battery.

Sergeant Wilbert Huff, First Degree Assault with Battery.

Officer John Brownell, First Degree Assault and Aggravated Assault.

Sergeant Richard Stensland, First Degree Assault, Aggravated Assault, First Degree Battery and Mayhem.

Parker did not dwell on the charges facing the indicted policemen, or on the scores of civil suits that beating victims Dinardo Sanchez, Juan Carbijal, Dennis Rice, Ezekiel Garcia, Clinton Rice and Reyes Chasco have filed against individual policemen and the Los Angeles Police Department. He announced that the following officers would receive interdepartmental trial boards, and, if not vindicated, would be severely disciplined within the Department.

Sergeant Walter Crumley, Sergeant Walter Dukeshearer, Sergeant Francis Doherty, Officer Charles Heinz, Officer Joseph Hernandez, Sergeant Willis Tristano, Officer Frederick Turentine, Lieutenant James Frieling, Officer Wendell White, Officer John Heineke and Sergeant John Vincennes.

Parker closed his press conference praising Sergeant Edmund J. Exley, the Central Division officer who came forward to testify before the grand jury. 'It took great courage to do what Ed Exley did,' the chief said. 'The man has my greatest admiration.'

EXTRACT: L.A. *Examiner*, April 11:

FIVE 'BLOODY CHRISTMAS' INDICTMENTS DISMISSED; PARKER REVEALS RESULTS OF TRIAL BOARD ACTIONS

The District Attorney's Office announced today that five future defendants in last year's 'Bloody

Christmas' police brutality scandal will not stand trial. Officer Michael Krugman, Officer Henry Pratt and Sergeant Ward Tucker, all forced to resign from the Los Angeles Police Department as the result of being charged, had their indictments dismissed on the basis of abandoned testimony. Deputy D.A. Ellis Loew, who had been set to prosecute them, explained. 'Many minor witnesses, prisoners at the Central Station Jail last Christmas, cannot be located.'

In a related development, LAPD Chief William H. Parker announced the results of his 'massive shake-up' of police personnel. The following indicted and non-indicted officers were found guilty of various interdepartmental infractions pertaining to their behavior last Christmas morning.

Sergeant Walter Crumley: six months suspension from duty without pay, transferred to Hollenbeck Division.

Sergeant Walter Dukeshearer, six months suspension from duty without pay, transferred to Newton Street Division.

Sergeant Francis Doherty, four months suspension from duty without pay, transferred to Wilshire Division.

Officer Charles Heinz, six months suspension from duty without pay, transferred to the Southside Vagrant Detail.

Officer Joseph Hernandez, four months suspension from duty without pay, transferred to 77th Street Division.

Sergeant Wilbert Huff, nine months suspension from duty without pay, transferred to Wilshire Division.

Sergeant Willis Tristano, three months suspension from duty without pay, transferred to Newton Street Division.

Officer Frederick Turentine, three months suspension from duty without pay, transferred to East Valley Division.

Lieutenant James Frieling, six months suspension from duty without pay, transferred to the LAPD Academy Instruction Bureau.

Officer John Heineke, four months suspension from duty without pay, transferred to Venice Division.

Sergeant Elmer Lentz, nine months suspension from duty without pay, transferred to Hollywood Division.

Officer Wendell White, no suspension, transferred to the Homicide Adjunct Surveillance Detail.

Sergeant John Vincennes, no suspension, transferred to Administrative Vice.

EXTRACT: L.A. *Times*, May 3:

POLICE SCANDAL DEFENDANT
RECEIVES SUSPENDED SENTENCE

Officer John Brownell, 38, the first Los Angeles policeman involved in the 'Bloody Christmas' scandal to face public trial, pleaded guilty at arraignment today and asked Judge Arthur J. Fitzhugh to sentence him immediately on the First Degree Assault and Aggravated Assault charges he was facing.

Brownell is the older brother of LAPD patrolman Frank D. Brownell, one of two officers injured in a bar brawl with six young men last Christmas Eve. Judge Fitzhugh, taking into account the facts that Officer Brownell was under psychological duress over the injury of his brother and that he had been discharged from the Los Angeles Police Department without pension, read the County Probation Department's report, which recommended formal probation and no jail time. He then gave Brownell a year in the County Jail, sentence suspended, and ordered him to report to the county's chief probation officer, Randall Milteer.

EXTRACT: L.A. *Examiner*, May 29:

STENSLAND CONVICTED – JAIL FOR L.A. POLICEMAN

. . . the eight-man, four-woman jury found Stensland guilty on four counts: First Degree Assault, Aggravated Assault, First Degree Battery and Mayhem, the charges stemming from the former police detective's alleged maltreatment of Central Jail prisoners during last year's 'Bloody Christmas' scandal. In biting testimony, Sergeant E. J. Exley of the LAPD described Stensland's 'rampage against unarmed men.' Stensland's attorney, Jacob Kellerman, attacked Exley's credibility, stating that he was locked in a storeroom throughout most of the morning the events took place. In the end, the jurors believed Sergeant Exley, and Kellerman, citing the suspended sentence received by Bloody Christmas defendant John Brownell, asked Judge Arthur Fitzhugh to take mercy on his client. The judge did not oblige. He sentenced Stensland, already dismissed from the LAPD, to a year in the County Jail and remanded him to the custody of the Sheriff's deputies who would escort him to Wayside Honor Rancho. As he was led away, Stensland shouted obscenities regarding Sergeant Exley, who could not be reached for comment.

FEATURE: *Cavalcade Weekend Magazine*, L.A. *Mirror*, July 3:

TWO EXLEY GENERATIONS SERVE THE SOUTHLAND

The first thing that strikes you about Preston Exley

and his son Edmund is that they don't talk like cops, even though Preston served with the Los Angeles Police Department for fourteen years and Ed has been with the LAPD since 1943, shortly before he went off to war and won himself the Distinguished Service Cross in the Pacific Theater. In fact, before the Exley clan emigrated to America, their family tree spawned generations of Scotland Yard detectives. So police work is in the clan's blood, but even more so is a thirst for advancement.

Item: Preston Exley took an engineering degree at USC, studying by night while he pounded a dangerous downtown beat by day.

Item: The late Thomas Exley, Preston's eldest son, achieved the highest scholastic average in the history of the LAPD Academy, and a plaque commemorating him is hung in the Academy's administration building. Tragically, Thomas was killed in the line of duty soon after his graduation. Further item: The second highest average was earned by Ed Exley himself, a summa cum laude UCLA graduate – at nineteen! – in 1941. Evidence going back generations: the Exleys don't talk like cops because they are not typical policemen.

Both men have been in the news lately. Preston, 58, has teamed up with world-renowned cartoonist/movie-maker/TV show host Raymond Dieterling to build Dream-a-Dreamland, the monumental amusement park that broke ground six months ago, with completion and opening scheduled for late April of next year. Exley Senior began his career in the construction business after he left the LAPD in 1936, taking his chief aide, Lieutenant Arthur De Spain, with him. At his spacious Hancock Park mansion, Preston Exley spoke with *Mirror* correspondent Dick St. Germain.

'I had an engineering degree and Art knew building materials,' he said. 'We had our combined life savings and borrowed from some independent investors who appreciated the wildcat mentality. We started Exley Construction and built cheap houses, then better houses, then office buildings, then the Arroyo Seco Freeway. We flourished beyond my wildest dreams. Now Dream-a-Dreamland, the gentle dreams of millions of people realized on two hundred acres. In a way, its a hard one to top.'

Exley smiled. 'Ray Dieterling is a visionary,' he said. 'Dream-a-Dreamland will give people the chance to live the many worlds he has created through films and animation. The mountain that he's calling Paul's World is a perfect example. Paul Dieterling, Ray's son, died tragically in an avalanche back in the mid-30s. Now there will be a mountain that serves as a benevolent testimony to the boy, a mountain that brings people joy, with a percentage of the revenues earned going to children's charities. That's a hard one to top.'

But will he try to top it?

Exley smiled again. 'I'm addressing the Los Angeles County Board of Supervisors and the State Legislature next week,' he said. 'The subject will be the cost of Southern California mass rapid transit and the best way to link the Southland by freeway. Frankly, I want the job and I'm ready to offer the county an enticing bid.'

And then?

Exley smiled and sighed. 'And then there's all these politico fellows who've been pestering me,' he said. 'They think I'd be a natural for mayor, governor, senator or whatever, even though I keep telling them that Fletcher Bowron, Dick Nixon and Earl Warren are friends of mine.'

But is he ruling politics out?

'I rule nothing out,' Preston Exley said. 'Setting limitations is against my nature.'

And, as our reporters discovered, his son Edmund, now a detective sergeant with the LAPD's Hollywood Division, feels the same way. Recently in the news

79

for testifying in a trial related to the 'Bloody Christmas' police scandal, Ed Exley sees blue skies ahead – although he plans to keep police work his sole career. Speaking to our correspondent at his family's Lake Arrowhead cabin, Exley Junior said, 'I want nothing other than to be a valuable, ranking detective presented with challenging cases. My father had the Loren Atherton case' – a reference to the 1934 child murderer who claimed six victims, including child star Wee Willie Wennerholm – 'and I'd like to be in a position to work cases of that importance. Being in the right place at the right time is important, and I have a deep need to solve things and create order out of chaotic situations, which I believe is a good drive for a detective to have.'

Exley was certainly in the right place at the right time in the fall of 1943, when, the sole survivor of a bayonet attack on his platoon, he single-handedly wiped out three trenches full of Japanese infantry. He was in the right place at the right time for justice when he courageously testified against fellow officers in a massive police brutality scandal. Exley says of the two incidents: 'That's the past, and right now I'm building for my future. I'm getting solid experience working Hollywood Detectives, and my father, Art De Spain and I spend evenings performing mock questionings to help me perfect my interrogation techniques. My father wants the world, but all I want is the most this police department has to offer.'

Preston Exley and Ed Exley survive Thomas, and Marguerite (nee Tibbetts) Exley, the clan's matriarch, who died of cancer six years ago. Do they feel the loss in their personal lives?

Preston said, 'God, yes, every day. They are both irreplaceable.'

On that subject, Edmund was more reflective. 'Thomas was Thomas,' he said. 'I was seventeen when he died and I don't think I ever knew him. My mother was different. I knew her, she was kind and brave and strong, and there was something sad about her. I miss her, and I think the woman I marry will probably be like her, only a bit more volatile.'

Two generations for this week's Profile – two men going places and serving the Southland while they do it.

BANNER: L.A. *Times*, July 9:

LOEW ANNOUNCES D.A.'S CANDIDACY

BANNER: Society page,
L.A. *Herald-Express*, September 12:

GALA LOEW/MORROW WEDDING ATTRACTS HOLLYWOOD, LEGAL CROWDS

EXTRACT: L.A. *Times*, November 7:

McPHERSON AND LOEW TOP D.A.'S FIELD: WILL CLASH IN SPRING ELECTION

William McPherson, seeking his fourth term as Los Angeles district attorney, will face upstart Deputy D.A. Ellis Loew in next March's general election, the two colleagues leading an eight-man field by a wide margin.

McPherson, 56, received 38 percent of the votes cast; Loew, 41, received 36 percent. Their closest rival was Donald Chapman, the former city parks commissioner, with 14 percent. The remaining five candidates, considered long shots with little chance of winning, received a total of 12 percent of the votes cast between them.

McPherson, in a scheduled press conference, predicted a down-to-the-wire campaign and stressed that he is an incumbent civil servant first and a political candidate second. Loew, at home with his wife, Joan, echoed those sentiments, predicted victory next March and thanked the voters at large and the law enforcement community in particular for their support.

1953

LAPD Annual Fitness Report,
Marked *Confidential*, dated
1/3/53, filed by Lt. Dudley
Smith, copies to Personnel and
Administration Divisions:

1/2/53
ANNUAL FITNESS REPORT
DUTY DATES: 4/4/52–12/31/52
SUBJECT: White, Wendell A., Badge 916
GRADE: Police Officer (Detective) (Civil Serv. Rate 4)
Division: Detective Bureau (Homicide Adjunct Surveillance Detail)
COMMANDING OFFICER: Lt. Dudley L. Smith, Badge 410.

Gentlemen:
This memorandum serves both as a fitness report on Officer White and an update on the first nine months of the Surveillance Detail's existence. Of the sixteen men working the squad, I consider White my finest officer. To date he has been attentive, thorough, and has put in long hours without complaint. He has a perfect attendance record, and has often worked two-week stretches of eighteen-hour days. White transferred to Surveillance under the cloud of last year's unfortunate Christmas mess, and Deputy Chief Green, citing the four excessive-force complaints filed against him, had some misgivings about the transfer (i.e.: that White's propensity for violence and the potentially violent nature of the assignment would

82

prove to be a disastrous combination). This has not proven to be the case, and I unhesitatingly give Officer White straight 'A' markings in every fitness category. He has often evinced spectacular bravery. By way of example, I would like to cite several instances of White's performance above and beyond the call of duty.

1. 5/8/52. On a liquor store stakeout, Officer White (who is plagued by old football injuries) chased a fleeing armed suspect for a half mile. The suspect fired repeatedly back at Officer White, who did not return his fire for fear of hitting innocent civilians. The suspect took a woman hostage and held a gun to her head, which held off the backup officers who had caught up with Officer White. White then walked through a side alley while his partners attempted to calm the suspect down. The suspect refused to release the woman, and White shot and killed him at point-blank range. The woman was unharmed.

2. Numerous instances. One of the key duties of the Surveillance Detail is to meet paroled prison inmates upon their return to Los Angeles and try to convince them of the folly of committing violent crimes in our city. This job requires great physical presence, and Officer White has, frankly, been instrumental in scaring many hardened criminals into a docile parole. He has spent much off-duty time tailing parolees with particularly violent records, and he is responsible for the arrest of John 'Big Dog' Cassese, a twice-convicted rapist and armed robber. On 7/20/52, White, while surveilling Cassese inside a cocktail lounge, overheard him attempting to suborn a minor female into prostitution. Cassese attempted to resist arrest, and Officer White subdued him through physical means. Later, White and two other Surveillance officers (Sgt. Michael Breuning, Officer R. J. Carlisle) questioned Cassese extensively about his post-parole activities. Cassese confessed to the rape/murders of three women. (See Homicide arrest report

168-A, dated 7/22/52.) Cassese was tried, convicted and executed at San Quentin.

3. 10/18/52. Officer White, while surveilling parolee Percy Haskins, observed Haskins in a known criminal assembly with Robert Mackey and Karl Carter Goff. All three men possessed long armed-robbery records, and White sensed that a major felony was in the making and proceeded on that assumption. He tailed Haskins, Mackey and Goff to a market at 1683 S. Berendo. The three robbed the market, and White attempted to arrest them outside. The three refused to relinquish their weapons. White shot and killed Goff and severely wounded Mackey. Haskins surrendered. Mackey later died of his wounds and Haskins pleaded guilty to armed robbery with priors and was given a life sentence.

In summary, Officer White has taken the high ground and has been instrumental in making the Surveillance Detail's first year a resounding success. I will be returning to my regular Homicide duties effective 3/15/53 and would like Officer White to join my squad as a regular Homicide detective. In my opinion, he has the makings of a fine case man.

Respectfully,
Dudley L. Smith, Badge 410,
Lieutenant, Homicide Division

LAPD Annual Fitness Report,
marked *Confidential*, dated 1/6/53,
filed by Capt. Russell Millard,
copies to Personnel and Administration
Divisions:

1/6/53
ANNUAL FITNESS REPORT
DUTY DATES: 4/13/52–12/31/52
SUBJECT: Vincennes, John, Badge 2302
GRADE: Detective Sergeant (Civil Serv. Rate 5)

DIVISION: Detective Bureau (Administrative Vice)
COMMANDING OFFICER: Capt. Russell A. Millard, Badge 5009

Gentlemen:

An overall 'D+' fitness rating for Sergeant Vincennes, along with some comments.

A. Since he doesn't drink, Vincennes is excellent at liquor violation operations.

B. Vincennes oversteps his bounds where narcotics are concerned, insisting on making possession arrests when dope is found collaterally at Ad Vice crime scenes.

C. He has not fulfilled my fears that he would neglect his Ad Vice duties to offer assistance to his Bureau mentor, Lt. Dudley Smith. This is to Vincennes' credit.

D. Vincennes is not terribly resented for his testimony in the Christmas assaults matter, because he lost his much coveted Narco assignment and because none of the officers he specifically informed on went to jail.

E. Vincennes is continually pressing me to return him to Narco. I will not sign his transfer papers until he makes a major case at Ad Vice – this is a long-standing Ad Vice transfer stipulation. Vincennes has had Deputy D.A. Ellis Loew exert pressure on me to transfer him, and I have refused. I will continue to refuse, even if Loew is elected D.A.

F. There are rumors that Vincennes leaks interdepartmental information to the *Hush-Hush* scandal rag. I have warned him: never leak word of our work or I will have your hide.

G. In conclusion, Vincennes has proven himself a barely adequate Ad Vice officer. His attendance is good, his reports are well written (and, I suspect, padded). He is too well known to operate bookmakers and adequate at working prostitution sweeps. He has not neglected his duties to fulfill his TV show commitments, which is to his credit. Ad Vice has a probable pornography crackdown coming up within the next few months and Vincennes has a chance to prove his mettle (and earn his major case transfer requirement) on that. Again, an overall 'D+' rating.

Respectfully,
Russell A. Millard, Badge 5009,
Commanding Officer,
Administrative Vice

LAPD Annual Fitness Report,
marked *Confidential*, dated 1/11/53,
filed by Lt. Arnold Reddin,
Commander, Hollywood Division Detective
Squad, copies to Personnel and
Administration Divisions:

1/11/53
ANNUAL FITNESS REPORT
DUTY DATES: 3/1/52–12/31/52
SUBJECT: Exley, Edmund J., Badge 1104
GRADE: Detective Sergeant (Civil Serv. Rate 5)
DIVISION: Detective (Hollywood Squad)
COMMANDING OFFICER: Lt. Arnold D. Reddin, Badge 556

Gentlemen:
On Sergeant Exley:
This man has obvious gifts as a detective. He is thorough, intelligent, seems to have no personal life and works very long hours. He is only thirty years old and in his nine months as a detective he has amassed a brilliant arrest record, with a 95 percent conviction rate on the cases (mostly minor felony property crimes) he has made. He is a thorough and succinct report writer.

Exley works poorly with partners and well by himself, so I have let him conduct interviews alone. He is a peerless interrogator and to my mind has gotten many miraculous confessions (without physical force). All well and good, and my overall fitness grade on Exley is a solid 'A.'

But he is roundly hated by his fellow officers, the result of his serving as an informant in the Christmas shake-up, and he is despised for receiving a Bureau assignment out of it. (It seems to be common knowledge that Exley made the Detective Bureau as a result of his informing.) Also, Exley does not like to employ force with suspects, and most of the men consider him a coward.

Exley has passed the lieutenant's exam with very high marks and an opening is probably coming up for him. I think he is both too young and too inexperienced to be a detective lieutenant and that such a promotion would create great resentment. I think he would be a roundly hated supervisor.

Respectfully,
Lt. Arnold D. Reddin, Badge 556

EXTRACT: L.A. *Daily News*, February 9:

IT'S OFFICIAL: CONSTRUCTION KING EXLEY TO LINK SOUTHLAND WITH SUPERHIGHWAYS

Today, the Tri-County Highway Commission announced that Preston Exley, ex-San Francisco paperboy and L.A. cop, would be the man to build the freeway system that will link Hollywood to downtown L.A., downtown to San Pedro, Pomona to San Bernardino and the South Bay to the San Fernando Valley.

'Details will be forthcoming,' Exley told the *News* by phone. 'I'll be holding a televised press conference tomorrow, and representatives of the State Legislature and the Tri-County Commission will be there with me.'

February 1953 issue, *Hush-Hush* Magazine:

L.A. D.A. TAKES TIME OFF FROM CAMPAIGN – RELAXING WITH COPPER CUTIE!!!
by Sidney Hudgens

Bill McPherson, the district attorney for the City of Los Angeles, likes them long and leggy, zesty and chesty – and dark and dusky. From Harlem's Sugar Hill to L.A.'s Darktown, the 57-year-old married man with three teenaged daughters is known as a sugar daddy who likes to toss around that long slush-fund green – in dark hot spots where the drinks are tall, the jazz is cool, reefer smoke hangs humid and black-white romance bebops to the jungle throb of a wailing tenor sax.

Can you dig it, hepcat? McPherson, engaged in a reelection campaign, the fight of his political life against ace crimebuster Ellis Loew, needs time to relax. Does he go to the pool at the staid Jonathan Club? No. Does he take the family to Mike Lyman's or the Pacific Dining Car? No. Where *does* he go? To the Darktown Strutter's Ball.

It's all shakin' south of Jefferson, hepcat. It's a different world down there. Get your hair marcelled, get yourself a purple sharkskin suit and trip the dark fantastic. D.A. Bill McPherson does – every Thursday nite.

But let's talk facts. Marion McPherson, Darktown Bill's long-suffering hausfrau, thinks Billy Boy spends Thursday nites watching Mexican bantamweights pound each other silly at the Olympic Auditorium. She's wrongsky – Bad Billy craves amour, not mayhem, on his Thursdays.

Fact numero uno – Bill McPherson is a regular

at Minnie Roberts' Casbah – the swankiest colored cathouse on L.A.'s southside. Call it sinuendo, hepcat – but we've heard he likes the thirty-five-dollar milkbath, plied by two very large Congo cuties. Fact numero twosky – McPherson was seen listening to Charlie 'Bird' Parker (a notorious hophead) at Tommy Tucker's Playroom, on cloud ten from the Playroom's potent Plantation Punch. His date that night was one Lynette Brown, age eighteen, a dusky deelite with two juvenile arrests for possession of marijuana. Lynette told a secret *Hush-Hush* correspondent, 'Bill like his black. He say, "Once you had black you can't go back." He dig jazz and he like to party slow. He really married? He really distric' 'turney?'

He sure is, sweet thing. But for how much longer? There's a bunch of Thursdays between now and Election Day, and will Bad Bebop Billy be able to control his dark desires until then?

Remember, dear reader, you heard it first here – off the record, on the Q.T. and *very Hush-Hush*.

EXTRACT: L.A. *Herald-Express*, March 1:

BLOODY CHRISTMAS POLICEMAN TO LEAVE JAIL SOON

On April 2, Richard Alex Stensland leaves Wayside Honor Rancho a free man. Convicted last year on four assault charges related to the 1951 Bloody Christmas police brutality scandal, he walks out an ex-cop with an uncertain future.

Stensland's former partner, Officer Wendell White, spoke to the *Herald*. He said, 'It was the luck of the draw, that —— Christmas thing. I was there, and I could have been the guy that swung. It was Dick, though. He made a good cop out of me. I owe him for that and I'm —— mad at what happened to him. I'm still Dick's friend, and I bet he's still got lots of friends in the Department.'

And among the civilian population, it appears. Stensland told a *Herald* reporter that upon his release he'll go to work for Abraham Teitlebaum, the owner of Abe's Noshery, a delicatessen in West Los Angeles. Asked whether he bears grudges against any of the people who put him in jail, Stensland said, 'Only one. But I'm too law-abiding to do anything about it.'

L.A. *Daily News*, March 6:

SCANDAL TURNS CLOSE D.A.'S RACE TO LANDSLIDE

It was expected to go down to the wire: incumbent city D.A. William McPherson vs. Deputy D.A. Ellis Loew, the winner to hold the job as top elected crime-fighter in the Southland for the next four years. Both men campaigned on the issues: how to deploy the city's legal budget the best way, how to most efficaciously fight crime. Both men, predictably, claimed they would fight crime the hardest. The L.A. law enforcement establishment considered McPherson soft on crime and too liberal in general and threw their support to Loew. Union organizations supported the incumbent. McPherson stood pat on his status quo record and played off his nice-guy personality, and Loew tried a young firebrand routine that didn't work: he came off as theatrical and vote-hungry. It was a gentleman's campaign until the February issue of *Hush-Hush* magazine hit the stands.

Most people take *Hush-Hush* and other scandal sheets with a grain of salt, but this was election time. An article alleged that D.A. McPherson, happily married for twenty-six years, cavorted with young Negro women. The D.A. ignored the article, which was accompanied by photographs of him and a Negro girl, taken at a nightclub in south central Los Angeles. Mrs. McPherson did not ignore the article – she filed for divorce. Ellis Loew did not mention the article in his campaign, and McPherson began to slip in the polls. Then, three days before the election, Sheriff's deputies raided the Lilac View Motel on the Sunset Strip, acting on the tip of an 'unknown informant' who called in with word of an illegal assignation in room 9. The assignators proved to be D.A. McPherson and a young Negro prostitute, age 14. The deputies arrested McPherson on statutory rape charges and heard out the story of Marvell Wilkins, a minor with two soliciting arrests.

She told them that McPherson picked her up on South Western Avenue, offered her twenty dollars for an hour of her time and drove her to the Lilac View. McPherson pleaded amnesia: he recalled having 'several martinis' at a dinner meeting with supporters at the Pacific Dining Car restaurant, then getting into his car. He remembers nothing after that. The rest is history: reporters and photographers arrived at the Lilac View Motel shortly after the deputies, McPherson became front-page news and on Tuesday Ellis Loew was elected city district attorney by a landslide.

Something seems fishy here. Scandal-rag journalism should not dictate the thrust of political campaigns, although we at the *Daily News* (admitted McPherson supporters) would never abridge their right to print whatever filth they desire. We have tried to locate Marvell Wilkins, but the girl, released from custody, seems to have disappeared off the face of the earth. Without pointing fingers, we at the *Daily News* ask District Attorney-elect Loew to initiate a grand jury investigation into this matter, if for no other reason than his desire to assume his new office with no dark clouds overhead.

Part Two

Nite Owl Massacre

Chapter Fourteen

The whole squadroom to himself.

A retirement party downstairs – he wasn't invited. The weekly crime report to be read, summarized, tacked to the bulletin board – nobody else ever did it, they knew he did it best. The papers ballyhooing the Dream-a-Dreamland opening – the other cops Moochie mouse-squeaked him ad nauseam. Space Cooley playing the party; pervert Deuce Perkins roaming the halls. Midnight and nowhere near sleepy – Ed read, typed.

4/9/53: a transvestite shoplifter hit four stores on Hollywood Boulevard, disabled two salesclerks with judo chops. 4/10/53: an usher at Grauman's Chinese stabbed to death by two male Caucasians – he told them to put out their cigarettes. Suspects still at large; Lieutenant Reddin said he was too inexperienced to handle a homicide – he didn't get the job. 4/11/53: a stack of crime sheets – several times over the past two weeks a carload of Negro youths were seen discharging shotguns into the air in the Griffith Park hills. No IDs, the kids driving a '48–'50 purple Mercury coupe. 4/11–4/13/53: five daytime burglaries, private homes north of the Boulevard, jewelry stolen. Nobody assigned yet; Ed made a note: bootjack the job, dust before the access points got pawed. Today was the fourteenth – he might have a chance.

Ed finished up. The empty squadroom made him happy: nobody who hated him, a big space filled with desks and filing cabinets. Official forms on the walls – empty spaces you filled in when you notched an arrest and made somebody confess. Confessions could be ciphers, nothing past an admission of the crime. But if you twisted your man the right way – loved him and hated him to precisely the right degree – then he would tell you things – small details – that would create a reality to buttress your case and give you that much more intelligence to bend the next suspect with. Art De Spain and his father taught how to find the spark point. They had boxloads of old steno transcripts: kiddie rapers, heisters, assorted riffraff who'd confessed to them. Art would rabbit-punch – but he used the threat more than the act. Preston Exley rarely hit – he considered it the criminal defeating the policem in and creating disorder. They read elliptical answers and made him guess the questions; they gave him a rundown of common criminal experiences – wedges to get the flow started. They showed him that men have levels of weakness that are acceptable because other men condone them and levels of weakness that produce a great shame, something to hide from all but a brilliant confessor. They honed his instinct for the jugular of weakness. It got so sharp that sometimes he couldn't look at himself in the mirror.

The sessions ran late – two widowers, a young man without a woman. Art had a bug on multiple murders – he had his father rehash the Loren Atherton case repeatedly: horror snatches, witness testimony. Preston obliged with psychological theories, grudgingly – he wanted his glory case to stay sealed off, complete, in his mind. Art's old cases were scrutinized – and *he* reaped the efforts of three fine minds: confessions straight across, 95 percent convictions. But so far his drive to crack criminal knowledge hadn't been challenged – much less sated.

Ed walked down to the parking lot, sleep coming on. 'Quack, quack,' behind him – hands turned him around.

A man in a kid's mask – Danny Duck. A left-right knocked off his glasses; a kidney shot put him down. Kicks to the ribs drove him into a ball.

Ed curled hard, caught kicks in the face. A flashbulb popped; two men walked away: one quacking, one laughing. Easy IDs: Dick Stensland's bray, Bud White's football limp. Ed spat blood, swore payback.

Chapter Fifteen

Russ Millard addressed Ad Vice squad 4 – the topic pornography.

'Picture-book smut, gentlemen. There's been a bunch of it found at collateral crime scenes lately: narcotics, bookmaking and prostitution collars. Normally this kind of stuff is made in Mexico, so it's not our jurisdiction. Normally it's an organized crime sideline, because the big mobs have the money to manufacture it and the connections to get it distributed. But Jack Dragna's been deported, Mickey Cohen's in prison and probably too puritanical anyway, and Mo Jahelka's foundering on his own. Stag pix aren't Jack Whalen's style – he's a bookie looking to get his hands on a Vegas casino. And the stuff that's surfaced is too high quality for the L.A. area print mills: Newton Street Vice rousted them, they're clean, they just don't have the facilities to make magazines of this quality. But the backdrops in the pictures indicate L.A. venue: you can see what looks like the Hollywood Hills out some windows, and the furnishings in a lot of the places look like your typical cheap Los Angeles apartments. So our job is to track this filth to its source and arrest whoever made it, posed for it and distributed it.'

Jack groaned: the Great Jerk-off Book Caper of 1953. The other guys looked hot to glom the smut, maybe fuel up their wives. Millard popped a Digitalis. 'Newton Street dicks questioned everyone at the collateral rousts, and they all denied possessing the stuff. Nobody at the print mills knows where it was made. The mags have been shown around the Bureau and our station vice squads, and we've got zero IDs on the posers. So, gentlemen, look yourself.'

Henderson and Kifka had their hands out; Stathis

looked ready to drool. Millard passed the smut over. 'Vincennes, is there someplace you'd rather be?'

'Yeah, Captain. Narcotics Division.'

'Oh? Anyplace else?'

'Maybe working whores with squad two.'

'Make a major case, Sergeant. I'd love to sign you out of here.'

Oohs, ahhs, cackles, oo-la-las; three men shook their heads no. Jack grabbed the books.

Seven mags, high-quality glossy paper, plain black covers. Sixteen pages apiece: photos in color, black and white. Two books ripped in half; explicit pictures: men and women, men and men, girls and girls. Insertion close-ups: straight, queer, dykes with dildoes. The Hollywood sign out windows; Murphy-bed fuck shots, cheap pads: stucco-swirled walls, the hot plate on a table that came with every bachelor flop in L.A. Par for the stag-book course – but the posers weren't glassy-eyed hopheads, they were good-looking, well-built young kids – nude, costumed: Elizabethan garb, Jap kimonos. Jack put the ripped mags back together for a bingo: Bobby Inge – a male prostitute he'd popped for reefer – blowing a guy in a whalebone corset.

Millard said, 'Anybody familiar, Vincennes?'

An angle. 'Nothing, Cap. But where did you get these torn-up jobs?'

'They were found in a trash bin behind an apartment house in Beverly Hills. The manager, an old woman named Loretta Downey, found them and called the Beverly Hills P.D. They called us.'

'You got an address on the building?'

Millard checked an evidence form. '9849 Charleville. Why?'

'I just thought I'd take that part of the job. I've got good connections in Beverly Hills.'

'Well, they do call you "Trashcan." All right, follow up in Beverly Hills. Henderson, you and Kifka try to locate the arrestees in the crime reports and try to find out *again* where they got the stuff – I'll get you carbons in a minute. Tell them there'll be no additional charges filed if they talk. Stathis, take that filth by the costume supply companies and see if you can get a matchup to their inventory, then find out who rented the costumes the . . . performers were wearing. Let's try it this way first – if we have to go through mugshots for IDs we'll lose a goddamn week. Dismissed, gentlemen. Roll, Vincennes. And don't get sidetracked – this is Ad Vice, not Narco.'

Jack rolled: R&I, Bobby Inge's file, his angle flushed out: Beverly Hills, see the old biddy, see what he could find out and concoct a hot lead that told him what he already knew – Bobby Inge was guilty of conspiracy to distribute obscene material, a felony bounce. Bobby would snitch his co-stars and the guys who took the pix – one major class transfer requirement dicked.

The day was breezy, cool; Jack took Olympic straight west. He kept the radio going; a newscast featured Ellis Loew: budget cuts at the D.A.'s Office. Ellis droned on; Jack flipped the dial – a kibosh on thoughts of Bill McPherson. He caught a happy Broadway tune, thought about him anyway.

Hush-Hush was his idea: McPherson liked colored poon, Sid Hudgens loved writing up jig-fuckers. Ellis Loew knew about it, approved of it, considered it another favor on deposit. McPherson's wife filed for divorce; Loew was satisfied – he took a lead in the polls. Dudley Smith wanted more – and set up the tank job.

An easy parlay:

Dot Rothstein knew a colored girl doing a stretch at Juvenile Hall: soliciting beefs, Dot and the girl kept a thing sizzling whenever she did time. Dot got the little twist sprung; Dudley and his ace goon Mike Breuning fixed up a room at the Lilac View Motel: the most notorious fuck pad on the Sunset Strip, county ground where the city D.A. would be just another john caught with his pants down. McPherson attended a Dining Car soiree; Dudley had Marvell Wilkins – fourteen, dark, witchy – waiting outside. Breuning alerted the West Hollywood

Sheriff's and the press; the Big V dropped chloral hydrates in McPherson's last martini. Mr. D.A. left the restaurant woozy, swerved his Cadillac a mile or so, pulled over at Wilshire and Alvarado and passed out. Breuning cruised up behind him with the bait: Marvell in a cocktail gown. He took the wheel of McPherson's Caddy, hustled Bad Bill and the girl to their tryst spot – the rest was political history.

Ellis Loew wasn't told – he figured he just got lucky. Dot sent Marvell down to Tijuana, all expenses paid – skim off the Woman's Jail budget. McPherson lost his wife and his job; his statch rape charge was dismissed – Marvell couldn't be located. Something snapped inside the Bigggg V –

The snap: one shitty favor over the line. The reason: Dot Rothstein in the ambulance October '47 – she knew, Dudley probably knew. If they knew, the game had to be played so the rest of the world wouldn't know – so Karen wouldn't.

He'd been her hero a solid year; somehow the bit got real. He stopped sending the Scoggins kids money, closing out his debt at forty grand – he needed cash to court Karen, being with her gave him some distance on the Malibu Rendezvous. Joan Morrow Loew stayed bitchy; Welton and the old lady grudgingly accepted him – and Karen loved him so hard it almost hurt. Working Ad Vice hurt – the job was a snore, he hot-dogged on dope every time he got a shot. Sid Hudgens didn't call so much – he wasn't a Narco dick now. After the McPherson gig he was glad – he didn't know if he could pull another shakedown.

Karen had her own lies going – they helped his hero bit play true. Trust fund, beach pad paid for by Daddy, grad school. Dilettante stuff: he was thirty-eight, she was twenty-three, in time she'd figure it out. She wanted to marry him; he resisted; Ellis Loew as an in-law meant bagman duty until he dropped dead. He knew why his hero role worked: Karen was the audience he'd always wanted to impress. He knew what she could take, what she couldn't; her love had shaped his performance so that

100

all he had to do was act natural – and keep certain secrets hidden.

Traffic snagged; Jack turned north on Doheny, west on Charleville. 9849 – a two-story Tudor – stood a block off Wilshire. Jack double-parked, checked mailboxes.

Six slots: Loretta Downey, five other names – three Mr. & Mrs., one man, one woman. Jack wrote them down, walked to Wilshire, found a pay phone. Calls to R&I and the DMV police information line; two waits. No criminal records on the tenants; one standout vehicle sheet: Christine Bergeron, the mailbox 'Miss,' four reckless-driving convictions, no license revocation. Jack got extra stats off the clerk: the woman was thirty-seven years old, her occupation was listed as actress/car hop, as of 7/52 she was working at Stan's Drive-in in Hollywood.

Instincts: carhops don't live in Beverly Hills; maybe Christine Bergeron hopped some bones to stretch the rent. Jack walked back to 9849, knocked on the door marked 'Manager.'

An old biddy opened up. 'Yes, young man?'

Jack flashed his badge. 'L.A. Police, ma'am. It's about those books you found.'

The biddy squinted through Coke-bottle glasses. 'My late husband would have seen to justice himself, Mr. Harold Downey had no tolerance for dirty things.'

'Did you find those magazines yourself, Mrs. Downey?'

'No, young man, my cleaning lady did. *She* tore them up and threw them in the trash, where I found them. I questioned Eula about it after I called the Beverly Hills police.'

'Where did Eula find the books?'

'Well . . . I . . . don't know if I should . . . '

A switcheroo. 'Tell me about Christine Bergeron.'

Harumph. 'That woman! And that boy of hers! I don't know who's worse!'

'Is she a difficult tenant, ma'am?'

'She entertains men at all hours! She roller-skates on the floor in those tight waitress outfits of hers! She's got

101

a no-goodnik son who never goes to school! Seventeen years old and a truant who associates with lounge lizards!'

Jack held out a Bobby Inge mugshot; the biddy held it up to her glasses. 'Yes, this is one of Daryl's no-goodnik friends, I've seen him skulking around here a dozen times. Who *is* he?'

'Ma'am, did Eula find those dirty books in the Bergeron apartment?'

'Well . . . '

'Ma'am, are Christine Bergeron and the boy at home now?'

'No, I heard them leave a few hours ago. I have keen ears to make up for my poor eyesight.'

'Ma'am, if you let me into their apartment and I find some more dirty books, you could earn a reward.'

'Well . . . '

'Have you got keys, ma'am?'

'Of course I have keys, I'm the manager. Now, I'll let you look if you promise not to touch and I don't have to pay withholding tax on my reward.'

Jack took the mugshot back. 'Whatever you want, ma'am.'

The old woman walked upstairs, up to the second-floor units. Jack followed; granny unlocked the third door down. 'Five minutes, young man. And be respectful of the furnishings – my brother-in-law owns this building.'

Jack walked in. Tidy living room, scratched floor – probably roller-skate tracks. Quality furniture, worn, ill-cared-for. Bare walls, no TV, two framed photos on an end table – publicity-type shots.

Jack checked them out; old lady Downey stuck close. Matching pewter frames – two good-looking people.

A pretty woman – light hair in a pageboy, eyes putting out a cheap sparkle. A pretty boy who looked just like her – extra blond, big stupid eyes. 'Is this Christine and her son?'

'Yes, and they are an attractive pair, I'll give them that. Young man, what is the amount of that reward you mentioned?'

Jack ignored her and hit the bedroom: through the drawers, in the closet, under the mattress. No smut, no dope, nothing hinky – negligees the only shit worth a sniff.

'Young man, your five minutes are up. And I want a written guarantee that I will receive that reward.'

Jack turned around smiling. 'I'll mail it to you. And I need another minute or so to check their address book.'

'No! No! They could come home at any moment! I want you to leave this instant!'

'Just one minute, ma'am.'

'No, no, no! Out with you this second!'

Jack made for the door. The old bat said, 'You remind me of that policeman on that television program that's so popular.'

'I taught him everything he knows.'

He felt a quickie shaping up.

Bobby Inge rats off the smut peddlers, turns state's, some kind of morals rap on him and Daryl Bergeron: the kid was a minor, Bobby was a notorious fruitfly with a rap sheet full of homo-pandering beefs. Wrap it up tight: confessions, suspects located, lots of paperwork for Millard. The big-time Big V cracks the big-time filth ring and wings back to Narco a hero.

Up to Hollywood, a loop by Stan's Drive-in – Christine Bergeron slinging hash on skates. Pouty, provocative – the quasi-hooker type, maybe the type to pose with a dick in her mouth.

Jack parked, read the Bobby Inge sheet. Two outstanding bench warrants: traffic tickets, a failure-to-appear probation citation. Last known address 1424 North Hamel, West Hollywood – the heart of Lavender Gulch. Three fruit bars for 'known haunts' – Leo's Hideaway, the Knight in Armor, B.J.'s Rumpus Room – all on Santa Monica Boulevard nearby. Jack drove to Hamel Drive, his cuffs out and open.

A bungalow court off the Strip: county turf, 'Inge – Apt 6' on a mailbox. Jack found the pad, knocked, no

answer. 'Bobby, hey, sugar,' a falsetto trill – still no bite.
A locked door, drawn curtains – the whole place dead
quiet. Jack went back to his car, drove south.

Fag bar city: Inge's haunts in a two-block stretch. Leo's
Hideaway closed until 4:00; the Knight in Armor empty.
The barkeep vamped him – 'Bobby who?' – like he really
didn't know. Jack hit B.J.'s Rumpus Room.

Tufted Naugahyde inside – the walls, ceiling, booths
adjoining a small bandstand. Queers at the bar; the
barman sniffed cop right off. Jack walked over, laid his
mugshots out face up.

The barman picked them up. 'That's Bobby something.
He comes in pretty often.'

'How often?'

'Oh, like several times a week.'

'The afternoon or the evening?'

'Both.'

'When was the last time he was here?'

'Yesterday. Actually, it was around this time yesterday.
Are you – '

'I'm going to sit at one of those booths over there and
wait for him. If he shows up, keep quiet about me. Do
you understand?'

'Yes. But look, you've cleared the whole dance floor
out already.'

'Write it off your taxes.'

The barkeep giggled; Jack walked over to a booth near
the bandstand. A clean view: the front door, back door,
bar. Darkness covered him. He watched.

Queer mating rituals:

Glances, tête-à-têtes, out the door. A mirror above the
bar: the fruits could check each other out, meet eyes and
swoon. Two hours, half a pack of cigarettes – no Bobby
Inge.

His stomach growled; his throat felt raw; the bottles on
the bar smiled at him. Itchy boredom: at 4:00 he'd hit
Leo's Hideaway.

3:53 – Bobby Inge walked in.

104

He took a stool; the barman poured him a drink. Jack walked up.

The barman, spooked: darting eyes, shaky hands. Inge swiveled around. Jack said, 'Police. Hands on your head.'

Inge tossed his drink. Jack tasted scotch; scotch burned his eyes. He blinked, stumbled, tripped blind to the floor. He tried to cough the taste out, got up, got blurry sight back – Bobby Inge was gone.

He ran outside. No Bobby on the sidewalk, a sedan peeling rubber. His own car two blocks away.

Liquor brutalizing him.

Jack crossed the street, over to a gas station. He hit the men's room, threw his blazer in a trashcan. He washed his face, smeared soap on his shirt, tried to vomit the booze taste out – no go. Soapy water in the sink – he swallowed it, guzzled it, retched.

Coming to: his heart quit skidding, his legs firmed up. He took off his holster, wrapped it in paper towels, went back to the car. He saw a pay phone – and made the call on instinct.

Sid Hudgens picked up. *'Hush-Hush*, off the record and on the QT.'

'Sid, it's Vincennes.'

'Jackie, are you back on Narco? I need copy.'

'No, I've got something going with Ad Vice.'

'Something good? Celebrity oriented?'

'I don't know if it's good, but if it gets good you've got it.'

'You sound out of breath, Jackie. You been shtupping?'

Jack coughed – soap bubbles. 'Sid, I'm chasing some smut books. Picture stuff. Fuck shots, but the people don't look like junkies and they're wearing these expensive costumes. It's well-done stuff, and I thought you might have heard something about it.'

'No. No, I've heard bupkis.'

Too quick, no snappy one-liner. 'What about a male prostie named Bobby Inge or a woman named Christine Bergeron? She carhops, maybe peddles it on the side.'

'Never heard of them, Jackie.'

'Shit. Sid, what about independent smut pushers in general. What do you know?'

'Jack, I know that that is secret shit that I know nothing about. And the thing about secrets, Jack, is that everybody's got them. Including you. Jack, I'll talk to you later. Call when you get work.'

The line clicked off.

EVERYBODY'S GOT SECRETS – INCLUDING YOU.

Sid wasn't quite Sid, his exit line wasn't quite a warning.

DOES HE FUCKING KNOW?

Jack drove by Stan's Drive-in, shaky, the windows down to kill the soap smell. Christine Bergeron nowhere on the premises. Back to 9849 Charleville, knock knock on the door of her apartment – no answer, slack between the lock and the doorjamb. He gave a shove; the door popped.

A trail of clothes on the living room floor. The picture frame gone.

Into the bedroom, scared, his gun in the car.

Empty cabinets and drawers. The bed stripped. Into the bathroom.

Toothpaste and Kotex spilled in the shower. Glass shelves smashed in the sink.

Getaway – fifteen-minute style.

Back to West Hollywood – fast. Bobby Inge's door caved in easy; Jack went in gun first.

Clean-out number two – a better job.

A clean living room, pristine bathroom, bedroom showing empty dresser drawers. A can of sardines in the icebox. The kitchen trashcan clean, a fresh paper bag lining it.

Jack tore the pad up: living room, bedroom, bathroom, kitchen – shelves knocked over, rugs pulled, the toilet yanked apart. He stopped on a flash: garbage cans, full, lined both sides of the street –

There or gone.

Figure an hour-twenty since his run-in with Inge: the fuck wouldn't run straight to his crib. He probably got off the street, cruised back slow, risked the move out with his car parked in the alley. He figured the roust was for his old warrants or the smut gig; he knew he was standing heat and couldn't be caught harboring pornography. He wouldn't risk carrying it in his car – the odds on a shake were too strong. The gutter or the trash, right near the top of the cans, maybe more skin IDs for Big Trashcan Jack.

Jack hit the sidewalk, rooted in trashcans – gaggles of kids laughed at him. One, two, three, four, five – two left before the corner. No lid on the last can; glossy black paper sticking out.

Jack beelined.

Three fucking mags right on top. Jack grabbed them, ran back to his car, skimmed – the kids made goo-goo eyes at the windshield. The same Hollywood backdrops, Bobby Inge with boys and girls, unknown pretties screwing. Halfway through the third book the pix went haywire.

Orgies, hole-to-hole daisy chains, a dozen people on a quilt-covered floor. Disembodied limbs: red sprays off arms, legs. Jack squinted, eye-strain, the red was colored ink, the photos doctored – limb severings faked, ink blood flowing in artful little swirls.

Jack tried for IDs; obscene perfection distracted him: ink-bleeding nudes, no faces he knew until the last page: Christine Bergeron and her son fucking, standing on skates planted on a scuffed hardwood floor.

Chapter Sixteen

A photograph, dropped in his mailbox: Sergeant Ed Exley bleeding and terrified. No printing on the back, no need for it: Stensland and White had the negative, insurance that he'd never try to break them.

Ed, alone in the squadroom, 6:00 A.M. The stitches on his chin itched; loose teeth made eating impossible. Thirty-odd hours since the moment – his hands still trembled.

Payback.

He didn't tell his father; he couldn't risk the ignominy of going to Parker or Internal Affairs. Revenge on Bud White would be tricky: he was Dudley Smith's boy, Smith just got him a straight Homicide spot and was grooming him for his chief strongarm. Stensland was more vulnerable: on probation, working for Abe Teitlebaum, an ex-Mickey Cohen goon. A drunk, begging to go back inside.

Payback – already in the works.

Two Sheriff's men bought and paid for: a dip in his mother's trust fund. A two-man tail on Dick Stens, two men to swoop on his slightest probation fuckup.

Payback.

Ed did paperwork. His stomach growled: no food, loose trousers weighted down by his holster. A voice out the squawk box: loud, spooked.

'Squad call! Nite Owl Coffee Shop one-eight-two-four Cherokee! Multiple homicides! See the patrolmen! Code three!'

Ed banged his legs getting up. No other detectives on call – it was his.

Patrol cars at Hollywood and Cherokee; blues setting up crime scene blockades. No plainclothesmen in sight – he might get first crack.

Ed pulled up, doused his siren. A patrolman ran over.

'Load of people down, maybe some of them women. I found them, stopped for coffee and saw this phony sign on the door, "Closed for Illness." Man, the Nite Owl *never* closes. It was dark inside and I knew this was a hinky deal. Exley, this ain't your squawk, this has gotta be downtown stuff, so – '

Ed pushed him aside, pushed over to the door. Open, a sign taped on: 'Closed Due to Illness.' Ed stepped inside, memorized.

A long, rectangular interior. On the right: a string of tables, four chairs per. The side wall mural-papered: winking owls perched on street signs. A checkered linoleum floor; to the left a counter – a dozen stools. A service runway behind it, the kitchen in back, fronted by a cook's station: fryers, spatulas on hooks, a platform for laying down plates. At front left: a cash register.

Open, empty – coins on the floor mat beside it.

Three tables in disarray: food spilled, plates dumped; napkin containers, broken dishes on the floor. Drag marks leading back to the kitchen; one high-heeled pump by an upended chair.

Ed walked into the kitchen. Half-fried food, broken dishes, pans on the floor. A wall safe under the cook's counter – open, spilling coins. Crisscrossed drag marks connecting with the other drag marks, dark black heel smudges ending at the door of a walk-in food locker.

Ajar, the cord out of the socket – no cool air as a preservative. Ed opened it.

Bodies – a blood-soaked pile on the floor. Brains, blood and buckshot on the walls. Blood two feet deep collecting in a drainage trough. Dozens of shotgun shells floating in blood.

NEGRO YOUTHS DRIVING PURPLE '48–'50 MERC COUPE SEEN DISCHARGING SHOTGUNS INTO AIR IN GRIFFITH PARK HILLS SEVERAL TIMES OVER PAST TWO WEEKS.

Ed gagged, tried for a body count.

No discernible faces. Maybe five people dead for the cash register and safe take and what they had on them –

'Holy shit fuck.'

A rookie type – pale, almost green. Ed said, 'How many men outside?'

'I . . . I dunno. Lots.'

'Don't get sick, just get everybody together to start canvassing. We need to know if a certain type of car was seen around here tonight.'

'S-s-sir, there's this Detective Bureau man wants to see you.'

Ed walked out. Dawn up: fresh light on a mob scene. Patrolmen held back reporters; rubberneckers swarmed. Horns blasted; motorcycles ran interference: meat wagons cut off by the crowd. Ed looked for high brass; newsmen shouting questions stampeded him.

Pushed off the sidewalk, pinned to a patrol car. Flash-bulbs pop pop pop – he turned so his bruises wouldn't show. Strong hands grabbed him. 'Go home, lad. I've been given the command here.'

Chapter Seventeen

The first all-Bureau call-in in history – every downtown-based detective standing ready. The chief's briefing room jammed to the rafters.

Thad Green, Dudley Smith by a floor mike; the men facing them, itchy to go. Bud looked for Ed Exley – a chance to scope out his wounds. No Exley – scotch a rumor he caught the Nite Owl squeal.

Smith grabbed the mike. 'Lads, you all know why we're here. "Nite Owl Massacre" hyperbole aside, this is a heinous crime that requires a hard and swift resolution. The press and public will demand it, and since we already have solid leads, we will give it to them.

'There were six people dead in that locker – three men and three women. I have spoken to the Nite Owl's owner, and he told me that three of the dead are likely Patty Chesimard and Donna DeLuca, female Caucasians, the late-shift waitress and cash register girl, and Gilbert Escobar, male Mexican, the cook and dishwasher. The three other victims – two men, one woman – were almost certainly customers. The cash register and safe were empty and the victims' pockets and handbags were picked clean, which means that robbery was obviously the motive. SID is doing the forensic now – so far they have nothing but rubber glove prints on the cash register and food locker door. No time of death on the victims, but the scant number of customers and another lead we have indicates 3:00 A.M. as the time of the killings. A total of forty-five spent 12-gauge Remington shotgun shells were found in the locker. This indicates three men with five-shot-capacity pumps, all of them reloading twice. I do not have to tell you how gratuitous forty of those rounds were, lads. We are dealing with stark raving mad beasts here.'

Bud looked around. Still no Exley, a hundred men

jotting notes. Jack Vincennes in a corner, no notebook. Thad Green took over.

'No blood tracks leading outside. We were hoping for footprints to run eliminations against, but we didn't find any, and Ray Pinker from SID says the forensic will take at least forty-eight hours. The coroner says IDs on the customer victims will be extremely difficult because of the condition of the bodies. But we do have one very hot lead.

'Hollywood Division has taken a total of four crime reports on this, so listen well. Over the past two weeks a carload of Negro youths were seen discharging shotguns into the air up at Griffith Park. There were three of them, and the shotguns were pumps. The punks were not apprehended, but eyeball witnesses ID'd them as driving a 1948 to 1950 Mercury coupe, purple in color. And just an hour ago Lieutenant Smith's canvassing crew found a witness: a news vendor who saw a purple Merc coupe, '48–'50 vintage, parked across from the Nite Owl last night around 3:00 A.M.'

The room went loud: a big rumbling. Green gestured for quiet. 'It gets better, so listen well. There are no '48 to '50 purple Mercurys on the hot sheet, so it is very doubtful that we're dealing with a stolen car, and the state DMV has given us a registration list on '48 to '50 Mercurys statewide. Purple was an original color on the '48 to '50 coupe models, and those models were favored by Negroes. Over sixteen hundred are registered to Negroes in the State of California, and in Southern California there are only a very few registered to Caucasians. There are one hundred and fifty-six registered to Negroes in L.A. County, and there are almost a hundred of you men here. We have a list compiled: home and work addresses. The Hollywood squad is cross-checking for rap sheets. I want fifty two-man teams to shake three names apiece. There's a special phone line being set up at Hollywood Station, so if you need information on past addresses or known associates, you can call there. If you get hot suspects, bring them here to the Hall. We've got a string of interrogation rooms set up, along with a man to head the interro-

112

gations. Lieutenant Smith will give out the assignments in a second, and Chief Parker would like a word with you. Any questions first?'

A man yelled, 'Sir, who's running the interrogations?'

Green said, 'Sergeant Ed Exley, Hollywood squad.'

Catcalls, boos. Parker walked up to the mike. 'Enough on that. Gentlemen, just go out and get them. Use all necessary force.'

Bud smiled. The real message: kill the niggers clean.

Chapter Eighteen

Jack's list:

George NMI Yelburton, male Negro, 9781 South
Beach; Leonard Timothy Bidwell, male Negro, 10062
South Duquesne; Dale William Pritchford, male Negro,
8211 South Normandie.

Jack's temporary partner: Sergeant Cal Denton, Bunco
Squad, a former guard at the Texas State Pen.

Denton's car down to Darktown, the radio humming:
jazz on the 'Nite Owl Massacre.' Denton hummed: Leonard Bidwell used to fight welterweight, he saw him go ten
with Kid Gavilan – he was one tough shine. Jack brooded
on his back-to-Narco ticket: Bobby Inge, Christine Bergeron gone, no smut leads from the other squad guys. The
orgy pix – beautiful in a way. His own private leads,
fucked up by some crazy spooks killing six people for a
couple hundred bucks. He could still taste the booze, still
hear Sid Hudgens: 'We've all got secrets.'

Snitch call-ins first: his, Denton's. Shine stands, pool
halls, hair-processing parlors, storefront churches –
informants palmed, leaned on, queried. The Darktown
shuffle – purple car/shotgun rebop, hazy, distorted – riffraff gone on Tokay and hair tonic. Four hours down, no
hard names, back to the names on the list.

9781 Beach – a tar-paper shack, a purple '48 Merc on
the lawn. The car stood sans wheels, a rusted axle sunk
in the grass. Denton pulled up. 'Maybe that's their alibi.
Maybe they fucked up the car after they did the Nite Owl
so we'd think they couldn't drive it nowhere.'

Jack pointed over. 'There's weeds wrapped around the
brake linings. Nobody drove that thing up to Hollywood
last night.'

'You think?'

'I think.'

'You sure?'

'Yeah, I'm sure.'

Denton hauled to the South Duquesne address – another tar-paper dive. A purple Mercury in the driveway – a coon coach featuring fender skirts, mud flaps, 'Purple Pagans' on a hood plaque. Bolted to the porch: a heavy bag/speed bag combo. Jack said, 'There's your welter-weight.'

Denton smiled; Jack walked up, pushed the buzzer. Dog barks inside – a real monster howling. Denton stood flank: the driveway, a bead on the door.

A Negro man opened up: wiry, a tough hump restraining a mastiff. The dog growled; the man said, 'This 'cause I ain' paid my alimony? That a goddamn po-lice offense?'

'Are you Leonard Timothy Bidwell?'

'That's right.'

'And that's your car in the driveway?'

'That's right. And if you a po-lice doin' repos on the side you barkin' up the wrong tree, 'cause my baby is paid for outright with my purse from my losin' effort 'gainst Johnny Saxton.'

Jack pointed to the dog. 'Put him back inside and close the door, walk out and put your hands on the wall.'

Bidwell did it extra slow; Jack frisked him, turned him around. Denton walked over. 'Boy, you like 12-gauge pumps?'

Bidwell shook his head. 'Say what?' Jack threw a change-up. 'Where were you last night at 3:00 A.M.?'

'Right here at my crib.'

'By yourself? If you got laid you got lucky. Tell me you got lucky, before my buddy gets pissed.'

'I gots custody of my kids fo' the week. They was with me.'

'Are they here?'

'They asleep.'

Denton prodded him – a gun poke to the ribs. 'Boy, you know what happened last night? Bad juju, and I ain't woofin'. You own a shotgun, boy?'

'Man, I don't need no fuckin' shotgun.'

115

Denton poked harder. 'Boy, don't you use curse words with me. Now, before we get your pickaninnies out here, you gonna tell me who you lent your automobile to last night?'

'Man, I don' lend my sled to nobody!'

'Then who'd you lend your 12-gauge pump shotguns to? Boy, you spill on that.'

'Man, I tol' you I don't own no shotgun!'

Jack stepped in. 'Tell me about the Purple Pagans. Are they a bunch of guys who like purple cars?'

'Man, that is just a name for our club. I gots a purple car, some other cats in the club gots them too. Man, what is this all about?'

Jack took out his DMV sheet – the Merc owners all typed up. 'Leonard, did you read the papers this morning?'

'No. Man, what is – '

'Sssh. You listen to the radio or watch television?'

'I ain't got either of them. What's that – '

'Sssh. Leonard, we're looking for three colored guys who like to pop off shotguns and a Merc like yours, a '48, a '49, or a '50. I know you wouldn't hurt anybody, I saw you fight Gavilan and I like your style. We're looking for some *bad* guys. Guys with a car like yours, guys who might belong to your club.'

Bidwell shrugged. 'Why should I help you?'

'Because I'll cut my partner loose on you if you don't.'

'Yeah, and you get me a fuckin' snitch jacket, too.'

'No jacket, and you don't have to say anything. Just look at this list and point. Here, read it over.'

Bidwell shook his head. 'They's bad, so I jus' tell you. Sugar Ray Coates, drives a '49 coupe, a beautiful ride. He gots two buddies, Leroy and Tyrone. Sugar loves to party with a shotgun, I heard he gets his thrills shootin' dogs. He tried to get in my club, but we turned him down 'cause he is righteous trash.'

Jack checked his list – bingo on 'Coates, Raymond NMI, 9611 South Central, Room 114.' Denton had his own sheet out. 'Two minutes from here. We haul, we might get there first.'

Hero headlines. 'Let's do it.'

The Tevere Hotel: an L-shaped walk-up above a washateria. Denton coasted into the lot; Jack saw stairs going up – just one floor of rooms, a wide-open doorway.

Up and in – a short corridor, flimsy-looking doors. Jack drew his piece; Denton pulled two guns: a .38, an ankle rig automatic. They counted room numbers; 114 came up. Denton reared back; Jack reared back; they kicked the same instant. The door flew off its hinges for a pure clean shot: a colored kid jumping out of bed.

The kid put up his hands. Denton smiled, aimed. Jack blocked him – two reflex pulls tore the ceiling. Jack ran in; the kid tried to run; Jack nailed him: gun-butt shots to the head. No more resistance – Denton cuffed his hands behind his back. Jack slipped on brass knucks and made fists. 'Leroy, Tyrone. *Where?*'

The kid dribbled teeth – 'One-two-one' came out bloody. Denton yanked him up by his hair; Jack said, 'Don't you fucking kill him.'

Denton spat in his face; shouts boomed down the hall. Jack ran out, around the 'L,' a skid to a stop in front of 121 –

A closed door. Background noise huge – no way to take a listen. Jack kicked; wood splintered; the door creaked open. Two coloreds inside – one asleep on a cot, one snoring on a mattress.

Jack walked in. Sirens whirring up very close. The mattress kid stirred – Jack bludgeoned him quiet, bashed the other punk before he could move. The sirens screeched, died. Jack saw a box on the dresser.

Shotgun shells: Remington 12-gauge double-aught buck. A box of fifty, most of them gone.

Chapter Nineteen

Ed skimmed Jack Vincennes' report. Thad Green watched, his phone ringing off the hook.

Solid, concise – Trash knew how to write a good quickie.

Three male Negroes in custody: Raymond 'Sugar Ray' Coates, Leroy Fontaine, Tyrone Jones. Treated for wounds received while resisting arrest; snitched by another male Negro – who described Coates as a shotgun toter who liked to blast dogs. Coates was on the DMV sheet; the informant stated that he ran with two other men – 'Tyrone and Leroy' – also living at the Tevere Hotel. The three were arrested in their underwear; Vincennes turned them over to prowl car officers responding to shots fired and searched their rooms for evidence. He found a fifty-unit box of Remington 12-gauge double-aught shotgun shells, forty-odd missing – but no shotguns, no rubber gloves, no bloodstained clothing, no large amounts of cash or coins and no other weaponry. The only clothing in the rooms: soiled T-shirts, boxer shorts, neatly pressed garments covered by dry cleaner's cellophane. Vincennes checked the incinerator in back of the hotel; it was burning – the manager told him he saw Sugar Coates dump a load of clothes in at approximately 7:00 this morning. Vincennes said Jones and Fontaine appeared to be inebriated or under the influence of narcotics – they slept through gunfire and the general ruckus of Coates resisting arrest. Vincennes told late-arriving patrolmen to search for Coates' car – it was not in the parking lot or anywhere in a three-block radius. An APB was issued; Vincennes stated that all three suspects' hands and arms reeked of perfume – a paraffin test would be inconclusive.

Ed laid the report on Green's desk. 'I'm surprised he didn't kill them.'

The phone rang – Green let it keep going. 'More head-lines this way, he's shacking with Ellis Loew's sister-in-law. And if the coons doused their paws with perfume to foil a paraffin test, we can thank Jack for that – he gave that little piece of information to *Badge of Honor*. Ed, are you up for this?'

Ed's stomach jumped. 'Yes, sir. I am.'

'The chief wanted Dudley Smith to work with you, but I talked him out of it. As good as he is, the man is off the deep end on coloreds.'

'Sir, I know how important this is.'

Green lit a cigarette. 'Ed, I want confessions. Fifteen of the rounds we retrieved at the Nite Owl were nicked at the strike point, so if we get the guns we've got the case. I want the location of the guns, the location of the car and confessions before we arraign them. We've got seventy-one hours before they see the judge. I want this wrapped up by then. *Clean*.'

Specifics. 'Rap sheets on the kids?'

Green said, 'Joyriding and B&E for all three. Peeping Tom beefs for Coates and Fontaine. And they're not kids – Coates is twenty-two, the others are twenty. This is a gas chamber bounce pure and clean.'

'What about the Griffith Park angle? Shell samples to compare, witnesses to the guys letting off the shotguns.'

'Shell samples might be good backup evidence, if we can find them and the coloreds don't confess. The park ranger who called in the complaints is coming down to try for an ID. Ed, Arnie Reddin says you're the best interrogator he's ever seen, but you've never worked any-thing this – '

Ed stood up. 'I'll do it.'

'Son, if you do, you'll have my job one day.'

Ed smiled – his loose teeth ached. Green said, 'What happened to your face?'

'I tripped chasing a shoplifter. Sir, who's talked to the suspects?'

'Just the doctor who cleaned them up. Dudley wanted Bud White to have first shot, but – '

'Sir, I don't think – '

'Don't interrupt me, I was about to agree with you. No, I want *voluntary* confessions, so White is out. You've got first shot at all three. You'll be observed through the two-ways, and if you want a partner for a Mutt and Jeff, touch your necktie. There'll be a group of us listening through an outside speaker, and a recorder will be running. The three are in separate rooms, and if you want to play them off on each other, you know the buttons to hit.'

Ed said, 'I'll break them.'

His stage: a corridor off the Homicide pen. Three cubicles set up – mirror-fronted, speaker-connected – flip switches, and a string of suspects could hear their partners rat each other off. The rooms: six-by-six square, welded-down tables, bolted-down chairs. In 1, 2 and 3: Sugar Ray Coates, Leroy Fontaine, Tyrone Jones. Rap sheets taped to the wall outside – Ed memorized dates, locations, known associates. A deep breath to kill stage fright – in the #1 door.

Sugar Ray Coates cuffed to a chair, dressed in baggy County denims. Tall, light-complected – close to a mulatto. One eye swollen shut; lips puffed and split. A smashed nose – both nostrils sutured. Ed said, 'Looks like we both took a beating.'

Coates squinted – one-eyed, spooky. Ed unlocked his cuffs, tossed cigarettes and matches on the table. Coates flexed his wrists. Ed smiled. 'They call you Sugar Ray because of Ray Robinson?'

No answer.

Ed took the other chair. 'They say Ray Robinson can throw a four-punch combination in one second. I don't believe it myself.'

Coates lifted his arms – they flopped, dead weight. Ed opened the cigarette pack. 'I know, they cut off the circulation. You're twenty-two, aren't you, Ray?'

Coates: 'Say what and so what,' a scratchy voice. Ed scoped his throat – bruised, finger marks. 'Did one of the officers do a little throttling on you?'

No answer. Ed said, 'Sergeant Vincennes? The snazzy dresser guy?'

Silence.

'Not him, huh? Was it Denton? Fat guy with a Texas drawl, sounds like Spade Cooley on TV?'

Coates' good eye twitched. Ed said, 'Yeah, I commiserate – that guy Denton is one choice creep. You see *my* face? Denton and I went a couple of rounds.'

No bite.

'Goddamn that Denton. Sugar Ray, you and I look like Robinson and LaMotta after that last fight they had.'

Still no bite.

'So you're twenty-two, right?'

'Man, why you ask me that!'

Ed shrugged. 'Just getting my facts straight. Leroy and Tyrone are twenty, so they can't burn on a capital charge. Ray, you should have pulled this caper a couple of years ago. Get life, do a little Youth Authority jolt, transfer to Folsom a big man. Get yourself a sissy, orbit on some of that good prison brew.'

'Sissy' hit home: Coates' hands twitched. He picked up a cigarette, lit it, coughed. 'I never truck with no sissies.'

Ed smiled. 'I know that, son.'

'I ain't your son, you ofay fuck. You the sissy.'

Ed laughed. 'You know the drill, I'll give you that. You've done juvie time, you know I'm the nice guy cop trying to get you to talk. That fucking Tyrone, I almost believed him. Denton must have knocked a few of my screws loose. How could I fall for a line like that?'

'Say what, man? What line you mean?'

'Nothing, Ray. Let's change the subject. What did you do with the shotguns?'

Coates rubbed his neck – shaky hands. 'What shotguns?'

Ed leaned close. 'The pumps you and your friends were shooting in Griffith Park.'

'Don't know 'bout no shotguns.'

'You don't? Leroy and Tyrone had a box of shells in their room.'

'That their bidness.'

Ed shook his head. 'That Tyrone, he's a pisser. You did the Casitas Youth Camp with him, didn't you?'

A shrug. 'So what and say what?'

'Nothing, Ray. Just thinking out loud.'

'Man, why you talkin' 'bout Tyrone? Tyrone's bidness is Tyrone's bidness.'

Ed reached under the table, found the audio switch for room 3. 'Sugar, Tyrone told me you went sissy up at Casitas. You couldn't do the time so you found yourself a big white boy to look after you. He said they call you "Sugar" because you gave it out so sweet.'

Coates hit the table. Ed hit the switch. 'Say what, *Sugar*?'

'Say I *took* it! *Tyrone* give it! Man, I was the fuckin' boss jocker on my dorm! Tyrone the sissy! Tyrone give it for candy bars! Tyrone love it!'

Switch back up. 'Ray, let's change the subject. Why do you think you and your friends are under arrest?'

Coates fingered the cigarette pack. 'Some humbug beef, maybe like dischargin' firearms inside city limit, some humbug like that. Wha's Tyrone say 'bout that?'

'Ray, Tyrone said lots of things, but let's get to meat and potatoes. Where were you at 3:00 A.M. last night?'

Coates chained a smoke butt to tip. 'I was at my crib. Asleep.'

'Were you on hop? Tyrone and Leroy must have been, they were passed out while those officers arrested you. Some crime partners. Tyrone calls you a fairy, then him and Leroy sleep through you getting beat up by some cracker shitbird. I thought you colored guys stuck together. Were you hopped up, Ray? You couldn't take what you did, so you got yourself some dope and – '

'Take what! What you mean! Tyrone and Leroy fuck with them goofballs, not me!'

Ed hit the 2 and 3 switches. 'Ray, you protected Tyrone and Leroy up at Casitas, didn't you?'

Coates coughed out a big rush of smoke. 'You ain't woofin' I did. Tyrone give his boodie and Leroy so scared he almos' throw hisself off the roof and drink hisself blind on pruno. Stupid down-home niggers got no more sense than a fuckin' dog.'

Switches back up. 'Ray, I heard you like to shoot dogs.'

A shrug. 'Dogs got no reason to live.'

'Oh? You feel that way about people, too?'

'Man, what you sayin'?'

Switches down. 'Well, you must feel that way about Leroy and Tyrone.'

'Shit, Leroy and Tyrone almos' too stupid to live.'

Switches up. 'Ray, where's the shotguns you were shooting in Griffith Park?'

'They – I . . . I don't own no shotguns.'

'Where's your 1949 Mercury coupe?'

'I let . . . it just be safe.'

'Come on, Ray. A cherry rig like that? Where is it? I'd keep a nice sled like that under lock and key.'

'I said it safe!'

Ed slapped the table – two palms flat down. 'Did you sell it? Ditch it? It's a felony transport car. Ray, don't you think – '

'I didn't do no felony!'

'The hell you say! Where's the car?'

'I ain't sayin'!'

'Where's the shotguns?'

'I ain't – I don't know!'

'Where's the car?'

'I ain't sayin'!'

Ed drummed the table. 'Why, Ray? You got shotguns and rubber gloves in the trunk? You got wallets and purses and blood all over the seats? Listen to me, you dumb son of a bitch, I'm trying to save you a gas chamber bounce like your buddies – they're underage and you're not, and somebody has to fry for this – '

'I don't know what you talkin' 'bout!'

Ed sighed. 'Ray, let's change the subject.'

Coates lit another cigarette. 'I don' like your subjects.'

'Ray, why were you burning clothes at 7:00 this morning?'

Coates trembled. 'Say what?'

'Say this. You, Leroy and Tyrone were arrested this morning. None of you had last night's clothes with you. You were seen burning a big pile of clothes at 7:00. Add that to the fact that you hid the car that you, Tyrone and Leroy were cruising around in last night. Ray, it doesn't look good, but if you give me something good to give the D.A., it'll make me look good and I'll say, "Sugar Ray wasn't a punk like his sissy partners." Ray, just give me something.'

'Such as what, since I innocent of all this rebop you shuckin' me with.'

Ed flipped 2 and 3. 'Well, you've said bad things about Leroy and Tyrone, you've implied that they're hopheads. Let's try this: where do they get their stuff?'

Coates stared at the floor. Ed said, 'The D.A. hates hop pushers. And you met Jack Vincennes, the Big V.'

'Crazy fuckin' fool.'

Ed laughed. 'Yeah, Jack is a little on the crazy side. Personally, I think anyone who wants to ruin their life with narcotics should have the right, it's a free country. But Jack's good buddies with the new D.A., and they've both got hard-ons for hop pushers. Ray, give me one to give the D.A. Just a little one.'

Coates hooked a finger; Ed let the switches up and leaned in. Sugar Ray, a whisper. 'Roland Navarette, lives on Bunker Hill. Runs a hole-up for parole 'sconders and sells red devils, and that ain't for the fuckin' D.A., that's 'cause Tyrone shoot off his fat fuckin' mouth.'

Switches down. 'All right, Ray. You've told me that Roland Navarette sells barbiturates to Leroy and Tyrone, so now we're making some progress. And you're scared shitless, you know this is gas chamber stuff and you haven't even asked me what it's all about. Ray, you have a big guilty sign around your neck.'

Coates cracked his knuckles; his good eye darted, flickered. Ed killed the audio. 'Ray, let's change the subject.'

'How 'bout baseball, motherfucker?'

'No, let's talk about pussy. Did you get laid last night

or did you put that perfume on yourself to fuck up a paraffin test?'

Heebie-jeebie shakes.

Ed said, 'Where were you at 3:00 last night?'

No answer, more shakes.

'Strike a nerve, Sugar Ray? *Perfume? Women?* Even a piece of shit like you has to have some women he cares about. You got a mother? Sisters?'

'Man, don't you talk 'bout my mother!'

'Ray, if I didn't know you I'd say you were protecting some nice girl's virtue. She was your alibi, you were shacked somewhere. But Tyrone and Leroy have got that same perfume on their mitts, and I'm betting against a gang bang, I'm betting you learned about paraffin tests up in road camp, I'm betting you've got just enough decency to feel some guilt over killing three innocent women.'

'I AIN'T KILLED NOBODY!'

Ed pulled out the morning *Herald.* 'Patty Chesimard, Donna DeLuca and one unidentified. Read this while I take a breather. When I come back you'll get the chance to tell me about it and make a deal that just might save your life.'

Coates, Tremor City – all twitches, soaked denims. Ed threw the paper in his face and walked out.

Thad Green in the hall; Dudley Smith, Bud White at the listening post. Green said, 'We got an eyeball confirmation from that ranger – those *were* the guys in Griffith Park. And you were great.'

Ed smelled his own sweat. 'Sir, Coates was hinked on the women. I can feel it.'

'So can I, so just keep going.'

'Have we turned the guns or the car?'

'No, and the 77th Street squad is shaking down their relatives and K.A.'s. We'll get them.'

'I want to lean on Jones next. Will you do something for me?'

'Name it.'

'Set up Fontaine. Unlock his cuffs and let him read the morning paper.'

Green pointed to the #3 mirror. '*He'll* break soon. Sniveling bastard.'

Tyrone Jones – weeping, a piss puddle on the floor by his chair. Ed looked away. 'Sir, have Lieutenant Smith read the paper into his speaker, nice and slow, especially the lines about the car spotted by the Nite Owl. I want this guy primed to fold.'

Green said, 'You've got it.' Ed checked out Tyrone Jones – dark-skinned, flabby, pockmarked. Bawling – cuffed in, welded down.

A whistle up the hall. Dudley Smith spoke into a microphone – silent lip movements. Ed fixed on Jones.

The kid twisted, heaved, buckled, like a film clip they showed at the Academy: an electric chair malfunction, a dozen jolts before the man fried. A sharp whistle up the corridor – Jones slumped, legs splayed, chin down.

Ed walked in. 'Tyrone, Ray Coates ratted you off. He said the Nite Owl was your idea, he said you got the idea while you were cruising Griffith Park. Tyrone, tell me about it. I think it was Ray's idea. He made you do it. Tell me where the guns and car are and I think we can save your life.'

No answer.

'Tyrone, this is a gas chamber job. If you don't talk to me you'll be dead in six months.'

No answer – Jones kept his head down.

'Son, all you have to do is tell me where the guns are and tell me where Sugar left the car.'

No answer.

'Son, this can be over in one minute. You tell me, and I get you transferred to a protective custody cell. Sugar won't be able to get you, Leroy won't be able to get you. The D.A. will let you turn state's. *You won't go to the gas chamber.*'

No response.

'Son, six people are dead and somebody has to pay. It can be you or it can be Ray.'

No answer.

'Tyrone, he called you a queer. He called you a sissy and a homo. He said you took it up the – '

'I DIDN' KILL NOBODY!'

A strong voice – Ed almost jumped back. 'Son, we have witnesses. We have evidence. Coates is confessing right now. He's saying you planned the whole thing. Son, save yourself. The guns, the car. *Tell me where they are.*'

'I didn' kill nobody!'

'Sssh. Tyrone, do you know what Ray Coates said about you?'

Jones lifted his head. 'I know he lie.'

'I think he lied, too. I don't think you're a queer. I think he's a queer, because he hates women. I think he liked killing those women. I think you feel bad about – '

'We didn' kill no women!'

'Tyrone, where were you last night at 3:00 A.M.?'

No answer.

'Tyrone, why did Sugar Ray hide his car?'

No answer.

'Tyrone, why did you guys hide the shotguns you were shooting in Griffith Park? We have a witness who ID'd you on that.'

No answer. Jones lolled his head – eyes shut, spilling tears.

'Son, why did Ray burn the clothes you guys were wearing last night?'

Jones keening now – animal stuff.

'They had blood on them, didn't they? You killed six goddamn people, you got sprayed. Ray did the clean-up, he tidied the loose ends, *he's* the one who hid the shotguns, he's the boss man, he's been giving the orders since you were giving out butthole up at Casitas. Spill, goddamn you!'

'WE DIDN' KILL NOBODY! I AIN'T NO FUCKIN' QUEER!'

Ed circled the table – walking fast, talking slow. 'Here's what I think. I think Sugar Ray's the boss, Leroy's just a dummy, you're the fat boy Sugar likes to tease. You all did road camp together, you and Sugar Ray got popped for Peeping Tom. Sugar liked looking at girls, you liked looking at boys. You both like looking at white folks, because that is the colored man's forbidden fruit. You had your 12-gauge pumps, you had your snazzy '49 Merc, you had some red devils you bought off Roland Navarette. You were up in Hollywood, white folks' neck of the woods. Sugar was teasing you about being fruit, you kept saying it was just because there were no girls around. Sugar says prove it, prove it, and you guys start peeping. You're getting mad, you're all flying on hop, it's late at night and there's nothing to look at, all those nice white folks have their curtains down. You drive by the Nite Owl, there's these nice white people inside – and it is just too fucking much to take. Poor fat sissy Tyrone, he takes over. He leads his boys into the Nite Owl. Six people are there – three of them women. You drag them into the locker, you hit the cash register and make the cook open the safe. You take their billfolds and purses and you spill some perfume on your hands. Sugar says, "Touch the girlies, sissy. Prove you ain't queer." You can't do it so you start shooting and everybody starts shooting and you love it because finally you're more than a poor queer fat little nigger and – '

'NO! NO NO NO NO NO NO!'

'Yes! Where's the guns? You fucking confess and turn over the evidence or you'll go to the fucking gas chamber!'

'No! Didn' kill nobody!'

Ed hit the table. 'Why'd you ditch the car?'

Jones lashed his head, spraying sweat.

'Why'd you burn the clothes?'

No answer.

'Where did the perfume come from?'

No answer.

'Did Sugar and Leroy rape the women first?'

'No!'

'Oh? You mean all three of you did?'

'We didn' kill nobody! We wasn't even there!'

'Where were you?'

128

No answer.

'Tyrone, where were you last night?'

Jones sobbed; Ed gripped his shoulders. 'Son, you know what's going to happen if you don't talk. So for God's sake admit what you did.'

'Didn' kill nobody. None of us. Wasn't even there.'

'Son, you did.'

'No!'

'Son, you did, so tell me.'

'We didn'!'

'Hush now. Just tell me – *nice and slowly*.'

Jones started babbling. Ed knelt by his chair, listened. He heard: 'Please God, I just wanted to lose my cherry'; he heard: 'Didn't mean to hurt her so's we'd have to die.' He heard: 'Not right punish what we didn' do . . . maybe she be okay, she don't die so I don't die, 'cause I ain't no queer.' He felt himself buzzing, electric chair, a sign on top: THEY DIDN'T DO IT.

Jones slipped into a reverie – Jesus, Jesus, Jesus, Father Divine. Ed hit the #2 cubicle.

Rank: sweat, cigarette smoke. Leroy Fontaine – big, dark, processed hair, his feet up on the table. Ed said, 'Be smarter than your friends. Even if you killed her, it's not as bad as killing six people.'

Fontaine tweaked his nose – bandaged, spread over half his face. 'This newspaper shit ain't shit.'

Ed closed the door, scared. 'Leroy, you'd better hope she was with you at the coroner's estimated time of death.'

No answer.

'Was she a hooker?'

No answer.

'Did you kill her?'

No answer.

'You wanted Tyrone to lose his cherry, but things got out of hand. Isn't that right?'

No answer.

'Leroy, if she's dead and she was colored you can cop a plea. If she was white you might have a chance. Remember, we can make you for the Nite Owl, and we can make

129

it stick. Unless you convince me you were somewhere else doing something bad, we'll nail you for what's in that newspaper.'

No answer – Fontaine cleaned his nails with a match-book.

A big lie. 'If you kidnapped her and she's still alive, that's not a Little Lindbergh violation. It's not a capital charge.'

No answer.

'Leroy, where are the guns and the car?'

No answer.

'Leroy, is she still alive?'

Fontaine smiled – Ed felt ice on his spine. 'If she's still alive, she's your alibi. I won't kid you, it could get bad: kidnap, rape, assault. But if you eliminate yourself on the Nite Owl now, you'll save us time and the D.A. will like you for it. Kick loose, Leroy. Do yourself a favor.'

No answer.

'Leroy, look how it can go both ways. I think you kidnapped a girl at gunpoint. You made her bleed up the car, so you hid the car. She bled on your clothes, so you burned the clothes. You got her perfume all over yourselves. If you didn't do the Nite Owl, I don't know why you hid the shotguns, maybe you thought she could identify them. Son, if that girl is alive she is the only chance you've got.'

Fontaine said, 'I thinks she alive.'

Ed sat down. *'You think?'*

'Yeah, I thinks.'

'Who is she? *Where is she?*'

No answer.

'Is she colored?'

'She Mex.'

'What's her name?'

'I don' know. College-type bitch.'

'Where did you pick her up?'

'I don' know. Eastside someplace.'

'Where did you assault her?'

'I don' know . . . old building on Dunkirk some-wheres.'

'Where's the car and the shotguns?'

'I don' know. Sugar, he took care of them.'

'If you didn't kill her, why did Coates hide the shot-guns?'

No answer.

'Why, Leroy?'

No answer.

'Why, son? Tell me.'

No answer.

Ed hit the table. 'Tell me, goddammit!'

Fontaine hit the table – harder. 'Sugar, he poked her with them guns! He 'fraid it be evidence!'

Ed closed his eyes. 'Where is she now?'

No answer.

'Did you leave her at the building?'

No answer.

Eyes open. 'Did you leave her someplace else?'

No answer.

Leaps: none of the three had cash on them, call their money evidence – stashed when Sugar burned the clothes. 'Leroy, did you sell her out? Bring some buddies by that place on Dunkirk?'

'We . . . we drove her 'roun'.'

'Where? Your friends' pads?'

'Tha's right.'

'Up in Hollywood?'

'We didn' shoot them people!'

'Prove it, Leroy. Where were you guys at 3:00 A.M.?'

'Man, I cain't tell you!'

Ed slapped the table. 'Then you'll burn for the Nite Owl!'

'We didn't do it!'

'Who did you sell the girl to?'

No answer.

'Where is she now?'

No answer.

'Are you afraid of reprisals? You left the girl some-

131

where, right? *Leroy, where did you leave her, who did you leave her with, she is your only chance to stay out of the fucking gas chamber!'*

'Man, I cain't tell you, Sugar, he like to kill me!'

'Leroy, where is she?'

No answer.

'Leroy, you turn state's you'll get out years before Sugar and Tyrone.'

No response.

'Leroy, I'll get you a one-man cell where nobody can hurt you.'

No response.

'Son, you have to tell me. I'm the only friend you've got.'

No response.

'Leroy, are you afraid of the man you left the girl with?'

No answer.

'Son, he can't be as bad as the gas chamber. *Tell me where the girl is.'*

The door banged open. Bud White stepped in, threw Fontaine against the wall.

Ed froze.

White pulled out his .38, broke the cylinder, dropped shells on the floor. Fontaine shook head to toe; Ed kept freezing. White snapped the cylinder shut, stuck the gun in Fontaine's mouth. 'One in six. Where's the girl?'

Fontaine chewed steel; White squeezed the trigger twice: clicks, empty chambers. Fontaine slid down the wall; White pulled the gun back, held him up by his hair. *'Where's the girl?'*

Ed kept freezing. White pulled the trigger – another little click. Fontaine, bug-eyed. 'S-ss-sylvester F-fitch, one-o-nine and Avalon, gray corner house please don' hurt me no – '

White ran out.

Fontaine passed out.

Riot sounds in the corridor – Ed tried to stand up, couldn't get his legs.

132

Chapter Twenty

A four-car cordon: two black-and-whites, two unmarkeds. Sirens to a half mile out; a coast up to the gray corner house.

Dudley Smith drove the lead prowler; Bud rode shotgun reloading his piece. A four-car flank: black-and-whites in the alley, Mike Breuning and Dick Carlisle parked streetside – rifles on the gray house door. Bud said, 'Boss, he's mine.'

Dudley winked. 'Grand, lad.'

Bud went in the back way – through the alley, a fence vault. On the rear porch: a screen door, inside hook and eye. He slipped the catch with his penknife, walked in on tiptoes.

Darkness, dim shapes: a washing machine, a blind-covered door – strips of light through the cracks.

Bud tried the door – unlocked – eased it open. A hall-way: light bouncing from two side rooms. A rug to walk on; music to give him more cover. He tiptoed up to the first room, wheeled in.

A nude woman spread-eagled on a mattress – bound with neckties, a necktie in her mouth. Bud hit the next room loud.

A fat mulatto at a table – naked, wolfing Kellogg's Rice Krispies. He put down his spoon, raised his hands. 'Nossir, don't want no trouble.'

Bud shot him in the face, pulled a spare piece – bang bang from the coon's line of fire. The man hit the floor dead spread – a prime entry wound oozing blood. Bud put the spare in his hand; the front door crashed in. He dumped Rice Krispies on the stiff, called an ambulance.

Chapter Twenty-one

Jack watched Karen sleep, putting their fight behind him.

Newspaper pix caused it: the Big V and Cal Denton rousting three colored punks – suspects in L.A.'s 'Crime of the Century.' Denton dragged Fontaine by his conk; Big V had neck holds on the other two. Karen said they reminded her of the Scottsboro Boys; Jack told her he saved their goddamned lives, but now that he knew they gang-raped a Mexican girl he wished he'd let Denton kill them outright. The argument deteriorated from there.

Karen slept curled away from him – covered tight like she thought he might hit her. Jack watched her while he dressed; his last two days hit him.

He was off the Nite Owl, back to Ad Vice. Ed Exley's interrogations tentatively cleared the spooks – pending questioning of the woman they'd been abusing. Bud White played some Russian roulette – the three clammed up. So far, there was no way to know if they had time to leave the woman, drive to the Nite Owl, return to Darktown and gang-rape. Maybe Coates or Fontaine left Jones in charge of the girl and pulled the snuffs with other partners. No luck finding the shotguns; Coates' purple Merc was still missing. No restaurant loot found at their hotel; the debris in the incinerator too far gone for blood-on-fabric analysis. The perfume on the jigs' hands skunked a late paraffin test. Huge pressure at the Bureau: solve the fucking case fast.

The coroner was trying to ID the patron victims, working from dental abstracts and their physical stats cross-checked against missing persons bulletins, call-ins. Made: the cook/dishwasher, waitress, cash register girl; nothing yet on the three customers, the autopsies showed no sexual abuse on the women. Maybe Coates/Jones/Fontaine weren't the triggers; Dudley Smith on the job – his men bracing armed robbers, nuthouse parolees, every known L.A. geek with a gun jacket. The news vendor who spotted the purple Merc across from the Nite Owl was requestioned; now he said it could have been a Ford or a Chevy. Ford and Chevy registrations being checked; *now* the park ranger who ID'd the spooks said he wasn't sure. Ed Exley told Green and Parker the purple car might have been placed by the Nite Owl to put the onus on the jigs; Dudley pooh-poohed the theory – he said it was probably just a coincidence. A sure-thing case unraveling into a shitload of possibilities.

Huge press coverage – Sid Hudgens had already called – zero hink on the smut, nothing like 'We've *all* got secrets.' A heroic version of the arrests for fifty scoots – Sid hung up quick.

The Nite Owl cost him a day on the smut. He'd checked the squadroom postings: no leads, none of the other men tracked the shit. He filed a phony report himself: nothing on Christine Bergeron and Bobby Inge, nothing on the other mags he found. Nothing on his filth dreams: his sweetheart Karen orgied up.

Jack kissed Karen's neck, hoping she'd wake up and smile.

No luck.

Canvassing first.

Charleville Drive, questions, no luck: none of the tenants in Christine Bergeron's building heard the woman and her son move out; none knew a thing about the men she entertained. The adjoining apartment houses – ditto straight across. Jack called Beverly Hills High, learned that Daryl Bergeron was a chronic truant who hadn't attended classes in a week; the vice-principal said the boy kept to himself, didn't cause trouble – he was never in school *to* cause trouble. Jack didn't tell him Daryl was too tired to cause trouble: fucking your mother on roller skates takes a lot out of a kid.

His next call: Stan's Drive-in. The manager told him Chris Bergeron splitsvilled day before yesterday, two seconds after getting a phone call. No, he didn't know who the caller was; yes, he would buzz Sergeant Vincennes if she showed up; no, Chris did not unduly fraternize with customers or receive visitors while carhopping.

Out to West Hollywood.

Bobby Inge's place, talks – fellow tenants and neighbors. Bobby paid his rent on time, kept to himself, nobody saw him move out. The swish next door said he 'played the field – he wasn't seeing anyone in particular.' Tweaks: 'smut books,' 'Chris Bergeron,' 'this little twist Daryl' – the fruit deadpanned him cold.

Call West Hollywood dead – after B.J.'s Rumpus Room Bobby wouldn't be caught near the fag-bar strip. Jack grabbed a hamburger, checked his Inge rap sheet – no K.A.'s listed. He studied his private filth stash, hard to concentrate, the contradictions in the pictures kept distracting him.

Attractive posers, trashy backdrops. Beautiful costumes that made you look twice at disgusting homo action. Artful orgy shots: inked-in blood, bodies connected over quilts – pix that made you squint to see female forms held in check by too much explicitness – the sex organ extravaganza made you want to see the women plain nude. The shit was pornography manufactured for money – but somewhere in the process an artist was involved.

A brainstorm.

Jack drove to a dime store, bought scissors, Scotch tape, a drawing pad. He worked in the car: faces cut from the mags, taped to the paper, men and women separated, repeats placed together to make IDs easier. Downtown to the Bureau for matchups: stag pix to Caucasian mug books. Four hours of squinting: eyestrain, zero identifications. Over to Hollywood Station, their separate Vice mugs, another zero; the West Hollywood Sheriff's Substation made zero number three. Bobby Inge aside, his smut beauties were virgins – no criminal records.

4:30 P.M. – Jack felt his options dwindling fast. Another idea caught: check Bobby Inge through the DMV; check

Chris Bergeron through again – a complete paper prowl. R&I/Inge one more time – updates on his sheet.

He hit a pay phone, made the calls. Bobby Inge was DMV clean: no citations, no court appearances. Complete Bergeron paper: traffic violation dates, the names of her surety bond guarantors. R&I's only Inge update: a year-old bail report. One name crossed over – Bergeron to Inge.

Bail on an Inge prostie charge – fronted by Sharon Kostenza, 1649 North Havenhurst, West Hollywood. The same woman paid a Bergeron reckless-driving bond.

Jack called R&I back, ran Sharon Kostenza and her address through – no California criminal record. He told the clerk to check the forty-eight-state list; that took a full ten minutes. 'Sorry, Sarge. Nothing at all on the name.'

Back to the DMV; a shocker: no one named Sharon Kostenza possessed or had ever possessed a California driver's license. Jack drove to North Havenhurst – the address 1649 did not exist.

Brain circuits: prostie Bobby Inge, Kostenza bailed him on a prostie beef, prosties used phony names, prosties posed for stag pix. North Havenhurst a longtime call-house block –

He started knocking on doors.

A dozen quickie interviews; tags on nearby fuck joints. Two, on Havenhurst: 1611, 1564.

6:10 P.M.

1611 open for business; the boss deadpanned Sharon Kostenza, Bobby Inge, the Bergerons. Ditto the faces clipped from the fuck mags – the girls working the joint panned out likewise. The madam at 1564 cooperated – the names and faces were Greek to her and her whores.

Another burger, back to West Hollywood Substation. A run through the alias file: another flat busted dead end.

7:20 – no more names to check. Jack drove to North Hamel, parked with a view: Bobby Inge's door.

He kept a fix on the courtyard. No foot traffic, street traffic slow – the Strip wouldn't jump for hours. He waited: smoking, smut pictures in his head.

At 8:46 a quiff ragtop cruised by – a slow trawl close to the curb. Twenty minutes later – one more time. Jack tried to read plate numbers – nix, too dark out. A hunch: he's looking for window lights. If he's looking for Bobby's, he's got them.

He walked into the courtyard, lucked out on witnesses – none. Handcuff ratchets popped the door: teeth cutting cheap wood. He felt for a wall light, tripped a switch.

The same cleaned-out living room; the pad in the same disarray. Jack sat by the door, waited.

Boredom time stretched – fifteen minutes, thirty, an hour. Knocks on the front windowpane.

Jack drew down: the door, eye-level. He faked a fag lilt: 'It's open.'

A pretty boy sashayed in. Jack said, 'Shit.'

Timmy Valburn, a.k.a. Moochie Mouse – Billy Dieterling's squeeze.

'Timmy, what the fuck are you doing here?'

Valburn slouched, one hip cocked, no fear. 'Bobby's a friend. He doesn't use narcotics, if that's what you're here for. And isn't this a tad out of your jurisdiction?'

Jack closed the door. 'Christine Bergeron, Daryl Bergeron, Sharon Kostenza. They friends of yours?'

'I don't know these names. Jack, what is this?'

'You tell me, you've been getting up the nerve to knock for hours. Let's start with where's Bobby?'

'I don't know. Would I be here if I knew where – '

'Do you trick with Bobby? You got a thing going with him?'

'He's just a friend.'

'Does Billy know about you and Bobby?'

'Jack, you're being vile. *Bobby is a friend*. I don't think Billy knows we're friends, but friends is all we are.'

Jack took out his notepad. 'So I'm sure you have a lot of friends in common.'

'No. Put that away, because I don't know any of Bobby's friends.'

'All right, then where did you meet him?'

'At a bar.'

'Name the bar.'

'Leo's Hideaway.'

'Billy know you chase stuff behind his back?'

'Jack, don't be crude. I'm not some criminal you can slap around, I'm a citizen who can report you for breaking into this apartment.'

Change-up. 'Smut. Picture-book stuff, regular and homo. That your bent, Timmy?'

One little eye flicker – not quite a wink. 'You get your kicks that way? You and Billy take shit like that to bed with you?'

No flinch. 'Don't be vile, Jack. It's not your style, but be nice. Remember what I am to Billy, remember what Billy is to the show that gives you the celebrity you grovel for. Remember who Billy knows.'

Jack moved extra slow: the smut mags and face sheets to a chair, a lamp pulled over for some light. 'Look at those pictures. If you recognize anybody, tell me. That's all I want.'

Valburn rolled his eyes, looked. The face sheets first: quizzical, curious. On to the costume skin books – nonchalant, a queer sophisticate. Jack stuck close, eyes on his eyes.

The orgy book last. Timmy saw inked-on blood and kept looking; Jack saw a neck vein working overtime.

Valburn shrugged. 'No, I'm sorry.'

A tough read – a skilled actor. 'You didn't recognize anybody?'

'No, I didn't.'

'But you did recognize Bobby.'

'Of course, because I know him.'

'But nobody else?'

'Jack, really.'

'Nobody familiar? Nobody you've seen at the bars your type goes to?'

'*My type?* Jack, haven't you been sucking around the Industry long enough to call a spade a spade and still be nice about it?'

Let it pass. 'Timmy, you keep your thoughts hidden. Maybe you've been playing Moochie Mouse too long.'

'What kind of thoughts are you looking for? I'm an actor, so give me a cue.'

'Not thoughts, *reactions*. You didn't blink an eye at some of the strangest stuff I've seen in fifteen years as a cop. Arty-farty red ink shooting out of a dozen people fucking and sucking. Is that everyday stuff to you?'

An elegant shrug. 'Jack, I'm *très* Hollywood. I dress up as a rodent to entertain children. Nothing in this town surprises me.'

'I'm not sure I buy that.'

'I'm telling you the truth. I don't know any of the people in those pictures, and I haven't seen those magazines before.'

'People of your type know people who know people. You know Bobby Inge, and he was in those pictures. I want to see your little black book.'

Timmy said, 'No.'

Jack said, 'Yes, or I give *Hush-Hush* a little item on you and Billy Dieterling as soul sisters. *Badge of Honor*, the *Dream-a-Dream Hour* and queers. You like that for a three-horse parlay?'

Timmy smiled. 'Max Peltz would fire you for that. He wants you to be nice. *So be nice.*

'You carry your book with you?'

'No, I don't. Jack, remember who Billy's father is. Remember all the money you can make in the Industry after you retire.'

Pissed now, almost seeing red. 'Hand me your wallet. Do it or I'll lose my temper and put you up against the wall.'

Valburn shrugged, pulled out a billfold. Jack glommed what he wanted: calling cards, names and numbers on paper scraps.

'I want those returned.'

Jack handed the wallet back light. 'Sure, Timmy.'

'You are going to fuck up very auspiciously one day, Jack. Do you know that?'

'I already have, and I made money on the deal. Remember that if you decide to rat me to Max.'

Valburn walked out – elegant.

Fruit-bar pickings: first names, phone numbers. One card looked familiar: 'Fleur-de-Lis. Twenty-four Hours a Day – Whatever You Desire. HO-01239.' No writing on the back – Jack racked his brain, couldn't make a connection.

New plan: call the numbers, impersonate Bobby Inge, drop lines about stag books – see who bit. Stick at the pad, see who called or showed up: long-shot stuff.

Jack called 'Ted – DU-6831' – busy signal; 'Geoff – CR-9640' – no bite on a lisping 'Hi, it's Bobby Inge.' 'Bing – Ax-6005' – no answer; back to 'Ted' – 'Bobby who? I'm sorry, but I don't think I know you.' 'Jim,' 'Nat,' 'Otto': no answers; he still couldn't make the odd card. Last-ditch stuff: buzz the cop line at Pacific Coast Bell.

Ring, ring. 'Miss Sutherland speaking.'

'This is Sergeant Vincennes, LAPD. I need a name and address on a phone number.'

'Don't you have a reverse directory, Sergeant?'

'I'm in a phone booth, and the number I want checked is Hollywood 01239.'

'Very well. Please hold the line.'

Jack held; the woman came back on. 'No such number is assigned. Bell is just beginning to assign five-digit numbers, and that one has not been assigned. Frankly, it may never be, the changeover is going so slow.'

'You're sure about this?'

'Of course I'm sure.'

Jack hung up. First thoughts: bootleg line. Bookies had them – bent guys at P.C. Bell rigged the lines, kept the numbers from being assigned. Free phone service, no way police agencies could subpoena records, no make on incoming calls.

A reflex call: The DMV police line.

'Yes? Who's requesting?'

'Sergeant Vincennes, LAPD. Address only on a Tim-

141

othy V–A–L–B–U–R–N, white male, mid to late twenties. I think he lives in the Wilshire District.'

'I copy. Please hold.'

Jack held; the clerk returned. 'Wilshire it is. 432 South Lucerne. Say, isn't Valburn that mouse guy on the Dieterling show?'

'Yeah.'

'Well . . . uh . . . what are you after him for?'

'Possession of contraband cheese.'

Chez Mouse: an old French Provincial with new money accoutrements – floodlights, topiary bushes – Moochie, the rest of the Dieterling flock. Two cars in the driveway: the ragtop prowling Hamel, Billy Dieterling's Packard Caribbean – a fixture on the *Badge of Honor* lot.

Jack staked the pad spooked: the queers were too well connected to burn, his smut job stood dead-ended – 'Whatever You Desire' some kind of dead-end tangent. He could level with Timmy and Billy, shake them down, squeeze their contacts: people who knew people who knew Bobby Inge – who knew who made the shit. He kept the radio tuned in low; a string of love songs helped him pin things down.

He wanted to track the filth because part of him wondered how something could be so ugly and so beautiful and part of him plain jazzed on it.

He got itchy, anxious to move. A throaty soprano pushed him out of the car.

Up the driveway, skirting the floodlights. Windows: closed, uncurtained. He looked in.

Moochie Mouse gimcracks in force, no Timmy and Billy. Bingo through the last window: the lovebirds in a panicky spat.

An ear to the glass – all he got was mumbles. A car door slammed; door chimes ting-tinged. A look-see in – Billy walking toward the front of the house.

Jack kept watching. Timmy pranced hands-on-hips; Billy brought a big muscle guy back. Muscles forked over

142

goodies: pill vials, a glassine bag full of weed. Jack sprinted for the street.

A Buick sedan at the curb – mud on the front and back plates. Locked doors – kick glass or go home empty.

Jack kicked out the driver's-side window. Glass on his front seat booty – a single brown paper bag.

He grabbed it, ran to his car.

Valburn's door opened.

Jack peeled rubber – east on 5th, zigzags down to Western and a big bright parking lot. He ripped the bag open.

Absinthe – 190 proof on the label, viscous green liquid.

Hashish.

Black-and-white glossies: women in opera masks blowing horses.

'Whatever You Desire.'

Chapter Twenty-two

Parker said, 'Ed, you were brilliant the other day. I disapprove of Officer White's intrusion, but I can't complain with the results. I need smart men like you, and . . . direct men like Bud. And I want both of you on the Nite Owl job.'

'Sir, I don't think White and I can work together.'

'You won't have to. Dudley Smith's heading up the investigation, and White will report directly to him. Two other men, Mike Breuning and Dick Carlisle, will work with White – however Dudley wants to play it. The Hollywood squad will be in on the job, reporting to Lieutenant Reddin, who'll report to Dudley. We've got divisional contacts assigned, and every man in the Bureau is calling in informant favors. Chief Green says Russ Millard wants to be detached from Ad Vice to run the show with Dud, so that's a possibility. That makes twenty-four full-time officers.'

'What specifically do I do?'

Parker pointed to a case graph on an easel. 'One, we have not found the shotguns or Coates' car, and until that girl those thugs assaulted clears them on the time element we have to assume that they are still our prime suspects. Since White's little escapade they've refused to talk, and they've been booked on kidnap and rape charges. I think – '

'Sir, I'd be glad to have another try at them.'

'Let me finish. Two, we still have no IDs on the other three victims. Doc Layman's working overtime on that, and we're logging in four hundred calls a day from people worried about missing loved ones. There's an outside chance that this might be more than just a set of robbery killings, and if that proves to be the case I want you on that end of things. As of now, you're liaison to SID, the

D.A.'s Office and the divisional contacts. I want you to go over every field report every day, assess them and share your thoughts with me personally. I want daily written summaries, copies to Chief Green and myself.'

Ed tried not to smile – the stitches in his chin helped. 'Sir, some thoughts before we continue?'

Parker leaned his chair back. 'Of course.'

Ed ticked points. 'One, what about searching for comparable shell samples in Griffith Park? Two, if the girl clears our suspects on the time element, what was that purple car doing across from the Nite Owl? Three, how likely are we to turn the guns and the car? Four, the suspects said they took the girl to a building on Dunkirk first. What kind of evidence did we get there?'

'Good points. But one, shell samples to compare is a long shot. With breech-load weapons the rounds might have expelled back into the car those punks were driving, the actual locations listed in the crime reports were vague, Griffith Park is all hillsides, we've had rain and mudslides over the past two weeks and that park ranger has waffled on ID'ing the three in custody. Two, the news vendor who ID'd the car by the Nite Owl says now that maybe it was a Ford or a Chevy, so our registration checks are now a nightmare. If you're thinking the car was placed there as a plant, I think that's nonsense – how would anyone know *to* plant it there? Three, the 77th Street squad is tearing up the goddamn southside for the car and the guns, muscling K.A.'s, the megillah. And four, there was blood and semen all over a mattress in that building on Dunkirk.'

Ed said, 'It all comes back to the girl.'

Parker picked up a report form. 'Inez Soto, age twenty-one. A college student. She's at Queen of Angels, and she just came out of sedation this morning.'

'Has anyone spoken to her?'

'Bud White went with her to the hospital. Nobody's talked to her in thirty-six hours, and I don't envy you the task.'

'Sir, can I do this alone?'

'No. Ellis Loew wants to prosecute our boys for Little Lindbergh – kidnapping and rape. He wants them in the gas chamber for that, the Nite Owl, or both. And he wants a D.A.'s investigator and a woman officer present. You're to meet Bob Gallaudet and a Sheriff's matron at Queen of Angels in an hour. I don't have to mention that the course of this investigation will be determined by what our Miss Soto tells you.'

Ed stood up. Parker said, 'Off the record, do you make the coloreds for the job?'

'Sir, I'm not sure.'

'You cleared them temporarily. Did you think I'd be angry with you for that?'

'Sir, we both want absolute justice. And you like me too much.'

Parker smiled. 'Edmund, don't dwell on what White did the other day. You're worth a dozen of him. He's killed three men line of duty, but that's nothing compared to what you did in the war. Remember that.'

Gallaudet met him outside the girl's room. The hall reeked of disinfectant – familiar, his mother died one floor down. 'Hello, Sergeant.'

'It's Bob, and Ellis Loew sends his thanks. He was afraid the suspects would get beaten to death and he wouldn't get to prosecute.'

Ed laughed. 'They might be cleared on the Nite Owl.'

'I don't care, and neither does Loew. Little Lindbergh with rape carries the death penalty. Loew wants those guys in the ground, so do I, so will you once you talk to the girl. So here's the sixty-four-dollar question. Did they do it?'

Ed shook his head. 'Based on their reactions, I'd lean against it. But Fontaine said they drove the girl around. "Sold her out" was the phrase he reacted to. I think it *could* have been Sugar Coates and a little pickup gang, maybe two of the guys they sold her to. None of the three had money on them when they were arrested, and either way – Nite Owl or gang rape – I think that money is stashed somewhere, covered with blood – like the bloody clothes Coates burned.'

Gallaudet whistled. 'So we need the girl's word on the time element *and* IDs on the other rapers.'

'Right. *And* our suspects are clammed, *and* Bud White killed the one witness who could have helped us.'

'That guy White's a pisser, isn't he? Don't look so spooked, being scared of him means you're sane. Now come on, let's talk to the young lady.'

They walked into the room. A Sheriff's matron blocked the bed – tall, fat, short hair waxed straight back. Gallaudet said, 'Ed Exley, Dot Rothstein.' The woman nodded, stepped aside.

Inez Soto.

Black eyes, her face cut and bruised. Dark hair shaved to the forehead, sutures. Tubes in her arms, tubes under the sheets. Cut knuckles, split nails – she fought. Ed saw his mother: bald, sixty pounds in an iron lung.

Gallaudet said, 'Miss Soto, this is Sergeant Exley.'

Ed leaned on the bed rail. 'I'm sorry we couldn't have given you more time to recuperate, and I'll try to make this as brief as possible.'

Inez Soto stared at him – dark eyes, bloodshot. A raspy voice: 'I won't look at any more pictures.'

Gallaudet: 'Miss Soto identified Coates, Fontaine and Jones from mugshots. I told her we might need her to look at some mugshots for IDs on the other men.'

Ed shook his head. 'That won't be necessary right now. Right now, Miss Soto, I need you to try to remember a chronology of the events that happened to you two nights ago. We can do this very slowly, and for now we won't need details. When you're more rested, we can go over it again. Please take your time and start when the three men kidnapped you.'

Inez pushed up on her pillows. 'They weren't men!'

Ed gripped the rail. 'I know. And they're going to be punished for what they did to you. But before we can do that we need to eliminate or confirm them as suspects on another crime.'

'I want them dead! I heard the radio! *I want them dead for that!*'

'We can't do that, because then the other ones who hurt you will go free. We have to do this correctly.'

A hoarse whisper. 'Correctly means six white people are more important than a Mexican girl from Boyle Heights. Those animals ripped me up and did their business in my mouth. They stuck guns in me. My family thinks I brought it on myself because I didn't marry a stupid *cholo* when I was sixteen. I will tell you nothing, *cabrón*.'

Gallaudet: 'Miss Soto, Sergeant Exley saved your life.'

'He ruined my life! Officer White said he cleared the *negritos* on a murder charge! Officer White's the hero – he killed the *puto* who took me up my ass!'

Inez sobbed. Gallaudet gave the cut-off sign. Ed walked down to the gift shop – familiar, his deathwatch. Flowers for 875: fat cheerful bouquets every day.

Chapter Twenty-three

Bud came on duty early, found a memo on his desk.

4/19/53

Lad –

Paperwork is not your forte, but I need you to run records checks (two) for me. (Dr. Layman has identified the three patron victims.) Use the standard procedure I've taught you and first check bulletin 11 on the squadroom board: it updates the overall status of the case and details the duties of the other investigating officers, which will prevent you from doing gratuitous and extraneous tasks.

1. Susan Nancy Lefferts, W.F., DOB 1/29/22, no criminal record. A San Bernardino native recently arrived in Los Angeles. Worked as a salesgirl at Bullock's Wilshire (background check assigned to Sgt. Exley).

2. Delbert Melvin Cathcart, a.k.a. 'Duke,' W.M., DOB 11/14/14. Two statutory rape convictions, served three years at San Quentin. Three procuring arrests, no convictions. (A tough ID: laundry markings and the body cross-checked against prison measurement charts got us our match.) No known place of employment, last known address 9819 Vendome, Silverlake District.

3. Malcolm Robert Lunceford, a.k.a. 'Mal,' W.M., DOB 6/02/12. No last known address, worked as a security guard at the Mighty Man Agency, 1680 North Cahuenga. Former LAPD officer (patrolman), assigned to Hollywood Division throughout most of his eleven-year career. Fired for incompetence 6/50. Known to be a late night habitué of the Nite Owl. I've checked Lunceford's personnel file and con-

cluded that the man was a disgraceful police officer (straight 'D' fitness reports from every C.O.). You check whatever paperwork exists on him at Hollywood Station (Breuning and Carlisle will be there to shag errands for you).

Summation: I still think the Negroes are our men, but Cathcart's criminal record and Lunceford's ex-policeman status mean that more than cursory background checks should be conducted. I want you as my adjutant on this job, an excellent baptism of fire for you as a straight Homicide detective. Meet me tonight (9:30) at the Pacific Dining Car. We'll discuss the job and related matters.

D.S.

Bud checked the main bulletin board. Nite Owl thick: field reports, autopsy reports, summaries. He found bulletin 11, skimmed it.

Six R&I clerks detached to check criminal records and auto registrations; the 77th Street squad shaking down jigtown for the shotguns and Ray Coates' Merc. Breuning and Carlisle muscling known gun jockeys; the area around the Nite Owl canvassed nine times without turning a single extra eyewitness. The spooks refused to talk to LAPD men, D.A.'s Bureau investigators, Ellis Loew himself. Inez Soto refused to cooperate on clearing up the time frame; Ed Exley blew a questioning session, said they should treat her kid-gloves.

Down the board: Malcolm Lunceford's LAPD personnel sheets. Bad news – Lunceford as a free-meal scrounger, general incompetent. A putrid arrest record; cited for dereliction of duty three times. An interdepartmental information request issued; four officers who worked with Lunceford responded. Grafter/buffoon: Mal drank on duty, shook down hookers for blowjobs, tried to shake down Hollywood merchants for his off-duty 'protection service' – letting him sleep on their premises while he was locked out of his apartment for nonpayment of rent. One complaint too many got Lunceford bounced

150

in June 1950; all four responding officers stated that he probably wasn't a deliberate Nite Owl victim: as a policeman he habituated all-night coffee shops – usually to scrounge chow; he was probably at the Nite Owl at 3:00 A.M. because he was hooked on sweet Lucy and sleeping in the weeds and the Nite Owl looked cozy and warm.

Bud drove to Hollywood Station – Inez on his mind, Dudley, Dick Stens along with her. Guts: she tried to claw herself off the gurney to get at Sylvester Fitch, strapped dead to a morgue cot; she screamed: 'I'm dead, I want them dead!' He hustled her to the ambulance, filched morphine and a hypo, shot her up while no one was looking. The worst of it should have been over – but the worst was still coming.

Exley would interrogate her, make her spit out details, look at sex offender pix until she cracked. Ellis Loew wanted an airtight case – that meant show-ups, courtroom testimony. Inez Soto: the first headliner witness for the most ambitious D.A. who ever breathed – all he could do was see her at the hospital, say 'Hi,' try to muffle the blows. A brave woman shoved at Ed Exley – fodder for a cowardly hard-on.

Inez to Stens.

Good revenge: Danny Duck masks, Exley whimpering. The photo good insurance; Dick still jacked up on blood – a taste that told him he was still on the muscle. His job at Kikey T.'s deli stunk – the dump was a known grifter hangout, a probation rap waiting to happen. Stens sleeping in his car, boozing, gambling – jail taught him absolutely shit.

Bud cut north on Vine; sunlight picked up his reflection in the windshield. His necktie stood out: LAPD shields, 2's. The 2's stood for the men he killed; he'd have to get some new ties made up – 3's to add on Sylvester Fitch. Dudley's idea: *esprit de corps* for Surveillance. Snappy stuff: women got a kick out of them. Dudley was a kick – in the teeth, in the brains.

He owed him more than he owed Dick Stens – the man frosted Bloody Christmas, got him Surveillance, then

Homicide. But when Dudley Smith brought you along you belonged to him – and he was so much smarter than everyone else that you were never sure what he wanted from you or how he was using you – shit got lost in all his fancy language. It didn't quite rankle, but you felt it; it scared you to see how Mike Breuning and Dick Carlisle gave the man their souls. Dudley could bend you, shape you, twist you, turn you, point you – and never make you feel like some dumb lump of clay. But he always let you know one thing: he knew you better than you knew yourself.

No streetside parking – every space taken. Bud parked three blocks over, walked up to the squadroom. No Exley, every desk occupied: men talking into phones, taking notes. A giant bulletin board all Nite Owl – paper six inches thick. Two women at a table, a switchboard behind them, a sign by their feet: 'R&I/DMV Requests.' Bud went over, talked over phone noise. 'I'm on the Cathcart check, and I want all you can get me, known associates, the works. This clown was popped twice for statch rape. I want full details on the complainants, plus current addresses. He had three pimping rousts, no convictions, and I want you to check all the local city and county vice squads to see if he's got a file. If he does, I want names on the girls he was running. If you get names, get DOBs and run them back through R&I, DMV, City/County Parole, the Woman's Jail. *Details*. You got it?'

The girls hit the switchboard; Bud hit the bulletin board: paper tagged 'Victim Lunceford.' One update: a Hollywood squad officer talked to Lunceford's boss at the Mighty Man Agency. Facts: Lunceford patronized the Nite Owl virtually every early A.M. – after he got off his 6:00–to–2:00 shift at the Pickwick Bookstore Building; Lunceford was a typical wino security guard not permitted to carry a sidearm; Lunceford had no known enemies, no known friends, no known lady friends, did not associate with his fellow Mighty Men, slept in a pup tent behind the Hollywood Bowl. The tent was checked out, inventoried:

a sleeping bag, four Mighty Man uniforms, six bottles of Old Monterey muscatel.

Adiós, shitbird – you were in *the* wrong place at *the* wrong time. Bud checked Lunceford's arrest record: nineteen minor felony pops in eleven years as a cop, scratch revenge as a motive, kill six to get one stunk as a motive anyway. Still no Exley, no Breuning and Carlisle. Bud remembered Dudley's memo: check the station files for Lunceford listings.

A good bet: field interrogation cards filed by officer surname. Bud hit the storage room, pulled the 'L' cabinet – no folder for 'Lunceford, Officer Malcolm.' An hour checking misfiles 'A' to 'Z' – zero. No F.I.'s – strange – maybe Wino Mal never filed his field cards.

Almost noon, time for a chow run – a sandwich, talk to Dick. Carlisle and Breuning showed up – loafing, drinking coffee. Bud found a free phone, buzzed snitches.

Snake Tucker heard bupkis; ditto Fats Rice and Johnny Stomp. Jerry Katzenbach said it was the Rosenbergs – they ordered the snuffs from death row, make Jerry back on the needle. An R&I girl hovered.

She handed him a tear sheet. 'There's not much. Nothing on Cathcart's K.A.'s, not much detail besides his rap sheet. I couldn't get much on the statutory rape complainants, except that they were fourteen and blonde and worked at Lockheed during the war. My bet is they were transients. Sheriff's Central Vice had a file on Cathcart, with nine suspected prostitutes listed. I followed up. Two are dead of syphilis, three were underaged and left the state as a probation stipulation, two I couldn't get a line on. The remaining two are on that page. Does it help?'

Bud waved Breuning and Carlisle over. 'Yeah, it does. Thanks.'

The clerk walked off; Bud checked her sheet, two names circled: Jane (a.k.a. 'Feather') Royko, Cynthia (a.k.a. 'Sinful Cindy') Benavides. Last known addresses, known haunts: pads on Poinsettia and Yucca, cocktail lounges.

Dudley's strongarms hovered. Bud said, 'The two names here. Shag them, will you?'

Carlisle said, 'This background check shit is the bunk. I say it's the shines.'

Breuning grabbed the sheet. 'Dud says do it, we do it.'

Bud checked their neckties – five dead men total. Fat Breuning, skinny Carlisle – somehow they looked just like twins. 'So do it, huh?'

Abe's Noshery, no parking, around the block. Dick's Chevy out back, booze empties on the seat: probation violation number one. Bud found a space, walked up and checked the window: Stens guzzling Manischewitz, bullshitting with ex-cons – Lee Vachss, Deuce Perkins, Johnny Stomp. A cop type eating at the counter: a bite, a glance at the known criminal assembly, another bite – clockwork. Back to Hollywood Station – pissed that he was still playing nursemaid.

Waiting for him: Breuning, two hooker types – laughing up a storm in the sweatbox. Bud tapped the glass; Breuning walked out.

Bud said, 'Who's who?'

'The blonde's Feather Royko. Hey, did you hear the one about the well-hung elephant?'

'What'd you tell them?'

'I told them it was a routine background check on Duke Cathcart. They read the papers, so they weren't surprised. Bud, it's the niggers. They're gonna burn for that Mex ginch, Dudley's just going through this rigamarole 'cause Parker wants a showcase and he's listening to that punk kid Exley with all his highfalut – '

Hard fingers to the chest. 'Inez Soto ain't a ginch, and maybe it ain't the jigs. So you and Carlisle go do some police work.'

Kowtow – Breuning shambled off smoothing his shirt. Bud walked into the box. The whores looked bad: a peroxide blonde, a henna redhead, too much makeup on too many miles.

Bud said, 'So you read the papers this morning.'

Feather Royko said, 'Yeah. Poor Dukey.'

'It don't sound like you're exactly grieving for him.'

'Dukey was Dukey. He was cheap, but he never hit you. He had a thing about chiliburgers, and the Nite Owl had good ones. One chiliburg too many, RIP Dukey.'

'Then you girls buy all that robbery stuff in the papers?'

Cindy Benavides nodded. Feather said, 'Sure. That's what it was, wasn't it? I mean, don't you think so?'

'Probably. What about enemies? Duke have any?'

'No, Dukey was Dukey.'

'How many other girls was he running?'

'Just us. We are the meager remnants of Dukey-poo's stable.'

'I heard Duke ran nine girls once. What happened? Rival pimp stuff?'

'Mister, Dukey was a dreamer. He liked young stuff personally, and he liked to run young stuff. Young stuff gets bored and moves on unless their guy gets mean. Dukey could get mean with other men, but never with females. RIP Dukey.'

'Then Duke must've had something else going. A two-girl string wouldn't cover him.'

Feather picked at her nail polish. 'Dukey was jazzed up on some new business scheme. You see, he always had some kind of scheme going. He was a dreamer. And the schemes made him happy, made him feel like the meager coin Cindy and me turned for him wasn't so bad.'

'Did he give you details?'

'No.'

Cindy had her lipstick out, smearing on another coat. 'Cindy, he tell *you* anything?'

'No' – a little squeak.

'Nothing about enemies?'

'No.'

'What about girlfriends? Duke have any young stuff going lately?'

Cindy grabbed a tissue, blotted. 'N-no.'

'Feather, you buy that?'

'I guess Dukey wasn't talking up nobody. Can we go now? I mean – '

'Go. There's a cabstand up the street.'

The girls moved out fast; Bud gave them a lead, ran to his car. Up to Sunset across from the cabstand; a two-minute wait. Cindy and Feather walked up.

Separate cabs, different directions. Cindy shot due north on Wilcox, maybe toward home – 5814 Yucca. Bud took a shortcut; the cab showed right on time. Cindy walked to a green De Soto, took off westbound. Bud counted to ten, followed.

Up to Highland, the Cahuenga Pass to the Valley, west on Ventura Boulevard. Bud stuck close; Cindy drove middle lane fast. A last-second swerve to the curb by a motel – rooms circling a murky swimming pool.

Bud braked, U-turned, watched. Cindy walked to a left-side room, knocked. A girl – fifteenish, blonde – let her in. Young stuff – Duke Cathcart's statch rape type.

Eyeball Surveillance.

Cindy walked out ten minutes later – zoom – a U-turn back toward Hollywood. Bud knocked on the girl's door.

She opened it – teary-eyed. A radio blasted: 'Nite Owl Massacre,' 'Crime of the Southland's Century.' The girl focused in. 'Are you the police?'

Bud nodded. 'Sweetie, how old are you?'

No more focus – her eyes went blurry.

'Sweetie, what's your name?'

'Kathy Janeway. Kathy with a "K." '

Bud closed the door. 'How old are you?'

'Fourteen. Why do men always ask you that?'

A prairie twang.

'Where are you from?'

'North Dakota. But if you send me back I'll just run away again.'

'Why?'

'You want it in VistaVision? Duke said lots of guys get their jollies that way.'

'Don't be such a tough cookie, huh? I'm on your side.'

'That's a laugh.'

156

Bud scoped the room. Panda bears, movie mags, school-girl smocks on the dresser. No whore threads, no dope paraphernalia. 'Was Duke nice to you?'

'He didn't make me do it with guys, if that's what you mean.'

'You mean you only did it with him?'

'No, I mean my daddy did it to me and this other guy made me do it with guys, but Duke bought me away from him.'

Pimp intrigue. 'What was the guy's name?'

'No! I won't tell you and you can't make me and I forgot it anyway!'

'Which one of those, sweetie?'

'I don't want to tell!'

'Sssh. So Duke was nice to you?'

'Don't shush me. Duke was a panda bear, all he wanted was to sleep in the same bed with me and play pinochle. Is that so bad?'

'Honey – '

'My daddy was worse! My Uncle Arthur was *lots* worse!'

'Hush, now, huh?'

'You can't make me!'

Bud took her hands. 'What did Cindy want?'

Kathy pulled away. 'She told me Duke was dead, which any dunce with a radio knows. She told me Duke said that if anything happened to him she should look after me, and she gave me ten dollars. She said the police bothered her. I said ten dollars isn't very much, and she got insulted and yelled at me. And how'd you know Cindy was here?'

'Never mind.'

'The rent here's nine dollars a week and I – '

'I'll get you some more money if you'll – '

'Duke was *never* that cheap with me!'

'*Kathy, hush now and let me ask you a few questions and maybe we'll get the guys who killed Duke. All right? Huh?*'

A kid's sigh. 'Okay, all right, ask me.'

Bud, soft. 'Cindy said Duke told her to look after you

157

if something happened to him. Do you think he figured something was gonna happen?'

'I don't know. Maybe.'

'Why maybe?'

'Maybe 'cause Duke was nervous lately.'

'Why was he nervous?'

'I don't know.'

'Did you ask him?'

'He said, "Just biz." '

Feather on Cathcart: 'Jazzed on some new business scheme.' 'Kathy, was Duke starting some new kind of thing up?'

'I don't know, Duke said girls don't need shoptalk. And I *know* he left me more than a crummy ten dollars.'

Bud gave her a Bureau card. 'That's my number at work. You call me, huh?'

Kathy plucked a panda off the bed. 'Duke was so messy and such a slob, but I didn't care. He had a cute smile and this cute scar on his chest, and he never yelled at me. My daddy and Uncle Arthur always yelled at me, so Duke never did. Wasn't that a nice thing to do?'

Bud left her with a hand squeeze. Halfway out to the street he heard her sobbing.

Back to the car, a brainstorm on the Cathcart play so far. Call Duke's 'new gig' and pimp intrigue weak maybes; call Nite Owl chiliburgers 99 percent sure the ink on his death warrant. A pimp statch raper and a grifter ex-cop for victims – strange – but par for the Hollywood Boulevard 3:00 A.M. course. Call it busywork for Dudley – maybe Cindy was hinked on more than the cash she held back. He could muscle the money out of her, glom some pimp scuttlebutt, close out the Cathcart end and ask Dud to send him down to Darktown. Simple – but Cindy was who-knows-where and Kathy had him dancing to her tune: savior with no place to go. He snapped to something missing from the bulletins: no checkout on Cathcart's apartment. A chance Duke's whore book might be there

– leads on his gig and the pimp he bought Kathy from – a good time-killer.

Bud headed over Cahuenga. He saw a red sedan hovering back – he thought he'd seen it by the motel. He speeded up, made a run by Cindy's pad – no green De Soto, no red sedan. He drove to Silverlake checking his rearview. No tail car – just his imagination.

9819 Vendome looked virgin – a garage apartment behind a small stucco house. No reporters, no crime scene ropes, no locals out taking some sun. Bud popped the door with his hand.

A typical bachelor flop: living room/bedroom combo, bathroom, kitchenette. Lights on for a quick inventory – the way Dudley taught him.

A Murphy bed in the down position. Cheapie seascapes on the walls. One dresser, a walk-in closet. No doors on the bathroom and kitchenette – neat, clean. The whole pad looked spanking neat – at odds with Kathy: 'Duke was so messy and such a slob.'

Detail prowls – another Dudley trick. A phone on an end table, check the drawers: pencils, no address book, no whore book. A stack of Yellow Page directories, a toss – L.A. County, Riverside County, San Bernardino County, Ventura County. San Berdoo the only book used – ruffled pages, a cracked spine. Check the rufflings: 'Printshop' listings thumbed through. A connection, probably nothing: victim Susan Lefferts, San Berdoo native.

Bud eyeball-prowled, click/click/click. The bathroom and kitchen immaculate; neatly folded shirts in the dresser. The carpet clean, a bit grimy in the corners. A final click: the crib had been checked out, cleaned up – maybe tossed by a pro.

He went through the closet: jackets and slacks slipping off hangers. Cathcart had a nifty wardrobe – someone had been trying on his threads or this was the real Duke – Kathy's slob – and the tosser didn't bother with his clothes.

Bud checked every pocket, every garment: lint, spare

159

change, nothing hot. A click: a test to test the tosser. He walked down to the car, got his evidence kit, dusted: the dresser a sure thing for latents. One more click: scouring powder wipe marks. Nail the pad as professionally print-wiped.

Bud packed up, got out, brainstormed some more – pimp war clicks, clickouts – Duke Cathcart had two skags in his stable, no stomach for pushing a fourteen-year-old nymphet – he was a pimp disaster area. He tried to click Duke's pad tossed to the Nite Owl – no gears meshed, odds on the coons stayed high. If the tossing played, tie it to Cathcart's 'new gig' – Feather Royko talked it up – she came off as clean as Sinful Cindy came off hinky. Cindy next – and she owed Kathy money.

Dusk settling in. Bud drove to Cindy's pad, saw the green De Soto. Moans out a half-cracked window – he shoved the sill up, vaulted in.

A dark hallway, grunt-grunt-grunt one door down. Bud walked over, looked in. Cindy and a fat man wearing argyles, the bed about ready to break. Fattie's trousers on the doorknob – Bud filched a billfold, emptied it, whistled.

Cindy shrieked; Fats kept pumping. Bud: 'SHITBIRD, WHAT YOU DOIN' WITH MY WOMAN!!!!'

Things speeded up.

Fattie ran out holding his dick; Cindy dove under the sheets. Bud saw a purse, dumped it, grabbed money. Cindy shrieked willy-nilly. Bud kicked the bed. 'Duke's enemies. Spill and I won't roust you.'

Cindy poked her head out. 'I . . . don't . . . know . . . nothin'.''

'The fuck you don't. Let's try this: somebody broke into Duke's place, you give me a suspect.'

'I . . . don't . . . know.'

'Last chance. You held back at the station, Feather came clean. You went to Kathy Janeway's motel and stiffed her with a ten-spot. What else you hold back on?'

'Look – '

'Give.'

'Give on what?'

'Give on Duke's new gig and his enemies. Tell me who used to pimp Kathy.'

'I don't know who pimped her!'

'Then give on the other two.'

Cindy wiped her face – smeared lipstick, runny makeup. 'All I know's this guy was going around talking up cocktail-bar girls, acting like Duke. You know, the same one-liners, real Dukey shtick. I heard he was trying to get girls to do call jobs for him. He didn't talk to me or Feather, this is just stale-bread stuff I heard, like from two weeks ago.'

Click: 'This Guy' maybe the pad tosser, 'This Guy' trying on Cathcart's clothes. 'Keep going on that.'

'That is all I heard, just the way I heard it.'

'What did the guy look like?'

'I don't know.'

'Who told you about him?'

'I don't even know that, they were just girls gabbing at the next table at this goddamned bar.'

'All right, easy. Duke's new gig. Give on that.'

'Mister, it was just another Dukey pipe dream.'

'Then why didn't you tell me before?'

'You know the old adage "Don't speak ill of the dead"?'

'Yeah. You know the bull daggers at the Woman's Jail?'

Cindy sighed. 'Dukey pipe dream number six thousand – smut peddler. Is that a yuck? Dukey said he was going to push this weird smut. That's all I know, we had a two-second conversation on the topic and that's all Duke said. I didn't press it 'cause I know a pipe dream when I hear one. Now will you get out of here?'

Loose Bureau talk: Ad Vice working pornography. 'What kind of smut?'

'Mister, I told you I don't know, it was just a two-second conversation.'

'You gonna pay Kathy back what Duke left you?'

'Sure, Good Samaritan. Ten here, ten there. If I gave her the money all at once she'd just blow it on movie mags anyway.'

'I might be back.'
'I wait with bated breath.'

Bud drove to a mailbox, sent the cash out special delivery: Kathy Janeway, Orchid View Motel, plenty of stamps and a friendly note. Four hundred plus – a small fortune for a kid.

7:00 – time to kill before he met Dudley. The Bureau for a time-killer: Ad Vice, the squadroom board.

Squad 4 on the smut job – Kifka, Henderson, Vincennes, Stathis – four men tracking stag books, all reporting no leads. Nobody around, he could check by in the morning, it was probably nothing anyway. He walked over to Homicide, called Abe's Noshery.

Stens answered. 'Abe's.'

'Dick, it's me.'

'Oh? Checking up on me, *Officer?*'

'Dick, come on.'

'No, I mean it. You're a Dudley man now. Maybe Dud don't like the people I push my corned beef to. Maybe Dud wants skinny, thinks I'll talk to you. It ain't like you're your own man no more.'

'You been drinking, partner?'

'I drink kosher now. Tell Exley that. Tell him Danny Duck wants to dance with him. Tell him I read about his old man and Dream-a-fucking-Dreamland. Tell him I might come to the opening, Danny Duck requests the presence of Sergeant Ed cocksucker Exley for one more fucking dance.'

'Dick, you're way out of line.'

'The fuck you say. One more dance, Danny Duck's gonna break his glasses and chew his fuckin' throat – '

'Dick, goddammit – '

'Hey, fuck you! I read the papers, I saw the personnel on that Nite Owl job. You, Dudley S., Exley, the rest of Dudley's hard-ons. You're fucking partners with the cocksucker who put me away, you're sucking the same gravy case, so if you th – '

Bud threw the phone out the window. He walked down

162

to the lot kicking things – then the Big Picture kicked him.

He should have swung for Bloody Christmas.

Dudley saved him.

Make Exley the Nite Owl hero so far – he'd be the one to send Inez back through Hell.

Strangeness on the Cathcart end, the case might go wide, more than a psycho robbery gang. *He* could make the case, twist Exley, work an angle to help out Stens. Which meant:

Not greasing Ad Vice for smut leads.

Holding back evidence from Dudley.

BEING A DETECTIVE – NOT A HEADBASHER – ON HIS OWN.

He fed himself drunk talk for guts:

It ain't like you're your own man.

It ain't like you're your own man.

It ain't like you're your own man.

He was scared.

He owed Dudley.

He was crossing the only man on earth more dangerous than he was.

Chapter Twenty-four

Ray Pinker walked Ed through the Nite Owl, reconstructing.

'Bim, bam, I'm betting it happened like this. First, the three enter and show their weaponry. One man takes the cash register girl, the kitchen boy and the waitress. This guy hits Donna DeLuca with his shotgun butt – she's standing by the cash register, and we found a piece of her scalp on the floor there. She gives him the money and the money from her purse, he shoves her and Patty Chesimard to the locker, picking up Gilbert Escobar in the kitchen en route. Gilbert resists – note the drag marks, the pots and pans on the floor. A pop to the head – bim, bam – that little pool of blood you see outlined in chalk. The safe is exposed under the cook's stand, one of the three employee victims opens it, note the spilled coins. Bim, bam, Gilbert resists some more, another gun-butt shot, note the circle marked 1–A on the floor, we found three gold teeth there, bagged them and matched them: Gilbert Luis Escobar. The drag marks start there, old Gil has quit fighting, bim, bam, suspect number one plants victims one, two and three inside the food locker.'

Back to the restaurant proper – still sealed three nights post-mortem. Gawkers pressed up to the windows; Pinker kept talking. 'Meanwhile, gunmen two and three are rounding up victims four through six. The drag marks going back to the locker and the spilled food and dishes speak for themselves. You might not be able to see it because the linoleum's so dark, but there's blood under the first two tables: Cathcart and Lunceford, sitting separately, two gun-butt shots. We know who was where through blood typing. Cathcart drops by table two, Lunceford by table one. Now – '

164

Ed cut in. 'Did you dust the plates for more confirmation?'

Pinker nodded. 'Smudges and smears, two viable latents on dishes under Lunceford's table. That's how we ID'd him – we got a match to the set they took when he joined the LAPD. Cathcart and Susan Lefferts had their hands blown off, no way to cross-check on that, their dishes were too smudged anyway. We tagged Cathcart on a partial dental and his prison measurement chart, Lefferts on a full dental. Now, you see the shoe on the floor?'

'Yes.'

'Well, from an angle study it looks like Lefferts was flailing to get to Cathcart at the next table, even though they were sitting separately. Dumb panic, she obviously didn't know him. She started screaming, and one of the gunmen stuck a wad of napkins from that container there in her mouth. Doc Layman found a big wad of swallowed tissue in her throat at autopsy, he thinks she might have gagged and suffocated just as the shooting started. Bim, bam, Cathcart and Lefferts are dragged to the locker, Lunceford walks, the poor bastard probably thinks it's just a stickup. At the locker, purses and wallets are taken – we found a scrap of Gilbert Escobar's driver's license floating in blood just inside the door, along with six wax-saturated cotton balls. The gunmen had the brains to protect their ears.'

The last bit didn't play: his coloreds were too impetuous. 'It doesn't seem like enough men to do the job.'

Pinker shrugged. 'It worked. Are you suggesting one or more of the victims knew one or more of the killers?'

'I know, it's unlikely.'

'Do you want to see the locker? It'll have to be now, we promised the owner he could have the place back.'

'I saw it that night.'

'I saw the pictures. Jesus, you couldn't tell they were human. You're working the Lefferts background check, right?'

Ed looked out the window; a pretty girl waved at him. Dark-haired, Latin – she looked like Inez Soto. 'Right.'

'And?'

'And I spent a full day in San Bernardino and got nowhere. The woman used to live with her mother, who was half-sedated and wouldn't talk to me. I talked to acquaintances, and they told me Sue Lefferts was a chronic insomniac who listened to the radio all night. She had no boyfriends in recent memory, no enemies ever. I checked her apartment in L.A., which was just about what you'd expect for a thirty-one-year-old salesgirl. One of the San Berdoo people said she was a bit of a round-heels, one said she belly-danced at a Greek restaurant a few times for laughs. Nothing suspicious.'

'It keeps coming back to the Negroes.'

'Yes, it does.'

'Any luck on the car or the weapons?'

'No, and 77th Street's checking trashcans and sewer grates for the purses and wallets. And I know an approach we can make and save the investigation a lot of time.'

Pinker smiled. 'Check Griffith Park for the nicked shells?'

Ed turned to the window – the Inez type was gone. 'If we place those shells, then it's either the Negroes in custody or another three.'

'Sergeant, that is one large long shot.'

'I know, and I'll help.'

Pinker checked his watch. 'It's 10:30 now. I'll find the occurrence reports on those shootings, try to pinpoint the locations and meet you with a sapper squad tomorrow at dawn. Say the Observatory parking lot?'

'I'll be there.'

'Should I get clearance from Lieutenant Smith?'

'Do it on my say-so, okay? I'm reporting directly to Parker on this.'

'The park at dawn then. Wear some old clothes, it'll be filthy work.'

Ed ate Chinese on Alvarado. He knew why he was heading that way: Queen of Angels was close, Inez Soto might be awake. He'd called the hospital: Inez was healing up

166

quickly, her family hadn't visited, her sister called, said Mama and Papa blamed her for the nightmare – provocative clothing, worldly ways. She'd been crying for her stuffed animals; he had the gift shop send up an assortment – gifts to ease his conscience – he wanted her as a major witness in his first big homicide case. And he just wanted her to like him, wanted her to disown four words: 'Officer White's the hero.'

He stalled with a last cup of tea. Stitches, dental work – his wounds were healing, made small: his mother and Inez blurred together. He'd gotten a report: Dick Stens hung out with known armed robbers, bet with bookies, took his salary in cash and frequented whorehouses. When his men had him pinned cold they'd call County Probation and fix an arrest.

Which paled beside 'Officer White's the hero' and Inez Soto with the fire to hate him.

Ed paid the check, drove to Queen of Angels.

Bud White was walking out.

They crossed by the elevator. White got the first word in. 'Give your career a rest and let her sleep.'

'What are you doing here?'

'Not looking to pump a witness. Leave her alone, you'll get your chance.'

'This is just a visit.'

'She sees through you, Exley. You can't buy her off with teddy bears.'

'Don't you want the case cleared? Or are you just frustrated that there's nobody else for you to kill?'

'Big talk from a brownnosing snitch.'

'Did you come here to get laid?'

'Different circumstances, I'd eat you for that.'

'Sooner or later, I'll take you and Stensland down.'

'That goes two ways. War hero, huh? Those Japs must've rolled over for you.'

Ed flinched.

White winked.

167

Tremors – all the way up to her room. Ed looked before he knocked.

Inez was awake – reading a magazine. Stuffed animals strewn on the floor, one creature on the bed: Scooter Squirrel as a footrest. Inez saw him, said, 'No.'

Faded bruises, her features coming back hard. 'No what, Miss Soto?'

'No, I won't go through it with you.'

'Not even a few questions?'

'No.'

Ed pulled a chair up. 'You don't seem surprised to see me here so late.'

'I'm not, you're the subtle type.' She pointed to the animals. 'Did the district attorney reimburse you for those?'

'No, that was out of my own pocket. Did Ellis Loew visit you?'

'Yes, and I told him no. I told him that the three *negrito putos* drove me around, took money from other *putos* and left me with the *negrito puto* that Officer White killed. I told him that I can't remember or won't remember or don't want to remember any more details, he can take his pick and that is *absolutamente* all there is to it.'

Ed said, 'Miss Soto, I just came to say hello.'

She laughed in his face. 'You want the rest of the story? An hour later my brother Juan calls and tells me I can't go home, that I disgraced the family. Then *puto* Mr. Loew calls and says he can put me up in a hotel if I cooperate, then the gift shop girl brings me those *puto* animals and says they're gifts from the nice policeman with the glasses. I've been to college, *pendejo*. Don't you think I can follow the chain of events?'

Ed pointed to Scooter Squirrel. 'You didn't throw him away.'

'He's special.'

'Do you like Dieterling characters?'

'So what if I do!'

'Just asking. And where do you put Bud White in your chain of events?'

Inez fluffed her pillows. 'He killed a man for me.'

'He killed him for himself.'

'And that *puto* animal is dead just the same. Officer White just comes by to say hello. He warns me about you and Mr. Loew. He tells me I should cooperate, but he doesn't press the subject. He hates you, subtle man. I can tell.'

'You're a smart girl, Inez.'

'You want to say "for a Mexican," I know that.'

'No, you're wrong. You're just plain smart. And you're lonely, or you would have asked me to leave.'

Inez threw her magazine down. 'So what if I am!'

Ed picked it up. Dog-eared pages: a piece on Dream-a-Dreamland. 'I'm going to recommend that we give you some time to get well and recommend that when this mess goes to court you be allowed to testify by written deposition. If we get enough Nite Owl corroboration from other sources, you might not have to testify at all. And I won't come back if you don't want me to.'

She stared at him. 'I've still got no place to go.'

'Did you read that article on the Dream-a-Dreamland opening?'

'Yes.'

'Did you see the name "Preston Exley"?'

'Yes.'

'He's my father.'

'So what? I know you're a rich kid, blowing your money on stuffed animals. So what? Where will I go?'

Ed held the bed rail. 'I've got a cabin at Lake Arrowhead. You can stay there. I won't touch you, and I'll take you to the Dream-a-Dreamland opening.'

Inez touched her head. 'What about my hair?'

'I'll get you a nice bonnet.'

Inez sobbed, hugged Scooter Squirrel.

Ed met the sappers at dawn, groggy from dreams: Inez, other women. Ray Pinker brought flashlights, spades, metal detectors; he'd had Communications Division issue a public appeal: witnesses to the Griffith Park shotgun blastings were asked to come forth to ID the blasters. The occurrence report locations were marked out into grids – all steep, scrub-covered hillsides. The men dug, uprooted, scanned with gizmos going tick, tick, tick – they found coins, tin cans, a .32 revolver. Hours came, went; the sun beat down. Ed worked hard – breathing dirt, risking sunstroke. His dreams returned, circles leading back to Inez.

Anne from the Marlborough School Cotillion – they did it in a '38 Dodge, his legs banged the doors. Penny from his UCLA biology class: rum punch at his frat house, a quick backyard coupling. A string of patriotic roundheels on his bond tour, a one-night stand with an older woman – a Central Division dispatcher. Their faces were hard to remember; he tried and kept seeing Inez – Inez without bruises, no hospital smock. It was dizzying, the heat was dizzying, he was filthy, exhausted – it all felt good. More hours went – he couldn't think of women or anything else. More time down, yells in the distance, a hand on his shoulder.

Ray Pinker holding out two spent shotgun shells and a photo of a shotgun shell strike surface. A perfect match: identical firing pin marks straight across.

Chapter Twenty-five

Two days since the Fleur-de-Lis grab – no way to tell how far he could take it.

Two days, one suspect: Lamar Hinton, age twenty-six, arrested for strongarm assault, a conviction on an ADW, a deuce at Chino – paroled 3/51. Current employment: telephone installer at P.C. Bell – his parole officer suspected he moonlighted rigging bootleg bookie lines. A mugshot match: Hinton the muscle boy at Timmy Valburn's house.

Two days, no break on his stalemate: a made case would ticket him back to Narco, making *this* case meant Valburn and Billy Dieterling for material witnesses – well-connected homos who could flush his Hollywood career down the toilet.

Two days of page prowling – every roundabout approach tapped out. He checked the collateral case reports, talked to the arrestees – more denials – nobody admitted buying the smut. One day wasted; nothing at Ad Vice to goose his leads: Stathis, Henderson, Kifka reported zero, Millard was trying to co-boss the Nite Owl – pornography was not on his mind.

Two days since: midway through day two he hit hard – the bootleg number, Muscle Boy.

No Fleur-de-Lis phone listing; brain gymnastics tagged his personal connection – the first time he saw the calling card.

Tilt:

Xmas Eve '51, right before Bloody Christmas. Sid Hudgens set up a reefer roust – he popped two grasshoppers, found the card at their pad, thought nothing else of it.

Scary Sid: 'We've all got secrets, Jack.'

He pushed ahead anyway, that undertow driving him:

he wanted to know who made the smut – and why. He hit the P.C. Bell employment office, cross-checked records against physical stats until he hit Lamar Hinton – tilt, tilt, tilt, tilt, tilt –

Jack looked around the squadroom – men talking Nite Owl, Nite Owl, Nite Owl, the Big V chasing hand-job books.

The orgy pix.

Vertigo.

Jack chased.

Hinton's route: Gower to La Brea, Franklin to the Hollywood Reservoir. His A.M. installations: Creston Drive, North Ivar. Jack found Creston on his car map: Hollywood Hills, a cul-de-sac way up.

He drove there, saw the phone truck: parked by a pseudo-French chateau. Lamar Hinton on a pole across the street – monster huge in broad daylight.

Jack parked, checked the truck – the loading door wide open. Tools, phone books, Spade Cooley albums – no suspicious-looking brown paper bags. Hinton stared at him; Jack went over badge first.

Hinton trundled down the pole; six-four easy, blond, muscles on muscles. 'You with Parole?'

'Los Angeles Police Department.'

'Then this ain't about my parole?'

'No, this is about you cooperating to avoid a parole rap.'

'What do you – '

'Your parole officer don't really approve of this job you've got, Lamar. He thinks you might start doing some bootlegs.'

Hinton flexed muscles: neck, arms, chest. Jack said, 'Fleur-de-Lis, "Whatever You Desire." You desire no violation, you talk. You don't talk, then back to Chino.'

One last flex. 'You broke into my car.'

'You're a regular Einstein. Now, you got the brains to be an informant?'

Hinton shifted; Jack put a hand on his gun. 'Fleur-de-

172

Lis. Who runs it, how does it work, what do you push? Dieterling and Valburn. Tell me and I'm out of your life in five minutes.'

Muscles thought it through: his T-shirt bulged, puckered. Jack pulled out a fuck mag – an orgy pic spread full. 'Conspiracy to distribute pornographic material, possession and sales of felony narcotics. I've got enough to send you back to Chino until nineteen-fucking-seventy. Now, did you move this smut for Fleur-de-Lis?'

Hinton bobbed his head. 'Y-y-yeah.'

'Smart boy. Now, who made it?'

'I d-don't know. Really, honest, I d-don't.'

'Who posed for it?'

'I don't kn-know, I just d-d-delivered it.'

'Billy Dieterling and Timmy Valburn. *Go*.'

'J-just c-customers. Queers, you know, they like to fag party.'

'You're doing great, so here's the big question. Who – '

'Officer, please don't – '

Jack pulled his .38, cocked it. 'You want to be on the next train to Chino?'

'N-no.'

'Then answer me.'

Hinton turned, gripped the pole. 'P-pierce Patchett. He runs the business. He-he's some kind of legit businessman.'

'Description, phone number, address.'

'He's maybe fifty-something. I th-think he lives in B-brentwood and I don't know his n-number 'cause I get paid b-by the m-mail.'

'More on Patchett. Go.'

'H-he sugar-p-pimps girls made up like movie stars. H-he's rich. I-I only met him once.'

'Who introduced you?'

'This guy Ch-chester I used to see at M-m-muscle Beach.'

'Chester who?'

'I don't know.'

Hinton: bunching, flexing – Jack figured hot seconds and he'd snap. 'What else does Patchett push?'

'L-lots of b-boys and girls.'

'What about through Fleur-de-Lis?'

'W-whatever you d-desire.'

'Not the sales pitch, what specifically?'

Pissed more than scared. 'Boys, girls, liquor, dope, picture books, bondage stuff!'

'Easy, now. Who else makes the deliveries?'

'Me and Chester. He works days. I don't like – '

'Where's Chester live?'

'I don't know!'

'*Easy, now.* Lots of nice people with lots of money use Fleur-de-Lis, right?'

'R-right.'

The records in the truck. 'Spade Cooley? Is he a customer?'

'N-no, I just get free albums 'cause I party with this guy Burt Perkins.'

'You fucking would know him. The names of some customers. *Go.*'

Hinton dug into the pole. Jack flashed: the monster turning, six .38s not enough. 'Are you working tonight?'

'Y-yes.'

'The address.'

'No . . . please.'

Jack frisked: wallet, change, butch wax, a key on a fob. He held the key up; Hinton bobbed his head bam bam – blood on the pole.

'The address and I'm gone.'

Bam bam – blood on the monster's forehead. '5261B Cheramoya.'

Jack dropped the pocket trash. 'You don't show up tonight. You call your parole officer and tell him you helped me, you tell him you want to be picked up on a violation, you have him put you up someplace. You're clean on this, and if I get to Patchett I'll make like one of the smut people snitched. *And if you clean that place out you are Chino-fucking-bound.*'

174

'B-but you *t-told* me.'

Jack ran to his car, gunned it. Hinton tore at the pole barehanded.

Pierce Patchett, fifty-something, 'some kind of legit businessman.'

Jack found a pay phone, called R&I, the DMV. A make: Pierce Morehouse Patchett, DOB 6/30/02, Grosse Pointe, Michigan. No criminal record, 1184 Gretna Green, Brentwood. Three minor traffic violations since 1931.

Not much. Sid Hudgens next – fuck his smut hink. A busy signal, a buzz to Morty Bendish at the *Mirror*.

'City Room, Bendish.'

'Morty, it's Jack Vincennes.'

'The Big V! Jack, when are you going back to the Narco Squad? I need some good dope stories.'

Morty wanted shtick. 'As soon as I get squeaky-clean Russ Millard off my case and make a case for him. And *you* can help.'

'Keep talking, I'm all ears.'

'Pierce Patchett. Ring a bell?'

Bendish whistled. 'What's this about?'

'I can't tell you yet. But if it breaks his way, you've got the exclusive.'

'You'd feed me before you feed Sid?'

'Yeah. Now I'm all ears.'

Another whistle. 'There's not much, but what there is is choice. Patchett's a big handsome guy, maybe fifty, but he looks thirty-eight. He goes back maybe twenty-five years in L.A. He's some kind of judo or jujitsu expert, he's either a chemist by trade or he was a chemistry major in college. He's worth a boatload of greenbacks, and I know he lends money to businessman types at thirty percent interest and a cut of their biz, I know he's bankrolled a lot of movies under the table. Interesting, huh? Now try this on: he's rumored to be some kind of periodic heroin sniffer, rumored to dry out at Terry Lux's clinic.

175

All in all, he's what you might wanta call a powerful behind-the-scenes strange-o.'

Terry Lux – plastic surgeon to the stars. Sanitarium boss: booze, dope cures, abortions, detoxification heroin available – the cops looked the other way, Terry treated L.A. politicos free. 'Morty, that's all you've got?'

'Ain't that enough? Look, what I don't have, Sid might. Call him, but remember I got the exclusive.'

Jack hung up, called Sid Hudgens. Sid answered: *'Hush-Hush*. Off the record and on the QT.'

'It's Vincennes.'

'Jackie! You got some good Nite Owl scoop for the Sidster?'

'No, but I'll keep an ear down.'

'Narco skinny maybe? I want to put out an all-hophead issue – shvartze jazz musicians and movie stars, maybe tie it in to the Commies, this Rosenberg thing has got the public running hot with a thermometer up their ass. You like it?'

'It's cute. Sid, have you heard of a man named Pierce Patchett?'

Silence – seconds ticking off long. Sid, too Sid-like. 'Jackie, all I know on the man is that he is very wealthy and what I like to call "Twilight." He ain't queer, he ain't Red, he don't know anybody I can use in my quest for prime sinuendo. Where'd you hear about him?'

Bullshitting him – he could taste it. 'A smut peddler told me.'

Static – breath catching sharp. 'Jack, smut is from hunger, strictly for sad sacks who can't get their ashes hauled. Leave it alone and write when you get work, *gabishe*?'

Hang up – bang! – a door slamming, cutting you off, some line you couldn't cross back to. Jack drove to the Bureau, MALIBU RENDEZVOUS stamped on that door.

The Ad Vice pen stood empty, just Millard and Thad Green in a huddle by the cloakroom. Jack checked the assignment board – more no-leads – walked around to the supply room on the QT. Unlocked – easy to pull off a snatch. Downwind: the high brass talking Nite Owl.

'Russ, I know you want in. But Parker wants Dudley.'

'He's too volatile on Negroes, Chief. We both know it.'

'You only call me "Chief" when you want something, *Captain.*'

Millard laughed. 'Thad, the sappers found matching spents in Griffith Park, and I heard 77th Street turned the wallets and purses. Is that true?'

'Yes, an hour ago, in a sewer. Blood-caked, print-wiped. SID matched to the victims' blood. It's the coloreds, Russ. I know it.'

'I don't think it's the ones in custody. Do you see them leaving a rape scene on the southside, then driving the girl around to let their friends abuse her, *then* driving all the way to Hollywood to pull the Nite Owl job – when two of them are high on barbiturates?'

'It's a stretch, I'll admit that. We need to nail down the outside rapists and get Inez Soto to talk. So far she's refused. But Ed Exley is working on her, and Ed Exley is very good.'

'Thad, I won't let my ego get in the way. I'm a captain, Dudley's a lieutenant. We'll share the command.'

'I worry about your heart.'

'A heart attack five years ago doesn't make me a cripple.'

Green laughed. 'I'll talk to Parker. Jesus, you and Dudley. What a pair.'

Jack found what he wanted: a tape recorder/phone tapper, bolt-on style, headphones. He hustled it out a side door, no witnesses.

Dusk, Cheramoya Avenue: Hollywood, a block off Franklin. 5261: a Tudor four-flat, two pads upstairs, two down. No lights – probably too late to glom 'Chester' the day man. Jack rang the B buzzer – no response. An ear to the door, a listen – no sounds, period. In with the key.

Jackpot: one glance told him Hinton played it straight

177

– no cleanout. Pervert fucking Utopia – floor-to-ceiling shelves jammed with goodies.

Maryjane: leaf, prime buds. Pills – bennies, goofballs, red devils, yellow jackets, blue heavens. Patent dope: laudanum, codeine mixture, catchy brand names: Dreamscope, Hollywood Sunrise, Martian Moonglow. Absinthe, pure alcohol in pints, quarts, half gallons. Ether, hormone pills, envelopes of cocaine, heroin. Film cans, smutty titles: *Mr. Big Dick, Anal Love, Gang Bang, High School Rapist, Rape Club, Virgin Cocksucker, Hot Negro Love, Fuck Me Tonite, Susie's Butthole Deelite, Boys in Love, Locker Room Lust, Blow the Man Down, Jesus Porks the Pope, Cocksucker's Paradise, Cornholers Meet the Ramrod Boys, Rex the Randy Rottweiler.* Old stag books: T.J. venues, women sucking cock, boys sucking cock, up-the-hole close-ups. Dusty – not a hot item; empty spaces alongside, maybe the good smut, *his smut*, was piled there: make Lamar for cleaning *that* out? Why? The rest of the shit spelled felony time to the year 2000. Snapshots – candid-type pix – real-life movie stars in the raw. Lupe Velez, Gary Cooper, Johnny Weissmuller, Carole Landis, Clark Gable, Tallulah Bankhead muff-diving, corpses going 69 on morgue slabs. A color pic: Joan Crawford and a notoriously well hung Samoan extra named 'O.K. Freddy' fucking. Dildoes, dog collars, whips, chains, amyl nitrite poppers, panties, brassieres, cock rings, catheters, enema bags, black lizard pumps with six-inch heels and a female mannequin covered by a tarp – plasterboard, rubber lips, glued-on pubic hair, a snatch made from a garden hose.

Jack found the bathroom and pissed. A mirror threw his face back: old, strange. He went to work: tapper to the phone, the oldie smut skimmed.

Cheap stuff, probably Mex-made: spic hairstyles on skinny junkie posers. Vertigo: he felt swirly, like a good hop jolt. The dope on the shelves made him drool; he mixed Karen in with the pictures. He paced the room, tapped a hollow place, pulled up the rug. Bingo on a cute hidey-hole: a basement, stairs leading to an empty black space.

The phone rang.

Jack hit the tapper, picked up. 'Hi. Whatever You Desire' – Lamar Hinton mimicked.

Click, a hang-up, he shouldn't have used the slogan. A half hour passed – the phone rang. 'Hi, it's Lamar' – casual.

A pause, click.

A chain of smokes – his throat hurt. The phone rang.

Try a mumble. 'Yeah?'

'Hi, it's Seth up in Bel Air. You feel like bringing something over?'

'Sure.'

'Make it a jug of the wormwood. Make it fast and you made a nice tip.'

'Uh . . . gimme the address again, would ya?'

'Who could forget digs like mine? It's 941 Roscomere, and don't dawdle.'

Jack hung up. Ring ring again.

'Yeah?'

'Lamar, tell Pierce I need to . . . Lamar, is that you, boychik?'

SID HUDGENS.

Lamar – with a tremor. 'Uh, yeah. Who's this?'

Click.

Jack pushed 'Replay.' Hudgens talked, recognition creeped in –

SID KNEW PATCHETT. SID KNEW LAMAR. SID KNEW THE FLEUR-DE-LIS RACKET.

The phone rang – Jack ignored it. Splitsville – grab the tapper, wipe the phone, wipe all the filth he'd touched. Out the door queasy – night air peaking his nerves.

He heard a car revving.

A shot took out the front window; two shots smashed the door.

Jack drew, fired – the car hauling, no lights.

Clumsy: two shots hit a tree and sprayed wood. Three

more pulls, no hits, the car fishtailing. Doors opening – eyewitnesses.

Jack got his car – skids, brodies, no lights until Franklin and a main traffic flow. No make on the shooter car: dark, no lights, the cars all around him looked alike: sleek, wrong. A cigarette slowed him down. He drove straight west to Bel Air.

Roscomere Road: twisty, all uphill, mansions fronted by palm trees. Jack found 941, pulled into the driveway.

Circular, looping a big pseudo-Spanish: one story, low slate roof. Cars in a row – a Jag, a Packard, two Caddies, a Rolls. Jack got out – nobody braced him. He hunkered down, took plate numbers.

Five cars: classy, no Fleur-de-Lis bags on plush front seats. The house: bright windows, silk swirls. Jack walked up and looked in.

He knew he'd never forget the women.

One almost Rita Hayworth à la *Gilda*. One almost Ava Gardner in an emerald-green gown. A near Betty Grable – sequined swimsuit, fishnet stockings. Men in tuxedos mingled – background debris. He couldn't stray his eyes from the women.

Astonishing make-believe. Hinton on Patchett: 'He sugar-pimps these girls made up to look like movie stars.' 'Made up' didn't cut it: call these women chosen, culti-vated, enhanced by an expert. Astonishing.

Veronica Lake walked through the light. Her face wasn't as close: she just oozed that cat-girl grace. Back-ground men flocked to her.

Jack pressed up to the glass. Smut vertigo, real live women. Sid, that door slamming, that line. He drove home, bad vertigo – achy, itchy, jumpy. He saw a *Hush-Hush* card on his door, 'Malibu Rendezvous' inked on the bottom.

He saw headlines:

DOPED-OUT DOPE CRUSADER SHOOTS INNO-CENT CITIZENS!

CELEBRITY COP INDICTED FOR KILLINGS!

GAS CHAMBER FOR THE BIG-TIME BIG V! RICH

KID GIRLFRIEND BIDS DEATH ROW AU REVOIR!

Chapter Twenty-six

An arm-in-arm entrance – Inez in her best dress and a veil to hide her bruises. Ed kept his badge out – it got them past the press. Attendants formed the guests into lines – Dream-a-Dreamland was open for business.

Inez was awestruck: quick breaths billowed her veil. Ed looked up, down, sideways – every detail made him think of his father.

A grand promenade – Main Drag, USA, 1920 – soda fountains, nickelodeons, dancing extras: the cop on the beat, a paperboy juggling apples, ingenues doing the Charleston. The Amazon River: motorized crocodiles, jungle excursion boats. Snow-capped mountains; vendors handing out mouse-ear beanies. The Moochie Mouse Monorail, tropical isles – acres and acres of magic.

They rode the monorail: the first car, the first run. high speed, upside down, right side up – Inez unbuckled herself giggling. The Paul's World toboggan; lunch: hot dogs, snow cones, Moochie Mouse cheese balls.

On to 'Desert Idyll,' 'Danny's Fun House,' an exhibit on outer space travel. Inez seemed to be tiring: gorged on excitement. Ed yawned – his own late night catching up.

A late squeal at the station: a shootout on Cheramoya, no perpetrators caught. He had to go to the scene: an apartment house, shots riddling a downstairs unit. Weird: .38s, .45s retrieved, the living room all shelving – empty except for some sadomasochist paraphernalia – and no telephone. The building's owner couldn't be traced; the manager said he was paid by mail, cashier's checks, he got a free flop and a C-note a month, so he was happy and didn't ask questions – he couldn't even name the dump's tenant. The condition of the apartment indicated a rapid clean-out – but no one saw a thing. Four hours of report writing – four hours snatched from the Nite Owl.

The exhibit was a bore – a sop to culture. Inez pointed to the ladies' room; Ed stepped outside.

A VIP tour on the promenade – Timmy Valburn shepherding bigwigs. The *Herald* front page hit him: Dream-a-Dreamland, the Nite Owl, like nothing else mattered.

He tried to reinterrogate Coates, Jones and Fontaine – they would not give him one word. Eyewitnesses responded to the appeal for IDs on the Griffith Park shooters and could not identify the three in custody: they said they 'can't quite be sure.' Vehicle checks now extended to '48–'50 Fords and Chevys – nothing hot so far. Jockeying for command of the case: Chief Parker supported Dudley Smith, Thad Green pumped up Russ Millard. No shotguns found, no trace of Sugar Ray's Merc. Wallets and purses belonging to the victims were found in a sewer a few blocks from the Tevere Hotel – combine that with the matching shells found in Griffith Park and you got what the papers didn't report: Ellis Loew bullying Parker to bully him: 'It's all circumstantial so far, so have your boy Exley keep working on that Mexican girl, it looks like he's getting next to her, have him talk her into a questioning session under sodium pentothal, let's get some juicy Little Lindbergh details and fix the Nite Owl time frame once and for all.'

Inez sat down beside him. They had a view: the Amazon, plaster mountains. Ed said, 'Are you all right? Do you want to go back?'

'What I want is a cigarette, and I don't even smoke.'

'Then don't start. Inez – '

'Yes, I'll move into your cabin.'

Ed smiled. 'When did you make up your mind?'

Inez tucked her veil under her hat. 'I saw a newspaper in the bathroom, and Ellis Loew was gloating about me. He sounded happy, so I figured I'd put some distance between us. You know, I never thanked you for my bonnet.'

183

'You don't have to.'

'Yes I do, because I'm naturally bad-mannered around Anglos who treat me nice.'

'If you're waiting for the punch line, there isn't any.'

'Yes, there is. And for the record again, I won't tell you about it, I won't look at pictures, and I won't testify.'

'Inez, I submitted a recommendation that we let you rest up for now.'

'And "for now's" a punch line, and the other punch line's that you go for me, which is okay, because I've looked better in my time and no Mexican man would ever want a Mexican girl who was gang-raped by a bunch of *negrito putos*, not that I've ever gone for Mexican guys anyway. You know what's scary, Exley?'

'I told you, it's Ed.'

Inez rolled her eyes. 'I've got a creep brother named Eduardo, so I'll call you Exley. You know what's scary? What's scary is that I feel good today because this place is like a wonderful dream, but I know that it's got to get really bad again because what happened was a hundred times more real than this. Do you understand?'

'I understand. For now, though, you should try trusting me.'

'I don't trust you, Exley. Not "for now," maybe not ever.'

'I'm the only one you can trust.'

Inez flipped her veil down. 'I don't trust you because you don't hate them for what they did. Maybe you think you do, but you're helping your career out at the same time. Officer White, he hates them. He killed a man who hurt me. He's not as smart as you, so maybe I can trust him.'

Ed reached a hand out – Inez slid away. 'I want them dead. *Absolutamente muerto. Comprende?*'

'I *comprende*. Do you *comprende* that your beloved Officer White is a goddamned thug?'

'Only if you *comprende* that you're jealous of him. Look, oh God.'

Ray Dieterling, his father. Ed stood up; Inez stood up

starry-eyed. Preston said, 'Raymond Dieterling, my son Edmund. Edmund, will you introduce the young lady?'

Inez, straight to Dieterling. 'Sir, it's a pleasure to meet you. I've been . . . oh, I'm just a big fan.'

Dieterling took her hand. 'Thank you, dear. And your name?'

'Inez Soto. I've seen . . . oh, I'm just a big fan.'

Dieterling smiled, sad – the girl's story front-page news. He turned to Ed. 'Sergeant, a pleasure.'

A good handshake. 'Sir, an honor. And congratulations.'

'Thank you, and I share those congratulations with your father. Preston, your son has an eye for the ladies, doesn't he?'

Preston laughed. 'Miss Soto, Edmund has rarely evinced such good taste.' He handed Ed a slip of paper. 'A Sheriff's officer called the house looking for you. I took the message.'

Ed palmed the paper; Inez blushed through her veil. Dieterling smiled. 'Miss Soto, did you enjoy Dream-a-Dreamland?'

'Yes, I did. Oh God, yes.'

'I'm glad, and I want you to know that you have a good job here anytime you wish. All you have to do is say the word.'

'Thank you, thank you, sir' – Inez wobbly. Ed steadied her, looked at his message: 'Stensland on toot at Raincheck Room, 3871 W. Gage. Felony assembly, parole off. Alerted. Waiting for you – Keefer.'

The partners walked off bowing; Inez waved to them. Ed said, 'I'll take you back, but I've got a little stop to make first.'

They drove back to L.A., the radio going, Inez beating time on the dashboard. Ed played scenes: Stensland crushed with snappy one-liners. An hour to Raincheck Room – Ed parked behind a Sheriff's unmarked. 'I'll only be a few minutes. You stay here, all right?'

Inez nodded. Pat Keefer left the bar; Ed got out, whistled.

Keefer came over; Ed steered him away from Inez. 'Is he still there?'

'Yeah, skunk drunk. I'd just about given up on you, you know.'

'A dark alley by the bar. 'Where's the Parole man?'

'He told me to take him, this is county jurisdiction. His pals took off, so there's just him.'

Ed pointed to the alley. 'Bring him out cuffed.'

Keefer went back in; Ed waited by the alleyway door. Shouts, thuds, Dick Stens muscled out: smelly, disheveled. Keefer pulled his head back; Ed hit him: upstairs, downstairs, flails until his arms gave out. Stens hit the ground retching; Ed kicked him in the face, stumbled away. Inez on the sidewalk. Her one-liner: 'Officer White's the thug?'

Chapter Twenty-seven

Bud fed the woman coffee – get her out, go see Stens at the lock-up.

Carolyn something, she looked okay at the Orbit Lounge, morning light put ten years on her. He picked her up on a flash: he just got the word on Dick, if he couldn't find a woman he was going to find Exley and kill him. She wasn't bad in bed – but he had to think of Inez to charge up enthusiasm, it made him feel cheap, the odds on Inez ever doing it for love were about six trillion to one. He stopped thinking about her – the rest of the night was all bad talk and brandy.

Carolyn said, 'I think I should go.'

'I'll call you.'

The doorbell rang.

Bud walked Carolyn over. Across the screen: Dudley Smith and a West Valley dick – Joe DiCenzo.

Dudley smiled; DiCenzo nodded. Carolyn ducked out – like she knew they knew the score. Bud scoped his front room: the fold-out down, a bottle, two tumblers.

DiCenzo pointed to the bed. 'There's his alibi, and I didn't think he did it anyway.'

Bud shut the door. 'Did *what*? Boss, what is this?'

Dudley sighed. 'Lad, I'm afraid I'm the bearer of bad tidings. Last night a young lassie named Kathy Janeway was found in her motel room, raped and beaten to death. Your calling card was found in her purse. Sergeant DiCenzo took the squeal, knew you were a protégé of mine and called me. I visited the crime scene, found an envelope addressed to Miss Janeway, and recognized your rather unformed handwriting immediately. Explain with brevity, lad – Sergeant DiCenzo is heading the investigation and wants you eliminated as a suspect.'

A body shot – little Kathy sobbing. Bud got his lies

187

straight. 'I was on the Cathcart background check and this hooker who worked for Cathcart told me the Janeway girl was Cathcart's last squeeze, but he didn't pimp her. I talked to the girl, but she didn't know nothing worth reporting. She told me the hooker was holding cash from Cathcart for her, but she wouldn't kick loose. I shook her down and mailed the money to the kid.'

DiCenzo shook his head. 'Do you routinely shake down hookers?'

Dudley sighed. 'Bud has a sentimental weakness for females, and I find his account plausible within the limitations of that limitation. Lad, who was this "hooker" you mentioned?'

'Cynthia Benavides, a.k.a. "Sinful Cindy." '

'Lad, you didn't include mention of her in any of the reports you've filed. Which have been rather threadbare, I might add.'

Lies: hold back on smut, Cathcart's pad tossed, the pimp who sold Kathy to Duke. 'I didn't think she was important stuff.'

'Lad, she is a tangential Nite Owl witness. And haven't I taught you to be thorough in your reports?'

Mad now – Kathy on a morgue slab. 'Yeah, you have.'

'And what precisely have you accomplished since that dinner meeting of ours – which is when you *should* have reported on Miss Janeway and Miss Benavides?'

'I'm still checking out Lunceford and Cathcart K.A.'s.'

'Lad, Lunceford's known associates are extraneous to this investigation. Have you learned of anything else on Cathcart?'

'No.'

Dudley to DiCenzo. 'Lad, are you satisfied that Bud isn't your man?'

DiCenzo pulled out a cigar. 'I'm satisfied. And I'm satisfied he ain't the smartest human being ever to breathe. White, toss me a bone. Who do you think did the girl?'

The red sedan: the motel, Cahuenga. 'I don't know.'

'A succinct answer. Joe, let me have a few minutes alone with my friend, would you please?'

DiCenzo walked out smoking; Dudley leaned against the door. 'Lad, you cannot shake down prostitutes for money to pay off underaged mistresses. I understand your sentimental attachment to women, and I know that it is an essential component of your policeman's persona, but such overinvolvement cannot be tolerated, and as of this moment you are off the Cathcart and Lunceford checks and back on the Darktown end of the case. Now, Chief Parker and I are convinced that the three Negroes in custody are our perpetrators, or, at the very most, another jigaboo gang is responsible. We still have no murder weapons and no shake on Coates' car, and Ellis Loew wants more evidence for a grand jury presentation. Our fair Miss Soto will not talk, and I'm afraid we must urge her to take pentothal and endure a questioning session. Your job is to check files and question known Negro sex offenders. We need to find the men our unholy three let abuse Miss Soto, and I think the job is right up your alley. Will you do this for me?'

Big words – more body shots. 'Sure, Dud.'

'Good lad. Clock in and out at 77th Street Station, and make your reports more detailed.'

'Sure, Boss.'

Smith opened the door. 'I tendered that reprimand with much affection, lad. Do you know that?'

'Sure.'

'Grand. You are much in my thoughts, lad. Chief Parker has given me approval on a new containment measure, and I've already signed on Dick Carlisle and Mike Breuning. Once we close the Nite Owl, I'm going to ask you to join us.'

'That sounds good, Boss.'

'Grand. And lad? I'm sure you know that Dick Stensland was arrested and Ed Exley had a part in it. You are not to retaliate. Do you understand?'

The red sedan – call it a maybe.

Cathcart's pad tossed and wiped, his clothes prowled – ?????

189

Sinful Cindy: Duke's smut peddler pipe dream.

Feather Royko on Duke: 'Hopped up on some new biz.'

The Dukey shtick man trying to recruit B-girls. Ad Vice checked out: zero on their smut job. Trashcan Jack V., ace report padder, asked for a transfer to the Nite Owl – he said the job was from hunger. Russ Millard's last c.o.'s summary: 86 the gig – call it a wash.

He lied to Dudley and strolled on it.

If he'd ratted little Kathy to Juvie she'd be reading a movie mag somewhere.

THE PIMP WHO SOLD HER TO DUKE: 'THIS GUY MADE ME DO IT WITH GUYS.'

EXLEY EXLEY EXLEY EXLEY EXLEY EXLEY EXLEY –

Sinful Cindy's rap sheet – four known haunt whore bars listed. Her pad first – no Cindy. Hal's Nest, the Moonmist Lounge, the Firefly Room, the Cinnabar at the Roosevelt – no Cindy. An old Vice cop's story: whores congregating at Tiny Naylor's Drive-in – the carhops scouted tricks for them. Over to Tiny's, Cindy's De Soto outside – a food tray hooked to the door.

Bud parked beside her. Cindy saw him, dumped her tray, rolled up her window. Wham – the De Soto in reverse. Bud sprinted, popped the hood, yanked the distributor – the car stalled dead.

Cindy rolled down her window. 'You stole my money! You ruined my lunch!'

Bud dropped a five on her lap. 'Lunch is on me.'

'Mister big shot! Mister big spender!'

'Kathy Janeway got raped and beaten to death. Give on the guy who used to pimp her, give on her tricks.'

Cindy put her head on the wheel. The horn beeped; she came back up pale, no tears. 'Dwight Gilette. He's some kind of colored guy passing. I don't know nothing about her old tricks.'

'Gilette drive a red car?'

'I don't know.'

'You got an address?'

'I heard he lives in this tract in Eagle Rock. It's white only, so he plays it that way. But I know he didn't kill her.'

'How do you figure?'

'He's a swish. He's careful about his hands, and he'd never put it in a girl.'

'Anything else?'

'He carried a knife. His girls call him "Blue Blade" 'cause his name's Gilette.'

'You don't seem surprised Kathy got it that way.'

Cindy touched her eyes – bone dry. 'She was born for it. Dukey softened her up, so she quit hating men. A few more years and she would've learned. Shit, I should have treated her better.'

'Yeah, me too.'

Eagle Rock, an R&I check: Dwight Gilette, a.k.a. 'Blade,' a.k.a. 'Blue Blade,' 3245 Hibiscus, Eagle's Aerie Housing Development. Six suborning arrests, no convictions, listed as a male Caucasian – if he was a shine he was passing with style. Bud found the tract, the street: cozy stucco cubes, Hibiscus a prime spot: a smoggy L.A. view.

3245: peach paint job, steel flamingos on the lawn, a blue sedan in the driveway. Bud walked up, pushed the buzzer – jingly chimes sounded.

A high-yellow guy opened up. Thirtyish, short, plump, slacks and a silk shirt with a Mr. B. collar. 'I heard on the radio, so I thought you fellows might be coming by. The radio said midnight, and I have an alibi. He lives a block away and I can have him here toot-sweet. Kathy was a sweet kid and I don't know who'd do a thing like that. And don't you fellows usually come in pairs?'

'You finished?'

'No. My alibi is my lawyer, he still lives a block away and he's very well placed in the American Civil Liberties Union.'

Bud shouldered him into the house, whistled.

Fruit heaven: deep pile rugs, Greek god statues. Male

nudes on the wall – paint on velvet flocking. Bud said, 'Cute.'

Gilette pointed to the phone. 'Two seconds or I call my attorney.'

Quick throw. 'Duke Cathcart. You sold Kathy to him, right?'

'Kathy was headstrong, Duke made me an offer. Duke's dead in that awful Nite Owl thing, so don't tell me you suspect me of that.'

No hink. 'I heard Duke was pushing smut. You hear that?'

'Smut is déclassé and the answer is no.'

More no hink. 'Give me some trade talk on Duke. What've you heard?'

Gilette stood one hip jutting. 'I heard a guy was asking around about Duke, coming on like Duke, maybe thinking about crashing his stable, not that he had much of a stable left, I've heard. Now will you please leave me alone before I call my friend?'

The phone rang – Gilette walked to the kitchen, grabbed an extension. Bud walked in slow. Nice stuff: Frigidaire, coil burner stove on full blast: eggs, boiling water, stew.

Gilette made kissy sounds, hung up. 'Are *you* still here?'

'Nice pad, Dwight. Business must be good.'

'Business is excellent, thank you very much.'

'Good. I need skinny on Kathy's old tricks, so cough up your whore book.'

Gilette hit a switch above the sink. A motor growled; he shoved scrapings down a garbage hole. Bud flipped the switch up. 'Your whore book.'

'No, *nein, nyet* and never.'

Bud hooked him to the gut. Gilette rolled with it, grabbed a knife, swung. Bud sidestepped, kicked at his balls. Gilette doubled up; Bud hit the garbage switch. The motor *scree'd*; Bud jammed the queer's knife hand down the chute.

SCREEEE – the sink shot back blood, bone. Bud yanked the hand out minus fingers – SCREEEEE fifty times louder. Stumps to the burner coils, stumps to the icebox sizzling. 'GIVE ME THE FUCKING WHORE BOOK' – through a SCREEEEEEEE echo chamber.

Gilette, eyes rolling back. 'Drawer . . . by TV . . . ambulance.'

Bud dropped him, ran to the living room. Empty drawers, back to the kitchen – Gilette on the floor eating paper.

Choke hold: Gilette spat out a half-chewed page. Bud picked up the wad, stumbled outside, burned flesh making him gag. He smoothed the paper out: names, phone numbers – smeared, two legible: Lynn Bracken, Pierce Patchett.

Chapter Twenty-eight

Jack at his desk, counting lies.

At work: a string of dead-end reports; legit zeros from the other squad guys totaled luck: Millard wanted to dump the smut job. Count duty no-shows as lies – he'd spent a full day chasing names – matches to the cars in Bel Air. Four names tagged; no luck at a modeling agency specializing in movie star lookalikes – none of the girls came close to his beauties. Put the names aside, chalk up the day as a wash – Sid Hudgens made pursuit a dead issue. He just wanted to see the women again – add that one to his lies to Karen.

They spent the morning at her beach place. Karen wanted to make love; he put her off with bullshit: he was distracted, he'd asked to be detached to the Nite Owl because justice was so important. Karen tried to undress him; he told her he had a sprained back; he didn't say he wasn't interested because all he wanted to do was use her, make her do it with other women, recreate fuck book scenarios. His biggest lie: he didn't tell her that he'd finally stepped in shit that didn't turn to clover, that he'd played an angle that played him back to the gas chamber door, that his home-to-Narco ticket read adiós, lovebirds – because she'd trace 10/24/47 to all his other lies and his carefully constructed nice-guy Big V would go down in flames.

He didn't tell her he was terrified. She didn't sense it – his front was still strong.

Other fronts holding – dumb luck.

Sid hadn't called, his monthly *Hush-Hush* came on schedule – no note, some 'sinuendo' on Max Peltz and teenage poon – nothing scary. He checked the report on the Fleur-de-Lis shoot-out: bright boy Ed Exley caught the squeal. Exley baffled: no make on the drop-pad tenants, the shelves cleaned out – only some bondage shit left – make the rest of the filth down the hidey-hole. Make Lamar Hinton for the shots – a free ride – the Big V was off the case, the Big V had a new mission.

Sid Hudgens knew Pierce Patchett and Fleur-de-Lis; Sid Hudgens knew the Malibu Rendezvous. Sid had a load of private dirt files stashed. The Big V's job: find *his* file, destroy it.

Jack checked his plate list, names matched to DMV pics.

Seth David Krugliak, the owner of the Bel Air manse – fat, oily, a movie biz lawyer. Pierce Morehouse Patchett, Fleur-de-Lis Boss – Mr. Debonair. Charles Walker Champlain, investment banker – shaved head, goatee. Lynn Margaret Bracken, age twenty-nine – Veronica Lake. No criminal records.

'Hello, lad.'

Jack swiveled around. 'Dud, how are you? What brings you to Ad Vice?'

'A confab with Russ Millard, my colleague on the Nite Owl now. And on that topic, I heard you want in.'

'You heard right. Can you swing it?'

Smith passed him a mimeo sheet. 'I already have, lad. You're to join in the search for Coates' car. Every garage within the radius on this page is to be checked – with or without the owner's consent. You're to begin immediately.'

A map carbon: southside L.A. in street grids. 'Lad, I need a personal favor.'

'Name it.'

'I want you to keep a tail on Bud White. He's gotten personally involved in the unfortunate killing of a child prostitute, and I need him stable. Will you stick to him nights, great tailer that you are?'

Bad Bud – always a sucker for strays. 'Sure, Dud. Where's he working out of?'

'77th Street Station. He's been assigned to roust jigaboos with sex offender records. He's on daywatch at 77th, and you'll be clocking in and out there as well.'

195

'Dud, you're a lifesaver.'
'Would you care to elaborate on that, lad?'
'No.'

Chapter Twenty-nine

Memo:

'From: Chief Parker. To: Dep. Chief Green, Capt. R. Millard, Lt. D. Smith, Sgt. E. Exley. Conference: Chief's Office, 4:00 P.M., 4/23/53. Topic: Questioning of witness Inez Soto.' His father's note: 'She's wonderful and Ray Dieterling's much taken with her. But she's a material witness and a Mexican, and I advise you not to get too attached to her. And under no circumstances should you shack up with her. Cohabitation is against departmental regs and being with a Mexican woman could seriously stall your career.'

Parker kicked things off. 'Ed, the Nite Owl case is narrowing down to the Negroes in custody or some other colored gang. Now, word has it that you've gotten close to the Soto girl. Lieutenant Smith and I deem it imperative that she undergo questioning in order to clear up the time element, alibi or not alibi the three in custody, and identify the other men who assaulted her. We think pentothal is the best way to get results, and pentothal works best when a subject is at ease. We want you to convince Miss Soto to cooperate. She probably trusts you, so you'll have credibility.'

Inez post-Stensland: shell-shocked, hard-pressed to move to Arrowhead. 'Sir, I think all our evidence so far is circumstantial. I think we should get other corroboration before I approach Miss Soto, and I want to try questioning Coates, Jones and Fontaine again.'

Smith laughed. 'Lad, they refused to talk to you the other day, and now they have a pinko public defender who's advising them to stay mute. Ellis Loew wants a grand jury presentation – Nite Owl and Little Lindbergh – and you can facilitate it. Kid gloves have gotten us

197

nowhere with our fair Miss Soto, and it's time we quit coddling her.'

Russ Millard: 'Lieutenant, I agree with Sergeant Exley. If we keep pressing on the southside, we'll turn rape witnesses and maybe find Coates' car and the murder weapons. My instincts tell me the girl's recollections of that night might be too muddled to do us any good, and if we make her remember, it might wreck her life more than it's been wrecked already. Can you picture Ellis Loew badgering her in front of the grand jury? Not very pretty, is it?'

Smith laughed – straight at Millard. 'Captain, you politicked very hard to share this command with me, and now you advance a sob sister sensibility. This is a brutal mass murder that requires a swift and hard resolution, not a sorority party. And Ellis Loew is a brilliant attorney and a compassionate man. I'm sure he would handle Miss Soto with care.'

Millard swallowed a pill, chased it with water. 'Ellis Loew is a headline-grubbing buffoon, not a policeman, and he should not be directing the thrust of this investigation.'

'Fair Captain, I deem that comment near seditious in its – '

Parker raised a hand. 'Gentlemen, enough. Thad, will you take Captain Millard and Lieutenant Smith down the hall and buy them coffee while I talk to the sergeant here?'

Green ushered the two outside. Parker said, 'Ed, Dudley's right.'

Ed kept quiet. Parker pointed to a stack of newspapers. 'The press and the public demand justice. We'll look very bad if we don't clear this up soon.'

'Sir, I know.'

'Do you care about the girl?'

'Yes.'

'You know that sooner or later she'll have to cooperate?'

'Sir, don't underestimate her. She's steel inside.'

Parker smiled. 'Then let's see how much steel you possess. Convince her to cooperate, and if we get enough corroboration to convince Ellis Loew he's got a show-stopper grand jury case, I'll jump you on the promotion list. You'll be a detective lieutenant immediately.'

'And a command?'

'Arnie Reddin retires next month. I'll give you the Hollywood detective squad.'

Ed tingled.

'Ed, you're thirty-one. Your father didn't make lieutenant until he was thirty-three.'

'I'll do it.'

Chapter Thirty

Pervert patrol:

Cleotis Johnson, registered sex offender, pastor of the New Bethel Methodist Episcopal Church of Zion, had an alibi for the night Inez Soto was kidnapped: he was in the 77th Street drunk tank. Davis Walter Bush, registered sex offender, alibied up by a half dozen witnesses: they were engaged in an all-night crap game in the rec room of the New Bethel Methodist Episcopal Church of Zion. Fleming Peter Hanley, registered sex offender, spent that night at Central Receiving: a drag queen bit his dick; a team of emergency room docs labored to save the organ so he could notch up a few more convictions for sodomy with mayhem.

Pervert patrol, a call to Eagle Rock Hospital: Dwight Gilette made it there. A skate: the swish didn't die on him.

Four more RSOs alibied; a run by the Hall of Justice Jail. Stens flying high on raisinjack – a jailer fixed him a toilet brew cocktail. Rants: Ed Exley, Danny Duck porking Ellis Loew.

Home, a shower, DMV checks: Pierce Patchett, Lynn Bracken. Calls – a pal working Internal Affairs, West Valley Station. Good results: no Gilette complaint, three men on the Kathy snuff.

Another shower – he could still smell the day on himself.

Bud drove to Brentwood: squeeze Pierce Morehouse Patchett, no criminal record – strange for a name in a pimp's whore book. 1184 Gretna Green, a big Spanish mansion: all pink, lots of tile.

He parked, walked up. Porch lights came on: soft focus on a man in a chair. He matched Patchett's DMV stats, looked shitloads younger than his DOB. 'Are you a police officer?'

His cuffs were hooked on his belt. 'Yeah. Are you Pierce Patchett?'

'I am. Are you soliciting for police charities? The last time, you people called at my office.'

Pinned eyes – maybe zoned on some kind of hop. Body-builder muscles, a tight shirt to show them off. An easy voice – he came on like he always sat in the dark waiting for cops to call. 'I'm a Homicide detective.'

'Oh? Who was killed and why do you think I can help you?'

'A girl named Kathy Janeway.'

'That's only half an answer, Mr. – ?'

'It's Officer White.'

'Mr. White, then. Again, why do you think I can help you?'

Bud pulled up a chair. 'Did you know Kathy Janeway?'

'No, I did not. Did she claim to know me?'

'No. Where were you last night at midnight?'

'I was here, hosting a party. If push comes to shove, which I hope it won't, I'll supply you with a guest list. Why do you – '

Bud cut in: 'Delbert "Duke" Cathcart.'

Patchett sighed. 'I don't know him either. Mr. White – '

'Dwight Gilette, Lynn Bracken.'

A big smile. 'Yes, I know those people.'

'Yeah? Then keep going.'

'Now let me interrupt. Did one of them give you my name?'

'I shook down Gilette for his whore book. He tried to chew up the page that had your name and this Bracken woman's name on it. Patchett, why's a shit pimp have your phone number?'

Patchett leaned forward. 'Do you care about criminal matters peripheral to the Janeway killing?'

'No.'

'Then you wouldn't feel obliged to report them.'

The fucker had style. 'That's right.'

'Then listen closely, because I'll only say it once, and if it gets repeated I'll deny it. I run call girls. Lynn Bracken is one of them. I bought Lynn from Gilette a few years ago, and if Gilette tried to chew up my name it was because he knows that I hate and fear the police, and he thought – correctly – that I would squash him like a bug if I thought he put the police on to me. Now, I treat my girls very well. I have grown daughters myself, and I lost a baby girl to crib death. I do not like the thought of women being hurt and I frankly have a great deal of money to indulge my fancies. Did this Kathy Janeway girl die badly?'

Beaten to death, semen in the mouth, rectum, vagina. 'Yeah, very bad.'

'Then find her killer, Mr. White. Succeed, and I'll give you a handsome reward. If that goes against your moral grain, I'll donate the money to a police charity.'

'Thanks, but no thanks.'

'Against your code?'

'I don't have one. Tell me about Lynn Bracken. She street?'

'No, call. Gilette was ruining her with bad clients. *I'm* very selective who my girls truck with, by the way.'

'So you bought her off Gilette.'

'That's correct.'

'Why?'

Patchett smiled. 'Lynn looks very much like the actress Veronica Lake, and I needed her to fill out my little studio.'

'What "little studio"?'

Patchett shook his head. 'No. I admire your intrusive style and I sense you're on your best behavior, but that's all I'll give you. I've cooperated, and if you persist I'll meet you with my attorney. Now, would you like Lynn Bracken's address? I doubt that she knows anything about the late Miss Janeway, but if you like I'll call her and tell her to cooperate.'

Bud pointed to the house. 'I got her address. You get this address running call girls?'

'I'm a financier. I have an advanced degree in chemistry, I worked as a pharmacist for several years and invested wisely. "Entrepreneur" sums me up best, I think. And don't tweak me with criminal slang, Mr. White. Don't make me regret I leveled with you.'

Bud scoped him. Two to one he *was* leveling, thought cops were bugs that leveling worked with sometimes. 'Okay, then I'll wrap it up.'

'Please do.'

Notebook out. 'You said Gilette was pimping Lynn Bracken, right?'

'I dislike the word "pimp," but yes.'

'Okay, were any of your other girls street-pimped, call-pimped?'

'No, all my girls are either models or girls that I saved from general Hollywood heartbreak.'

Switcheroo. 'You don't read the papers too good, right?'

'Correct. I try to avoid bad news.'

'But you heard of the Nite Owl Massacre.'

'Yes, because I do not dwell in a cave.'

'That guy Duke Cathcart was one of the victims. He was a pimp, and lately a guy's been asking around about him, trying to get girls to do call jobs for him. Now Gilette street-pimped Kathy Janeway, and you know him. I'm thinking maybe you might do business with some other people who might give me a line on this guy.'

Patchett crossed his legs, stretched. 'So you think "this guy" might have killed Kathy Janeway?'

'No, I don't think that.'

'Or you think he's behind that Nite Owl thing. I thought Negro youths were supposed to be the killers. What crime are you investigating, Mr. White?'

Bud gripped the chair – fabric ripped. Patchett put his hands up, palms out. 'The answer to your questions is no. Dwight Gilette is the only person of that breed I've ever dealt with. Low-level prostitution is not my field of expertise.'

'What about B&E?'

'B and E?'

'Breaking and entering. Cathcart's apartment was tossed, and the walls were wiped.'

Patchett shrugged. 'Mr. White, you're speaking in Sanskrit now. I simply don't know what you're talking about.'

'Yeah? Then what about smut? You know Gilette, Gilette sold you Lynn Bracken, Gilette sold Kathy Janeway to Cathcart. Cathcart was supposed to be starting up a smut biz.'

'Smut' buzzed him – little eye flickers. Bud said, 'Ring a bell?'

Patchett picked up a glass, swirled ice cubes. 'No bells, and your questions are getting further and further afield. Your approach has been novel, so I've tolerated it. But you're wearing me thin and I'm beginning to think that your motives for being here are quite muddled.'

Bud stood up pissed, no handle on the man. Patchett said, 'One of your tangents is personal with you, isn't it?'

'Yeah.'

'If it's the Janeway girl, I meant what I said. I may suborn women into illicit activities, but they're handsomely compensated, I treat them very well and make sure the men they deal with show them every due respect. Good night, Mr. White.'

Thoughts for the ride: how did Patchett get his number so quick, did his evidence suppression bit backfire – Dudley suspicious, wise to how far he'd go to hurt Exley. Lynn Bracken lived on Nottingham off Los Feliz; he found the address easy – a modern-style triplex. Colored lights beamed out the windows – he looked before he rang.

Red, blue, yellow – figures cut through the beams. Bud watched his very own stag show.

A Veronica Lake dead ringer, nude on her tiptoes: slender, full-breasted. Blond – hair in a perfect pageboy cut. A man moving inside her, straining, crouching for the fit.

Bud watched; street sounds faded. He blotted out the

204

man, studied the woman: every inch of her body in every shade of light. He drove home tunnel-vision – nothing but her.

Inez Soto on his doorstep.

Bud walked over. She said, 'I was at Exley's place in Lake Arrowhead. He said there was no strings, then he showed up and told me I had to take this drug to make me remember. I told him no. Did you know you're the only Wendell White in the Central Directory?'

Bud straightened her hat, tucked a loose piece of veil under the crown. 'How'd you get down here?'

'I took a cab. A hundred of Exley's dollars, so at least he's good for something. Officer White, I don't want to remember.'

'Sweetie, you already do. Come on, I'll fix you up with a place.'

'I want to stay with you.'

'All I've got's a fold-out.'

'Fine by me. I figure there has to be a first time again.'

'Give it a rest and get yourself a college boy.'

Inez stood up. 'I was starting to trust him.'

Bud opened the door. The first thing he saw was the bed – trashed from Carolyn or whatever her name was. Inez plopped down on it – seconds later she was sleeping. Bud tucked her in, stretched out in the hall with his suitcoat for a pillow. Sleep came slow – his long strange day kept replaying. He went out seeing Lynn Bracken; toward dawn he stirred and found Inez curled up next to him.

He let her stay.

Chapter Thirty-one

He knew he was dreaming, knew he couldn't stop. He kept flinching with the replay.

Inez at the cabin: 'Coward,' 'Opportunist,' 'Using me to further your career.' Her out-the-door salvo: 'Officer White's ten times the man you are, with half the brains and no big-shot daddy.' He let her go, then chased: back to L.A., the Soto family shack. Three pachuco brothers came on strong; old man Soto supplied an epitaph: 'I don't have that daughter no more.'

The phone rang. Ed rolled over, grabbed it. 'Exley.'

'It's Bob Gallaudet. Congratulate me.'

Ed pushed his dream away. 'Why?'

'I passed the bar exam, making me both an attorney and a D.A.'s Bureau investigator. Aren't you impressed?'

'Congratulations, and you didn't call at 8:00 A.M. to tell me that.'

'Right you are, so listen close. Last night a lawyer named Jake Kellerman called Ellis Loew. He's representing two witnesses, brothers, who say they've got a viable Duke Cathcart connection to Mickey Cohen. They say they can clear the Nite Owl. They've got some outstanding L.A. warrants for pushing Benzedrine, and Ellis is giving them immunity on that, plus possible immunity on any conspiracy charges that might stem from their connection to the Nite Owl. We're having a meeting at the Mirimar Hotel in an hour – the brothers and Kellerman, you, me, Loew and Russ Millard. Dudley S. won't be there. Thad Green's orders – he thinks Millard's the better man for this.'

Ed swung out of bed. 'So who are these brothers?'

'Peter and Baxter Englekling. Heard of them?'

'No. Is this an interrogation?'

Gallaudet laughed. 'Wouldn't you love that. No, it's

Kellerman reads a prepared statement, we hobknob with Loew over whether to let them turn state's and take it from there. I'll brief you. Mirimar parking lot in forty-five minutes?'

'I'll be there.'

Forty-five on the button. Gallaudet met him in the lobby – no handshake, straight to it. 'Want to hear what we've got?'

'Go.'

They talked walking. 'They're waiting for us, a steno included, and what we've got are Pete and Bax Englekling, age thirty-six, age thirty-two, San Bernardino-based . . . quasi-hoods, I guess you'd call them. They both did Youth Authority time for pushing maryjane back in the early '40s, and except for the bennie pushing warrants, they've stayed clean. They own a legit printshop up in San Berdoo, they're what you'd call genius fix-it guys, and their late father was a real piece of work. Get this: he was a college chemistry teacher and some kind of pioneering pharmaceuticalist who developed early anti-psychotic drugs. Impressive, right? Now get this: Pops, who kicked off in the summer of '50, developed dope compounds for the old mobs – and Mickey C. was his protector back in his bodyguard days.'

'This won't be dull. But do *you* make Cohen for the Nite Owl? He's in prison, for one thing.'

'Exley, I make those colored guys in custody. Gangsters *never* kill innocent citizens. But frankly, Loew likes the idea of a mob angle. Come on, they're waiting.'

Into suite 309, the meeting in a small living room. One long table – Loew and Millard across from three men: a middle-aged lawyer, near twins in overalls – thinning hair, beady eyes, bad teeth. A steno by the bedroom door, perched with her machine set to go.

Gallaudet carried chairs over. Ed nodded around, sat by Millard. The lawyer checked papers; the brothers lit cigarettes. Loew said, 'For the official record, it is 8:53 A.M., April 24, 1953. Present are myself, Ellis Loew, district attorney for the City of Los Angeles, Sergeant Bob Gallaudet of the D.A.'s Bureau, Captain Russ Millard and Sergeant Ed Exley of the Los Angeles Police Department. Jacob Kellerman represents Peter and Baxter Englekling, potential prosecution witnesses in the matter of the multiple homicides perpetrated at the Nite Owl Coffee Shop on April 14 of this year. Mr. Kellerman will read a prepared statement given to him by his clients, they will initial the stenographer's transcript. As a courtesy for this voluntary statement, the District Attorney's Office is dismissing felony warrant number 16114, dated June 8, 1951, against Peter and Baxter Englekling. Should this statement result in the arrests of the perpetrators of the aforementioned multiple homicides, Peter and Baxter Englekling will be granted immunity from prosecution in all matters pertaining to the said, including accessory, conspiracy and all collateral felonies and misdemeanors. Mr. Kellerman, do your clients understand the aforesaid?'

'Yes, Mr. Loew, they do.'

'Do they understand that they may be asked to submit to questioning after their statement has been read?'

'They do.'

'Read the statement, Counselor.'

Kellerman put on bifocals. 'I've eliminated Peter and Baxter's more colorful colloquialisms and cleaned up their language and syntax, please bear that in mind.'

Loew tugged at his vest. 'We're capable of discerning that. Please continue.'

Kellerman read: 'We, Peter and Baxter Englekling, do swear that this statement is entirely true. In late March of this year, approximately three weeks before the Nite Owl killings, we were approached at our legitimate business, the Speedy King Printshop in San Bernardino. The man who approached us was one Delbert "Duke" Cathcart, who said that he had gotten our names from "Mr. XY," an acquaintance from our youth camp sentence days. Mr. XY had informed Cathcart that we ran a printshop which featured a high-speed offset press of our own design, which was true. Mr. XY had also told

208

Cathcart that we were always interested in quote turning a quick buck unquote, which was also true.'

Chuckles. Ed wrote, 'Vict. Susan Lefferts from S. Berdoo – connection?' Loew said, 'Continue, Mr. Keller-man. We're all capable of laughing and thinking at the same time.'

Kellerman: 'Cathcart showed us photographs of people engaged in explicit sexual activities, some of them homo-sexual in nature. Some of the photographs were quote arty-farty unquote. I.E.: people in colorful costumes and animated red ink embossed on some of the snapshots. Cathcart said that he heard we could manufacture high-quality magazine-type books very fast, and we said this was true. Cathcart also stated that a number of magazine-type books had already been manufactured, using the obscene photographs, and quoted us the cost involved. We knew we could make the books at one eighth of that cost.'

Ed passed Millard a note: 'Isn't Ad Vice working a pornography job?' The brothers smirked; Loew and Gal-laudet whispered. Millard passed a note back: 'Yes – no leads from a 4 man team. A cold trail tracking the ("strange costumed" per the statement) books – we're dropping it. Also, no field reports submitted so far link Cathcart to pornography.'

Kellerman sipped water. 'Cathcart then told us that he heard our late father, Franz "Doc" Englekling, was friends with Meyer Harris "Mickey" Cohen, Los Angeles mobster currently incarcerated at McNeil Island Peniten-tiary. We said this was true. Cathcart then made his basic proposal. He said that distribution of the pornographic books would have to be quote very close unquote, because the quote strange cats unquote who took the photographs and did the pasteup work seemed like they had lots to hide. He did not elaborate on this further. He said that he had access to a network of quote rich perverts unquote who would pay large sums for the books and proposed that we could also manufacture quote regular fuck-suck shit unquote, that could be distributed in large quantities.

Cathcart claimed to have access to quote pervert mailing list unquote, quote junkies and whores unquote to serve as models, and access to quote classy call girls unquote, who might pose for a lark if their quote crazy sugar daddyo unquote agreed. Again, Cathcart did not elaborate on any of his claims, nor did he mention specific names or locations.'

Kellerman flipped pages. 'Cathcart told us that he would be the procurer, talent scout and middleman. We would be the manufacturers of the books. We were also to visit Mickey Cohen at McNeil Island and get him to release funds to get the business started. We were also to solicit his advice on starting a distribution system. In exchange for the above Cohen would be given a quote bonaroo unquote percentage cut.'

Ed passed a note: 'No follow-up names – it's too convenient.' Millard whispered, 'And the Nite Owl is not Mickey's style.' Bax Englekling chuckled; Pete poked his ears with a pencil. Kellerman read: 'We visited Mickey Cohen in his cell at McNeil, approximately two weeks before the Nite Owl killings. We proposed the idea to him. He refused to help and became very angry when we told him the idea was conceived by Duke Cathcart, whom he referred to as quote a notorious statch rape-o shitbird unquote. In conclusion, we believe that gunmen employed by Mickey Cohen perpetrated the Nite Owl Massacre, a kill-six-to-get-one ruse undertaken out of his hatred for Duke Cathcart. Another possibility is that Cohen talked up Cathcart's proposed scheme on the prison yard and word got out to Cohen rival Jack "The Enforcer" Whalen, who, always looking for new rackets to crash, assassinated Cathcart and five innocent bystanders as subterfuge. We believe that if the killings were the result of pornography intrigue, we too might become victims. We swear that this deposition is true and not rendered under physical or mental duress.'

The brothers clapped. Kellerman said, 'My clients welcome questions.'

Loew pointed to the bedroom. 'After I talk to my colleagues.'

They walked in; Loew closed the door. 'Conclusions. Bob, you first.'

Gallaudet lit a cigarette. 'Mickey Cohen, despite his many faults, does not murder people out of pique, and Jack Whalen's only interested in gambling rackets. I believe their story, but everything we've dug up on Cathcart makes him look like a pathetic chump who couldn't get something this big going. I say it's tangent stuff at best. I still make the boogies for the job.'

'I agree. Captain, your opinion.'

Millard said, 'I like one possible scenario – with major reservations. *Maybe* Cohen talked up the job on the yard at McNeil, word got to the outside and somebody took it from there. *But* – if this deal is smut-connected, then the Englekling boys would either have been killed or approached by now. I've been running a stag book investigation out of Ad Vice for two weeks and my squad has heard nothing on this and hit one brick wall after another. I think Ed and Bob should talk to Whalen, then fly up to McNeil and talk to Mickey. I'll question those lowlifes in the next room, and I'll talk to my Ad Vice men. I've read every field report filed by every man on the Nite Owl, and there is not one mention of pornography. I think Bob's right. It's a tangent we're dealing with.'

'Agreed. Bob, you and Exley talk to Cohen and Whalen. Captain, did you have capable men on your job?'

Millard smiled. 'Three capable men and Trashcan Jack Vincennes. No offense, Ellis. I know he's involved with your wife's sister.'

Loew flushed. 'Exley, do you have anything to add?'

'Bob and the captain covered my points, but there's two things I want to mention. One, Susan Lefferts was from San Berdoo. Two, if it's not the Negroes in custody or another colored gang, then the car by the Nite Owl was a plant and we are dealing with one huge conspiracy.'

'I think we have our killers. And on that note, are you making progress with Miss Soto?'

'I'm working at it.'

'Work harder. Good efforts are for schoolboys, results are what counts. Go to it, gentlemen.'

Ed drove to his apartment – a change of clothes for the run to McNeil. He found a note on the door.

Exley –
    I still think you're everything I said you were, but I called the house and talked to my sister and she said you came by and were obviously concerned about my welfare, so I'm thawing a little bit. You've been nice to me (when you weren't covering angles or beating up people) and maybe I'm an opportunist myself and I'm just using you for shelter until I get better and can accept Mr. Dieterling's offer, so since I live in a glass house I shouldn't throw stones at you. That's as close to an apology as I'm going to give you and I will continue to refuse to cooperate. Get the picture? Is Mr. Dieterling for real about a job at Dream-a-Dreamland? I'm going shopping today with the rest of the money you gave me. Keeping busy makes me think about it less. I'll come by tonight. Leave a light burning.
                                                Inez

Ed changed and taped his spare key to the door. He left a light burning.

Chapter Thirty-two

Jack in his car, waiting to tail Bud White. Mangled hands, fruit-caked clothes – a shift breaking down garage doors, high-spirited darkies japping the search teams – rooftop hit-and-runs. No luck on Coates' Merc; Millard's bomb still exploding, lucky he heard by phone – he would have shit his pants otherwise.

'Vincennes, two witnesses have contacted Ellis Loew. They said Duke Cathcart was involved in some kind of unrealized scheme to push that smut we've been chasing. My guess is that it doesn't connect to the Nite Owl, but have you come up with anything?'

He said, 'No.' He asked if the other guys on the squad hit pay dirt. Millard said, 'No.'

He didn't tell him his reports were all bullshit. He didn't tell him he didn't care if the smut gig and the Nite Owl were doubled up from here to Mars. He didn't tell him he wouldn't rest easy until he had Sid Hudgens' file in his hand and the niggers sucked gas – guilty or not.

Eyes on the bullpen back door: blues hauling in sex geeks. Bud White inside – rubber hose work. He blew his tail last night – Dudley was pissed. Tonight he'd stick close, then hit Hudgens: get the Malibu Rendezvous wiped.

White walked out. Good light: Jack saw blood on his shirt. He hit the ignition, waited.

Chapter Thirty-three

No colored lights – white light behind closed curtains. Bud pushed the buzzer.

The door opened – backlight on Lynn Bracken. 'Yes? Are you the policeman Pierce told me about?'

'That's right. Did Patchett tell you what it was about?'

She held the door open. 'He said you weren't quite sure yourself, and he said I should be candid and cooperate with you.'

'You do everything he tells you?'

'Yes, I do.'

Bud walked in. Lynn said, 'The paintings are real and I'm a prostitute. I've never heard of Kathy what's-her-name, and Dwight Gilette would never sexually abuse a female. If he were going to kill one, he would have used a knife. I have heard of that man Duke Cathcart, essentially that he was a loser with a soft spot for his girls. And that's all the news that's fit to print.'

'You finished?'

'No. I have no information on Dwight's other girls, and all I know about that Nite Owl thing is what I read in the papers. Satisfied?'

Bud almost laughed. 'You and Patchett had *some* talk. Did he call you last night?'

'No, this morning. Why?'

'Never mind.'

'It's Officer White, isn't it?'

'It's Bud.'

Lynn laughed. '*Bud*, do you believe what Pierce and I have told you?'

'Yeah, pretty much.'

'And you know why we're humoring you.'

'You use words like that, you might make me mad.'

'Yes. But you know.'

'Yeah, I know. Patchett's running whores, maybe other stuff on the side. You don't want me to report you on it.'

'That's right. Our motives are selfish, so we're cooperating.'

'You want some advice, Miss Bracken?'

'It's Lynn.'

'Miss Bracken, here's my advice. Keep cooperating and don't fucking ever try to bribe me or threaten me or I'll have you and Patchett in shit up to your ears.'

Lynn smiled. Bud caught it – Veronica Lake in some turkey he saw, Alan Ladd comes home from the war to find his bitch wife snuffed. 'Do you want a drink, *Bud*?'

'Yeah, plain scotch.'

Lynn walked to the kitchen, came back with two short ones. 'Are they making progress on the girl's killing?'

Bud knocked his back. 'There's three men on it. It's a sex job, so they'll round up all the usual perverts. They'll give it a decent shot for a couple of weeks, then let it go.'

'But you won't let it go.'

'Maybe, maybe not.'

'Why are you so concerned?'

'Old stuff.'

'Old personal stuff?'

'Yeah.'

Lynn sipped her drink. 'Just asking. And what about the Nite Owl thing?'

'That's coming down to these nig – colored guys we arrested. It's a big fucking mess.'

'You say "fuck" a lot.'

'You fuck for money.'

'There's blood on your shirt. Is that an integral part of your job?'

'Yeah.'

'Do you enjoy it?'

'When they deserve it.'

'Meaning men who hurt women.'

'Bright girl.'

'Did they deserve it today?'

'No.'

215

'But you did it anyway.'

'Yeah, just like the half dozen guys you screwed today.'

Lynn laughed. 'Actually, it was two. Off the record, did you beat up Dwight Gilette?'

'Off the record, I stuck his hand down a garbage disposal.'

No gasp, no double take. 'Did you enjoy it?'

'Well . . . no.'

Lynn coughed. 'I'm being a bad hostess. Would you like to sit down?'

Bud sat on the sofa; Lynn sat an arm's length over. 'Homicide detectives are different. You're the first man I've met in five years who didn't tell me I look like Veronica Lake inside of a minute.'

'You look better than Veronica Lake.'

Lynn lit a cigarette. 'Thank you. I won't tell your lady friend you said that.'

'How do you know I got a lady friend?'

'Your jacket is a mess and reeks of perfume.'

'You're wrong. This is me taking a pass on a pass.'

'Which you . . . '

'Yeah, which I seldom fucking do. Keep cooperating, Miss Bracken. Tell me about Pierce Patchett and this racket of his.'

'Off the – '

'Yeah, off the record.'

Lynn smoked, sipped scotch. 'Well, putting what he's done for me aside, Pierce is a Renaissance man. He dabbles in chemistry, he knows judo, he takes good care of his body. He loves having beautiful women beholden to him. He had a marriage that failed, he had a daughter who died very young. He's very honest with his girls, and he only lets us date well-behaved, wealthy men. So call it a savior complex. Pierce loves beautiful women. He loves manipulating them and making money off them, but there's real affection there, too. When I first met Pierce I told him my little sister was killed by a drunken driver. He actually cried. Pierce Patchett is a hardcase businessman, and yes, he runs call girls. But he's a good man.'

216

It played straight. 'What else has Patchett got going?'

'Nothing illegal. He puts business deals and movie deals together. He advises his girls on business matters.'

'Smut?'

'God, not Pierce. He likes to *do* it, not look at it.'

'Or sell it?'

'Yes, or sell it.'

Almost too smooth – like Patchett's smut hink needed a whitewash. 'I'm starting to think you're snowing me. There's gotta be a perv deal here. Sugar-pimping's one thing, but you make this guy out to be fucking Jesus. Let's start with Patchett's "little studio." '

Lynn put out her cigarette. 'Suppose I don't want to talk about that?'

'Suppose I give you and Patchett to Administrative Vice?'

Lynn shook her head. 'Pierce thinks you have your own private vendetta going, that it's in your best interest to eliminate him as a suspect in whatever it is you're investigating and keep quiet about his dealings. He thinks you won't inform on him, that it would be stupid for you to do it.'

'Stupid is my middle name. What else does Patchett think?'

'He's waiting for you to mention money.'

'I don't do shakedowns.'

'Then why – '

'Maybe I'm just fucking curious.'

'So be it. Do you know who Dr. Terry Lux is?'

'Sure, he runs a dry-out farm in Malibu. He's dirty to the core.'

'Correct on both counts, and he's also a plastic surgeon.'

'He did a plastic on Patchett, right? Nobody his age looks that young.'

'I don't know about that. What Terry Lux *does* do is alter girls for Pierce's little studio. There's Ava and Kate and Rita and Betty. Read that as Gardner, Hepburn, Hayworth and Grable. Pierce finds girls with middling resemblances to movie stars, Terry performs plastic surgery for exact resemblances. Call them Pierce's concubines. They sleep with Pierce and selected clients – men who can help him put together movie and business deals. Perverse? Perhaps. But Pierce takes a cut of all his girls' earnings and invests it for them. He makes his girls quit the life at thirty – no exceptions. He doesn't let his girls use narcotics and he doesn't abuse them, and I owe him a great deal. Can your policeman's mentality grasp those contradictions?'

Bud said, 'Jesus fucking Christ.'

'No, Mr. White. Pierce Morehouse Patchett.'

'Lux cut you to look like Veronica Lake?'

Lynn touched her hair. 'No, I refused. Pierce loved me for it. I'm really a brunette, but the rest is me.'

'And how old are you?'

'I'll be thirty next month, and I'll be opening up a dress shop. See how time changes things? If you'd met me a month from now, I wouldn't be a whore. I'd be a brunette who didn't look quite so much like Veronica Lake.'

'Jesus Christ.'

'No, Lynn Margaret Bracken.'

Too quick – almost a blurt. 'Look, I want to see you again.'

'Are you asking me for a date?'

'Yeah, because I can't afford what Patchett charges.'

'You could wait a month.'

'No, I can't.'

'No more shoptalk, then. I don't want to be somebody's suspect.'

Bud made a check mark in the air: Patchett crossed off for Kathy and the Nite Owl. 'Deal.'

Chapter Thirty-four

Mickey Cohen's cell.

Gallaudet laughed: velvet-covered bed, velvet-flocked shelves, commode with a velvet-flocked seat. Heat through a wall vent – Washington State, still cold in April. Ed was tired: they talked to Jack 'The Enforcer' Whalen, eliminated him, flew a thousand miles. 1:00 A.M. – two cops waiting for a psychopathic hoodlum busy with a late pinochle game. Gallaudet patted Cohen's pet bulldog: Mickey Cohen, Jr., snazzy in a velvet-flocked sweater. Ed checked his Whalen notes.

Rambling – they couldn't shut him up. Whalen laughed off the Englekling theory, digressed on L.A. organized crime.

Mob activity in a general lull since Mickey C. hit stir. The insider view: the Mick power broke, Swiss bank money tucked away – cash to rebuild with. Morris Jahelka, Cohen underboss, given a fiefdom – he promptly blew it, investing badly, no funds to pay his men. Whalen said *he* was doing well and offered his Cohen theory.

He figured Mickey was parceling out bookmaking, loansharking, dope and prostitution franchises – small, choosy who they dealt with; when paroled he'd consolidate, grab the money the franchise men invested for him, rebuild. Whalen based his theory on hink: Lee Vachss, ex-Cohen trigger, seemed to have gone legit; Johnny Stompanato and Abe Teitlebaum ditto – two wrong-o's who couldn't walk a straight line. Make all three of them still on the grift – maybe safeguarding Cohen's interests. Chief Parker – afraid the lull might lead to Mafia encroachment – just fielded a new front line against out-of-town muscle: Dudley Smith and two of his goons set up shop at a motel in Gardena: they beat gang guys half to death, stole their money for police charity contributions, put them back on

the bus, train or plane to wherever they came from – all
very much on the QT.

Whalen concluded:

He's allowed to operate because somebody had to provide gambling services or a bunch of crazy independents
would shoot L.A. to shit. 'Containment' – a Dudley S.
word – said it all: the police establishment knew he only
shot when shot at; he *played the game*. The idea of him or
Mickey blasting six people over jack-off books was pure
bullshit. Still, things were too quiet, shit had to be
brewing.

Mickey Cohen, Jr., yipped; Ed looked up. Mickey
Cohen walked in, holding a box of dog biscuits. He said,
'I have never killed no man that did not deserve killing
by the standards of our way of life. I have never distributed no obscene shit to be used for the purpose of mastur-
bation and only took a confabulation with Pete and Bax
Englekling because of my fondness for their late father,
may God rest his soul even though he was a fucking kraut.
I do not kill innocent bystanders because it's a mitzvah
not to and because I adhere to the Ten Commandments
except when it is bad for business. Warden Hopkins told
me why you was here and I made you wait because you
must be stupid morons to make me for this vicious and
stupid caper, obviously the handiwork of stupid shvartzes.
But since Mickey Junior likes you I will give you five
minutes of my time. Come to Daddy, bubeleh!'

Gallaudet howled. Cohen knelt on the floor, put a biscuit in his mouth. The dog ran to him, grabbed the
biscuit, kissed him. Mickey nuzzled the beast; Cohen
Junior squealed, pissed. Ed saw a man on the catwalk:
Davey Goldman, Mickey's chief accountant, at McNeil
on his own tax beef.

Goldman sidled away. Gallaudet said, 'Mickey, the
Englekling brothers said you went crazy when they mentioned Duke Cathcart was behind their idea.'

Cohen spat biscuit crumbs. 'Are you familiar with the
old saying "blowing off steam"?'

Ed said, 'Yes, but what about other names? Did the Engleklings mention any other names besides Cathcart?'

'No, and Cathcart I never met myself. I heard he had a statch rape jacket, so I judged him on that. The Bible says, "Judge not, lest ye be judged," so since I am willing to be judged, I say, "Judge on, O Mickster."'

'Did you give the brothers any advice on setting up a distribution system?'

'No! As God and my beloved Mickey Junior are my witnesses, no!'

Gallaudet: 'Mick, here's the key question. Did you talk up the deal on the yard? Who else did you tell about it?'

'I told nobody! Jerk-off books are from sin and hunger! I even chased Davey away when those meshugeneh brothers came calling! Davey's my ears, that's how much I respect the cardinal virtue of confidentiality!'

Gallaudet said, 'Ed, I called Russ Millard while you were talking to the warden. He said he checked with his Ad Vice guys on the pornography job, and they've got nothing. No Cathcart, no leads on the books. Russ went through all the Nite Owl field reports and got nothing. Bud White background checked Cathcart, and he reported nothing. Ed, Susie Lefferts from San Berdoo is just a coincidence. Cathcart couldn't make a smut deal happen if he tried. This whole thing was the Engleklings' buying out of some old warrants and a dog show.'

Ed nodded. Mickey Cohen, Sr., cradled Mickey Cohen, Jr. 'Fathers and sons are food for thought, are they not a veritable feast? My canine offspring and me, old Doc Franz and his gap-toothed white trash lowlifes. Franz was a chemical genius, great things he did for the drool case mentally disturbed. When a boatload of Big H was stole from me way back, I thought of Franz, and how if I had his brains instead of my own poetic genius I would have recreated my own white powder to sell. Go home, boy-chiks. Dirty books will not win you your murder case. It's the shvartzes, it's the fucking shvoogies.'

Chapter Thirty-five

Bottles: whisky, gin, brandy. Flashing signs: Schlitz, Pabst Blue Ribbon. Sailors downing cold beers, happy folks juicing their lights out. Hudgens' pad a block away – booze would give him the guts. He knew it before he tailed Bud White – now he had a thousand times the reason.

The barman yelled, 'Last call.' Jack killed his club soda, pressed the glass to his neck. His day hit him – again.

Millard says Duke Cathcart was involved in some scheme to push *his* smut.

Bud White visits Lynn Bracken, one of the lookalike whores. He stays inside two hours; the whore walks him out. He tails White home, starts thinking evidence: White knows Bracken, she knows Pierce Patchett, he knows Hudgens. Sid knows about the Malibu Rendezvous, Dudley Smith probably knows. Big Dud's reason for the tail job: White bent out of shape on a *hooker* snuff.

Pulsing beer signs: neon monsters. Brass knucks in the car, the Sidster might fold, kick loose with his file –

Jack bolted: Hudgens' place, no lights on, Sid's Packard at the curb. The door – brass knucks for a knocker.

Thirty seconds – nothing. Jack tried the door – no give – shouldered the jamb. The door popped open.

That smell.

Slow motion: handkerchief out, gun out, elbow to the wall – the switch, no prints. Switch down, lights on.

Sid Hudgens hacked up on the floor – a rug soaked black, the floor a blood slick.

Arms and legs severed, out at weird angles off his torso.

Split open crotch to neck, bones showing white through red.

Cabinets upended behind him – folders dumped on a clean patch of rug.

Jack bit his arms to kill screams.

No blood tracks, say the killer got out the back door. Hudgens naked, coated red-black. Limbs off his torso, strands of gore at the cut points, swirls like his inked-in fuck books –

Jack bolted.

Around the house, down the driveway. The back door: ajar, spilling light. Inside: a water-slick floor – no blood prints, tracks covered. He walked in, found grocery bags under the sink. Shaky steps to the living room. File cabinet dirt: folders, folders, folders – one, two, three, four, five bags – two trips to his car.

A quiet L.A. street at 2:20 A.M., calm down mumbo jumbo.

Fifty trillion people had motives. Nobody knew he'd seen the inked-in books. The mutilations would get written off– just psycho stuff.

He had to find his file.

Jack doused lights, sawed the front door with his handcuffs – let them think it's a burglar. He took off, no destination, just driving.

Just driving wore thin. He found a motel strip, a hot-sheet flop: Oscar's Sleepytime Lodge.

He paid a week's rent, hauled his bags in, took a shower and put his stale clothes back on. A cockroach palace: bugs, grease on the wall above the bed. He smelled himself: stale working on foul. He locked the door, prowled dirt.

Hush-Hush back issues, clippings, pilfered police documents. Files: Montgomery Clift as the smallest dick in Hollywood, Errol Flynn as a Nazi agent. A hot item: Flynn and some homo writer named Truman Capote. Commies, Commie sympathizers, celebrity spook fuckers ranging from Joan Crawford to former D.A. Bill McPherson. Hopheads galore: shit on Charlie Parker, Anita O'Day, Art Pepper, Tom Neal, Barbara Payton, Gail Russell. Intact *Hush-Hush* articles: 'Mafia Ties to the Vatican!!!,' 'Lavender Liturgy: Is "Rock" Hudson Really "Rockette"?,' 'Grasshopper Alert: Beware of Hollywood's Tea Bag Babies.' Complete files, too tame to be Hudgens' secret stash – Commies, queers, lezbos, dopesters, satyrs, nymphos, misogynists, mob-bought politicos.

Nothing on Sergeant Jack Vincennes.

Nothing on *Badge of Honor* – a big Hudgens fixation – he knew Sid had a file on Brett Chase.

Strange.

More strange: *Hush-Hush* ran a smear on Max Peltz – there was nothing on him.

Nothing on Pierce Patchett, Lynn Bracken, Lamar Hinton, Fleur-de-Lis.

Jack measured his filth pile. Big – make the killer a file thief, if he got any files it wasn't many – his pile looked like it would jam the cabinets to bursting.

ALIBI.

Jack stuffed his files in the closet. 'Do Not Disturb' on the door, back to his apartment.

5:10 A.M.

Under the knocker: 'Jack – remember our date Thurs.' 'Jack sweetie – are you hibernating? XXXX–K.' He walked in, grabbed the phone, dialed 888.

'Police Emergency.'

A hepcat drawl. 'Man, I want to report a murder. If I'm lyin', I'm flyin'.'

'Sir, is this legitimate?'

'Yeah, if I'm – '

'What is your address, sir?'

'My address is nowhere, but I was gonna burglarize this house, then I saw this body.'

'Sir – '

'421 South Alexandria, got that?'

'Sir, where are – '

Jack hung up, stripped, lay down on the bed. Figure twenty minutes for the bluesuits, ten to ID Hudgens. They putz around, make it as a big case, call Homicide. The desk man thinks brass, shakes a boss case man out of bed. Thad Green, Russ Millard, Dudley S. – they'd all think Big V pronto – his phone would ring in a hot hour.

Jack lay there – sweating up a clean set of sheets. Ring ring – at 6:58.

Jack, yawning. 'Yeah?'

'Vincennes, it's Russ Millard.'

'Yeah, Cap. What time is it? What's – '

'Never mind. Do you know where Sid Hudgens lives?'

'Yeah, Chapman Park somewhere. Cap, what's – '

'421 South Alexandria. *Now*, Vincennes.'

Shave, shower, clothes that stayed dry. Forty minutes to the scene – a fuckload of cop cars on Sid Hudgens' lawn. Morgue men hefting plastic bags: blood, body parts.

Jack parked on the lawn. An attendant wheeled out a gurney: gore wrapped in sheets. Russ Millard by the door; two comers – Don Kleckner, Duane Fisk – down the driveway. Patrolmen shooed away spectators; reporters crowded the sidewalk. Jack walked up to Millard. 'Hudgens?' – not too much shock, a pro.

'Yes, your buddy. A bit chewed up, I'm afraid. A burglar called it in. He was about to tap the house, then he saw the body. Pry marks on the doorjamb, so I buy it. Don't look inside if you've eaten.'

Jack looked. Dried blood, white tape outlines: arms, legs, torso – the severing points marked. Millard said, 'Somebody *hated* him. You see those drawers over there? I think the killer snuffed him for his files. I had Kleckner call the *Hush-Hush* publisher. He's going to open up the office and give us copies of the recent stuff Hudgens was working on.'

Old Russ wanted a comment. Jack crossed himself: his first time since the orphanage, where the fuck did it come from.

'Vincennes, you were his friend. What do you think?'

'I think he was scum! Everybody hated him! You've got all L.A. for suspects!'

'Easy, now, *easy*. I know you've leaked information to

225

Hudgens, I know you two did business. If we don't wrap this in a few days, I'm going to want a statement.'

Duane Fisk spieling Morty Bendish – make book on a *Mirror* scoop. Jack said, 'I'll kick loose. What am I going to do, impede the progress of an official investigation?'

'Your sense of duty is admirable. Now, let's talk about Hudgens. Girls, boys, what did he like?'

Jack lit a cigarette. 'He liked dirt. He was a goddamned degenerate. Maybe he pulled his pud while he looked at his own goddamn shitrag, I don't know.'

Don Kleckner walked up, a copy of *Hush-Hush* spread open: 'TV Mogul Loves to Ogle – And Then Some!!! And Teen Queens Are His Scene!!!' 'Captain, I bought this at that newsstand on the corner. And the publisher told me *Badge of Honor* was a bee in Hudgens' bonnet.'

'This is good. Don, you start canvassing. Vincennes, come here.'

Over to the lawn. Millard said, 'This keeps coming back to people you know.'

'I'm a cop and I'm Hollywood. I know lots of people, and I know Max Peltz likes young trim. So what? He's sixty years old and he's no killer.'

'We'll decide that this afternoon. You're block searching on the Nite Owl, right? Looking for Coates' car?'

'Yeah.'

'Then go back to that now and report to the Bureau at 2:00. I'm going to ask some key people from *Badge of Honor* to come in for some friendly questioning. You can help grease things.'

Billy Dieterling, Timmy Valburn – 'People He Knew' closing in. 'Sure, I'll be there.'

Morty Bendish ran up. 'Jackie, does this mean I'll get *all* your exclusives now?'

Garage door break-ins, niggers hurling fruit – *real* work back at the motel. He was heading into Darktown when it hit him.

He cut east, parked by the Royal Flush. Claude

226

Dineen's Buick up on blocks – he was probably dealing shit in the men's room.

Jack walked in. Everything froze: the Big V meant grief. The barman poured a double Old Forester; Jack downed it – cutting off five years kosher. The juice warmed him. He kicked the men's room door in.

Claude Dineen geezing up.

Jack kicked him prone, yanked the spike from his arm. A frisk, no resistance – Claude was up on cloud ten. Bingo: tinfoil Benzedrine. He swallowed a roll dry, flushed the hypo down the toilet. He said, 'I'm back.'

He hit the motel juiced, primed to figure angles. File go-round number two.

Nothing new jumped out; one instinct buzzed him: Hudgens didn't keep his 'secret' files at home. If the killer snuffed him for a particular file, he tried to torture the location out of him first. The killer didn't glom a lot of files – the cabinets wouldn't hold much more than what he stole. Sid's Big V file was still at large – if the killer found it he might keep it, might throw it away.

Jump: Hudgens/Patchett connected, pornography/vice rackets the connection. Put the Cathcart/Nite Owl connection aside: Millard/Exley called it a bust – denials from Whalen and Mickey C., Cathcart never got his smut gig going. Millard's report: the Englekling brothers didn't know who took the pictures; Cathcart got ahold of some of the stag books, went crazy with a harebrained scheme. Put that aside and what he had was:

Bobby Inge, Christine and Daryl Bergeron – gone. Lamar Hinton, the probable shooter at the Fleur-de-Lis drop – undoubtedly gone. Timmy Valburn, a Fleur-de-Lis customer, rousted by him – a connection to Billy Dieterling, a *Badge of Honor* cameraman, catch him at Millard's questioning party – *stay calm on that*. Say Timmy told Billy about the roust; Billy was there when he trashed Hinton's car, *keep calm*, the queers had shitloads to lose by admitting their connection to Fleur-de-Lis – which Russ Millard did not know existed.

227

Brainstorming, chain-smoking.

Mutilations on Hudgens' body matched the inked-in poses in the fuck books he found outside Bobby Inge's pad. *No other cops had seen those specific books* – Millard viewed the stiff, tagged the chopped limbs as straight amputations.

Hudgens warned him away from Fleur-de-Lis. Lynn Bracken was a Patchett whore – maybe she knew Sid.

Wild card: Dudley Smith told him to tail Bud White. His reason: White running maverick on a hooker killing. Bracken was a hooker, Patchett ran hookers. But: *Dudley did not mention any tie-ins to the Nite Owl or pornography – Patchett/Bracken/smut/Fleur-de-Lis et fucking al were probably Greek to him. The Englekling brothers/Cathcart wash aside, smut/Patchett/Bracken/Fleur-de-Lis/Hudgens in no way made its way into the incredible glut of interdivision posted Nite Owl paperwork.*

Sky high: Benzedrine, cop logic. 11:20 – time to kill before the Bureau. Two real leads – Pierce Patchett, Lynn Bracken.

Bracken was closer.

Jack drove to her apartment, settled in behind her car. Give her an hour, play it by ear if she left.

Time Benzedrine-flew; Bracken's door stayed shut. 12:33 – a kid chucked a newspaper at it. If Morty Bendish speedballed his story and that kid pitched the *Mirror* –

The door opened; Lynn Bracken picked the paper up, yawned back inside. The paperboy swooped by, carrier sacks in plain view: Los Angeles *Mirror-News*. Be in there, Morty.

Bang! – Bracken slammed the door, ran to her car. She gunned it, swerved west on Los Feliz. Jack cut her two seconds slack, tailed her.

Southwest: Los Feliz to Western to Sunset, Sunset straight out – ten miles over the speed limit. Odds on: a fear run to Patchett's place, she didn't want to use the phone.

Jack looped south, shortcutted, made 1184 Gretna

228

Green burning rubber. A huge Spanish manse, a huge front lawn – Lynn Bracken hadn't showed yet.

A skidding heart: he forgot what you paid to eat bennies. He parked, checked out the house: nobody out and about. Up to the door, a duck around the side – find some windows.

All closed. A gardener working around back – no way to circuit without being seen. A car door slammed; Jack ran to a front window: closed, a part in the curtains he could squint through.

The doorbell rang; Jack squinted in. Patchett walked to the door, opened it. Lynn Bracken shoved her newspaper at him – zoom into a panic duet: mute lip movements, fear very large. Jack put an ear to the glass – all he heard was his own heart thumping. No need for sound: they didn't know Sid was dead, they're scared anyway, they didn't kill him.

They walked into the next room – full curtains, no way to look or listen. Jack ran to his car.

He made the Bureau ten minutes late. The Homicide pen was jam-packed *Badge of Honor*: Brett Chase, Miller Stanton, David Mertens the set man, Jerry Marsalas his nurse – one long bench crammed tight. Standing: Billy Dieterling, the camera crew, a half dozen briefcase men: attorneys for sure. The gang looked nervous; Duane Fisk and Don Kleckner paced with clipboards. No Max Peltz, no Russ Millard.

Billy D. shot him the fisheye; the rest of the gang waved. Jack waved back; Kleckner buttonholed him. 'Ellis Loew wants to see you. Booth number six.'

Jack walked down. Loew was staring out a back wall mirror – a lie detector stall across the glass. Polygraph time: Millard questioning Peltz, Ray Pinker working the machine.

Loew noticed him. 'I'd rather Max didn't have to go through that. Can you fix it?'

Protecting a slush-fund contributor. 'Ellis, I've got no

truck with Millard. If Max's lawyer advised him to do it, he'll have to do it.'

'Can Dudley fix it?'

'Dud's got no truck with him either, Millard's the pious type. And before you ask me, I don't know who killed Sid, and I don't care. Has Max got an alibi?'

'Yes, but one that he would rather not use.'

'How old is she?'

'Quite young. Would – '

'Yeah, Russ would file on him for it.'

'My God, all this for scum like Hudgens.'

Jack laughed. 'Counselor, one of his little mudslings got you elected.'

'Yes, politics makes for strange bedfellows, but I doubt if he'll be grieved. You know, we've got nothing. I talked to those attorneys outside, and they all assured me their clients have valid alibis. They'll give statements and be eliminated, the rest of the *Badge of Honor* people will be alibied and then we'll only have the rest of Hollywood to deal with.'

An opening. 'Ellis, you want some advice?'

'Yes, give me your appropriately cynical view.'

'Let it play out. Push on the Nite Owl, that's the one the public wants cleared. Hudgens was shit, the investigation'll be a shit show and we'll never get the killer. Let it play out.'

The door opened; Duane Fisk put two thumbs down. 'No luck, Mr. Loew. Alibis straight across, and they sound like good ones. The coroner estimated Hudgens' death at midnight to 1:00 A.M., and these people were all in plain view somewhere else. We'll go for corroboration, but I think it's a wipe.'

Loew nodded; Fisk walked out. Jack said, 'Let it go.'

Loew smiled. 'What's your alibi? Were you in bed with my sister-in-law?'

'I was in bed alone.'

'I'm not surprised – Karen said you've been moody and scarce lately. You look edgy, Jack. Are you afraid your arrangement with Hudgens will be publicized?'

'Millard wants a deposition, I'll give him one. You buy Sid and me as lodge brothers?'

'Of course. Along with Dudley Smith, myself and several other well-known choirboys. You're right on Hudgens, Jack. I'll broach it to Bill Parker.'

A yawn – the bennies were losing their kick. 'It's a dog of a case, and you don't want to prosecute it.'

'Yes, since the victim did facilitate *my* election, and he might have left word that *you* leaked word to him on Mr. McPherson's quote dark desires. Jack . . . '

'Yeah, I'll keep my nose down, and if your name turns up on paper I'll destroy it.'

'Good man. And if I . . . '

'Yeah, there is something. Track the reports on the investigation. Sid kept some secret dirt files, and if your name's anywhere, it's there. And if I get a lead on where, I'll be there with a match.'

Loew, pale. 'Done, and I'll talk to Parker this afternoon.'

Ray Pinker rapped on the mirror, pressed a graph to the glass: twin needle lines – no wild fluctuations. Out the speaker: 'Not guilty, but no give on his alibi. Was he *en flagrante*?'

Loew smiled. Russ Millard, speaker loud. 'Go to work, Vincennes. Nite Owl block canvassing, if you recall. Your cockamamie TV show hasn't panned out so far, and I want a written statement on your dealings with Hudgens. *By 0800 tomorrow.*'

Darktown beckoned.

South to 77th. Jack popped another roll and picked up his search map; the desk sergeant told him the spooks were getting feistier, some pinko agitators put a bug up their ass, more garbage attacks, the garage men were going out in threes: one detective, two patrolmen, teams on opposite sides of the street. Meet his guys at 116th and Wills – they'd been one man short since noon.

The bennies kicked in – Jack zoomed back up. He drove to 116 and Wills: a stretch of cinderblock shacks, windows stuffed with cardboard. Dirt alleys, a bicycle brigade: colored kids packing fruit. His guys up ahead: two patrolmen on the left, two blues and a plainclothes on the right. Armed: tin snips, rifles. Jack parked, made the left-side team a threesome.

Pure shitwork.

Knock on the door, get permission to search the garage. Three quarters of the locals played possum; back to the garage, open the door, cut the lock. The right-side team didn't ask – they went in snips first, dawdled, brandished their hardware at the bicycle kids. The left-side kids tried to look mean; one kid chucked a tomato over their heads. The blues fired over his head – taking out a pigeon coop, chewing up a palm tree. Dusty garage after dusty garage after dusty garage – no '49 Merc license DG114.

Twilight, a block of deserted houses – broken windows, weed jungle lawns. Jack started feeling punk: achy teeth, chest pings. He heard rebel yells across the street; the right-side team triggered shots. He looked at his partners – then they all tore ass over.

The Holy Grail in a rat-infested garage: a purple '49 Merc, jig rig to the hilt. California license DG114 – registered to Raymond 'Sugar Ray' Coates.

Two patrolmen whipped out bottles.

A couple of bicycle kids jabbered: the bonaroo paint job, a white cat hanging around the alley.

The left-side guys broke into a rain dance.

Jack squinted through a side window. Three pump shotguns on the floor between the seats: big bore, probably 12-gauge.

Yells – deafening; back slaps – bonecrusher hard. The kids yelled along; a patrolman let them slug from his bottle. Jack took a big gulp, emptied his gun at a streetlight, got it with his last shot. Whoops, rebel yells; Jack let the kids play quick draw with his piece. Sid Hudgens buzzed him – he took a big drink, chased him away.

Chapter Thirty-six

A private room at the Pacific Dining Car. Dudley Smith, Ellis Loew, Bud across the table. Blistered hands, three days of hose work: sex offenders blurred in his head.

Dudley said, 'Lad, we found the car and the shotguns an hour ago. No prints, but one of the firing pins perfectly matches the nicked shells we found at the Nite Owl. We took the victims' purses and wallets out of a sewer grate near the Tevere Hotel, which means that we have a damn near airtight case. But Mr. Loew and I want the whole hog. We want confessions.'

Bud shoved his plate away. It all came back to the spooks – scotch his shot at Exley. 'So you'll put bright boy on the niggers again.'

Loew shook his head. 'No, Exley's too soft. I want you and Dudley to question them, inside the jail, tomorrow morning. Ray Coates has been in the infirmary with an ear infection, but they're releasing him back into general population early tomorrow. I want you and Dud there bright and early, say 7:00.'

'What about Carlisle and Breuning?'

Dudley laughed. 'Lad, you're a much more frightful presence. This job has the name "Wendell White" on it, as does another assignment I've kicked off lately. One you'll be interested in.'

Loew said, 'Officer, it's been Ed Exley's case so far, but now you can share the glory. And I'll grant you a favor in return.'

'Yeah?'

'Yes. Dick Stensland has been handed a six-count probation indictment. Do it, and I'll drop four of those charges and put him in front of a lenient judge. He'll be sentenced to no more than ninety days.'

Bud stood up. 'Deal, Mr. Loew. And thanks for dinner.'

Dudley beamed. 'Until 7:00 tomorrow, lad. And why are you leaving so abruptly, is it a hot date you have?'

'Yeah, Veronica Lake.'

She opened the door, all Veronica: spangly gown, blonde curl over one eye. 'If you'd called first, I wouldn't look this ridiculous.'

She looked edgy. Her dye job was off: uneven, dark at the roots. 'Bad date?'

'An investment banker Pierce wants to curry favor with.'

'Did you fake it good?'

'He was so self-absorbed that I didn't have to fake it.'

Bud laughed. 'You turn thirty, you do it strictly for thrills.'

Lynn laughed, still edgy, she might touch him first just to have something to do with her hands. 'If men don't try to be Alan Ladd, they might get the real Lynn Margaret.'

'Worth the wait?'

'You know it is, and you're wondering if Pierce told me to be receptive.'

He couldn't think of a comeback.

Lynn took his arm. 'I'm glad you thought of that, and I like you. And if you wait in the bedroom I'll scrub off Veronica and that investment banker.'

She came to him naked, a brunette, her hair still wet. Bud forced himself to go slow, take time with his kisses, like she was a lonely woman he wanted to love to death. Lynn played off his timing: her kisses back, her touches. Bud kept thinking she was faking – he rushed to taste her so he'd know.

Lynn moaned, put his hands on her breasts, set up a rhythm for his fingers. Bud followed her lead, loved it when she gasped and came over and over, hair-trigger. Real – so real he forgot about himself; he heard something like 'In me, please in me.' He rubbed himself hard on the

234

bed, went in her, kept his hands on her breasts like she taught him. Hard inside her – he let himself go just as her legs pulsed and her hips pushed him up off the sheets – then his face pressing wet hair, their arms locked on each other tight.

They rested, talked. Lynn talked up her diary: a thousand pages back to high school in Bisbee, Arizona. Bud rambled on the Nite Owl, his strongarm job in the morning – sitting-duck stuff he couldn't take much more of. Lynn's look said, 'Then just give it up'; he didn't have an answer, so he spieled on Dudley, the heartbreaker rape girl with a crush on him, how he'd hoped the Nite Owl would swing another way so he could use it to juke this guy he hated. Lynn talked back with little touches; Bud told her he was letting the Kathy snuff go for now, it was too easy to go crazy on – crazy like his play with Dwight Gilette. Lynn pressed on his family; he told her 'I don't have one'; he ran down his outlaw job: Cathcart, his pad tossed, his smut dream, the San Berdoo Yellow Pages open to printshops clicking in to the Englekling brothers plea bargain, then clicking out, back to the colored punks they had on ice. He knew she knew the gist: he was frustrated because he wasn't that smart, he wasn't really a Homicide detective – he was the guy they brought in to scare other guys shitless. After a while, the talk petered out – Bud felt restless, pissed at himself for spilling too much too fast. Lynn seemed to sense it: she bent down and drove him crazy with her mouth. Bud stroked her hair, still a little wet, glad she didn't have to fake it with him.

Chapter Thirty-seven

Evidence – the victims' belongings found near the Tevere Hotel; Coates' Merc and the shotguns located: forensic verification on the piece that shot the strangely marked rounds. No grand jury on earth would refuse to hand down Murder One. The Nite Owl case was made.

Ed at his kitchen table, writing a report: Parker's last summary. Inez in the bedroom, her bedroom now, he couldn't get up the nerve to say: 'Just let me sleep with you, we'll see how things go, wait on the other.' She'd been moody – reading books on Raymond Dieterling, getting up nerve to ask the man for a job. The news on the guns didn't bolster her – even though it meant no testimony. Evidence – her outside wounds had healed, there was no physical pain to distract her. She kept feeling it happen.

The phone rang; Ed grabbed it. An extra click – Inez picking up in the bedroom.

'Hello?'

'Russ Millard, Ed.'

'Captain, how are you?'

'It's Russ to sergeants and up, son.'

'Russ, have you heard about the car and the guns? The Nite Owl's history.'

'Not exactly, and that's why I called. I just talked to a Sheriff's lieutenant I know, a man on the Jail Bureau. He told me he heard a rumor. Dudley Smith's taking Bud White in to beat confessions out of our boys. Tomorrow morning, early. I had them moved to another cellblock where they can't get at them.'

'Jesus Christ.'

'The savior indeed. Son, I have a plan. We go in early, confront them with the new evidence and try for legitimate confessions. You play the bad guy, I'll play savior.'

Ed squared his glasses. 'What time?'

'Say 7:00?'

'All right.'

'Son, it means making an enemy out of Dudley.'

The bedroom line clicked off. 'So be it. Russ, I'll see you tomorrow.'

'Sleep well, son. I need you alert.'

Ed hung up. Inez in the doorway, wearing his robe – huge on her. 'You can't do this to me.'

'You shouldn't eavesdrop.'

'I was expecting a call from my sister. Exley, you can't.'

'You wanted them in the gas chamber, they're going there. You didn't want to testify, now I doubt if you'll have to.'

'I want them hurt. I want them to suffer.'

'No. It's wrong. This is a case that demands absolute justice.'

She laughed. 'Absolute justice fits you like this robe fits me, *pendejo*.'

'You got what you wanted, Inez. Let it go at that and get on with your life.'

'What life? Living with you? You'll never marry me, you're so deferential around me that I want to scream and every time I've got myself convinced you're a pretty decent guy you do something that makes me say, "*Madre mia*, how can I be so dumb?" And now you'd deny me this? *This little thing?*'

Ed held up his report. 'Dozens of men built this case. Those animals will be dead by Christmas. *Todos*, Inez. *Absolutamente*. Isn't that enough?'

She laughed – harder. 'No. Ten seconds and they go to sleep. Six hours they beat me and fucked me and stuck things in me. No, it's not enough.'

Ed stood up. 'So you'll let Bud White jeopardize our case. Ellis Loew probably arranged this, Inez. He's thinking airtight grand jury presentation, a two day trial with half of it him grandstanding. He'd jeopardize what he's already got for that. Be smart and recognize it.'

'No, you recognize that the fix is in. The *negritos* die

because that's the way it is. I'm just a witness nobody needs anymore, so maybe tomorrow Officer White takes a few licks for my justice.'

Ed made fists. 'White's a brutal disgrace of a policeman and a slimy, womanizing son of a bitch.'

'No, he's just a guy who calls a spade a spade and doesn't look six ways before he crosses the street.'

'He's shit. *Mierda*.'

'Then he's my *mierda*. Exley, I *know* you. You don't give a damn about justice, you just care about yourself. You're only doing that thing tomorrow to hurt Officer White, and you're only doing it because you know that he knows what you are. You treat me like you want to love me, then you give me nothing but money and social connections, which you've got plenty of and won't miss. You take no risks for me, and Officer White risks his *estúpido* life and doesn't weigh the consequences, and when I get better you'll want to fuck me and set me up someplace where you won't have to be seen in public with me, which is revolting to me, and if for no other reason I love *estúpido* Officer White because at least he has the sense to know what you are.'

Ed walked up to her. 'And what am I?'

'Just a run-of-the-mill coward.'

Ed raised a fist, flinched when she flinched. Inez pulled off her robe. Ed looked, looked away – at the wall and his framed army medals. A target – he threw them across the room. Not enough. He took a bead on a window, reared back, hit soft padded curtains instead.

Chapter Thirty-eight

Jack woke up seeing smut.

Karen in orgy shots – Veronica Lake loving her. Blood: fuck pix as coroner's pix, beautiful women drenched red. The first real thing he saw was daybreak – then Bud White's car parked by Lynn Bracken's pad.

Cracked lips, bone aches head to toe. He swallowed his last bennies, brought back his last thoughts before oblivion.

Nothing in the files, Patchett and Bracken his only Hudgens leads. Patchett had servants living in. Bracken lived alone – he'd brace her when White left her bed.

Jack brainstormed a tailing report – lies to snow Dudley Smith. A door slammed – a sound like a gunshot. Bud White walked to his car.

Jack hit the seat prone. The car pulled away, seconds, another gunshot/door slam. A quick look: a brunette Lynn Bracken heading out.

Over to her car, up to Los Feliz, east. Jack followed: the right lane, dawdling back. Sparse early morning traffic: call the woman too distracted to spot him.

Due east, into Glendale. North on Brand, a swerve to the curb in front of a bank. Jack pulled around the corner to a sighting point – the corner store, a grocer's – milk cartons stacked by the door.

He squatted down, watched the sidewalk. Lynn B. was talking to a man: nervous, a shaky little guy. He opened the bank and hustled her in; a Ford and Dodge were parked further down – no way to nail plate numbers. Lamar Hinton walked outside lugging boxes.

Files, files, files – it had to be.

Bracken and the bank geek hauled boxes: a run to the Dodge and Lynn's Packard. The geek locked up the bank, hit the Ford and U-turned southbound; Hinton and Bracken formed a chain – separate cars heading north.

Seconds tick tick tick – Jack counted to ten, chased.

He caught them a mile out – weaving, creeping up, falling back – downtown Glendale, north into foothills. Traffic dwindled; Jack found a lookout spot: a clean view of the road winding upward. He parked, watched: the cars kept climbing, took a fork, disappeared.

He followed their route straight to a campsite – picnic tables, barbecue pits. Two cars behind a pine row; Bracken and Hinton carrying boxes – muscle boy dangling a gas can off one pinky.

Jack ditched his car, snuck up behind some scrub pines. Bracken and Hinton dumped: paper in a big charcoal pit. They turned their backs; Jack sprinted over, ducked down.

They came back, another load: Bracken with a lighter out, Hinton's arms full. Jack stood up, kicked, pistol-whipped – the balls, left/right/left to the face. Hinton went down dropping paper; Jack broke his arms – knees to the elbows, jerks at the wrists.

Hinton went white – shock coming on.

Bracken had hold of the gas can and a lighter.

Jack stood in front of the pit, his .38 cocked.

Standoff.

Lynn held the can, the cap loose, spilling fumes. Flick – a flame on the lighter. Jack drew down – right in her face.

Standoff.

Hinton tried to crawl. Jack's gun hand started shaking. 'Sid Hudgens, Patchett and Fleur-de-Lis. It's either me or Bud White, and I can be bought.'

Lynn killed the flame, lowered the gas. 'What about Lamar?'

Hinton: pawing at the dirt, spitting blood. Jack lowered his gun. 'He'll live. And he shot at me, so now we're quits.'

'He didn't shoot at you. Pierce . . . I just know he didn't.'

'Then who did?'

'I don't know. Really. And Pierce and I don't know who killed Hudgens. The first we heard of it was the newspapers yesterday.'

The pit – folders on charcoal. 'Hudgens' private dirt, right?'

'Yes.'

'Yes and keep going.'

'No, let's talk about your price. Lamar told Pierce about you, and Pierce figured out that you were that policeman who always seems to wind up in the scandal sheets. So as you say, you can be bought. Now, for how much?'

'What I want's in with those files.'

'And what do you – '

'I know about you and the other girls Patchett runs. I know all about Fleur-de-Lis and the shit Patchett pushes, including the smut.'

No fluster – the woman put out a stone face. 'Some of your stag books have pictures with animated ink. Red, like blood. I saw pictures of Hudgens' body. He was cut up to match those photos.'

The stone face held. 'So now you're going to ask me about Pierce and Hudgens.'

'Yeah, and who doctored up the photos in the books.'

Lynn shook her head. 'I don't know who made those books, and neither does Pierce. He bought them bulk from a rich Mexican man.'

'I don't think I believe you.'

'I don't care. Do you want money besides?'

'No, and I'm betting whoever made those photographs killed Hudgens.'

'Maybe somebody who got excited by the pictures killed him. Do you care either way? Why am I betting Hudgens had dirt on you, and that's what's behind all this?'

'Smart lady. And I'm betting Patchett and Hudgens didn't play golf or – '

Lynn cut him off. 'Pierce and Sid were planning on working a deal together. I won't tell you any more than that.'

241

Extortion – it had to be. 'And those files were for that?'

'No comment. I haven't looked at the files, and let's keep this a stalemate and make sure nobody gets hurt.'

'Then tell me what happened at the bank.'

Lynn watched Hinton try to crawl. 'Pierce knew that Sid kept his private files in safe-deposit boxes at that B of A. After we read that he'd been killed, Pierce figured the police would locate the files. You see, Sid had files on Pierce's dealings – dealings legitimate policemen would disapprove of. Pierce bribed the manager into letting us have the files. And here we are.'

Jack smelled paper, charcoal. 'You and Bud White.'

Lynn made fists, pressed them to her legs. 'He has nothing to do with any of this.'

'Tell me anyway.'

'Why?'

'Because I don't make you two as the hot item of 1953.'

A smile from deep nowhere – Jack almost smiled back. Lynn said, 'We're going to strike a deal, aren't we? A truce?'

'Yeah, a non-agression pact.'

'Then make this part of it. Bud approached Pierce, investigating the murder of a young girl named Kathy Janeway. He'd gotten Pierce's name and mine from a man who used to know her. Of course, we didn't kill her, and Pierce didn't want a policeman coming around. He told me to be nice to Bud . . . and now I'm starting to like him. And I don't want you to tell him anything about this. *Please*.'

She even begged with class. 'Deal, and you can tell Patchett the D.A. thinks the Hudgens case is a loser. It's heading for the back burner, and if I find what I want in that pile, today didn't happen.'

Lynn smiled – this time he smiled back. 'Go look after Hinton.'

She walked over to him. Jack dug into the folders, found name tabs, kept digging. A spate of *T*'s and a run of *V*'s, the kicker. 'Vincennes, John.'

Eyewitness accounts: squarejohns at the beach that

night. Nice folks who saw him drill Mr. & Mrs. Harold J. Scoggins, nice folks who told Sid about it for cash, nice folks who didn't tell the 'authorities' for fear of 'getting involved.' The results of the blood test Sid bribed the examining doctor into suppressing: the Big V with a snootful of maryjane, Benzedrine, liquor. His own doped-up statement in the ambulance: confessions to a dozen shakedowns. Conclusive proof: Jack V. snuffed two innocent citizens outside the Malibu Rendezvous.

'I got Lamar back to my car. I'll drive him to a hospital.'

Jack turned around. 'This is too good to be true. Patchett's got carbons, right?'

That smile again. 'Yes, for his deal with Hudgens. Sid gave him carbons of every file except the files he kept on Pierce himself. Pierce wanted the carbons as his insurance policy. I'm sure he didn't trust Sid, and since we have all of Hudgens' files right here, I'm sure Pierce's files are in there.'

'Yeah, and you have a carbon on mine.'

'Yes, Mr. Vincennes. We do.'

Jack tried to ape that smile. 'Everything I know about you, Patchett, his rackets and Sid Hudgens is going into a deposition, *multiple* copies to *multiple* safe-deposit boxes. If anything happens to me or mine, they go to the LAPD, the D.A.'s Office and the L.A. *Mirror*.'

'Stalemate, then. Do you want to light the match?'

Jack bowed. Lynn doused the files, torched them. Paper sizzled, fireballed – Jack stared until his eyes stung.

'Go home and sleep, Sergeant. You look terrible.'

Not home – Karen's.

He drove there woozy, keyed up. He started to feel the close-out: bad debts settled bad, a clean slate. He got the idea just like he got the idea to shake down Claude Dineen. He didn't say the words, didn't rehearse it. He turned the radio on so he'd keep the notion fresh.

A stern-voiced announcer:

' . . . and the southside of Los Angeles is now the focus of the largest manhunt in California history. We repeat, an hour and a half ago, just after dawn, Raymond Coates, Tyrone Jones and Leroy Fontaine, the accused killers in the Nite Owl massacre case, escaped from the Hall of Justice Jail in downtown Los Angeles. The three had been moved to a minimum security cellblock to await requestioning and made their escape by the means of knotted-together bedsheets and a jump out a second-story window. Here, recorded immediately after the escape, are the comments of Captain Russell Millard of the Los Angeles Police Department, co-supervisor of the Nite Owl investigation.

' "I . . . assume full responsibility for this incident. I was the one who ordered the three suspects sequestered in a minimum security unit. I . . . every effort will be made to recapture them with all due speed. I . . . " '

Jack turned the radio off. Close-out: pious Russ Millard's career. Call-out: figure the whole Bureau yanked from bed for the dragnet. He yawned the rest of the way to Karen's, rang her bell seeing double.

Karen opened up. 'Sweetie, *where have you been?*'

Jack plucked curlers out of her hair. 'Will you marry me?'

Karen said, 'Yes.'

Chapter Thirty-nine

Ed, staked out at 1st and Olive. His father's shotgun for
backup, a replay on his hunch.

Sugar Ray Coates: 'Roland Navarette, lives on Bunker
Hill. Runs a hole-up for parole absconders.'

A whispered snitch: the speakers didn't catch it, doubtful Coates remembered he said it. R&I, Navarette's mugshot, address: a rooming house midway down Olive, half
a mile from the Hall of Justice Jail. A dawn breakout –
they couldn't make Darktown unseen. Figure all four of
them armed.

Scared – like Guadalcanal '43.

Outlaw – he didn't report the lead.

Ed drove to mid-block. A clapboard Victorian: four
stories, peeling paint. He jumped the steps, checked out
the mail slots: R. Navarette, 408.

Inside, his suitcoat around the shotgun. A long hallway,
glass-fronted elevator, stairs. Up those stairs – he couldn't
feel his footsteps. The fourth-floor landing – nobody in
sight. Down to 408, drop the suitcoat. Inez screaming
primed him – he kicked the door in.

Four men eating sandwiches.

Jones and Navarette at a table. Fontaine on the floor.
Sugar Coates by the window, picking his teeth.

No weapons in sight. Nobody moved.

Odd sounds – 'You're under arrest' strangling out.
Jones put his hands up. Navarette raised his hands. Fon-
taine laced his hands behind his head. Sugar Ray said,
'Cat got your goddamn tongue, sissy?'

Ed jerked the trigger: once, twice – buckshot took off
Coates' legs. Recoil – Ed braced against the doorway,
aimed. Fontaine and Navarette stood up screaming; Ed
SQUEEZED the trigger, blew them up in one spread.
Recoil, a bad pull: half the back wall came down.

Blood spray thick – Ed stumbled, wiped his eyes. He saw Jones make the elevator.

He ran after him: slid, tripped, caught up. Jones was pushing buttons, screaming prayers – inches from the glass, 'Please Jesus.' Ed aimed point-blank, squeezed twice. Glass and buckshot took his head off.

Strong legs now, fuck civilian screams all around him.

Ed ran downstairs, into a crowd: blues, plainclothesmen. Hands pounded his back; men shouted his name. A voice close by: 'Millard's dead. Heart attack at the Bureau.'

Chapter Forty

Rain for the funeral. A graveside service: Dudley Smith's eulogy, a priest's last words.

Every Bureau man attended: Thad Green's orders. Parker called out the press: a little ceremony after they planted Russ Millard. Bud watched Ed Exley comfort the widow – his best profile to the cameras.

A week of cameras, headlines: Ed Exley, 'L.A.'s Greatest Hero' – World War II stalwart, the man who slayed the Nite Owl slayers and their accomplice. Ellis Loew told the press the three confessed before they escaped – nobody mentioned the niggers were unarmed. Ed Exley was made.

The priest's spiel picked up steam. The widow started weeping – Exley put an arm around her shoulders. Bud walked away.

Lightning, more rain – Bud ducked into the chapel. Parker's soiree was set up: lectern, chairs, a table laid out with sandwiches. More lightning – Bud looked out the window, saw the casket hit the dirt. Ashes to fucking ashes – Stens got six months, scuttlebutt had Exley and Inez a hot item: kill four jigs, get the girl.

The mourners headed up – Ellis Loew slipped, took a pratfall. Bud hit on the good stuff: Lynn, West Valley on the Kathy snuff. Let the bad shit go for now.

Into the chapel: raincoats and umbrellas dumped, a rush for seats. Parker and Exley stood by the lectern. Bud sprawled in a chair at the back.

Reporters, notepads. Front row seats: Loew, the widow Millard, Preston Exley – hot news for Dream-a-Dreamland.

Parker spoke into the mike. 'This is a sad occasion, an occasion of mourning. We mourn a kind and good man and a dedicated policeman. We mark his passing with

247

regret. The loss of Captain Russell A. Millard is the loss of Mrs. Millard, the Millard family and all of us here. It will be a hard loss to bear, but bear it we will. There is a passage I recall from somewhere in the annals of literature. That passage is "If there was no God, how could I be a Captain?" It is God who will see us through our grief and our loss. The God who allowed Russ Millard to become a captain, His captain.'

Parker pulled out a small velvet case. 'And life continues through our losses. The loss of one splendid policeman coincides with the emergence of another one. Edmund J. Exley, detective sergeant, has amassed a brilliant record in his ten years with the Los Angeles Police Department, three of those years given over to service in the United States Army. Ed Exley received the Distinguished Service Cross for gallantry in the Pacific Theater, and last week he evinced spectacular bravery in the line of duty. It is my honor to present him with the highest measure of honor this Police Department can bestow: our Medal of Valor.'

Exley stepped forward. Parker opened the case, took out a gold medallion hung from a blue satin ribbon and placed it around his neck. The men shook hands – Exley had tears in his eyes. Flashbulbs popped, reporters scribbled, no applause. Parker tapped the mike.

'The Medal of Valor is a very high expression of esteem, but not one with practical everyday applications. Spiritual ramifications aside, it does not reward the recipient with the challenge of good, hard police work. Today I am going to utilize a rarely used chief's prerogative and reward Ed Exley with *work*. I am promoting him two entire ranks, to captain, and assigning him as the Los Angeles Police Department's floating divisional commander, the assignment formerly held by our much loved colleague Russ Millard.'

Preston Exley stood up. Civilians stood up; the Bureau men stood on cue – Thad Green flashed them two thumbs. Scattered applause, lackluster. Ed Exley stood ramrod straight; Bud stayed sprawled in his chair. He took out his gun, kissed it, blew pretend smoke off the barrel.

Chapter Forty-one

A gala lawn wedding, a Presbyterian service – old man Morrow called the shots and picked up the tab. June 19, 1953: the Big V ties the knot.

Miller Stanton best man; Joanie Morrow – swacked on champagne punch – matron of honor. Dudley Smith the hit of the reception – stories, Gaelic songs. Parker and Green came at Ellis Loew's request; boy captain Ed Exley showed up. The Morrows' social circle pals rounded out the guest list – and swelled old Welton's huge backyard to bursting.

Marriage vows for his close-out. Bad debts settled good: new calendar days, his 'insurance policy deposition' stashed in fourteen different bank vaults. Scary vows: he pumped himself up at the altar.

Parker buried the Hudgens killing. Bracken and Patchett stalemated. Dudley called off his tail on White, bought his phony reports: no Lynn, White prowling bars at night. He staked Lynn's place for a couple of days, it looked like she had a good thing going with Bud – who always was a sucker.

Like himself.

The minister said the words; they said the words; Jack kissed his bride. Hugs, backslaps – well wishers swept them away from each other. Parker drummed up some warmth; Ed Exley worked the crowd, no sign of his Mexican girl. Nicknames now: 'Shotgun Ed,' 'Triggerman Eddie.' 'L.A.'s Greatest Hero' smiles on a bagman cop marrying up.

Jack found a spot above the pool house – a little rise with a view. Two celebrants stuck out: Karen, Exley. Give him credit: he seized the opportunity, made the Department look bold. *He* wouldn't have had the stomach for it – or the rage.

Exley. White. Himself.

Jack counted secrets: his own, whatever lived at that edge where pornography touched a dead scandal monger and lightly brushed the Nite Owl Massacre. He thought of Bud White, Ed Exley. He set up a wedding day prayer: the Nite Owl dead and buried, safe passage for ruthless men in love.

CALENDAR

1954

EXTRACT: L.A. *Herald-Express*, June 16:

EX-POLICEMAN ARRESTED FOR MURDEROUS ROBBERY SPREE

Richard Alex Stensland, 40, former Los Angeles police detective and a defendant in the 1951 'Bloody Christmas' police scandal, was arrested early this morning and charged with six counts of armed robbery and two counts of first-degree murder. Arrested with him at his hideout in Pacoima were Dennis 'The Weasel' Burns, 43, and Lester John Miciak, 37. The other men were charged with four armed-robbery counts and two counts of first-degree murder.

The arrest raid was led by Captain Edmund J. Exley, divisional floating commander for the Los Angeles Police Department, currently assigned to head up the LAPD's Robbery Division. Assisting Captain Exley were Sergeants Duane Fisk and Donald Kleckner. Exley, whose testimony in the Bloody Christmas scandal sent Stensland to jail in 1952, told reporters: 'Eyewitnesses identified photographs of the three men. We have conclusive proof that these men are responsible for stickups at six central Los Angeles liquor stores, including the robbery of Sol's Liquors in the Silverlake District on

June 9. The proprietor of that store and his son were shot and killed during that robbery and eyewitnesses place both Stensland and Burns at the scene. Intensive questioning of the suspects will begin soon, and we expect to clear up many other unsolved robberies.'

Stensland, Burns and Miciak offered no resistance during their arrest. They were taken to the Hall of Justice Jail, where Stensland was restrained from attacking Captain Exley.

BANNER: L.A. *Mirror-News*, June 21:

STENSLAND CONFESSES, DESCRIBES REIGN OF ROBBERY TERROR

BANNER: L.A. *Herald-Express*, September 23:

LIQUOR STORE KILLERS CONVICTED; DEATH PENALTY FOR EX-POLICEMAN

EXTRACT: L.A. *Times*, November 11:

STENSLAND DIES FOR LIQUOR STORE KILLINGS – GUNMAN FORMER POLICEMAN

At 10:03 yesterday morning, Richard Stensland, 41 and a former Los Angeles police officer, died in the gas chamber at San Quentin Prison for the June 9 murders of Solomon and David Abramowitz. The killings took place during a liquor store holdup. Stensland was convicted and sentenced on September 22 and refused to appeal his sentence.

The execution went off smoothly, although Stensland appeared inebriated. Present among the press and prison officials were two LAPD detectives: Captain Edmund J. Exley, the man responsible for Stensland's capture, and Officer Wendell White, the condemned killer's former partner. Officer White visited Stensland in his death row cell on execution eve and stayed through the night with him. Assistant Warden B. D. Terwilliger denied that Officer White supplied Stensland with intoxicating liquor and denied that White viewed the execution while drunk himself. Stensland verbally abused the prison chaplain who was present and his last words were obscenities directed at Captain Exley.

1955

Hush-Hush Magazine, May 1955 Issue:

WHO KILLED SID HUDGENS?

Justice in the City of the Fallen Angels reminds us of a line from that sin-sational sepia show *Porgy and Bess*. Like 'a man,' it's 'a sometime thing.' As in for instance: if you're a well-connected contributor to demon D.A. Ellis Loew's slush fund and you get murdered – killer beware!!! – L.A. Chief of Police William H. Parker will spare no expense unearthing the fiend who put you on the night train to the Big Adiós. But if you're a crusading journalist writing for this magazine and you get chopped into Ken-L ration in your own living room – killer rejoice!!! – Chief Parker and his moralistic, misanthropic, mindless mongolians will sit on their hands (well worn from palming payoffs) and whistle 'justice is a sometime thing' while the killer whistles Dixie.

It has now been two years since Sid Hudgens was fatally slashed in his Chapman Park living room. Two years ago the LAPD had its (sticky, graft-ridden) hands full with the infamous Nite Owl murder case, which was resolved when one of their members took the law into his own (overweeningly ambitious, opportunistic) hands and shotgunned the shotgunners to the Big Au Revoir. Sid Hudgens' murder was assigned to two flunky detectives with a total of zero 'made' homicide cases between them. They, of course, did not find the killer or killers, spent most of their days here at the *Hush-Hush* office reading back issues for clues, scarfing coffee and doughnuts and ogling the comely editorial assistants who flock to *Hush-Hush* because we know where the bodies are buried . . .

We at *Hush-Hush* tap the inside pulse of the City of the Fallen Angels, and we *have* investigated the Sidster's death on our own. We have gotten nowhere, and we ask the Los Angeles Police Department the following questions:

Sid's pad was ransacked. What happened to the ultra on the QT, ultra secret and ultra *Hush-Hush* files the Sidster was supposed to be keeping – sinuendo even too scalding for us to publish?

Why didn't D.A. Ellis Loew, elected largely on the strength of a *Hush-Hush* article exposing the peccadillos of his incumbent opponent, give us a backscratch in return and use his legal juice to force the LAPD to track down the Sidster's slayer?

Celebrity cop John 'Jack' Vincennes, the famous dope scourge 'Big V,' was a close friend of Sid's and was responsible for many of his crusading exposés on the menace of narcotics. Why didn't Jack (heavily connected to Ellis Loew – *we* won't utter the word 'bagman,' but feel free to *think* it) investigate the killing on his own, out of palship for his beloved buddy the Sidster?

Unanswerable questions for now – unless *you*, the reading public, take up the cry. Look for updates in future issues – and remember, dear reader, you heard it first here: off the record, on the QT and *very Hush-Hush.*

Hush-Hush Magazine, December 1955 issue:

JUSTICE WATCH: BEWARE THE LOEW/VINCENNES COMBINE!!!!

We've pussyfooted long enough, dear reader. In our May issue we marked the second anniversary of the fiendish murder of ace *Hush-Hush* scribe Sid Hudgens. We lamented the fact that his killing remains unsolved, gently prodded the Los Angeles Police Department, D.A. Ellis Loew and his brother-in-law by marriage LAPD Sergeant Jack Vincennes to do something about it, asked a few pertinent questions and got no response. Seven months have passed without justice being done, so here's some more questions:

Where *are* Sid Hudgens' *ultra* sin-tillating and sin-sational secret files – the files too hot for even scalding *Hush-Hush* to handle?

Did D.A. Loew quash the Hudgens murder investigation because the crusading Sidster recently published an exposé on *Badge of Honor* producer/director Max Peltz and his bent for teenage girls, and Peltz was a (five figure!!!) contributor to Loew's 1953 D.A.'s campaign fund?

Has Loew ignored our pleas for justice because he's too busy gearing up for his spring 1957 reelection campaign? Is Jack 'We won't use the word "Bagman" ' Vincennes again shaking down Hollywoodites for contributions for brother-in-law Ellis and thus unable to investigate the Sidster's death?

More on the Big-time Big V:

Is Vincennes, dope-buster supreme, on the sauce and feuding with his much younger rich-girl wife, who persuaded him to leave his beloved Narco Division, but now frets over his working the hazardous LAPD Surveillance Detail????

Fuel for thought, dear reader – and a gentle prodding for belated justice. The search for justice for Sid Hudgens continues. Remember, dear reader: you heard it first here, off the record, on the QT and *very Hush-Hush*.

1956

GANGLAND DROUGHT AS COHEN PAROLE APPROACHES: WILL FEAST FOLLOW FAMINE WITH THE MICKSTER REDUX?

You, dear reader, probably haven't noticed, since you're a law-abiding citizen who relies on *Hush-Hush* to keep you abreast of the dark and sin-sational side of life. This publication has been accused of being sin-ical, but we're also sin-cere in our desire to inform you of the perils of crime, organized and otherwise, which is why this periodical periodically offers a 'Crimewatch' feature. This month we offer a palpably percolating potpourri centering on malicious L.A. mob activity or the lack of it, our focus the currently incarcerated Meyer Harris Cohen, 43, also known as the misanthropic Mickster, the inimitable Mickey C.

The Mick has been reposing at McNeil Island Federal pen since November of 1951, and he should be paroled sometime next year, certainly by the end of 1957. You all know Mickey by reputation: he's the dapper little gent who ruled the L.A. rackets circa '45 to '51, until Uncle Sammy popped him for income tax evasion. He's a headline grabber, he's a big mocher, face it: he's a mensch. And he's up at McNeil, freezing his toches in the admittedly plush cell, his pet bulldog Mickey Cohen, Jr., keeping his tootsies warm, his money man Davey Goldman, also convicted of tax beefs, warming a cell down the hall. L.A. gangland activity has been – enjoying? *enduring?* – a strange lull since Mickey packed his PJs for Puget Sound, and we at *Hush-Hush*, privy to many unnamable insider sources, have a theory as to what's been shaking. Listen close, dear reader: this is off the record, on the QT and *very Hush-Hush.*

November '51: adiós Mickey, pack a toothbrush

and don't forget to write. Before catching the McNeil Island Express, the Mickster informs his number two man, Morris Jahelka, that he (Mo) will remain titular boss of Kingdom Cohen, which Mickey has 'long-term loan' divested to various legit, non-criminal businessmen that he trusts, to be quietly run by out-of-town muscle on a drastically scaled-down basis. Mickey may come off like a vicious buffoon, but Mrs. Cohen's little boy has a head on his simian shoulders.

Are you on our wavelength so far, dear reader? Yes? Good, now listen even more closely.

Mickey languishes in his cell, living the prison life of Riley, and time goes by. The Mick gets percentage fees from his 'franchise holders,' funneled straight to Swiss bank accounts, and when he's paroled he'll get 'give-back fees' and have Kingdom Cohen returned to him on a platter. He'll rebuild his evil empire and happy days will be here again.

Such is the power of the ubiquitous Mickey C. that for several years no upstart gangsters try to crash his lulled-down, on-siesta rackets. Jack 'The Enforcer' Whalen, however, a well-known thug/gambler, some-how knows of Mickey's plan to let sleeping dogs snooze while he's stuck in stir and the police are gratefully twiddling their thumbs with no mobster nests to swat. Whalen does not attack the diminutized Kingdom Cohen – he simply builds up a rival, strictly bookmaking kingdom with no fear of reprisals.

Meanwhile, what has happened to some of the Mickster's chief goons? Well, nebbish-like Mo Jah-elka keeps triplicate sets of books for the franchise holders, whiz at figures that he is, and Davey Gold-man, stuck in stir with his boss, walks Mickey Cohen, Jr., around the McNeil Island yard. Abe Teitlebaum, Cohen muscle goon, owns a delicatessen that features greasy sandwiches named after Borscht Belt com-edians, and Lee Vachss, Mr. Ice Pick To The Ear, sells patent medicine. *Our* favorite Mickey misan-thrope, Johnny Stompanato (sometimes known as

257

'Oscar' because of his Academy Award-size append-age), nurses a long-term case of the hots for Lana Turner, and may have returned to his old pre-Cohen ways: running blackmail/extortion rackets. Assuming that Whalen and Mickey don't collide upon the Mick's release, things look hunky-dory and copa-cetic, don't they? Gangland amity all around?

Perhaps *no*.

Item: in August of 1954 John Fisher Diskant, an alleged Cohen franchise holder, was gunned down outside a motel in Culver City. No suspects, no arrests, current disposition: the case reposes in the open file of the Culver City P.D.

Item: May 1955: two alleged Cohen prostitution bosses, franchise holders both – Nathan Janklow and George Palevsky – are gunned down outside the Torch Song Tavern in Riverside. No suspects, no arrests, current disposition: the Riverside County sheriff says case closed due to lack of evidence.

Item: July 1956: Walker Ted Turow, known drug peddler who had recently stated his desire to 'push white horse very large and become a bonaroo racket-eer' is found shot to death at his pad in San Pedro. You guessed it: no clues, no suspects, no arrests, current disposition with the LAPD's Harbor Div-ision: open file, we're not holding our breath.

Now, dig it, children: all four of these gang-con-nected or would be gang-connected chumps were shot dead by three-man trigger gangs. The cases were barely investigated because the respective investigat-ing agencies considered the victims lowlifes whose deaths did not merit justice. We wish we could say that ballistics reports indicate that the same guns were used for all three shootings, but they weren't – although .30-30 ripples pistols were the killers' M.O. all three times. And we at *Hush-Hush* know that no interagency effort has been launched to catch the killers. In fact, we at *Hush-Hush* are the first even to connect the crimes in theory. Tsk, tsk. We *do* know that Jack Whalen and his chief factotums are alibied up tight as a crab's pincer for the times of the killings and that Mickey C. and Davey G. have been questioned and have no idea who the bad boys are. Intriguing, right, dear reader? So far, no overt moves have been made to take over siesta time Kingdom Cohen, but we have word that Mickey minion Morris Jahelka has packed up and moved to Florida, scared witless . . .

And the Mickster is soon to be paroled. What will happen then??????

Remember, dear reader, you saw it here first. Off the record, on the QT and *very Hush-Hush*.

1957

CONFIDENTIAL LAPD REPORT: compiled by
Internal Affairs Division, dated 2/10/57.
Investigating officer: Sgt. D. W. Fisk, Badge 6129,
IAD. Submitted at the request of Deputy Chief
Thad Green, Chief of Detectives.
Subject: White, Wendell A., Homicide Division

Sir:

When you initiated this investigation you stated that Officer White passing the sergeant's exam with high marks after two failing attempts and nine years in the Bureau startled you, especially in the light of Lt. Dudley Smith's recent promotion to captain. I have thoroughly investigated Officer White and have come up with many contradictory items which should interest you. Since you already have access to Officer White's arrest record and personnel sheet, I will concentrate solely on those items.

1. White, who is unmarried and without immediate family, has been intimately involved on a sporadic basis with one Lynn Margaret Bracken, age 33, for the past several years. This woman, the owner of Veronica's Dress Shop in Santa Monica, is rumored

(unsubstantiated by police records) to be an ex-prostitute.

2. White, who was brought into Homicide by Lt. Smith in 1952, has, of course, not turned into the superior case man that (now) Capt. Smith assumed he would be. His 1952–53 work under Lt. Smith with the Surveillance Detail was, of course, legendary, and resulted in White's killing two men in the line of duty. Since his (April 1953) shooting of Nite Owl case collateral suspect Sylvester Fitch, White has served under Lt./Capt. Smith with little formal distinction. However (rather amazingly), there have been no excessive force complaints filed against him (see White's personnel sheets 1948–51 for records of his previous dismissed complaints). It is known that during those years and up until the spring of 1953 White visited paroled wife beaters and verbally and/or physically abused them. Evidence points to the fact that these illegal forays have not recurred for almost four years. White remains volatile (as you know, he received a departmental reprimand for punching out windows in the Homicide pen when he received word that his former partner, Sgt. R. A. Stensland, had been sentenced to death), but it is known that he has sometimes avoided work with Lt./Capt. Smith's Mobster Squad, straining his relationship with Smith, his Bureau mentor. Citing the violent nature of the assignment, White has been quoted as saying, 'I've got no more stomach left for that stuff.' Interesting, when given White's reputation and past record.

3. In spring 1956, White took nine months' accumulated sick leave and vacation time when Capt. E. J. Exley rotated in as acting commander of Homicide. (A well-known hatred exists between White and Capt. Exley, deriving from the 1951 Christmas brutality affair.) During his time off from duty, White (whose Academy scores indicate only average intelligence and below average literacy) attended criminology and forensics classes at USC and took and

passed (at his own expense) the FBI's 'Criminal Investigation Procedures' seminar at Quantico, Virginia. White had failed the sergeant's exam twice before embarking on these studies, and on his third attempt passed with a score of 89. His sergeantcy should come in before the end of the 1957 calendar year.

4. In November 1954, R. A. Stensland was executed at San Quentin. White asked for and received permission to attend the execution. He spent the night before the execution on death row drinking with Stensland. (I was told the assistant warden overlooked this infraction of prison rules out of a regard for Stensland's ex-policeman status.) Capt. Exley also attended the execution, and it is not known if he and White had words before or after the event.

5. I saved the most interesting item for last. It is interesting in that it illustrates White's continued (and perhaps increasing) tendency to overinvolve himself in matters pertaining to abused and (now) murdered women. I.e., White has shown undue curiosity in a number of unsolved prostitute killings that he believes to be connected: murders that have taken place in California and various parts of the West over the past several years. The victim's names, DODs and locations of death are:

Jane Mildred Hamsher, 3/08/51, San Diego
Kathy NMI Janeway, 4/19/53, Los Angeles
Sharon Susan Palwick, 8/29/53, Bakersfield, Calif.
Sally NMI DeWayne, 11/02/55, Needles, Ariz.
Chrissie Virginia Renfro, 7/16/56, San Francisco

White has told other Homicide officers that he thinks evidential similarities point to one killer, and he has traveled (at his own expense) to the above-listed cities where the crimes occurred. Naturally, the detectives that White has talked to considered him a pest and were reluctant to share information with him, and it is not known whether he has made progress toward solving any of the above cases. Lt. J. S. DiCenzo, Commander of the West Valley Station squad, stated that he thinks White's hooker-killing fixation dates back to the time of the Nite Owl case, when White became personally concerned about the murder of a young prostitute (Kathy Janeway) he was acquainted with.

6. All in all, a surprising investigation. Personally, I admire White's initiative and persistence in pursuing a sergeantcy and his (albeit untoward) tenacity in the matter of the prostitute homicides. A list of my interview references will follow in a separate memo.

Respectfully,
Sgt. D. W. Fisk, 6129, IAD

CONFIDENTIAL LAPD REPORT: Compiled by Internal Affairs Division, dated 3/11/57. Investigating officer: Sgt. Donald Kleckner, Badge 688, IAD. Submitted at the request of William H. Parker, Chief of Police
Subject: Vincennes, John, Sergeant, Surveillance Detail.

Sir:
You stated that you wished to explore, in light of Sgt. Vincennes' deteriorating duty performance, the advisability of offering him early retirement by stress pension before the twentieth anniversary of his LAPD appointment comes up in May 1958. I deem that measure inappropriate at this time. Granted, Vincennes is an obvious alcoholic; granted also, his alcoholism cost him his job with *Badge of Honor* and thus cost the LAPD a small fortune in promotional considerations. Granted again, at 42 he is too old to be working a high-risk assignment such as the Surveillance Detail. As for his admittedly deteriorating performance, it is only deteriorating because Vincennes was, during his Narcotics Division heyday, a

bold and inspired policeman. From my interviews I
have concluded that he does not drink on duty and
that his deteriorating performance can best be
summed up by 'sluggishness' and 'bad reflexes.'
Moreover, should Vincennes reject an early retirement offer, my guess is that the pension board would
back him up.

Sir, I know that you consider Vincennes a disgrace
as a policeman. I agree with you, but advise you to
consider his connection to District Attorney Loew.
The Department needs Loew to prosecute our cases,
as your new chief aide, Capt. Smith, will tell you.
Vincennes continues to solicit funds and run errands
for Loew, and should Loew, as expected, be reelected
next week, he would most likely intercede if you
decided to pressure Vincennes out of the Department. My recommendation is as follows: keep Vincennes on Surveillance until 3/58, when a new commander is scheduled to rotate in with his own
replacement officers, then assign him to menial duties
in a patrol division until his 5/15/58 retirement date
arrives. At that time, Vincennes, humbled by a return
to uniformed duty, could probably be persuaded to
separate from the Department with all due speed.

Respectfully,
Donald J. Kleckner, IAD

BANNER: L.A. *Times*, March 15:

LOEW REELECTED IN LANDSLIDE; STATEHOUSE BID NEXT?

EXTRACT: L.A. *Times*, July 8:

MICKEY COHEN WOUNDED IN PRISON YARD ATTACK

McNeil Island Federal Prison officials announced

that yesterday mobsters Meyer Harris 'Mickey' Cohen and David 'Davey' Goldman were wounded in a vicious daylight attack.

Cohen and Goldman, both slated to be paroled in September, were watching a softball game on the prison yard when three hooded assailants wielding pipes and handmade 'shivs' descended. Goldman was stabbed twice in the shoulder and beaten viciously about the head, and Cohen escaped with superficial puncture wounds. Prison doctors said that Goldman's injuries are severe and that he may have suffered irreparable brain damage. The assailants escaped, and at this moment a massive investigation is being conducted to discover who they are. McNeil administrator R. J. Wolf said, 'We believe this was a so-called death contract, contracted to in-prison inmates by outside sources. Every effort will be made to get to the bottom of this incident.'

Hush-Hush Magazine, October 1957 issue:

MICKEY COHEN BACK IN L.A.!!! ARE HIS BAD OLD GOOD TIMES HERE TO STAY???

He was the most colorful mobster the City of Fallen Angels had ever seen, Hepcat – and to dig his act at the Mocambo or the Troc was like watching Daddy-o Stradivarius chop a fiddle from a tree trunk. He'd crack jokes written by gagster Davey Goldman, slip fat envelopes to the bagmen from the Sheriff's Department and do a wicked Lindy hop with his squeeze Audrey Anders or the other comely quail sashaying on the premises. Eyes would dart to his table and the ladies would surreptitiously survey his chief bodyguard, Johnny Stompanato, and wonder, 'Is he really *that* large?' Sycophants, stooges, glad-handers, pissanters and general rimbamboos would drop by the Mickster's side, to be rewarded with jokes, a backslap, a handout. The Mick was a soft touch for crippled kids, stray dogs, the Salvation Army and the United Jewish Appeal. The Mick also ran bookmaking, loansharking, gambling, prostitution and dope rackets and killed an average of a dozen people a year. Nobody's perfect, right, Hepcat? You leave your toenail trimmings on the bathroom floor, Mickey sends people on the night train to Slice City.

Dig it, Hepcat: people also tried to kill Mickey!!! A mensch like that? – No!!!! Yes, Hepcat, what goes around comes around. The trouble was, the Mick had more lives than the proverbial feline, kept dodging bombs, bullets and dynamite while those around him went down dead, survived six years at McNeil Island Pen, including a recent shiv/pipe attack – and now he's back! Sy Devore, watch out: the Mickster will be in for a few dozen shiny new sharkskin suits; Trocadero and Mocambo cigarette girls, get ready for some C-note tips. Mickey and his entourage will soon descend on the Sunset Strip, and – *very Hush-Hush* – yes, ladies, Johnny Stompanato is *that* large, but he only has eyes for Lana Turner, and word is that he and Lana have been playing more than footsie lately . . .

But back to Mickey C. Avid *Hush-Hush* readers will recall our October '56 Crimewatch feature, where we speculated on the gangland 'lull' that has been going on since the Mick went to stir. Well, some *still* unsolved deaths occurred, and that pipe/shiv attack that wounded Mickey and left his stooge Davey Goldman a vegetable? Well . . . they never got the hooded inmate assailants who attempted to send Mickey and his man to Slice City . . .

Call this a warning, children: he's a mensch, he's local color to the nth degree, he's the marvelous, malevolent benevolent Mickster. He's tough to kill, 'cause innocent bystanders take the hot lead with his name on it. Mickey's back, and his old gang might be forming up again. Hepcat, when you club hop on the sin-tillating Sunset Strip, bring a bulletproof vest in case Meyer Harris Cohen sits nearby.

EXTRACT: L.A. *Herald-Express*, November 10:

MOBSTER COHEN SURVIVES BOMB ATTEMPT

A bomb exploded under the home of paroled mobster Mickey Cohen early this morning. Cohen and his wife, Lavonne, were not injured, but the bomb did destroy a wardrobe room that housed three hundred of Cohen's custom-made suits. Cohen's pet bulldog, asleep nearby, was treated for a singed tail at Westside Veterinary Hospital and released. Cohen could not be reached for comment.

Confidential letter, addendum to the outside agency investigation report required on all incoming commanders of Internal Affairs Division, Los Angeles Police Department, requested by Chief William H. Parker.

11/29/57

Dear Bill –
God, we were sergeants together! It seems like a million years ago, and you were right. I did relish the chance to slip briefly back into harness and play detective again. I felt slightly treacherous interviewing officers behind Ed and Preston's back, but again you were right: firstly in your overall policy of outside agency validation for incoming I.A. chiefs, and secondly in choosing an ex-policeman predisposed to like Ed Exley to query brother officers on the man. Hell, Bill, we both love Ed. Which makes me happy to state that, basic investigation aside (the D.A.'s Bureau is conducting it, aren't they?), I have nothing but positives to report.

I spoke to a number of Detective Bureau men and a number of uniformed officers. One consensus of opinion held: Ed Exley is very well respected. Some officers considered his shooting of the Nite Owl suspects injudicious, most considered it bold and a few tagged it as intentionally grandstanding. Whatever, my opinion is that that act is what Ed Exley is most remembered for and that it has largely eclipsed the bad feelings he generated by serving as an informant in the Bloody Christmas matter. Ed's jump from sergeant to captain was greatly resented, but he is considered to have proven his mettle as divisional floater: the man has run seven divisions in under five years, established many valuable contacts and has earned the general respect of the men serving under him. Your basic concern: that his 'not one of the boys' nature would provoke anger when it was learned that he would be running I.A., seems so far to be unfounded. Word is out that Ed will take over I.A. early in '58, and it is tacitly assumed that he will vigorously pursue the assignment. My guess is that his reputation for sternness and intelligence will deter many potentially bent cops into sticking to the straight and narrow.

It is also known that Ed has passed the exam for promotion to inspector and is first on the promotion list. Here some notes of discord appear. It is generally viewed that Thad Green will retire in the next several years and that Ed might well be chosen to replace him as chief of detectives. The great majority of the men I spoke to voiced the opinion that Capt. Dudley Smith, older, much more experienced and more the leader type, should have the job.

Some personal observations to supplant your outside agency report. (1) Ed's relationship with Inez Soto is physically intimate, but I know he would never violate departmental regs by cohabiting with her. Inez is a great kid, by the way. She's become good friends with Preston, Ray Dieterling and

267

myself, and her public relations work for Dream-a-Dreamland is near brilliant. And so what if she's a Mexican? (2) I spoke to I.A. Sgts. Fisk and Kleckner about Ed – the two worked Robbery under him, are junior straight-arrow Exley types and are positively ecstatic that their hero is about to become their C.O. (3) As someone who has known Ed Exley since he was a child, and as an ex-police officer, I'll go on the record: he's as good as his father and I'd be willing to bet that if you made a tally you'd see that he's made more major cases than any LAPD detective ever. I'm also willing to bet that he's wise to this affectionate little ploy you've initiated: all good cops have intelligence networks.

I'll close with a favor. I'm thinking of writing a book of reminiscences about my years with the Department. Would it be possible for me to borrow the file on the Loren Atherton case? Without Preston and Ed knowing, please – I don't want them to think I've gone arty-farty in my waning years.

I hope this little addendum serves you well. Best to Helen, and thanks for the opportunity to be a cop again.

Sincerely,
Art De Spain

LAPD TRANSFER BULLETINS

1. Officer Wendell A. White, Homicide Division to the Hollywood Station Detective Squad (and to assume the rank of Sergeant), effective 1/2/58.

2. Sgt. John Vincennes, Surveillance Detail to Wilshire Division Patrol, effective when a replacement officer is assigned, but no later than 3/15/58.

3. Capt. Edmund J. Exley to permanent duty station: Commander, Internal Affairs Division, effective 1/2/58.

Part Three

Internal Affairs

Chapter Forty-two

The Dining Car had a New Year's hangover: drooping crepe paper, '1958' signs losing spangles. Ed took his favorite booth: a view of the lounge, his image in a mirror. He marked the time – 3:24 P.M., 1/2/58. Let Bob Gallaudet show up late – anything to stretch the moment.

In an hour, the ceremony: Captain E. J. Exley assumes a permanent duty station – Commander, Internal Affairs Division. Gallaudet was bringing the results of his outside agency validation – the D.A.'s Bureau had gone over his personal life with a magnifying glass. He'd pass – his personal life was squeaky clean, putting the Nite Owl boys in the ground outgunned his Bloody Christmas snitching – he'd known it for years.

Ed sipped coffee, eyes on the mirror. His reflection: a man a month from thirty-six who looked forty-five. Blond hair gone gray; crease lines in his forehead. Inez said his eyes were getting smaller and colder; his wire rims made him look harsh. He'd told her harsh was better than soft – boy captains needed help. She'd laughed – it was a few years ago, when they were still laughing.

He placed the conversation: late '54, Inez analytical – 'You're a ghoul for watching that man Stensland die.' A year and a half post-Nite Owl; today made four years and nine months. A look in the mirror, a claim on those years – and what he'd had with Inez.

His killings pushed Bud White out: four deaths eclipsed one death. Those first months she was all his: he'd proven himself to her specifications. He bought her a house down the block; she loved their gentle sex; she accepted Ray Dieterling's job offer. Dieterling fell in love with Inez and her story: a beautiful rape victim abandoned by her family dovetailed with his own losses – once divorced, once widowered, his son Paul dead in an avalanche, his son Billy

271

a homosexual. Ray and Inez became father and daughter
– colleagues, deep friends. Preston Exley and Art De
Spain joined Dieterling in devotion – a circle of hardcase
men and a woman who made them grateful for the chance
to feel gentle.

Inez took friendships from a fantasy kingdom: the buil-
ders, the second generation – Billy Dieterling, Timmy
Valburn. A chatty little clique: they talked up Hollywood
gossip, poked fun at male foibles. The word 'men' sent
them into gales of laughter. They made fun of policemen
and played charades in a house bought by Captain Ed
Exley.

All claims came back to Inez.

After the killings, he had nightmares: were they innocent? Impotent rage made his finger jerk the trigger; the
dramatic resolution made the Department look so good
that little facts like 'Unarmed' and 'Not Dangerous' would
never surface to crush him. Inez stilled his fears with a
statement: the rapists drove her to Sylvester Fitch's house
in the middle of the night and left her there – giving them
time to take down the Nite Owl. She never told the police
about it because she did not want to recount the especially
ugly things that Fitch did to her. He was relieved: *guilty*
dead men shored up the justice in his rage.

Inez.

Time passed, the glow wore off – her pain and his
heroism couldn't sustain them. Inez knew he'd never
marry her: a high-ranking cop, a Mexican wife – career
suicide. His love held by threads; Inez grew remote – a
sometime lover in practice. Two people molded by extraordinary events, a powerful supporting cast hovering: the
Nite Owl dead, Bud White.

White's face in the green room: pure hatred while Dick
Stensland sucked gas. A look at Dicky Stens dying, a look
his way, no words necessary. Leave time called in so
they wouldn't have to work together when he took over
Homicide. He'd surpassed his brother, grown closer to
his father. His major case record was astounding; in May
he'd be an inspector, in a few years he'd compete with

Dudley Smith for chief of detectives. Smith had always given him a wide berth and a wary respect couched in contempt – and Dudley was the most feared man in the LAPD. Did he know that his rival feared only one thing: revenge perpetrated by a thug/cop without the brains to be imaginative?

The bar was filling up: D.A.'s personnel, a few women. The last time with Inez was bad – she just serviced the man who paid the mortgage. Ed smiled at a tall woman – she turned away.

'Congratulations, Cap. You're Boy Scout clean.'

Gallaudet sat down – strained, nervous.

'Then why do you look so grim? Come on, Bob, we're partners.'

'*You're* clean, but Inez was put under loose surveillance for two weeks, just routine. Ed . . . oh shit, she's sleeping with Bud White.'

The ceremony – one big blur.

Parker made a speech: policemen were subject to the same temptations as civilians, but needed to keep their baser urges in check to a greater degree in order to serve as moral exemplars for a society increasingly undercut by the pervasive influence of Communism, crime, liberalism and general moral turpitude. A morally upright exemplar was needed to command the division that served as a guarantor of police morality, and Captain Edmund J. Exley, war hero and hero of the Nite Owl murder case, was that man.

He made a speech himself: more pap on morality. Duane Fisk and Don Kleckner wished him luck; he read their minds through his blur: they wanted his chief assistant spots. Dudley Smith winked, easy to read: 'I will be our next chief of detectives – not you.' Excuses for leaving took forever – he made it to her place with the blur clearing hard.

6:00 – Inez got home around 7:00. Ed let himself in, waited with the lights out.

Time dragged; Ed watched his watch hands move. 6:50 – a key in the door.

'Exley, are you skulking? I saw your car outside.'

'No lights. I don't want to see your face.' Noises – keys rattling, a purse dropped to the floor. 'And I don't want to see all that faggot Dreamland junk you've plastered on the walls.'

'You mean the walls of the house you paid for?'

'You said it, not me.'

Sounds: Inez resting herself against the door. 'Who told you?'

'It doesn't matter.'

'Are you going to ruin him for it?'

'*Him?* No, there's no way I could do it without making myself look even more foolish than I've been. And you can say his name.'

No answer.

'Did you help him with the sergeant's exam? He didn't have the brains to pass it on his own.'

No answer.

'How long? How many fucks behind my back?'

No answer.

'How long, *puta*?'

Inez sighed. 'Maybe four years. On and off, when we each needed a friend.'

'You mean when you didn't need me?'

'I mean when I got exhausted being treated like a rape victim. When I got terrified of how far you'd go to impress me.'

Ed said, 'I took you out of Boyle Heights and gave you a life.'

Inez said, 'Exley, you started to scare me. I just wanted to be a girl seeing a guy, and Bud gave me that.'

'Don't you say his name in this house.'

'You mean in *your* house?'

'I gave you a decent life. You'd be pounding tortillas on a rock if it wasn't for me.'

'*Querido*, you turn ugly so well.'

'How many other lies, Inez? How many other lies besides him?'

'Exley, let's break this off.'

'No, give me a rundown.'

No answer.

'How many other men? How many other lies?'

No answer.

'Tell me.'

No answer.

'You fucking whore, after what I did for you. *Tell me*.'

No answer.

'I let you be friends with my father. *Preston Exley is your friend because of me*. How many other men have you fucked behind my back? How many other lies after what I did for you?'

Inez, a small voice. 'You don't want to know.'

'Yes I do, you fucking whore.'

Inez pushed off the door. 'Here's the only lie that counts, and it's all for you. Not even my sweetie pie Bud knows it, so I hope it makes you feel special.'

Ed stood up. 'Lies don't scare me.'

Inez laughed. '*Everything* scares you.'

No answer.

Inez, calm. 'The *negritos* who hurt me couldn't have killed the people at the Nite Owl, because they were with me the whole night. They never left my sight. I lied because I didn't want you to feel bad that you'd killed four men for me. And you want to know what the *big* lie is? You and your precious absolute justice.'

Ed pushed out the door, hands on his ears to kill the roar. Dark, cold outside – he saw Dick Stens strapped down dead.

Chapter Forty-three

Bud checked out his new badge: 'Sergeant' where 'Police-man' used to be. He put his feet up on his desk, said goodbye to Homicide.

His cubicle was a mess – five years' worth of paper. Dudley said the Hollywood squad transfer was just tem-porary – his sergeantcy shocked the brass, Thad Green was juking him for his window-punching number: Dick Stens green room bound, left/right hooks into glass. A fair trade: he never became a crackerjack case man because the only cases that mattered were case closed and case/cases shitcanned. Transfer blues: leaving Bureau HQ meant no early crack at dead-body reports – a good way to keep tabs on the Kathy Janeway case and the hooker snuff string he knew tied to it.

Stuff to take with him:

His new nameplate – 'Sergeant Wendell White,' a pic-ture of Lynn: brunette, goodbye Veronica Lake.

A Mobster Squad photo: him and Dud at the Victory Motel. Mobster Squad goodies – brass knuckles, a ball-bearing sap – he might leave them behind.

Lock and key stuff:

His FBI and forensics class diplomas; Dick Stensland's legacy: six grand from his robbery take. Dick's last words – a note a guard passed him.

Partner –

I regret the bad things I done. I especially regret the people I hurt when I was a policeman who just got in my way when I was feeling mean and the Christmas guys and the liquor store man and his son. It's too late to change it all. So all I can do is say I'm sorry, which don't mean anything worthwhile. I'll try to take my punishment like a man. I keep thinking

276

it could be you instead of me who did what I did, that it was just the luck of the draw and I know maybe you've thought the same thing. I wish being sorry counted for more with guys like you and me. I payed the piper and called the tune and all that, but Exley kept the piper tune going when he didn't have to and if I got a last request it is that you get him for his share and don't be stupid and do something dumb like I would have did. Use your brains and that money I told you where to find and give it to him good, a good one in the keester from Sergeant Dick Stens. Good luck, partner. I can't hardly believe that when you read this I'll be dead.

Dick

Double-locked in the bottom drawer:

His file on the Janeway/hooker snuffs, his private Nite Owl file – textbook pure, like he learned in school.

Two cases that proved he was a real detective; Dick's shot at Ed Exley. He pulled them out, read them over – college boy stuff all the way.

The Janeway string.

When things sizzled down with Lynn, he started looking for stuff to jazz him. Prowling for women didn't cut it – ditto his on-and-off thing with Inez. He flunked the sergeant's exam twice, paid his way through school with Dick's stash, worked the Mobster Squad part-time: meeting trains, planes, buses, taking would-be racketeers to the Victory Motel, beating the shit out of them and escorting them back to planes, trains, buses. Dud called it 'containment'; he called it too much to take and still like looking at yourself in the mirror. Good cases never came his way at Homicide: Thad Green bootjacked them, assigned different men. His classes taught him interesting stuff about forensics, criminal psychology and procedure – he decided to apply what he'd learned to an old case that still simmered with him: the Kathy Janeway job.

He read Joe DiCenzo's case file: no leads, no suspects, written off as a random sex kill. He read the autopsy reconstruction: Kathy beaten to death, face blows, a man with rings on both fists. B+ secretor semen in the mouth, rectum, vagina – three separate ejaculations, the bastard took his time. He got a flash backed up by case histories: a sex fiend like that doesn't kill just once, then go back to twiddling his thumbs.

He started paper-prowling – the kind of thing he used to hate.

No similar solveds or unsolveds anywhere in the LAPD and Sheriff's Department files – the search took him eight months. He worked his way through other police agencies – Stens' money for a stake. Zero for Orange County, San Bernardino County; four months in and a match with the San Diego PD: Jane Mildred Hamsher, 19, hooker, DOD 3/8/51, the same handwork and three-way rape: no clues, no suspects, case closed.

He read LAPD and SDPD M.O. files and got nowhere; he remembered Dudley warning him off the Janeway case – ragging him for going crazy on woman basher jobs. He went ahead anyway; pay dirt on a tri-state teletype: Sharon Susan Palwick, 20, hooker, DOD 8/29/53, Bakersfield, California. The same specs: no suspects, no leads, case closed. Dud never mentioned the teletype – if he knew it existed.

He went to Diego and Bakerfield – read files, pestered detectives who worked the cases. They were bored with the jobs – and gave him the brush. He tried reconstructing the time and place element: who was in those cities on the dates of the killings. He checked old train, bus and airplane records, got no crossover names, put out standing tri-state teletypes requesting information on the killer's M.O., asking for call-ins should his killer ply that M.O. again. Nothing came in on the info request; three dead-body reports trickled in over the years: Sally NMI DeWayne, 17, hooker, Needles, Arizona, 11/2/55; Chrissie Virginia Renfro, 21, hooker, San Francisco, 7/14/56; Maria NMI Waldo, 20, hooker, Seattle two months ago: 11/28/57. The call-ins logged in late, the same results: goose egg. Every angle, every schoolboy approach tapped

278

– for nothing. Kathy Janeway and five other prostitutes raped, beaten to death – open stuff only with him.

A 116-page dead-end file to take to the Hollywood squad – his own case, dead for now.

And his major case – pages and pages he kept checking over. Dick Stens' case: nails in Ed Exley's coffin. He got goose bumps just saying the words.

The Nite Owl case.

Starting in on the Janeway job brought it back: the Duke Cathcart/smut connection, evidence withheld, insider stuff to fuck Exley. Timing was against him then: he didn't have the smarts to pursue it, the niggers escaped, Exley gunned them down. The Nite Owl case was closed – the weird side bits around it forgotten. Years passed; he went back to the Janeway snuff, discovered a string. And little Kathy made him think Nite Owl, Nite Owl, Nite Owl.

Brainwork.

Back in '53, Dwight Gilette and Cindy Benavides – Kathy Janeway K.A.'s – told him a guy who came on like Duke Cathcart was talking up muscling Cathcart's pimp business. What 'pimp business'? – Duke had only two skags in his stable, but he had been talking up going into the smut biz – at first it sounded like a pipe dream coming from a major-league pipe dreamer – but it got validated when the Englekling brothers came forward and told their story of Cathcart approaching them with a deal: they'd print the smut, he'd distribute it, they'd approach Mickey Cohen for financing.

Cut to facts:

He was inside Duke's pad post-Nite Owl. It was tidied up and print-wiped; Duke's clothes had been gone through. The San Bernardino Yellow Pages were ruffled – the pages for printing shops especially. Pete and Bax Englekling owned a printshop in San Berdoo; Nite Owl victim Susan Nancy Lefferts was originally from San Berdoo.

Cut to the coroner's report:

The examining pathologist based his identification of

Cathcart's body on two things: dental plate *fragments* cross-checked against Cathcart's prison dental records and the 'D.C.' monogrammed sports jacket the stiff was wearing. The plate fragments were standard California prison issue – any ex-con who'd done time in the state penal system could have plastic like that in his mouth.

Cut to his insider skinny:

Kathy Janeway mentioned a 'cute' scar on Duke's chest. There was no mention of that scar anywhere in Doc Layman's autopsy report – and Cathcart's chest was not obliterated by shotgun pellets. A final kicker: the Nite Owl stiff was measured at 5'8"; Cathcart's prison measurement chart listed him at 5'9¼".

Conclusion:

A Cathcart impersonator was killed at the Nite Owl.

Cut to:

Smut.

Cindy Benavides said Duke was getting ready to push it; Ad Vice was investigating smut back then – he'd read through Squad 4's reports – all the men reported no leads, Russ Millard died, the fuck book gig fell by the wayside. The Englekling brothers told their story of Duke Cathcart's smut approach, how they visited Mickey Cohen in prison, how he refused to bankroll the deal. They thought Cohen ordered the Nite Owl snuffs out of batshit moral convictions – a ridiculous idea – but what if some kind of Nite Owl plot got started with the Mick? Exley submitted a report that said he and Bob Gallaudet talked up that theory, but the jigs escaped around then – and the Nite Owl got pinned on them.

Cut to:

His theory.

What if Cohen told some prison punk about the Cathcart/Englekling plan – or his man Davey Goldman did? What if the punk got paroled, talked up crashing Duke's stable while he was really just shoring up juice for his Duke impersonation? What if he killed Duke, stole some of his clothes and ended up at the Nite Owl by chance – because Duke frequented the place, or more likely – *as part of some kind of criminal rendezvous that went bad, the killers leaving, coming back with shotguns, blasting the Cathcart impersonator and five innocent bystanders to make it look like a robbery?*

Flaw in his theory so far:

He'd checked McNeil parole records: only Negroes, Latins and white men too large or too small to be the Cathcart impersonator were released between the time of the Cohen–Englekling brothers meeting and the Nite Owl. But – Cohen could have talked up the Cathcart smut proposal, word could have leaked to the outside, the impersonation could have been four or five times fucking removed.

Theories on top of theories, theories that proved he had the brains to call himself a detective:

Say the Nite Owl snuffs came out of smut intrigue. That meant the niggers were innocent, the real killers planted the shotguns in Ray Coates' car – which meant that the purple Merc seen outside the Nite Owl was a coincidence – the killers couldn't have known that three spooks were recently seen discharging shotguns in Griffith Park and would rank as natural first suspects. Somehow the killers found Coates' car before the LAPD – and planted the shotguns, print-wiped. It could have happened a half dozen ways.

1. Coates, in jail, could have told his lawyer where the car was stashed; the killers or their front man could have approached him for the information – or could have coerced him into making Coates talk.

2. The jigs could have spilled the location to one of their fellow inmates – maybe a planted inmate in with the killers.

3. His favorite, because it was simplest: the killers were smarter than the LAPD, did their own garage search, checked out garages behind deserted houses first – while the police went at it in grids.

Or the spooks told other inmates, who got released and got approached by the killers; or – unlikely – a cop finger man told them how the block search was breaking down.

Impossible to check it all out: the Hall of Justice Jail destroyed its 1935–55 records to make way for more storage space.

Or the jigs really were guilty.

Or it was some other bunch of boogies riding around, blasting the air in Griffith Park, killing six people at the Nite Owl. Their 1948–50 Ford/Chevy/Merc was never !ocated because the purple paint job was homemade, never listed on a DMV form.

Brainwork from a guy who never thought he had much of a brain – and he didn't make a shine gang for the snuffs, because –

The Englekling brothers sold their printshop mid-'54, then dropped off the face of the earth. Two years ago, he issued a 'Whereabouts' bulletin: no results, no positive results on the cadaver bulletins he'd been tracking statewide: zilch on the brothers, no stiffs that might be the real Duke Cathcart. And – six months ago, following up in San Berdoo, he got a hot lead.

He found a San Berdoo townie who'd seen Susan Nancy Lefferts with a man matching Duke Cathcart's description – two weeks before the Nite Owl killings. He showed him some Cathcart mugshots; the man said, 'Close, but no cigar.' The Nite Owl forensic had Susan Nancy 'flailing' to touch the man sitting at the next table: Duke Cathcart, really the impersonator, supposedly unknown to her. Why were they sitting at *different tables*? The kicker: he tried to interview Sue Lefferts' mother, a chance to run the boyfriend by her. She refused to talk to him.

Why?

Bud packed up: mementoes, ten pounds of paper. Stalemates for now – no new whore leads, the Nite Owl dead until he braced Mickey Cohen. Out to the elevator – adiós, Homicide.

Ed Exley walked by staring.

He knows about Inez and me.

Chapter Forty-four

Stakeout: Hank's Ranch Market, 52nd and Central. A sign above the door: 'Welfare Checks Cashed.' January 3, relief day – check-cashers shooting craps on the sidewalk. Surveillance Squad 5 got a tip – some anonymous ginch said her boyfriend and his buddy were going to take the market off, she was pissed at the boyfriend for porking her sister. Jack in the point car, watching the door, Sergeant John Petievich parked on 52 – scowling like he wanted to kill something.

Lunch: Fritos, straight vodka. Jack yawned, stretched, cut odds: Aragon vs. Pimentel, what Ellis Loew wanted – he was supposed to meet him at a political soiree tonight. The vodka burned his stomach; he had to piss wicked bad.

Horn toots – his signal. Petievich pointed to the sidewalk. Two white men entered the market.

Jack walked across the street. Petievich walked over. A frame on the doorway, a look in. The robbers at the checkstand, backs to the door – guns out, spare hands full of money.

No proprietor. No customers. A squint down the far aisle – blood and brains on the wall. SILENCER. BACK DOOR MAN. Jack shot the heisters in the back.

Petievich screamed; back door footsteps; Jack fired blind, chased. Bottles broke over his head: blind shots, silencer rounds – no noise, muffled thwaps. Down the far aisle, two dead winos, a door closing. Petievich fired, blew the door off – a man sprinted across the alley. Jack emptied his piece; the man vaulted a fence. Shouts from the sidewalk; crapshooters cheering. Jack reloaded, jumped the fence, hit a backyard. A Doberman jumped at him, snarling, snapping teeth in his face – Jack shot him point-blank. The dog belched blood; Jack heard shots, saw the fence explode.

Two bluesuits hit the yard running. Jack dropped his gun; they fired anyway – wide – blowing out fence pickets. Jack put his hands up. 'Police officer! Police officer! Policeman!'

They came up slow, frisked him – peach-fuzz rookies. The taller kid found his ID. 'Hey, Vincennes. You used to be some kind of hotshot, didn't you?'

Jack cold-cocked him – a knee to the nuts. The kid went down; the other kid gawked.

Jack went looking for a place to drink.

He found a juke joint, ordered a line of shots. Two drinks killed his shakes; two more made him a toastmaster.

To the men I just killed: sorry, I'm really better at shooting unarmed civilians. I'm being squeezed into retirement, so I thought I'd 86 a couple of real bad guys before I capped my twenty.

To my wife: you thought you married a hero, but you grew up and learned you were wrong. Now you want to go to law school and be a lawyer like Daddy and Ellis. No sweat on the money: Daddy bought the house, Daddy upgrades your marriage, Daddy will pay for tuition. When you read the paper and see that your husband drilled two evil robbers, you'll think they're the first notches on his gun. Wrong – in '47 dope crusader Jack blasted two innocent people, the big secret he almost wants to spill just to get some life kicking back into his marriage.

Jack downed three more shots. He went where he always went when with a certain amount of shit in his system – back to '53 and smut.

He felt safe on the blackmail: his depositions for insurance, the Hudgens snuff buried – *Hush-Hush* resurrected it, got nowhere. Patchett and Bracken never approached him – they had the carbon of Sid's Big V file, kept their end of the bargain. He heard Lynn and Bud White were still an item; call the brainy whore and Patchett memories – bad news from that bad bloody spring. What drove him was the smut.

He kept it in a safe-deposit box. He knew it was there, knew it excited him – knew that loving it would trash his marriage. He threw himself into the marriage, building walls to keep them safe from that spring. A string of sober days helped; the marriage helped. Nothing he did changed things – Karen just learned who he was.

She saw him muscle Deuce Perkins; he said 'nigger' in front of her parents. She figured out his press exploits were lies. She saw him drunk, pissed off. He hated her friends; his one friend – Miller Stanton – dropped out of sight when he blew *Badge of Honor*. He got bored with Karen, ran to the smut, went crazy with it.

He tried to ID the posers again – still no go. He went to Tijuana, bought other fuck books – no go. He went looking for Christine Bergeron, couldn't find her, put out teletypes that got him bupkis. No way to have the real thing – he decided to fake it.

He bought hookers, shook down call girls. He fixed them up to look like the girls in his books. He had them three and four at a pop, chains of bodies on quilts. He costumed them, choreographed them. He aped the pictures, took his own pictures, recaptured; sometimes he thought of the blood pix and got scared: perfect matches to murder mutilations.

Real women never thrilled him like the pictures did; fear kept him from going to Fleur-de-Lis – straight to the source. He couldn't figure out Karen's fear – why she didn't leave him.

A last drink – bad thoughts adieu.

Jack cleaned up, walked back to his car. No hubcaps, broken wiper blades. Crime scene tape around Hank's Ranch Market; two black-and-whites in the lot. No reprimand note on his windshield – the vandals probably stole it.

He hit the bash at full swing: Ellis Loew, a suite packed with Republican bigshots. Women in cocktail gowns; men in dark suits. The Big V: chinos, a sport shirt sprayed with dog blood.

Jack flagged a waiter, grabbed a martini off his tray. Framed pictures on the wall caught his eye.

Political progress: *Harvard Law Review*, the '53 election, a howler shot: Loew telling the press the Nite Owl killers confessed before they escaped. Jack laughed, sprayed gin, almost choked on his olive. Behind him: 'You used to dress a bit more nicely.'

Jack turned around. 'I used to be some kind of hotshot.'

'Do you have an excuse for your appearance?'

'Yeah, I killed two men today.'

'I see. Anything else?'

'Yeah, I shot them in the back, plugged a dog and took off before my superior officers showed up. And here's a news flash: I've been drinking. Ellis, this is getting stale, so let's get to it. Who do you want me to touch?'

'Jack, lower your voice.'

'What is it, boss? The Senate or the statehouse?'

'Jack, it's not the time to discuss this.'

'Sure it is. Tell true. You're gearing up for the '60 elections.'

Loew, on the QT. 'All right, it's the Senate. I did have some favors to ask, but your current condition precludes my asking them. We'll talk when you're in better shape.'

An audience now: the whole suite. 'Come on, I'm dying to run bag for you. Who do I shake down first?'

'*Sergeant, lower your voice.*'

Raise that voice. 'Cocksucker, I shit where you breathe. I put Bill McPherson in the tank for you, I cold-cocked him and put him in bed with that colored girl, I fucking deserve to know who you want me to put the screws to next.'

Loew, a hoarse whisper. 'Vincennes, you're through.'

Jack tossed gin in his face. 'God, I fucking hope so.'

Chapter Forty-five

' . . . and we're more than the moral exemplars that Chief Parker spoke of the other day. We are the dividing line between the old police work and the new, the old system of promotion through patronage and enforcement through intimidation and a new emerging system: the elite police corps that impartially asserts its authority in the name of a stern and unbiased justice, that punishes its own with a stern moral vigor should they prove duplicitous to the higher moral standards an elite corps demands of its members. And, finally, we are the protectors of the public image of the Los Angeles Police Department. Know that when you read interdepartmental complaints filed against your brother officers and feel the urge to be forgiving. Know that when I assign you to investigate a man you once worked with and liked. Know that our business is stern, absolute justice, whatever the price.'

Ed paused, looked at his men: twenty-two sergeants, two lieutenants. 'Nuts and bolts now, gentlemen. Under my predecessor, Lieutenant Phillips and Lieutenant Stinson supervised field investigations autonomously. As of now, I will assume direct field command, with Lieutenant Phillips and Lieutenant Stinson serving as my execs on an alternating basis. Incoming complaints and information requests will be routed through my office first, I'll read the material and make my assignments accordingly. Sergeant Kleckner and Sergeant Fisk will serve as my personal assistants and will meet with me every morning at 0730. Lieutenant Stinson and Lieutenant Phillips, please meet me in my office in one hour to discuss my assuming command of your ongoing investigations. Gentlemen, you're dismissed.'

The meeting dispersed in silence; the muster room emptied. Ed replayed his speech, hitting key phrases. 'Absolute justice' hit with Inez Soto's voice.

Dump ashtrays, straighten chairs, tidy the bulletin board. Unfurl the flags by the lectern, check them for dust. Back to his speech, his father's voice: 'Duplicitous to the higher moral standards an elite corps demands of its members.' Two days ago, his speech would have been the truth. Inez Soto's speech made it a lie.

Flags, gold-fringed. Gold-plated opportunism: he killed those men out of a weak man's rage. As the Nite Owl killers they gave the rage meaning: absolute justice boldly taken. He twisted the meaning to support what the public was telling him: you're L.A.'s greatest hero, you're going to the top and beyond. Bud White's revenge, the man too stupid to grasp it: a simple cuckold accompanied by a woman's few words had him treading lies at the top, thrashing for a way to make his stale glory real.

Ed walked into his office: clean, neat – no order to secure. Complaint forms on his desk – he sat down, worked.

Jack Vincennes in big trouble.

1/3/58: while on a Surveillance Detail stakeout, Vincennes shot and killed two armed robbers – gunmen who had murdered three people at a southside market. Vincennes gave chase to a third gunman/robber, lost him, was approached by two patrolmen who did not know he was a police officer. The patrolmen fired at Vincennes, assuming him to be a member of the robbery gang; Vincennes dropped his gun and allowed himself to be frisked – then assaulted one of the officers and vacated the crime scene before Homicide and the coroner arrived. The third suspect remained at large; Vincennes went to a political gathering honoring D.A. Ellis Loew, his brother-in-law by marriage. Presumed to be drunk, he verbally abused Loew and threw a drink in his face – in full view of the guests.

Ed skimmed Vincennes' personnel file. A 5/58 pension securement date – goodbye, Trashcan Jack – you were close. Stacks of his Narcotics Squad reports: thorough, detailed to the point of being padded. Between the lines: Vincennes had a hard-on for minor dope violators – especially Hollywood celebrities and jazz musicians – substantiating an old rumor: he called *Hush-Hush* Magazine to be in on his gravy rousts. Vincennes was transferred to Administrative Vice as part of the Bloody Christmas shake-up; another stack of reports: bookmaking and liquor infraction operations, no zeal, plenty of verbal padding. Ad Vice assignment into the spring of '53: Russ Millard commanding the division, a pornography investigation running concurrent with the Nite Owl. And a *big* anomaly: assigned to trace smut, Vincennes repeatedly reported no leads, commented that the other men on the assignment were coming up empty, twice offered the opinion that the investigation should be dropped.

Antithetical Jack V. behavior.

Smut brushed shoulders with the Nite Owl.

Ed thought back.

The Englekling brothers, Duke Cathcart, Mickey Cohen. Smut dismissed as a viable Nite Owl lead – three dead Negroes, case closed.

Ed read the file again. Years of padded reports, one assignment bereft of paper. Vincennes returned to Narco in July '53 – he went back to his old ways, continued them straight through to the end of his duty with Surveillance.

Big-time anomaly.

Coinciding with the Nite Owl.

Spring '53, another connection: Sid Hudgens was murdered then – unsolved. Ed hit the intercom.

'Yes, Captain?'

'Susan, find out who besides Sergeant John Vincennes was assigned to the Fourth Squad at Administrative Vice in April of 1953. Do that, then locate them.'

A half hour for results. Sergeant George Henderson, Officer Thomas Kifka retired; Sergeant Lewis Stathis working Bunco. Ed called his C.O.; Stathis walked in ten minutes later.

A burly man – tall, stooped. Nervous – an I.A. bracing

289

out of nowhere was a spooker. Ed pointed him to a chair. Stathis said, 'Sir, this is about . . . '

'Sergeant, this has nothing to do with you. This has to do with an officer you worked Ad Vice with.'

'Captain, my Ad Vice tour was years ago.'

'I know, late '51 through the summer of '53. You transferred out just as I rotated in on my floater assignment. Sergeant, how closely did you work with Jack Vincennes?'

Stathis smiled. Ed said, 'Why are you grinning?'

'Well, I read in the paper that Vincennes juked these two heist guys, and talk around the Bureau has it that he bugged out on the scene unannounced. That's a big infraction, so I was smiling 'cause it figured he'd be the Ad Vice guy you'd be interested in.'

'I see. And did you work closely with him?'

Stathis shook his head. 'Jack was strictly the single-o type. You know, the beat of a different drummer. Sometimes we worked the same general assignments, but that was it.'

'Your squad worked a pornography investigation in the spring of '53, do you recall that?'

'Yeah, it was a colossal waste of time. Dirty skin books, a waste of time.'

'You yourself reported no leads.'

'Yeah, and neither did Trashcan or the other guys. Russ Millard got co-opted to that Nite Owl thing, and the skinbook caper fell through.'

'Do you recall Vincennes acting strangely during that time?'

'Not really. I remember he only showed up at the squadroom at odd times and that him and Russ Millard didn't like each other. Like I said, Vincennes was a loner. He didn't pal around with the guys on the squad.'

'Do you recall Millard making specific queries of the squad when two printshop operators came forward with smut information?'

Stathis nodded. 'Yeah, something to do with the Nite Owl that didn't pan out. We all told old Russ that those skin books could not be traced hell or high water.'

One hunch going dry. 'Sergeant, the Department was running a fever with the Nite Owl back then. Can you recall how Vincennes reacted to it? Any little thing out of the ordinary?'

Stathis said, 'Sir, can I be blunt?'

'Of course.'

'Well, then I'll tell you that I always figured Vincennes was a cheap-shot cop on the take somehow. Put that aside, I remember he was sort of nervous around the time of the skin book job. On the Nite Owl, I'd say he was bored with it. He was in on the arrest of those colored guys, he was there when our guys found the car and the shotguns, and he still seemed bored by it.'

Coming on again – no facts, just instincts. 'Sergeant, think. Vincennes' behavior around the time of the Nite Owl and the pornography investigation. Anything out of the ordinary with him. *Think.*'

Stathis shrugged. 'Maybe one thing, but I don't think it amounts to – '

'Tell me anyway.'

'Well, back then Vincennes had the cubicle next to mine, and sometimes I could hear him pretty good. I was at my desk and heard part of a conversation, him and Dudley Smith.'

'And?'

'And Smith asked Vincennes to put a tail on Bud White. He said White'd gotten personally involved in a hooker homicide and he didn't want him doing nothing rash.'

Skin prickles. 'What else did you hear?'

'I heard Vincennes agree, and the rest of it was garbled.'

'This was during the Nite Owl investigation?'

'Yes, sir. Right in the middle of it.'

'Sergeant, do you remember Sid Hudgens, the scandal sheet man, being killed around that time?'

'Yeah, an unsolved.'

'Do you recall Vincennes talking about it?'

'No, but the rumor was that him and Hudgens were buddies.'

Ed smiled. 'Sergeant, thank you. This was off the

record, but I don't want you to repeat our conversation. Do you understand?'

Stathis got up. 'I won't, but I feel bad about Vincennes. I heard he's topping out his twenty in a few months. Maybe he vamoosed 'cause shooting those heist guys got to him.'

Ed said, 'Good day, Sergeant.'

Something old, wrong.

Ed sat with his door open. Gold-braided flags just outside – opportunities knocked.

Vincennes might have dirt on Bud White.

Instincts: Trash running scared in the spring of '53.

Connect the 'skin-book caper' to the Nite Owl.

Inez Soto's indictment – he killed three innocent men.

If he cut Vincennes a break on his I.A. investigation –

Ed hit the intercom. 'Susan, get me District Attorney Loew.'

Chapter Forty-six

Mickey Cohen said, 'I got my own problems to worry about. The fershtunkener Nite Owl case and fershtunkener dirty books I don't know from the Bible, another book I never read. That rebop bored me five years ago, now it is an even further distance from hunger. I got my own problems, such as look at my poor baby.'

Bud looked. A raggedy-assed bulldog by the Mickster's fireplace – wheezing, his tail in a splint. Cohen said, 'That is Mickey Cohen, Jr., my heir who is not long for this canine world. A bomb attempt in November he survived, though a goodly number of my Sy Devore suits did not. His poor tail has remained steadily infected and his appetite is dyspeptic. Cops resurrecting old grief is not good for his health.'

'Mr. Cohen – '

'I like a man who addresses me with proper decorum. What did you say your name was again?'

'Sergeant White.'

'Sergeant White then, I will tell you there is no end to the grief in my life. I am like Jesus your goy savior carrying the weight of the world on his back. Back in prison these fershtunkener goons attack me and my man Davey Goldman, Davey gets his brains scrambled, gets paroled and starts walking around in public with his shlong hanging out, it's big, I don't blame him for advertising, but the Beverly Hills cops ain't so enlightened and now he's doing ninety days' observation at the Camarillo nut bin. As if that is not enough grief for your yiddisher Jesus to undergo, then feature that while I was in prison some colleagues looking after my interests were bumped off by persons unknown. And now my old boys won't form back together with me. My God, Kikey T., Lee Vachss, Johnny Stompanato – '

Kill the tirade. 'I know Johnny Stomp.'

Cohen hit the roof. 'Ferstunkener Johnny, Judas from the best-selling Bible is his middle name! Lana Turner is his Jezebel and not his Mary Magdalene, his cock leads him to grovel for her like a dowsing rod. Granted, he is even better hung than Davey G., but my blessed Jesus I took him away from being a two-bit extortionist and made him my bodyguard, and now he refuses to re-enlist, he'd rather nosh grease at Kikey's fucking deli and hobnob with Deuce Perkins, who I have it on good authority plays hide the salami with members of the canine persuasion. Did you say your name was White?'

'That's right, Mr. Cohen.'

'Wendell White? *Bud* White?'

'That's me.'

'Boychik, why didn't you tell me?'

Cohen Junior pissed in the fireplace. Bud said, 'I didn't think you'd heard of me.'

'Heard, shmeard, word gets out. Word is you're Dudley Smith's lad. Word is you and the Dudster and a couple of his other hard boys been keeping L.A. safe for democracy while this so-called crime drought's been going on. A motel in Gardena, a little blackjack work to the kidneys, va va va voom. Maybe now, maybe if I can get my old guys to quit noshing grease and associating with dog fuckers, I can get business going again. I should be nice to you so's you and the Dudster reciprocate. So what's with this Nite Owl rehash?'

His pitch – canned. 'I heard how the Englekling brothers visited you up at McNeil, how they talked up Duke Cathcart's deal. I was thinking that you or Davey Goldman might have talked it up on the yard and word got out that way.'

Mickey said, 'Nix. Not possible, 'cause I never told Davey. True, I am well known for my cell business confabs, but not a soul on this earth did I tell. I told that guy Exley that when we shmoozed on the topic years ago. And here's a bonus insight from the Mickster. It is my considered opinion that dirty books are a high-profit item

worth killing innocent bystanders over only if an established high-profit market already exists. Give the fucking
Nite Owl up, those shvartzes the hero kid bumped took
the ticket and probably did the job anyway.'

Bud said, 'I don't think Duke Cathcart was killed at
the Nite Owl. I think it was a guy impersonating him. I
think the guy killed Cathcart, took over his identity and
wound up at the Nite Owl. I was thinking the whole thing
got started up at McNeil.'

Cohen rolled his eyes. 'Not with me it didn't, boychik,
'cause I told nobody, and I can't feature Pete and Bax
stopping to spread the word out on the yard. Where'd
this clown Cathcart live?'

'Silverlake.'

'Then dig up the Silverlake Hills. Maybe you'll find a
nice vintage stiff.'

A flash – San Berdoo, Sue Lefferts' mother at her pad
– eyes darting to a built-on room. 'Thanks, Mr. Cohen.'

Cohen said, 'Forget the fershtunkener Nite Owl.'

Cohen Junior took a bead on Bud's crotch.

San Bernardino, Hilda Lefferts. Last time she shoved him
out pronto; this time he'd hit on the boyfriend: Susan
Nancy was seen with a guy matching Duke Cathcart's
description – press, intimidate.

A two-hour run. The San Berdoo Freeway would be
working soon – cut the trip in half. Exley Senior to Junior:
the coward knew about him and Inez, his look the other
day spelled it plain. They were both biding their time.
But if things fell his way he'd hit harder – Exley would
never tag him for the brains to hit smart.

Hilda Lefferts lived in a dump: a shingle shack with a
cinder block add-on. Bud walked up, checked out the
mailbox. Good intimidation stuff: Lockheed pension
check, Social Security check, County Relief check. He
pushed the buzzer.

The door opened a crack. Hilda Lefferts looked over
the chain. 'Told you before, now I'll say it again. I'm not

buying what you're selling, so let my poor daughter rest in peace.'

Bud fanned out the checks. 'County Relief told me to hold these back until you cooperate. No tickee, no washee.'

Hilda squealed; Bud popped the chain, walked in. Hilda backed away. 'Please. I need that money.'

Susan Nancy smiled down from four walls: vamp poses on a nightclub floor. Bud said, 'Come on, be nice, huh? You remember what I tried to ask you last time? Susan had a boyfriend here in San Berdoo right before she moved to L.A. You looked scared when I told you before, you look scared now. *Come on*. Five minutes on that and I'm gone. And nobody's gonna know.'

Hilda, eyeball circuits: the checks, the add-on room. 'Nobody?'

Bud forked over Lockheed. 'Nobody. Come on. I'll give you the other two after you tell me.'

Hilda spoke straight to her daughter – the picture by the door. 'Susie, you told me you met the man at a cocktail lounge and I told you I didn't approve. You said he was a nice man who'd paid his debt to society, but you wouldn't tell me his name. I saw you with him one day, and you called him Don or Dean or Dick or Dee, and he said, "No, Duke. Get used to it." Then I was out one day and old Mrs. Jensen next door saw you with the man here at the house and thought she heard a ruckus . . . '

Match it: 'debt to society' equals 'ex-con.' 'Did you ever learn the man's name?'

'No, I didn't. I . . . '

'Did Susan know two brothers named Englekling? They lived here in San Bernardino.'

Hilda squinted at the picture. 'Oh, Susie. No, I don't think I know that name.'

'Did Susan's boyfriend ever mention the name "Duke Cathcart" or mention a pornography business?'

'No! Cathcart was the name of one of the dead people where Susie died, and Susie was a good girl who would never associate with filth!'

Bud forked over County Relief. 'Easy now. Tell me about the ruckus.'

Hilda, tears coming on. 'I came home the next day, and I thought I saw dried blood on the floor of the new den, I'd just had it built with the money from my husband's insurance policy. Susan and the man came back and acted nervous. The man crawled around under the house and called a Los Angeles phone number, then he and Susan Nancy left. A week later she was killed . . . and . . . I, well, I thought all that suspicious behavior meant the killings . . . I just thought of conspiracies and reprisals, and when that nice man who became such a hero came by a few days later with his background check, I just stayed quiet.'

Goose bumps: Susie Lefferts' boyfriend the Cathcart impersonator. 'The ruckus': the boyfriend kills Cathcart – probably in San Berdoo to talk to the Engleklings. Susie at the Nite Owl, scoping out some kind of meeting, the boyfriend playing Cathcart – which meant the killers never saw the real Cathcart face-to-face.

THE BOYFRIEND CRAWLING AROUND UNDER THE HOUSE.

Bud got the phone, the operator, an L.A. number: P.C. Bell police information. A clerk came on. 'Yes, who's requesting?'

'Sergeant W. White, LAPD. I'm in San Bernardino at RAnchview 04617. I need a list of all calls to Los Angeles from that number, say from March 20 to April 12, 1953. Got that?'

The clerk said, 'I copy.' Seconds, two minutes plus, the clerk back on. 'Three calls, Sergeant. April 2 and April 8, all to the same number, HO-21118. That's a pay phone, the corner of Sunset and Las Palmas.'

Bud hung up. Phone booth calls a half mile from the Nite Owl; the deal or the meet worked out – extra cautious.

Hilda fretted Kleenex. Bud saw a flashlight on an end table. He grabbed it, ran with it.

Outside to the add-on, a foundation crawlspace – one tight fit. Down, under, in.

Dirt, wood pilings, a long burlap sack up ahead. Smells: mothballs, rot. An elbow crawl to the bag – mothballs and rot getting stronger. He poked the sack, saw a rat's nest explode.

All around him: rats blinded by light.

Bud ripped burlap. In with the flashlight, rats, a skull caked with gristle. Drop the flash, rip two-handed, rats and mothballs in his face. A huge rip, a bullet hole in the skull, a skeleton hand out a sleeve – 'D.C.' on flannel.

He crawled out gulping air. Hilda Lefferts was right there. Her eyes said, 'Please God, not that.'

Clean air; clean daylight almost blinding. White light gave him the idea – his shiv at Exley.

A scandal mag leak. A guy at *Whisper* owed him – a pinko rag, they bled for Commies and jigs and hated cops.

Hilda, about to shit her drawers. 'Was . . . there . . . anything under there?'

'Nothing but some rats. I want you to stay put, though. I'm gonna bring back some mugshots for you to look at.'

'May I have that last check?'

The envelope – flecked with rat droppings. 'Here. Compliments of Captain Ed Exley.'

Chapter Forty-seven

A nice interrogation room – no bolted-down chairs, no piss smell. Jack looked at Ed Exley. 'I knew I was in the shit, but I didn't think I rated the top dog.'

Exley: 'You're probably wondering why you haven't been suspended.'

Jack stretched. His uniform chafed – he hadn't worn it since 1945. Exley looked creepy – skinny, gray-haired, rimless glasses that made his eyes come off brutal. 'I was wondering. My guess is Ellis had second thoughts on the complaint he filed. Bad publicity and all that.'

Exley shook his head. 'Loew considers you a liability to his career and his marriage, and leaving that crime scene and assaulting that officer are enough in themselves to warrant a suspension and a dismissal.'

'Yeah? Then why haven't I been suspended?'

'Because for the moment I've interceded with Loew and Chief Parker. Any other questions?'

'Yeah, where's the tape recorder and the steno?'

'I didn't want them here.'

Jack pulled his chair up. 'Captain, what *do* you want?'

'I'll throw that back at you. Do you want to flush your career down the toilet or would you like to skate for a few months and cash out your twenty?'

Easy: Karen's face when he told her. 'Okay, I'll play. Now what do you want?'

Exley leaned close. 'In the spring of '53 your friend and business associate Sid Hudgens was murdered and two detectives who worked the case under Russ Millard told me you referred to Hudgens as "scum" and were visibly agitated on the morning his body was discovered. During this time frame Dudley Smith asked you to tail Bud White, and you agreed. During this time frame the Nite Owl case was active and you worked a pornography investigation with Ad Vice and repeatedly submitted no-lead reports, when your long-standing procedure was to jam every report you wrote full of filler. During this time two men, Peter and Baxter Englekling, came forward to offer state's evidence on an alleged pornography link to the Nite Owl. Russ Millard queried you on it, you went along with your "no leads" routine. Throughout the smut investigation you repeatedly urged that the job be dropped. Those same two detectives, Sergeants Fisk and Kleckner, overheard you urging Ellis Loew to soft-pedal the Hudgens investigation, and one of your fellow Ad Vice officers recalls you as being atypically nervous throughout the smut job and absent from the squadroom for unusually long periods of time. Put it all together for me, would you, Jack?'

Ten counts guilty – he knew he was gawking, blinking, twitching. 'How . . . the . . . fuck did you . . . '

'It doesn't matter. Now let's hear your interpretation of what I want.'

Jack caught some breath. 'Okay, so I tailed Bud White. Dud was afraid he'd go apeshit over some hooker snuff, 'cause White had that tendency where young stuff was concerned. Okay, so I tailed him and didn't pick up anything worth a damn. You and White hate each other, everyone knows it. You figure someday he'll try to get you for your job on Dick Stensland and you'll cut me slack with Loew and Parker in exchange for some dirt on him. *Is that what you want?*'

'Call that twenty percent of it and give me something you learned about White.'

'Such as?'

'How about him and women?'

'White likes women, but that's no news flash.'

'IAD ran a personal on White after he passed the sergeant's exam. The report had him seeing a woman named Lynn Bracken. Did White know her back in '53?'

Jack shrugged. 'I don't know. I never heard that name.'

'Vincennes, your face says you're a liar, but put the

300

Bracken woman aside, she doesn't interest me. Was White seeing Inez Soto during the time you were tailing him?'

He almost laughed. 'No, not while I had my tail on him. Is that what you're so worked up on? You think White and your – '

Exley raised a hand. 'I'm not going to ask you if you killed Hudgens, I'm not going to make you put that spring together for me, not yet and maybe never. Just give me your opinion on something. You were up to your ears on the smut job *and* you worked the Nite Owl. Do you make the three Negroes for the killings?'

Jack inched back – get away from those eyes. 'There's loose ends out there, I knew it then. If it wasn't the three you got, maybe it was some other spooks, maybe they knew where Coates hid his car and planted the shotguns. Maybe it's tied to the smut. Do you care? Those niggers raped your woman, so what you did was right. What's this about, Captain?'

Exley smiled. Jack pegged it: a man sticking one foot off a cliff, hopping on one leg. 'Captain, what's this – '

'No, my motives are my business, and here's my first guess. Hudgens was connected to the smut somehow, and he had a file on you. That's why you were all over that mess.'

Quicksand. 'Yeah, I did something really bad once. You know . . . shit, sometimes I think . . . sometimes I think I don't care who finds out anymore.'

Exley stood up. 'I've already squared the complaints against you. There'll be no trial board, no charges. Part of the agreement I made with Chief Parker is a stipulation that you voluntarily retire in May. I told him you'd agree, and I convinced him that you deserve a full pension. He didn't question my motives, and I don't want you to question them either.'

Jack stood up. 'And the trade?'

'If the Nite Owl ever goes wide, you and everything you know belong to me.'

Jack stuck out his hand. 'Jesus, you turned into a cold son of a bitch.'

CALENDAR

FEBRUARY–MARCH 1958

Whisper Magazine, February 1958 issue:

WRONG MAN KILLED IN
NITE OWL SLAUGHTER?
WEB OF MYSTERY SPREADS . . .

You remember the Nite Owl brouhaha, don't you?
On April 14, 1953, three shotgun-toting killers
entered the convivial Nite Owl Coffee Shop, just off
Hollywood Boulevard in sunny Los Angeles, robbed
and murdered three employees and three patrons and
got away with an estimated three hundred scoots,
which divided by six comes to about fifty bucks a
life. The Los Angeles Police Department threw itself
into the case with characteristic zeal, arrested three
young Negro men on suspicion of committing the
murders and also charged them with kidnapping and
raping a young Mexican girl. The LAPD was not
quite certain that the three Negroes – Raymond
'Sugar Ray' Coates, Tyrone Jones and Leroy Fontaine – committed the Nite Owl killings, but they
were sure that the young men were the rapists of Inez
Soto, 21, a college student. The Nite Owl investigation continued, with much attendant publicity and
great pressure on the LAPD to solve L.A.'s 'Crime
of the Century.'

The LAPD pursued fruitless leads for two weeks,
then discovered the murder weapons inside Ray
Coates' car, stored in an abandoned South Los
Angeles garage. Shortly after that, Coates, Jones and
Fontaine escaped from the Hall of Justice Jail . . .

Enter a young police detective: Sergeant Edmund
J. Exley of the LAPD. World War II hero, UCLA
grad, informant against his fellow cops in the 1951
'Bloody Christmas' police brutality scandal and the

son of construction mogul Preston Exley, the builder of Raymond Dieterling's mammoth Dream-a-Dreamland and the massive Southern California freeway system. The plot thickens . . .

Item: Sergeant Ed Exley was in love with rape victim Inez Soto.

Item: Sergeant Ed Exley located, shot and killed Raymond Coates, Tyrone Jones and Leroy Fontaine, with – poetic justice – a shotgun.

Item: Sergeant Ed Exley was promoted (two whole ranks!!!) to captain a week later, a large reward for his justice-by-the-sword resolution of a case the LAPD needed to solve quicksville in order to ensure perpetuation of its (overblown?) reputation.

Item: *Captain* Ed Exley (a rich kid with a substantial private trust fund left to him by his late mother) soon became very cozy with Inez Soto and bought her a house down the block from his apartment.

Item: we at *Whisper* have it on very good authority that Raymond Coates, Leroy Fontaine, Tyrone Jones and the man who was sheltering them – Roland Navarette – were unarmed when hero Ed Exley gunned them down . . . and, now, nearly five years since the Nite Owl killings, the plot thickens again . . .

Now, *Whisper* is the underdog of what the squaresville press calls 'Scandal Sheet Journalism.' We're not the mighty *Hush-Hush*, we're based out of New York and our beat is primarily the East Coast. But we do have our L.A. sources, and among them is a crusading private eye who wishes to remain anonymous. This man has been obsessed with the Nite Owl case for years, has investigated it extensively and has come up with some startling revelations. This man, whom we shall call 'Private Eye X,' spoke to *Whisper* correspondents and revealed the following:

Private Eye eye-tem: during the Nite Owl investigation, two brothers, *Peter and Baxter Englekling*, printshop operators from San Bernardino, California, came forth and told authorities an account of how

Nite Owl victim Delbert 'Duke' Cathcart approached them with a plan to print pornographic material, then theorized that the Nite Owl killings were the result of intrigue within the pornography underworld. The LAPD pooh-poohed the brothers' theory in their haste to pin the crime on the Negroes, and now the Engleklings seem to have disappeared off the face of the globe . . .

Private Eye eye-tem: Mrs. Hilda Lefferts, mother of San Bernardino born and bred *Nite Owl victim Susan Nancy Lefferts*, told Private Eye X that immediately before the killings her daughter had a mysterious, unnamed boyfriend who greatly resembled Duke Cathcart, and she even heard him tell Susan Nancy: 'Call me "Duke." Get used to the idea.'!!! Mrs. Lefferts could not identify the man from privately hoarded mugshots that Private Eye X showed her. X then developed what we consider an x-cellent and x-citing theory!

X theory eye-tem: we think that mystery boyfriend X killed Duke Cathcart in an attempt to take over his pornography business, impersonated Duke Cathcart and wound up at the Nite Owl Coffee Shop to do biz with the three men who perpetrated the slaughter. Susan Nancy sat nearby in order to watch her boyfriend wheel and deal. Private Eye X offers the following unimpeachable evidence as proof:

Mrs. Lefferts said boyfriend X looked just like Duke Cathcart.

The body identified as Cathcart's was too decimated to correctly ID. The coroner's final identification was based on a *partial* dental plate reconstruction cross-checked against Cathcart's prison dental records – yet other prison records listed Cathcart's height at 5'8" while the body discovered at the Nite Owl was 5'9¼". All in all, unmistakable proof that an impersonator, not Duke Cathcart, was killed at the Nite Owl Coffee Shop . . .

X-citing x-trapolations that we believe will lead to

some x-tremely interesting revelations, x-asperate the trigger-happy Los Angeles Police Department and perhaps x-onerate the three Negroes falsely accused of the Nite Owl killings. We at *Whisper* urge the Los Angeles District Attorney's Office to x-hume the bodies of the Nite Owl victims; we x-coriate Captain Ed Exley for his cold-blooded murder of four societal victims and x-pressly petition the LAPD: redeem your old wrongs in the name of justice! Reopen the Nite Owl case!!!

EXTRACT: San Francisco *Chronicle*, February 27:

GAITSVILLE SLAYINGS BAFFLE POLICE

Gaitsville, Calif., Feb. 27, 1958 – A bizarre double murder has the citizens of Gaitsville, a small town sixty miles north of San Francisco, scared – and the Marin County Sheriff's baffled.

Two days ago, the bodies of Peter and Baxter Englekling, 41 and 37, were discovered at their apartment next door to the printshop where they were employed as typesetters. The two brothers, in the words of Marin County Sheriff's Lieutenant Eugene Hatcher, were 'shady characters with criminal connections.' The lieutenant guardedly elaborated to *Chronicle* reporter George Woods.

'Both Engleklings had criminal records for narcotics offenses,' Lieutenant Hatcher said. 'Granted, they've been clean for a number of years, but they were still shady characters. For instance, they were working at the printing shop under assumed names. So far we have no clues, but we do think we're dealing with a torture-for-information scenario.'

The Englekling brothers worked at Rapid Bob's Printing on East Verdugo Road in Gaitsville and lived in the apartment building next door. Their employer, Robert Dunkquist, 53, knew the pair as Pete and Bax Girard, and discovered their bodies on Tuesday morning. 'Pete and Bax had worked for me for a year and they were as regular as clockwork. When they were late for work on Tuesday I knew something was up. Also, the shop had been ransacked and I wanted them to help me find the culprits.'

The Englekling brothers, whose true identities were revealed by a fingerprint teletype check, were shot to death, and Lieutenant Hatcher is certain the killer used a .38 revolver equipped with a silencer. 'Our ballistics man found iron shavings embedded in the rounds we took out of the victims. This indicates a silencer and also indicates why the neighbors never reported any shots.'

Lieutenant Hatcher would not reveal the status of his investigation, but he did state that all the standard investigatory approaches are being utilized. He stated that both victims were tortured prior to being shot, but would not describe the crime scene. 'We want to keep that knowledge private,' he said. 'Sometimes publicity-seeking lunatics confess to crimes like this, even though they didn't commit them. Keeping your facts private helps eliminate the guilty from the innocent.'

Peter and Baxter Englekling have no known living relatives, and their bodies are being held at the Gaitsville city coroner's office. Lieutenant Hatcher urged all parties who might have information concerning the homicides to contact the Marin County Sheriff's Department.

EXTRACT: San Francisco *Examiner*, March 1:

MURDER VICTIMS LINKED TO CELEBRATED LOS ANGELES CRIME

Peter and Baxter Englekling, murder victims killed in Gaitsville, California, on February 25, were material witnesses in the famous Nite Owl murder case that occurred in Los Angeles in April 1953,

Marin County Sheriff's Lieutenant Eugene Hatcher revealed today.

'We got an anonymous tip on it yesterday,' Lieutenant Hatcher told the *Examiner*. 'A man just called in the information, then hung up. We verified it with the D.A.'s Bureau down in L.A., and they said it was true. I don't think it has anything to do with our case, but I called the Los Angeles Police Department anyway and ran it by them. They gave me the brush-off, so I say the heck with them.'

EXTRACT: L.A. *Daily News*, March 6:

NITE OWL REDIVIVUS – SHOCKING NEW REVELATIONS POINT TO INNOCENT MEN KILLED

This is an ugly story. The *Daily News*, frankly Los Angeles' only exposé-oriented newspaper and the only Southland paper proud to call itself 'muckraking,' does not shy away from such stories. This story punctures the hero image of a man considered by many to be a perfect exemplar of law-and-order righteousness, and when heroes possess feet of clay, we at the *Daily News* believe that it is our duty to expose their shortcomings to public scrutiny. The issues here are great, as notable as the crime that spawned them, so we are frankly sending up a muckraking hue and cry. That hue and cry: the infamous Nite Owl murder case – six people brutally robbed and shotgunned to death at a Hollywood coffee shop in April 1953 – was solved incorrectly, at a great cost to justice. We want to see the case reopened and true justice achieved.

Raymond Coates, Leroy Fontaine and Tyrone Jones – do you recall those names? They were the three Negro youths, criminals and sex offenders to be sure, who were railroaded by the Los Angeles Police Department. Arrested shortly after the Nite

307

Owl murders, they offered a hellish alibi: they could not have committed the killings because they were engaged in the kidnap and gang rape of a young woman named Inez Soto. They abused Miss Soto at a deserted building in South Los Angeles, then confessed that they drove her around and 'sold her out' to their friends for more sexual abuse. They left Miss Soto with a man named Sylvester Fitch, and an LAPD officer shot and killed him while effecting the brave young woman's escape.

Miss Soto refused to cooperate with the police investigation, which at the time centered on the imperative of establishing where Coates, Jones and Fontaine were at the time of the Nite Owl killings. Were they with her and the other alleged rapists (none of whom, besides Fitch, were ever identified)? Did they have time to drive from South Los Angeles to Hollywood, commit the Nite Owl killings, then return to heap more abuse upon her? Was she conscious throughout the total sum of her degradation?

Unanswered questions – until now.

The police investigation spread into two forks: searching for evidence to corroborate Jones, Coates and Fontaine as the killers; searching for general evidence, standard police work based on the supposition that the three youths were guilty only of kidnap and rape, but not murder. Miss Soto still refused to cooperate. Both investigatory forks proved moot when Coates, Jones and Fontaine escaped from jail and were gunned down by our aforementioned hero: LAPD Sergeant Edmund Exley.

College man, World War II hero, son of the illustrious Preston Exley, Ed Exley used the Nite Owl case as a springboard for his ruthless personal ambition. He was promoted to captain at age 31 and as of this writing will soon become an inspector – at 36, the youngest in LAPD history. He is mentioned as a potential Republican office-seeker almost as often as his construction-king father. A few persistent rumors surround him: that the men killed were unarmed, that D.A. Ellis Loew dreamed up the Nite Owl confession that Coates, Jones and Fontaine allegedly made before they escaped. What is not generally known is that Ed Exley was in love with Inez Soto and condoned her lack of cooperation during the investigation, later bought her a house and has been intimately involved with her for close to five years.

And now, two recent developments have blown the Nite Owl case wide open.

Back in 1953, two men, brothers, came forward as material witnesses with information on the Nite Owl killings. Those men, Peter and Baxter Englekling, asserted that a pornography plot was at the base of the coffee shop massacre, per a scheme devised by one of the victims: ex-convict Delbert 'Duke' Cathcart. The LAPD chose to ignore this information. Then, almost five years later, Peter and Baxter Englekling were viciously murdered in the small upstate town of Gaitsville. Those killings, which took place on February 25, are unsolved with a complete absence of clues. But a long-unanswered question was about to be answered.

At San Quentin Penitentiary, a Negro prisoner named Otis John Shortell read a San Francisco newspaper account of the Englekling brothers' killings, an account which mentioned their tenuous connection to the Nite Owl case. The article got Otis John Shortell thinking. He requested an audience with the assistant warden and made a startling confession.

Otis John Shortell, in prison on an accumulation of grand-theft auto convictions and frankly desiring a sentence reduction as a reward for his cooperation, confessed that he was one of the men Coates, Fontaine and Jones 'sold' Inez Soto to. He was with Miss Soto and the three youths between the hours of 2:30 and 5:00 on the morning of the Nite Owl killings, *during the entire murder time frame*. He told the warden that he never came forward to exonerate the three for fear of rape charges being filed against him. He further stated that Coates had a large quantity of narcotics in his car and that that was the reason he never relinquished its location to the police. Shortell cited a recent conversion to Pentecostal Christianity as his reason for finally making his confession, but prison authorities were dubious. Shortell petitioned for an in-cell lie detector test to prove his veracity and was given a total of four polygraph examinations. He passed all four tests conclusively. Shortell's attorney, Morris Waxman, has sent notarized copies of the polygraph examiner's reports to the *Daily News* and the LAPD. We have advanced this article. What will the LAPD do?

We decry the injustice of shotgun justice. We decry the motives of triggerman Ed Exley. We openly challenge the Los Angeles Police Department to reopen the Nite Owl Murder Case.

EXTRACT: L.A. *Times*, March 11:

NITE OWL HUE AND CRY BUILDING

A welter of unrelated events and a fire fanned by a series of articles in the Los Angeles *Daily News* are pressuring the Los Angeles Police Department to reopen the 1953 Nite Owl murder case investigation.

LAPD Chief William H. Parker called the controversy 'a powder keg with a wet fuse. It's all a bunch of baloney. The testimony of a degenerate criminal and an unrelated double murder do not constitute a reason to reopen a case successfully solved five years ago. I stood by Captain Ed Exley's actions in 1953 and I stand by them now.'

Chief Parker's references allude to the February 25 murders of Peter and Baxter Englekling, material witnesses to the original Nite Owl investigation, and the recent testimony of San Quentin inmate Otis John Shortell, who claimed to be with the three formerly accused killers during the time frame of the Nite Owl murders. Citing Shortell's in-prison lie detector tests, his attorney Morris Waxman stated, 'Polygraphs don't lie. Otis is a religious man who carries a great burden of guilt for not coming forth to exonerate innocent men five years ago, and now he wants to see justice done. He has given three dead victims a lie detector validated alibi and now he wants to see the real killers punished. I will not cease publicizing this matter until the LAPD agrees to do their duty and reopen the case.'

Richard Tunstell, city editor of the Los Angeles *Daily News*, echoed that sentiment. 'We've got our teeth sunk into something important. We're not going to let go.'

BANNERS

L.A. *Daily News*, March 14:

J'ACCUSE – LAPD IN NITE OWL COVER-UP

L.A. *Daily News*, March 15:

OPEN LETTER TO TRIGGERMAN EXLEY

L.A. *Times*, March 16:

CONVICT'S LAWYER PETITIONS STATE ATTORNEY GENERAL FOR NITE OWL CASE REOPENING

L.A. *Herald-Express*, March 17:

PARKER TO THE PRESS: NITE OWL A DEAD ISSUE

L.A. *Daily News*, March 19:

**CITIZENS DEMAND JUSTICE – PICKETS
STALK THE LAPD**

L.A. *Herald-Express*, March 20:

**PARKER/LOEW IN HOT SEAT
GOVERNOR KNIGHT: NITE OWL
A 'POWDER KEG'**

L.A. *Mirror-News*, March 20:

**THE WAGES OF DEATH –
EXCLUSIVE PICS OF EXLEY/SOTO
LOVE NEST**

L.A. *Examiner*, March 20:

**POLICE SWITCHBOARDS
FLOODED: CITIZENS VOICE
NITE OWL OPINIONS**

L.A. *Times*, March 20:

**PARKER BACKS EXLEY AND HOLDS FIRM:
'NO NITE OWL REOPENING'**

L.A. *Daily News*, March 20:

**JUSTICE MUST PREVAIL!
DEMAND POLICE ACCOUNTABILITY!
REOPEN THE NITE OWL CASE NOW!**

Part Four

Destination: Morgue

Chapter Forty-eight

The phone rang: odds on the press 20 to 1. Ed picked up anyway. 'Yes?'

'Bill Parker, Ed.'

'Sir, how are you? And thanks for that quote in the *Times*.'

'I meant it, son. We're going to tough this thing out and let it pass. How's Inez taking it? The publicity, I mean.'

'My father said she's staying at Ray Dieterling's place in Laguna. And we broke it off a few months ago. It just wasn't working.'

'I'm sorry. Inez is a plucky girl, though. Compared to what she's been through, this thing should be cake.'

Ed rubbed his eyes. 'I'm not so sure it'll pass.'

'I think it will. The Gaitsville Police won't cooperate on the Englekling homicides and that Negro at Quentin has nil value as a witness. His polygraph seems valid, but his attorney is a grandstanding shyster only interested in getting his client out of – '

'Sir, all that aside, I don't think the men I killed did the Nite Owl and – '

'Don't interrupt me and don't tell me you're so suicidally naive as to think reopening the case will do one whit of good. Now, I'm waiting for it to pass and the attorney general up in Sacramento is waiting for it to pass. Bad publicity, petitions for justice and the like *always* peak out and pass.'

'And if it doesn't?'

Parker sighed. 'If the A.G. orders a state-run special investigation, I'll file an LAPD injunction against him and preempt him with an investigation of our own. I have

Ellis Loew's full support on that strategy – but it *will* pass.'

Ed said, 'I'm not so sure I want it to.'

Chapter Forty-nine

Mobster Squad duty: room 6, the Victory Motel. Bud, Mike Breuning, a Frisco boy cuffed to the hot seat – Joe Sifakis, three loanshark falls, snatched off a train at Union Station. Breuning worked the hose; Bud watched.

Fourteen hundred on the dresser – a police charity donation. A get-out-of-town pitch in high gear – dental work coming up. Bud checked his watch – 4:20 – Dudley was late. Sifakis screamed.

Bud walked into the bathroom. Four obscene walls: sex ditties, some dated. '53 entries – he thought Nite Owl straight off. Scary: the Nite Owl big-time news, Dud wanted to talk to him bad. He turned on the sink – cover the screams. He tested *his* Nite Owl string, found it watertight.

Nobody knew he leaked his story to *Whisper* – if the high brass knew he would have heard – and Cathcart's stiff was still under the house. Nobody knew he tipped the Gaitsville Sheriff's to the Englekling connection to the Nite Owl. Lucky breaks: the brothers dead, the spook up at Quentin – probably a legit alibi. He was clean on the evidence he suppressed in '53 – if Dudley had an inkling he was holding stuff back it probably tied to his fix on the Kathy snuff. Dud was the Nite Owl supervisor, he'd want the brouhaha to pass – a reopening would make him look like a supporting player chump – second banana to hero chump Ed Exley. Parker was trying to keep a reopening kiboshed, call the odds against it 5 to 1, 5 to 1 that Exley would come out smelling –

Sifakis screamed – the door shook.

Bud doused his head in the sink. A scrawl by the mirror: Meg Greunwitz fucks good – AX-74022. Girls' names on the walls; last week the L.A. Sheriff's bagged a dead hooker, add it to his list: Lynette Ellen Kendrick, age 21, DOD 3/17/58. Beaten, ring lacerations, three-hole rape – the county cops wouldn't give him the time of –

Sifakis started babbling. The bathroom got too hot to take.

Bud walked out. Sifakis, snitch-frenzied. ' . . . and I know things, I *hear* things. Like, dig, with the Mick out it's open season. Things was on this weird slowdown while he was inside, but these shooter teams took out these guys that was running his franchises, then these maverick guys, three triggers bang bang bang, they 86'd Mickey's men and these guys trying to crash his loanouts. Everybody used to respect Dud S. as a trucemaker, but now he don't do a damn thing. You want a prostie roust? Huh? Huh? You want a good tip on a . . . '

Breuning looked bored. Bud went out to the courtyard: crabgrass, barbed-wire fenced. Fourteen empty rooms – LAPD bought the property cheap.

'Lad.'

Dudley on the sidewalk. Bud lit a cigarette, walked over.

'Lad, I'm sorry I'm late.'

'It don't matter, you said it was serious.'

'Yes, it is all of that. How are you enjoying the Hollywood squad, lad? Is it to your liking?'

'I liked Homicide better.'

'Grand, and I'll see to it that you return sometime soon. And have you been relishing the spectacle of friend Exley ridiculed by the fourth estate?'

Smoke made him cough. 'Yeah, sure. Too bad the case won't get reopened and really make him squirm. Not that I'd want to see you stand heat for it, though.'

Dudley laughed. 'I see the conflicts inherent in your perspective. And I feel a certain ambivalence myself, especially since a little birdie in Sacramento has informed me that the attorney general will soon press to reopen the case. Ellis Loew has an injunction prepared should things get dicey, so I think it is safe to assume that the Nite Owl is regrettably our hot potato once again. Political infighting, lad. The pinko Democrats have taken the tack of jigaboos wrongly accused, intend to press the issue during the primary elections, and the Republican A.G. has sidestepped and counterpunched. Lad, do you possess any Nite Owl information that you haven't presented to me?'

Ready, prepared. 'No.'

'Ah, grand. That aside then, I have an assignment for you here at the Victory tonight. A very large and muscular man requires a bracing, and frankly Mike and Dick lack the presence to appropriately impress him. It's a small world, lad – I think this chap knew our friend Duke Cathcart back in '53. Maybe he can give you some information on your Kathy Janeway fixation. Does fair Kathy's fate still concern you, lad?'

Bud swallowed – dry.

'Lad, forget that I asked. Fixations like that are like prostitutes – they can reform, but their old ways still linger. Tonight at 10:00, lad. And be of good cheer. I have some extracurricular work for you soon, work that should rekindle your old fearsome habits.'

Bud blinked.

Dudley smiled, walked to room 6.

Prostitute equals Lynn. Janeway jibe equals just how much?

Joe Sifakis screamed – through four walls, out to the edge of the courtyard.

Chapter Fifty

Gallaudet slipped him the news: the Attorney General's Office was set to press for a reopening: state-financed, state-run. Ellis Loew was set to usurp their investigation – the LAPD, Nite Owl redux. Time to call it all in.

Ed in a coffee shop on La Brea. Jack Vincennes due, paperwork on the table: Nite Owl, notes on the Hudgens case.

Check mark: was the man at San Quentin telling the truth? Most likely yes – whatever his motives.

Check mark: did the Englekling killings tie in to the Nite Owl? No way to tell until the Marin Sheriff's shared their information.

Check mark: the purple car by the Nite Owl. A hunch: it was an innocent vehicle, the real killers followed the publicity, located Ray Coates' car before the LAPD, planted the shotguns. This meant – astoundingly – that they planted the spent shells found in Griffith Park. Hall of Justice Jail records '35 to '55 had been destroyed – if the killers gleaned the information as part of a jail connection, finding that connection would most likely prove impossible. Have Kleckner and Fisk thoroughly investigate every logical possibility pertaining to the purple car/planted shotguns.

Check mark: victim Malcolm Lunceford, ex-LAPD officer/wino security guard. Did he tie in to some kind of criminal conspiracy that resulted in the Nite Owl massacre? Answer: unlikely – he was a certified, long-term Nite Owl habitué, late nights always.

Ed sipped coffee, thought POWER. Abused: IAD was autonomous inside and outside the Department; he'd had Fisk and Kleckner working toward a possible reopening – LAPD's or his own. Vincennes admitted his tail on Bud White and lied about White knowing his sporadic

320

girlfriend – Lynn Bracken – during the spring of '53. Lynn Bracken was placed under loose surveillance; Fisk just submitted a report.

The woman was rumored to be an ex-prostitute; she co-owned a dress shop in Santa Monica. Her partner: Pierce Morehouse Patchett, age fifty-six. Kleckner secured a financial report: Patchett emerged as a wealthy investor known to pimp call girls to business associates. The financial kicker:

Patchett owned an apartment building in Hollywood. A weird shootout took place there – in the middle of the Nite Owl time frame. He caught the squeal himself: no suspects apprehended, sadomasochist gear in a shot-riddled downstairs unit. The manager claimed not to know the building's owner – he was paid by mail, suspected a dummy corporation issued him his paycheck. He knew the first name of the apartment's tenant – 'Lamar,' a 'big blond guy.' The manager blamed Lamar for the shootout; a Hollywood Division follow-up report stated that Lamar had not been seen since the incident. Incident closed.

Trashcan was late. Move to the Hudgens notes.

God-awful butchery, no hard suspects, Hudgens roundly hated. A lackluster investigation – heat fell briefly on Max Peltz and the *Badge of Honor* crew – *Hush-Hush* published an article 'exposing' Peltz and his lust for teenage girls. Peltz passed a polygraph test; the rest of the 'crew' proffered alibis. Between the lines – Parker considered the victim scum, short-shrifted the case.

Still no Trash. Ed skimmed the alibi sheet.

Max Peltz engaged in statutory rape – heavily implied, no charges filed. Script girl Penny Fulweider home with her husband; Billy Dieterling alibied – Timmy Valburn. Set designer David Mertens – a sickly man suffering from epilepsy and other ailments – alibied by Jerry Marsalas, his live-in male nurse. Star Brett Chase at a party; co-star Miller Stanton likewise. A bust – but Hudgens' death had to play central to Vincennes' spring '53.

Trashcan walked up, sat down. No prelims. 'You're calling it in?'

'I'm meeting with Parker tomorrow. I'm sure he's going to announce a reopening.'

Vincennes laughed. 'Then don't look so grim. If you're crazy enough to want it, at least act happy.'

Ed placed six shell casings on the table. 'Three of these are target rounds I retrieved from your last range practice, three are rounds I took out of a Hollywood Division evidence locker. Identical lands and grooves. April '53, Jack. You remember that shootout on Cheramoya?'

Trash grabbed the table. 'Keep going.'

'Pierce Patchett owns that building on Cheramoya, and it's a nicely hidden ownership. S&M gear was found on the premises, and Patchett is a K.A. of Lynn Bracken, Bud White's girlfriend, who you denied knowing. You were working a smut job for Ad Vice then, and smut and sadomasochist paraphernalia are in the same ballpark. The last time we talked you admitted that Hudgens had a file on you, that that was why you were all over the place then. Here's my big leap, so correct me if I'm wrong. Bracken and Patchett were K.A.'s of Hudgens.'

Vincennes dug his hands in – the table shook. 'So you're a smart fucker. So what?'

'So did Bud White know Hudgens?'

'No, I don't think – '

'What does White have on Patchett and Bracken?'

'I don't know. Exley, look – '

'No, *you* look. And you answer me. Did you get Hudgens' file on you?'

Trashcan, sweating. 'Yeah, I did.'

'Who from?'

'The Bracken woman.'

'How did you get it out of her?'

'Deposition threat. I wrote out a deposition on her and Patchett, everything I put together about them. I made carbons and stashed them in safe-deposit boxes.'

'And you – '

'Yeah, I've still got them. And they've still got a carbon on me.'

Educated guess. 'And Patchett was pushing that smut you were chasing?'

'Yeah. Exley, look – '

'No, Vincennes, *you* look. Do you still have copies of the smut books?'

'I've got the depositions and the books. You want them, I get my evidence suppression wiped. And half the Nite Owl collar.'

'A third. There's no way to make the case without White.'

Chapter Fifty-one

Room 6 at Victory. Dudley, a muscle creep chained to the hot seat. Dot Rothstein ogling *Playboy*. Bud watched her scope cheesecake: a bull-dyke cop in a Hughes Aircraft jumpsuit.

Dudley skimmed a rap sheet. 'Lamar Hinton, age thirty-one. One ADW conviction, a former telephone company employee strongly suspected of installing bootleg bookie lines for Jack "The Enforcer" Whalen. A parole absconder since April 1953. Lad, I think it is safe to refer to you as an organized crime associate, thus someone in need of reeducation in the ways of polite society.'

Hinton licked his lips; Dudley smiled. 'You came along peacefully, which is to your credit. You did not give us a song and dance about your civil rights, which, since you don't have any, speaks well of your intelligence. Now, my job is to deter and contain organized crime in Los Angeles, and I have found that physical force often serves as the most persuasive corrective measure. Lad, I will ask questions, you will answer them. If I am satisfied with your answers, Sergeant Wendell White will remain in his chair. Now, why did you abscond your parole in April 1953?'

Hinton stuttered. Bud threw backhands – eyes on the wall so he wouldn't have to see. Left/right/left/right/left/right – Dot flashed the cut-off sign.

Cease fire. Dudley: 'A little admonishing to show you what Sergeant White is capable of. Now, from here on in I will accommodate your stammer. Do you recall the question? Why did you abscond your parole in April 1953?'

Stut-stut-stutter: Hinton with his eyes squeezed shut.

'Lad, we're waiting.'

Hinton: 'H-h-had b-b-blow t-town.'

'Ah, grand. And what precipitated your need to leave?'

'J-just w-woman t-t-trouble.'

'Lad, I don't believe you.'

'Th-th-the t-truth.'

Dudley nodded. Bud threw backhands – pulled, fake full force. Dot said, 'This boy could take a lot of grief. Come on, sugar, make it easy on yourself. April '53. Why'd you blow town?'

Bud heard Breuning and Carlisle next door. It hit him: 4/53 – the Nite Owl.

'Lad, I overestimated the power of your memory, so let me help it along. Pierce Patchett. You were acquainted with him back then, weren't you?'

Bud, chills: evidence suppression, he shouldn't know Patchett existed –

Hinton jerked, thrashed.

'Ah, grand, I think we touched a nerve.'

Dot sighed. 'God, such muscles. I should have such muscles.'

Dudley howled.

Kill the chills: he's on the reopening – maybe Hinton works in. *If he knew about my evidence dance I wouldn't be here.*

Dot sapped Hinton: the arms, the knees. Muscles took it stoic: no yelps, no whimpers.

Dudley laughed. 'Lad, you have a high threshold for discomfort. Comment on the following, please: Pierce Patchett, Duke Cathcart and pornography. Be concise or Sergeant White will test that threshold.'

Hinton, no stutter. 'Fuck you, Irish cocksucker.'

Ho, ho, ho. 'Lad, you're a regular Jack Benny. Wendell, show our organized crime associate your opinion of unsolicited comedy acts.'

Bud grabbed Dot's sap. 'What are you looking for, boss?'

'Full and docile cooperation.'

'Is this the Nite Owl? You said Duke Cathcart.'

'I want full and docile cooperation on all topics. Have you objections to that?'

Dot said, 'White, just do it. God, I should have such muscles.'

Bud got close. 'Let me play him solo. Just a couple minutes.'

'A return to your old methods, lad? It's been a while since you evinced enthusiasm for this kind of work.'

Bud whispered. 'I'm gonna let him think he can take me, then shiv him. You and Dot wait outside, okay?'

Dudley nodded, walked Dot out. Bud turned the radio on: a commercial, used-car values at Yeakel Olds.

Hinton rattled his chains. 'Fuck you, fuck that Irish guy and fuck that fucking diesel dyke.'

Bud pulled up a chair. 'I don't like this stuff, so you be good and give me some answers on the side and I'll tell the man to cut you loose. You got that? No parole roust.'

'Fuck you.'

'Hinton, I think you know Pierce Patchett, and maybe you knew Duke Cathcart. You can tell me some side stuff and I'll – '

'Fuck your mother.'

Bud threw Hinton and his chair across the room. The hot seat landed sideways – slats popped off. Shelves collapsed – the radio broke, spewing static.

Bud uprighted the chair one-handed. Hinton pissed his pants. Bud heard himself talking, a weird voice like a brogue. 'Give me some pimp stuff, lad. Cathcart, a coon named Dwight Gilette – they both ran this girl Kathy Janeway. She got snuffed and I don't like that. You got information on them, *lad*?'

Eyeball to eyeball – Hinton's wide wide. No stutter, don't rile the fucking animal. 'Sir, I just had this driver job for Mr. Patchett, me and this guy Chester Yorkin. All we did was deliver these . . . these illegal things . . . and Cathcart, him I don't know from Adam. I heard Gilette was a swish, all I know's he used to get hooers for Spade Cooley's parties. You want skinny on Spade? I know he blows opium, he's a righteous degenerate dope fiend. He's playing the El Rancho now, you roust him. But I don't know no hooer killers and I don't know no girl Kathy Janeway.'

Bud shook the chair – Hinton kept snitching. 'Sir, Mr. Patchett, he ran call girls. Gorgeous tail, all fixed up like movie stars. His favorite was this gorgeous cunt Lynn, looked just like – '

Bud went straight for his face. The face went red, big men pressed in – arms around him – lifting him. The ceiling zooming down, cracked stucco swirls going black.

Questions and answers through black, shouts and whimpers through gauze – a wall that held faces back. Stag books, Cathcart, Pierce P. – the full drift couldn't get through. A strain to hear 'Lynn Bracken,' no yield on the name, the black going that much blacker. Mickey Cohen, '53 and why'd you run – he tore at the gauze for that name. Shrieks that made him burrow into softness – snapshots of Lynn all around him.

Lynn blond and a whore, brunette and herself. Lynn on his thing with Inez: 'Be kind to her and spare me the details.' Lynn filling up her diary while he punked out on reading it because he knew she had him down cold. Lynn thinking two steps ahead of him, drifting in and out of his life while he drifted in and out of hers. That black gauze throbbing – questions, answers. Black silence, cracked stucco swirls going light.

Room 7 at the Victory: cots for the Mobster Squad guys. The door to 6 wide open.

Bud rolled off his cot, stood up. His head throbbed, his jaw ached, he'd ripped up his pillow burrowing in. Into 6, a shambles: the hot seat, blood on the walls. No Hinton, no Dot, no Dudley and his boys. 1:10 A.M. – no way to figure out the questions and answers.

He drove home woozy, too trashed to think. He unlocked his door yawning – the overhead light went on. Something/somebody grabbed him.

Cuffs on his wrists. Ed Exley, Jack Vincennes – square in front of him. A side check: Fisk and Kleckner – I.A. shitbirds – pinning his arms.

Exley slapped him. Fisk grabbed his neck, popped a finger on his carotid.

A folder in his face. Exley: 'I.A. ran a personal on you when you made sergeant, so we already know about Lynn Bracken. Vincennes had a tail on you back in '53, and he's got you, Bracken and Pierce Patchett in this deposition here. You braced Patchett on the Kathy Janeway homicide, and you were all over the Nite Owl like a plague. I need what you know, and if you don't cooperate I'll begin an I.A. investigation into your evidence suppression immediately. The Department needs a scapegoat on the old Nite Owl job – and I'm too valuable to take the fall. If you don't cooperate, I'll use every bit of my juice to ruin you.'

The choke hold went slack – Bud tried to pull away. Kleckner and Fisk dug in. 'You fuck, I'll fucking kill you.'

Exley laughed. 'I don't think so, and if you play you get your evidence suppression chilled, part of the collar and a little plum – a liaison to those hooker snuffs you care so much about.'

Black gauze coming back. 'Lynn?'

'She's our first interrogation – with pentothal. If she's clean, she walks.'

He doesn't know about *Whisper*, I've still got that stiff in San Berdoo. 'And you and me when it's over.'

Chapter Fifty-two

No sleep – Vincennes' deposition wouldn't let him. The wake-up call he didn't need: a reporter at 6:00 A.M. Radio news riding over: reopening speculation, a *mano a mano* with his father – the freeway system near done, the Nite Owl hero now a villain. Parking lot pickets – Commie types demanding justice.

Early – for the most important meeting of his career.

Parker's conference room was set up – notepads on the table. Ed wrote 'Patchett,' 'Bracken,' 'Patchett's "deal" with Hudgens – extortion?'; he underlined 'Pornography pictures match Hudgens mutilations – have Vincennes bring smut books to Bureau.' White's contribution: 'Patchett hinked on smut in '53'; 'Patchett/Englekling bros and father chem background'; 'Duke Cathcart's pad tossed & San Berdoo Yellow Pages (printshops) ruffled.' White was still holding back – he knew it.

Deposition underlined: 'Patchett involved (through Fleur-de-Lis racket) in (contained) distribution of smut Ad Vice chasing in '53, smut Cathcart developed distribution scheme around, smut connected to mutilations on Hudgens' body.'

Conclusion:

A dense series of criminal conspiracies at least five years old resulting in no fewer than four and perhaps as many as a dozen major crimes.

The other men filed in – Parker, Dudley Smith, Ellis Loew. Nods, quick sit-downs.

Parker said, 'We're reopening. The A.G.'s Office wants to usurp the job, but Ellis has filed a restraining order against them, which should buy us two weeks' time. We've got two weeks to clear the case and recover the respect we lost. We've got two weeks before Sacramento comes down here and makes us a laughingstock. I want this case cleared, legally inviolate and in the hands of the grand jury within twelve days. Do you understand, gentlemen?'

Nods all around. Loew said, 'I'm personally in a difficult position here, since Coates, Jones and Fontaine *did* confess to me. On reflection, I must admit that they were stupid and naive boys psychologically susceptible to suggestion, so – '

Smith cut in. 'Ellis, that's blood under the bridge. We simply got the wrong coloreds, not the ones who fired off those shotguns in Griffith Park. The real culprits are some smart Darktown strutters who knew where Coates stashed his car, then planted the weapons. Lads who knew niggertown well and simply beat us to the location. The purple car seen by the Nite Owl was just a coincidence that the killers capitalized on. I think the Griffith Park car was stolen or out of state, and in any event I think it's not applicable. We have to begin by shaking down the southside again.'

Ed smiled – Smith's tack played into his plan. 'Essentially I agree, and I've got one of my I.A. men checking old registrations. But aren't we ahead of ourselves? Shouldn't we set up a chain of command first?'

Loew coughed. 'Ed, I think your shooting those thugs was a noble act, whatever your motives. But I think giving you the command would just make the press and the public more resentful. I think you should take a subsidiary role in this investigation.'

Outrage down pat. 'I'm tired of being the bad guy on the six o'clock news and I'm tired of my sex life in the papers. I'm also the best detective in the – '

Parker cut in. 'You are the best detective we have, and I understand your need to cut your losses. But Ellis is right, this is too personal with you. I've given Dudley the command. He'll recruit a team from Homicide and various squadrooms and take it from there.'

'And me? Do I get a piece of the case?'

Parker nodded. 'I'll give you anything within reason.'

The kill. 'I want the chance to develop my own evidence

330

with I.A. autonomy. I want the use of my two personal aides from I.A. and my choice of two officers to serve as field runners.'

'That's fine by me. Dudley?'

'Yes, I think that's fair. Lad, who did you have in mind for runners?'

'Jack Vincennes and Bud White.'

Smith almost gawked. Parker said, 'Strange bedfellows, but then it's a strange case. Twelve days, gentlemen. Not one minute longer.'

Chapter Fifty-three

Jack woke up on the couch, wrote Karen a note.

Sweetie –
Fairs fair & yeah I screwed up with Ellis. But this goddamn sofa for two months isn't fair & if the Department can forgive me then you should be able to too. I haven't had a drink for six weeks, which if you checked the calendar by my closet you'd know. I don't expect you to think that makes everything right with us, but give me some credit for trying. I'll try – you want to go to law school, great, but I bet you'll hate it. In May I'll retire, maybe I can get a police chief job in some hick town near a good law school. I'll try, but cut me some slack because this deep freeze number is driving me crazy & right now I can't afford to be crazy because I've been detached back to work plainclothes on something that's very important to me. I'll probably be working late for the next week or so, but I'll call & check in.
J.

He dressed, waited for the phone to ring. Coffee in the kitchen, a note from Karen.

J. –
I've been a bitch lately. I'm sorry and I think we should try to figure some things out. You were asleep when I got home or I would have invited you into the boudoir.

XXXXX – K

P.S. A girl at work showed me this magazine that I

thought you might be interested in seeing. I know
you know that man Exley it mentions and it certainly
is pertinent to what's been in the papers lately.

On the table: *Whisper* – 'All the Dirt That's Fit to
Print.' Jack thumbed it smiling, caught a Nite Owl
spread.

Hopped-up stuff – 'Crusading Private Eye,' 'Duke
Cathcart impersonator,' smut speculation. Ed Exley raked
over hot coals – Exley hatred big. A snap take: 'P.I.' Bud
White shivs Exley – a February issue on sale in January,
out before the Englekling brothers got clipped and that
shine up at Quentin dropped that alibi. East Coast circulation, you probably couldn't find the rag in L.A. Exley
and the high brass couldn't have seen it – or *he* would
have heard.

The phone rang – Jack grabbed it. 'Exley?'

'Yes, and you're officially detached. White talked to
Lynn Bracken. She's agreed to be pentothaled, and I want
you to bring her in. She'll be waiting at that Chinese
restaurant across from the Bureau in an hour. Meet her
there and bring her up to I.A., and if she's got a lawyer
get rid of him.'

'Look, I saw something I think you should see.'

'Just bring me the woman.'

The woman five years post-file burning – Lynn Bracken
sipping tea at Al Wong's. Jack watched her through the
window.

Still a showstopper. A brunette now, a thirty-fivish
beauty drawing stares. She saw him. Jack got flutters: his
file.

She walked out. Jack said, 'I didn't want this to
happen.'

'You let it. And aren't you afraid of what I know about
you?'

Something skewed: she was too calm five minutes from
a bracing. 'I've got this scary captain looking after me. If
it came out, I'm betting he'd kibosh it.'

333

'Don't make any bets you can't cover. And I'm only doing this because Bud told me he'd get hurt if I didn't.'

'What else did Bud tell you?'

'Bad things about your scary captain. Can we go now? I want to get this over with.'

They walked across the street, up the back Bureau stairs. Fisk met them outside I.A., steered them to Exley's office. A scary set-up: scary Captain Ed. Ray Pinker, a desk covered with medical stuff – vials, syringes. A polygraph machine – backup if the truth juice failed.

Pinker filled a hypo. Exley pointed Lynn to a chair. 'Please, Miss Bracken.'

Lynn sat down. Pinker swabbed her left arm, fitted a tourniquet. Exley, all business. 'I don't know what Bud White told you, but essentially this is an investigation involving several interrelated criminal conspiracies. If you provide us with viable information we're prepared to grant you immunity on any possible criminal charges you might accrue.'

Lynn made a fist. 'I can't very well lie. Can we get this over with, please?'

Pinker took her arm, injected her. Exley punched a tape machine. Lynn went dreamy-eyed – not quite pentothal gaga. Exley talked into a hand mike. 'Witness Lynn Bracken, March 22, 1958. Miss Bracken, please count backward from one hundred.'

Slurs right off. 'Hundred, ninety-nine, ninety-eight, ninety-sev, nine-six . . .'

Pinker checked her eyes, nodded. Jack grabbed a chair. Still too calm – he could taste it.

Exley coughed. '3/22/58, present with the witness are myself, Sergeant Duane Fisk, Sergeant John Vincennes and forensic chemist Ray Pinker. Duane, transcribe in shorthand.'

Fisk grabbed a notepad. Exley said, 'Miss Bracken, how old are you?'

A slight slur. 'Thirty-four.'

'And your occupation?'

'Businesswoman.'

'Do you own Veronica's Dress Shop in Santa Monica?'

'Yes.'

'Why did you choose the name "Veronica's"?'

'A personal joke.'

'Please elaborate.'

'It's a name from my old life.'

'How specifically?'

A dreamy smile. 'I used to be a prostitute made up to resemble Veronica Lake.'

'Who convinced you to do that?'

'Pierce Patchett.'

'I see. Did Pierce Patchett kill a man named Sid Hudgens in April 1953?'

'No. I mean I don't know. Why would he?'

'Do you know who Sid Hudgens was?'

'Yes. A scandal-sheet writer.'

'Did Patchett know Hudgens?'

'No. I mean if he did know him, he would have told me, a famous man like that.'

A lie – she couldn't be full on the juice. She had to know he knew she was lying – she was thinking he'd cover her to protect himself.

Exley: 'Miss Bracken, do you know who killed a girl named Kathy Janeway in the spring of 1953?'

'No.'

'Do you know a man named Lamar Hinton?'

'Yes.'

'Please elaborate.'

'He worked for Pierce.'

'In what capacity?'

'As a driver.'

'And when was this?'

'Several years ago.'

'Do you know where Hinton is now?'

'No.'

'Elaborate on your answer, please.'

'No, he went away, I don't know where he went.'

'Did Hinton attempt to kill Sergeant Jack Vincennes in April 1953?'

'No.'

She told him no back then.

'Who did try to kill him?'

'I don't know.'

'Who else worked or works as a driver for Patchett?'

'Chester Yorkin.'

'Please elaborate.'

'Chet, Chester Yorkin, he lives in Long Beach some-where.'

'Does Pierce Patchett suborn women into prostitution?'

'Yes.'

'Who killed the six people at the Nite Owl Coffee Shop in April 1953?'

'I don't know.'

'Does Pierce Patchett sell a variety of illegal items through a service known as Fleur-de-Lis?'

'I don't know.'

A huge lie. Hink on her face: veins pulsing.

Exley: 'Does Dr. Terry Lux perform plastic surgery on Patchett's prostitutes in order to increase their resem-blance to movie stars?'

Veins smoothing out. 'Yes.'

'Is Patchett in fact a long-term procurer of expensive call girls?'

'Yes.'

'Did Patchett distribute expensive and artfully prod-uced pornography during the spring of 1953?'

'I don't know.'

White knuckles. Jack grabbed a notepad, wrote: 'Patch-ett a chem whiz. L.B.'s lying & I think she's on dope to counter pentothal. Get blood sample.'

'Miss Bracken, does – '

Jack passed the note. Exley scanned it, passed it to Pinker. Pinker fixed up a spike.

'Miss Bracken, does Patchett possess secret files stolen from Sid Hudgens?'

'I don't kn – '

Pinker grabbed Lynn's arm, fed the needle. Lynn jerked up; Exley grabbed her. Pinker pulled out the spike;

Exley pinned Lynn to his desk. She thrashed and kicked – Fisk got behind her and cuffed her. Spitting now – she caught Exley in the face. Fisk wrestled her out to the hall.

Exley wiped his face – red, mottled. 'I wasn't sure myself. I thought she might have been confused.'

Jack handed him *Whisper*. 'I knew how she should answer better than you. Captain, you should see this.'

Scary: that red face, those eyes. Exley read the piece, tore the rag in half. 'White did this. You go up to San Bernardino and talk to Sue Lefferts' mother. I'm going to break that whore.'

San Berdoo in an uproar: Exley breaking that whore as a slide show. 'Hilda Lefferts' in the phone book, directions, the house: white shingles, a cinderblock add-on.

A granny type watering the lawn. Jack parked, taped up the rip job on *Whisper*. The old girl saw him and rabbited – a run for the door.

He ran over. She squealed, 'Let my Susie rest in peace!'

Jack shoved *Whisper* in her face. 'An L.A. policeman talked to you, right? Big man about forty? You told him your daughter had a boyfriend who looked like Duke Cathcart right before the Nite Owl. He told her "get used to calling me 'Duke.'" ' The policeman showed you mugshots and you couldn't make the boyfriend. Is this true? You read this and tell me.'

She read, fast, squinting away sunlight. 'But he said he was a policeman, not a private detective. Those were police-type pictures he showed me, and it wasn't my fault that I couldn't identify Susie's beau. And I want to go on record as stating that Susie was a virgin when she died.'

'Ma'am, I'm sure she was – '

'And I want it to go on record that that policeman or whatever checked underneath the new wing on my house and found not a thing amiss. Young man, you're a police-man, aren't you?'

Jack shook his head – it felt sludgy. 'Lady, what are you telling me?'

'I'm telling you that Mr. Private Eye Policeman or

whatever crawled around under my house two months or so ago, because I told him Susan Nancy's beau did the same thing right after this ruckus they had with this other fellow right before that Nite Owl thing that you people keep tormenting me over, may Susie and the other victims rest in peace. All he found were rodents, not signs of foul play, so there.'

So there.

Granny pointed to a crawlspace flush with the ground – so there.

It fucking could not be. Bud White did not have the brains to let a card that strong sit.

Jack took a flashlight down under – Hilda Lefferts stood watching, so there. Dust, rot, mothball stink – light on dirt, rats, rat eyes glowing. Burlap, mothballs, gristle-caked bones, a skull with a hole between the eyes.

Chapter Fifty-four

Ed watched Lynn Bracken through the two-way.

Kleckner was questioning her, a nice guy set-up for Mr. Bad Guy – himself. She'd been repentothaled; Ray Pinker was testing her blood. Three hours in a cell hadn't broken her – she was still lying with style.

Ed turned the speaker up. Kleckner: 'I'm not saying that I don't believe you, I'm just saying my policeman's experience has shown me that pimps usually hate women, so I don't buy Patchett as such a philanthropist.'

'You have to look at his background, how he lost a little girl to crib death. I'm sure your policeman's mentality can grasp the cause and effect, even if you can't accept it.'

'Let's talk about his background then. You've described Patchett as a financier with L.A. roots going back thirty years. You've said that he puts deals together, so be specific about the deals.'

Lynn sighed – pure panache. 'Movie financing deals, real estate and contracting deals. Here's one for all you movie fans in the audience. Pierce told me he'd financed a few of Raymond Dieterling's early shorts.'

Cozy: Bud White's girlfriend's pimp knew Preston Exley's good buddy. Kleckner changed tape. Ed studied the whore.

Beautiful – a good part of it hung on the fact that she wasn't perfect. Her nose was too pointed; she had crease lines on her forehead. Big shoulders, big hands – beautifully formed, all the more stunning for being large. Blue eyes that probably danced when a man said the right thing; she probably thought Bud White had primitive integrity and respected him for not trying to impress her with gifts he didn't have. She kept her clothing subtle because she knew it would make more of an impression

339

on the people she wanted to impress; she thought most men were weak and trusted her brains to slide her through anything. Suppositions leading up to a hunch: couple her brains with the counterdope in her system and you got a pentothal-immune witness dissembling with impunity – and style.

'Captain, you got a call. It's Vincennes.'

Fisk had his phone, stretched to the end of the cord. Ed took it. 'Vincennes?'

'Yeah, and listen close, 'cause that scandal sheet story was kosher and there's lots more.'

'White?'

'Yeah, White was that phony P.I., and he braced old lady Lefferts two months or so ago. She told him that story of her daughter's boyfriend who looked like Duke Cathcart and another doozie.'

'*What?*'

'Just listen. A couple weeks before the Nite Owl, a neighbor saw Susie and the boyfriend alone at the house and heard them get into a ruckus with another guy. The boyfriend was seen crawling around under the house later that same day. Now, when White braced the old lady, he called P.C. Bell and checked their records for toll calls from the house to L.A. mid-March to mid-April '53. I did the same thing and got three tollers, all to a pay phone in Hollywood near the Nite Owl. Now, you think that's hot, you – '

'Goddammit – '

'Captain, *listen*. White crawled around under the house and told granny there was nothing there. I went under and found a stiff, wrapped in mothballs to kill the stink and a fucking bullet hole in the head. I got Doc Layman up to San Berdoo. He brought Duke Cathcart's prison dental file, the Coroner's Office copy. It was a perfect match. The first ID was bogus, off a partial plate, just like that article said. Fuck, I can't believe White put all this together and just left the stiff there. Captain, you there?'

Ed grabbed Fisk. 'Where's Bud White?'

Fisk looked scared. 'I heard he went up north with Dudley Smith. The Marin Sheriff's decided to kick loose on the Engleklings.'

Back to Trashcan. 'That article said the woman saw some mugs.'

'Yeah, White brought back some shots marked "State Records Bureau." Now we both know the state sets run light, so my guess is White didn't want to bring her down here to check our books. Anyway, she couldn't ID the boyfriend, and if the boyfriend was one of the Nite Owl stiffs we'll have him, 'cause Nort Layman took prison dental plate fragments out of his head back in '53. Bring her down? Show her our books?'

'Do it.'

Fisk took the phone. Ray Pinker walked up, holding a chem sheet. 'Prestilphyozine, Captain. It's an extremely rare experimental antipsychotic drug used to tranquilize violent mental patients. Somebody professional slipped it to our lady friend, because only a pro would know this breed of phyozine would be likely to counteract pentothal. Skipper, you should sit down, you look like you're about to have a coronary.'

Chemistry whiz Patchett: the Englekling brothers' father: a chemist who developed antipsychotic compounds. Bud White's whore across the glass – alone now, a tape recorder spinning.

Ed walked in. Lynn said, 'You again?'

'That's right.'

'Don't you have to charge me or release me?'

'Not for another sixty-eight hours.'

'Aren't you violating my constitutional rights?'

'Constitutional rights have been waived for this one.'

'*This one?*'

'Don't play dumb. This one is Pierce Patchett distributing pornography, including picture-book photographs that exactly match the mutilations on a murder victim, namely his late "partner" Sid Hudgens. This one is one of the supposed Nite Owl victims tied in to a conspiracy to distribute that pornography and your friend Bud White

341

withholding major evidence on who the real victim was. Now, White told you to cooperate and you came here under the influence of a drug to counteract pentothal. That's against you, but you can still save yourself *and* White a lot of trouble by cooperating.'

'Bud can look after himself. And you look terrible. Your face is all red.'

Ed sat down, turned off the tape. 'You don't even feel the dosage, do you?'

'I feel like I've had four martinis, and four martinis just make me that much more lucid.'

'Patchett sent you in without a lawyer to buy time, I know it. He knows you were called in as part of the Nite Owl reopening, so he knows he's a material witness at least. Personally, I don't see him as a killer. I know a great deal about Patchett's various enterprises, and you can save him a great deal of trouble by cooperating with me.'

Lynn smiled. 'Bud said you were quite smart.'

'What else did he say?'

'That you were a weak, angry man competing with your father.'

Let it pass. 'Then let's concentrate on my smarts. Patchett is a chemist, and it may be reaching, but I'm betting he studied under Franz Englekling, a pharmacologist who developed drugs such as the antipsychotic compound Patchett put you under to beat the pentothal. Englekling had two sons, who were murdered in Northern California last month. Those two men came forward during the base Nite Owl investigation and mentioned a quote crazy sugar daddy-o unquote who had access to lots of quote high-class call girls unquote. Obviously Patchett, obviously tied to a would-be smut merchant named Duke Cathcart, one of the alleged Nite Owl victims. Obviously Patchett is all over this thing and in for some trouble he doesn't need and you can help circumvent.'

Lynn lit a cigarette. 'So you're very, very smart.'

'Yes, and I'm a very good detective with a five-year backlog of withheld evidence to work from. I know about

342

your file-burning episode, I know about Patchett's proposed extortion plan with Hudgens. I've read the deposition Vincennes bargained you with and I know all about Patchett's various enterprises, including Fleur-de-Lis.'

'So you're assuming that Pierce has some very damaging information on Vincennes.'

'Yes, which the district attorney and I will quash in the interest of protecting the reputation of the Los Angeles Police Department.'

Fluster: Lynn dropped her cigarette, fumbled her lighter. Ed said, 'You and Patchett can't win. I've got twelve days to square this thing right, and if I can't do it I'm going to start looking for subsidiary indictments. There's at least a dozen I can hang on Patchett, and believe me if I don't make this case I'll do anything I can to make myself look good.'

Lynn stared at him. Ed stared back. 'Patchett made you, didn't he? You were a pom-pom girl from Bisbee, Arizona, and a whore. He taught you how to dress and talk and think, and I am very impressed with the results. But I've got twelve days to keep my life out of the toilet, and if I can't do it I'm going to take you and Patchett down.'

Lynn turned on the tape player. 'Pierce Patchett's whore for the record. I'm not afraid of you and I've never loved Bud White more. It makes me happy that he withheld evidence and got the better of you, and you're a fool for underestimating him. I used to be jealous of him sleeping with Inez Soto, but now I respect the poor girl's good sense in leaving a moral coward for a man.'

Ed pressed 'Erase,' 'Stop,' 'Start.' 'For the record, sixty-seven hours to go and my next interrogation won't be so cordial.'

Kleckner opened the door, passed him a folder. 'Captain, Vincennes brought the Lefferts woman in. They're checking out mugs, and he said you wanted these.'

Ed stepped outside. A thick folder – glossy-paper smut.

The top books: pretty kids, explicit action, colorful costumes. Some of the heads had been cropped and taped

343

back on – per the deposition – Jack tried to ID the posers from mugshots and thought cropping would facilitate the effort. Ugly/arty stuff – just like Trashcan said.

The bottom books – plain black covers – Trashcan's garbage can find. The first inked-in shots – embossed red streaming from disembodied limbs, posers linked orifice to orifice. The homicide match: a spread-eagled boy in sync to the Hudgens crime scene stills.

Past astonishing – and whoever posed the smut pics killed Hudgens.

Ed hit the last book, froze. A nude pretty boy, arms spread – ink/blood gouting off his torso. Familiar, too familiar, not from a Hudgens coroner's shot. He turned pages and caught a foldout: boys, girls, offset limbs touching, ink designs linking them.

AND HE KNEW.

He ran down the hall to Homicide, found their 1934 records, found 'Atherton, Loren, 187 P.C. (multiple).' Three thick folders, then the photos – shot by Dr. Frankenstein himself.

Children immediately after their dismemberment.

Their arms and legs arranged just off their torsos.

White waxed paper under the bodies.

Blood fingerpainted around their limbs, red on white, intricate designs identical to the pornographic ink shots, limb spreads identical to the Hudgens severings.

Ed mangled his fingers slamming the cabinet, Code 2'd to Hancock Park.

A party at Preston Exley's mansion: valets parking cars, music in the back – probably a rose garden bash. Ed went in the front door and stopped short – his mother's library was gone.

Replacing it: a long space eclipsed by a model – lengths of highway over papier-mâché cities. Directional markers at the perimeters – the entire freeway system.

Perfection – it jerked him out of his filth-picture haze. Boats in San Pedro Harbor, the San Gabriel Mountains, tiny autos on asphalt. Preston Exley's greatest triumph on the eve of its completion.

Ed pushed a car – ocean to foothills. His father's voice: 'I thought you'd be working South Central today.'

Ed turned around. 'What?'

Preston smiled. 'I thought you'd be making up for your recent bad press.'

Non sequiturs – the Atherton photos came back. 'Father, excuse me, but I don't know what you're talking about.'

Preston laughed. 'We've seen each other so seldom lately that we've forgotten the amenities.'

'Father, there's something – '

'I'm sorry, I was referring to Dudley Smith's statement to the *Herald* today. He said the reopening investigation was being centered on the southside, that you're looking for another Negro gang.'

'No, that's not the way it's going.'

Preston put a hand on his shoulder. 'You look frightened, Edmund. You do not look like a ranking policeman and you did not come here to enjoy my completion celebration.'

The hand felt warm. 'Father, outside of the Department, who's seen the old Atherton photographs?'

'Now I'll say "what?" You're referring to the photographs in the case file? The ones I showed you and Thomas years ago?'

'Yes.'

'Son, what are you talking about? Those photographs are sealed LAPD evidence, never released to the press or the public. Now tell me – '

'Father, the Nite Owl is collateral to several other major crimes, and Negro gangs have nothing to do with it. One of them is – '

'Then explain the evidence the way I taught you. I've had cases like – '

'Nobody has ever had a case like this, I'm a better detective than you *ever* were and *I've* never had a case like this.'

Preston clamped both hands down – Ed felt his shoulders go numb. 'I'm sorry for that, but it's true and I've got a five-year-old mutilation homicide connected to the Nite Owl case that says so. The victim was cut *identically* to Loren Atherton's victims and *identical* to some ink-embossed pornographic photographs tangential to the Nite Owl. Which means that either somebody saw the Atherton pictures and took it from there or you got the wrong suspect in '34.'

The man didn't even blink. 'Loren Atherton was incontrovertibly guilty, with a confession and eyewitness verification. You and Thomas saw his photographs, and I doubt seriously that those photographs have ever left the Homicide pen downtown. Unless you hypothesize a policeman killer, which I find absurd, then the only explanation is that Atherton showed the photographs to some person or persons prior to his arrest. *You* got the wrong men in your glory case – I did not make that error. *Think* before you raise your voice to your father.'

Ed stepped back – his legs brushed the model, broke off a piece of freeway. 'I apologize, and I should be asking your advice, not competing with you. Father, is there anything about the Atherton case you haven't told me?'

'Apology accepted, and no, there isn't. You, Art and I went over the case constantly during our seminar period, and I expect that you know it as well as I do.'

'Did Atherton have *any* known associates?'

Preston shook his head. 'Emphatically no. He was the very model of a psychotic loner.'

A deep breath. 'I want to interview Ray Dieterling.'

'Why? Because one of his child stars was killed by Atherton?'

'No, because a witness identified Dieterling as a K.A. of a criminal tangential to the Nite Owl.'

'How long ago?'

'Thirty years or so.'

'This person's name?'

'Pierce Patchett.'

Preston shrugged. 'I've never heard of him and I don't

want you bothering Raymond. Emphatically no, a thirty-year-old acquaintanceship does not warrant bothering a man of Ray Dieterling's stature. *I'll* ask Ray about him and report back to you. Will that suffice?'

Ed looked at the model. Hypnotic: L.A. grown huge, Exley Construction containing it. His father's hands, gentle now. 'Son, you've come very far and you've earned my respect absolutely. You've taken a beating for Inez and those men you killed, and I think you're bearing up strongly. For now, though, I want you to consider this. The Nite Owl case got you where you are today and a quick resolution on the reopening will keep you there. Collateral homicide investigations, however compelling, might seriously distract you from your main objective and thus destroy your career. Please remember that.'

Ed squeezed his father's hands. 'Absolute justice. Remember that?'

Chapter Fifty-five

Both crime scenes sealed – the printshop, the pad next
door. One Marin sheriff – a fat guy named Hatcher. A
lab man talking nonstop.

Crime Scene 1: the back room at Rapid Bob's Printing.
Bud scoped Dudley nonstop, flashing back to *his* pitch:
'We thought you were going to kill him, so we stopped
you. I'm sorry if we were untoward, but you were a
handful. Hinton is associated with some very bad people,
and I'll elaborate in all due time.'

He didn't press it – Dud might have stuff on him.

Lynn in custody.

Exley's slap in the face.

The lab man pointed to a rack of dumped shelves.
' . . . okay, so the front of the shop looked hunky-dory,
so our perpetrator didn't bother with it. We found cigarette butts in an ashtray here, two brands, so let's assume
the Engleklings were working late. Let's assume the perpetrator picked the front door lock, tiptoed up and got
the drop on them. Glove prints on the jamb of the connecting door, so that backs it up. He comes in, he makes our
boys open those cabinets I showed you, he doesn't find
what he wants. He gets pissed and yanks those shelves to
the floor, glove prints on the fourth shelf up indicate a
right-handed man of average height. The brothers open
the boxes that spilled off – we got a whole load of smudged
latents that indicate Pete and Bax were a bit panicked by
this time. So, the perpetrator obviously didn't find what
he wanted and marched our boys across the driveway to
their apartment. Gentlemen, follow me.'

Out the door, across an alley. The lab guy carried a
flashlight; Bud stuck to the back.

Lynn cocky – convinced she could beat truth juice with
her brains.

Dud probably had his own insider leads – but he still kept talking up niggers.

The lab man said, 'Note the dirt on the driveway. On the morning the bodies were found our tech crew discovered and photographed three sets of footmarks too shallowly placed to make exemplers from. Two sets walking ahead of a single set, which indicates a march at gunpoint.'

Over to a bungalow court. Dudley stone quiet – on the plane he hardly talked.

Would *Whisper* hit?

Play the stiff under the house against Exley – *HOW?*

Tape on the door – Hatcher peeled it off. The lab man opened up with a pass key. Lights inside – Bud squeezed in first.

A shambles – all forensicked up.

Blood spills on a wall-to-wall carpet – tape-marked. Glass tubes on the floor – circled, held in see-through evidence bags. Scattered around: photo negatives – dozens – cracked, scalded surfaces. Overturned chairs, a dumped dresser, a sofa with the stuffing ripped out. Tucked in the largest rip: a glassine bag tagged 'Heroin.'

The lab guy spieled. 'Those tubes contain chemicals that we've ID'd as antipsychotic drugs. The negatives were mostly too blurred to identify, but we were able to figure out that most of them were pornographic photographs. The images were mostly burned off with chemicals taken from the refrigerator in the kitchen: our boys owned a whole cornucopia of corrosive solutions. I'll hypothesize here: Peter and Baxter Englekling were tortured before they were shot to death – that we know. I think the killer showed them each negative individually, asked them questions, then burned them – and the pictures. What was he looking for? I don't know, maybe he wanted the picture participants identified. We found a magnifying glass under the couch, so I'm leaning toward that theory now. Also, note the plastic bag marked "Heroin" extruding from the couch, the contents of which, of course, we locked up. Four bags total in a safe

349

little hidey-hole. The killer left a small fortune in salable dope behind.'

Into the kitchen, more chaos, the icebox open – spilling tubes, bottles marked with chemical symbols. Stacked by the sink: something like printing press plates.

The tech man pointed to the mess. 'Another hypothesis, gentlemen. In my crime scene report you'll note that I've listed no less than twenty-six separate chemical substances found on the premises. The killer tortured Pete and Bax Englekling with chemicals, and he knew which chemicals would scald flesh. I'd call his torture method a means of opportunity, so I'm betting the man had an engineering, a medical or a chemistry background. Now the bedroom.'

Bud thought: PATCHETT.

Back to the bedroom, blood drops in the hall along the way. A small room, a twelve-by-twelve slaughterhouse.

Two body outlines – one on the bed, one on the floor, dried blood tape-to-tape both places. Clothesline sash wrapped around the bedposts; more sash on the floor; taped circles on the bedsheets, the floor, a nightstand by the bed. A bullet hole circled on one wall; a forensic display on a corkboard: more scalded negatives.

Lab man: 'Just glove prints and Englekling prints on the negatives, we dusted every one of them, then placed most of them back in their original locations. The ones on the board were found here in the bedroom, which as you can tell was where the torture and the killings took place. Now, those small circles on the bed and elsewhere indicate sections of torso, arm and leg tissue scalded off the Englekling brothers, and if you look closely at the floor you'll be able to see patches of singed carpet caused by chemical spills. Both men were shot twice with a silencer-fitted .38 revolver. Baffling threads we took off the shells indicate the silencer and indicate why no shots were heard. The bullet hole in the wall is our one real lead, and it's easy to reconstruct what happened. Bax Englekling got free of his bonds, got ahold of the gun and fired a wounding shot before the killer got the gun back and shot him. The shell we took out of the wall had shredded Caucasian flesh and gray arm hair stuck to it, along with O-plus blood. Both Englekling boys were AB-minus, so we know the perpetrator was hit. The blood drops leading out to the living room and the negatives that he took out to look at indicate that it wasn't a major wound. Lieutenant Hatcher's crew found a blood-soaked O-plus towel in a sewer down the street, so that was his tourniquet. My last hypothesis is that this bastard really had a hard-on for those negatives.'

Hatcher spoke up. 'And we've got nothing. We've canvassed two dozen times, we've got no eyewitnesses and those goddamned brothers did not have a single K.A. that we've been able to turn. We hit doctors' offices, emergency rooms, train stations, airports and bus stations looking for sightings of a wounded man and got nothing. If the brothers had an address book, it was taken. Nobody saw anything or heard anything. Like my science buddy says, our guy really had a boner for those negatives, which might – and I emphasize "might" – have something to do with our victims coming forth on that Nite Owl case of yours years ago. They had a dirty-picture theory then, right?'

Dudley said, 'They did indeed, quite unsubstantiated.'

'And the L.A. papers said you just reopened the case.'

'Yes, that's correct.'

'Captain, I regret that we didn't decide to cooperate with you earlier, but put that aside. Have you got anything to give me on the new end of your case that I can use?'

Dudley smiled. 'Chief Parker has authorized me to secure a copy of your case file to read. He said that if I find evidential links to our homicides, he'll release a transcription of the Englekling brothers' 1953 testimony.'

'Which you say pertains to pornography, which our case sure as hell does.'

Dudley lit a cigarette. 'Yes, if it doesn't pertain to heroin just as much.'

Hatcher snorted. 'Captain, if our boy got his chops licked over white horse, he'd have stolen that stuff stashed in the couch.'

351

'Yes, or the killer was simply a frothing-at-the-mouth psychopath who evinced a psychopathic reaction to the negatives for unfathomable reasons of his own. Frankly, the heroin angle interests me. Have you any evidence that the brothers were either selling or manufacturing it?'

Hatcher shook his head. 'None, and as far as *our* case goes, I don't think it plays. Have you got a pornography angle on the reopening?'

'No, not as yet. Again, after I've read your case file I'll be in touch.'

Hatcher – ready to bust. 'Captain, you came all the way up here for our evidence, and you got nothing to give in return?'

'I came up here at the urging of Chief Parker, who pledges his full cooperation should your case warrant reciprocity.'

'Big words, sahib, that I don't like the sound of.'

Getting ugly – Dudley dug in with a big blarney smile. Bud walked out to the curb, dug in by their rental.

Scared, standing on GO.

Dudley walked out; Hatcher and the lab man locked the printshop. Bud said, 'I don't follow you at all these days, boss.'

'Starting when, lad?'

'Let's try last night with Hinton.'

Dudley laughed. 'You were your old cruel self last night. It warmed my heart and convinced me that the extracurricular work I have planned for you remains within your grasp.'

'What work?'

'In due time.'

'What happened to Hinton?'

'We released him well-chastised and terrified of Sergeant Wendell White.'

'Yeah, but what were you pressing him on?'

'Lad, you have your extracurricular secrets, I have mine. We'll hold a clarification session soon.'

GO. 'No. I just want to know where we both stand on the Nite Owl. *Now*.'

'Edmund Exley, lad. We both stand there.'

'What?' – scared to his own ears.

'*Edmund Jennings Exley*. He's been your raison d'être since Bloody Christmas, and he's why you don't tell me certain things. I love you, so I respect your omissions. Now reciprocate my love and respect my lack of clarification for the next twelve days and you'll see him destroyed.'

'What are you – ' a little kid's voice.

'You've never accorded him credit, so I'll tell you now. As a man he's less than negligible, but as a detective he far exceeds even myself. There. God and yourself witness plaudits for a man I despise. Now will you respect my omissions – as I respect yours?'

Past GO. 'No. Just fucking tell me what you want me to do. Just explain it.'

Dudley laughed, smiled. 'Do nothing for now but listen. I've found out that Thad Green will be retiring to take over the U.S. Border Patrol later this spring. Our new chief of detectives will be either Edmund Exley or myself. His upcoming inspectorship gives Exley the inside track, and Parker favors him personally. I plan on using certain aspects of our mutually withheld evidence to clear the Nite Owl posthaste, establish myself as the new frontrunner and ruin Exley in the process. Lad, bear with me for a few more days and I'll guarantee you your own personal revenge.'

The deal was Exley/Dudley vs. Exley.

No contest.

Past GO: the crumbs he spilled to Exley, Exley's promise – liaison, the hooker snuffs. 'Boss, is there a carrot in this for me?'

'Besides our friend's downfall?'

'Yeah.'

'And in exchange for a full disclosure? Beyond what you gave Exley as part of your field runner agreement?'

Jesus, what the man knew. 'Right.'

Ho Ho Ho. 'Lad, you drive a hard bargain, but will a

353

Chief of Detectives' Special Inquiry suffice? Say 187 P.C. multiple, various jurisdictions?'

Bud stuck out his hand. 'Deal.'

Dudley said, 'Stay away from Exley and treat yourself to a grand clean room at the Victory. I'll be by to see you in a day or so.'

'You take the car, I got business in Frisco first.'

He blew forty bucks on a cab, cruised the Golden Gate high on adrenaline. Double cross: a bad deal to survive, then a good deal to win – up from the minors to the majors. Exley had insider tips and sad Trashcan Jack; Dudley had insider juice that almost went psychic. Turnaround: he lied to Dudley to burn down Exley; five years later the man calls it in: lies forgiven, two cops, one torch. San Francisco bright in the distance, Dudley Smith's voice: 'Edmund Jennings Exley.' Chills just saying the name.

Over the bridge, a stop at a pay phone. Long-distance: Lynn's number, ten rings, no answer. 9:10 P.M., a spooker – she should have been home from the Bureau by dark.

Across town for the drop-off: San Francisco Police Department, Detective Division HQ. Bud pinned on his badge, walked in.

Homicide on floor three – arrows painted on the wall pointed him up. Creaky stairs, a huge squad bay. Nightwatch lull: two men up by the coffee.

They walked over. The younger guy pointed to his shield. 'L.A., huh? Help you with something?'

Bud held his ID out. 'You've got an old 187, like one a pal of mine on the L.A. Sheriff's caught. He asked me to check out your case file.'

'Well, the captain's not here now. Maybe you should try in the morning.'

The older man checked his ID. 'You're the guy that's bugs on prostie jobs. The captain said you keep calling up and you're a royal pain in the keester. What's the matter, you got another one?'

'Yeah, Lynette Ellen Kendrick, L.A. County last week. Come on, ten minutes with the file and I'm out of your hair.'

The young guy: 'Hey, catch the drift? The captain wanted you to see the file, he woulda sent you an invitation.'

The old guy: 'The captain's a jack-off. What's our victim's name and DOD?'

'Chrissie Virginia Renfro, July 16, '56.'

'Well then, I'll tell you what you do. You hit the records room around the corner, find your 1956 unsolved cabinet and go to the *R*'s. You don't take anything out and you skedaddle before junior here has a migraine. Got it?'

'Got it.'

Autopsy pictures: orifice rips, facial close-ups – pulp, no real face, ring fragments embedded in cheekbones. Wide-angle shots: the body, found at Chrissie's pad – a dive across from the St. Francis Hotel.

Pervert shakedown reports – local deviates brought in, questioned, released for lack of evidence. Foot fuckers, sadist pimps, Chrissie's pimp himself – in the Frisco City Jail when Chrissie was snuffed. Panty sniffers, rape-o's, Chrissie's regular johns – all alibied up, no names that crossed to the other case files he'd read.

Canvassing reports: local yokels, guests at the St. Francis. Six loser sheets, a grabber.

7/16/56: a St. Francis bellhop told detectives he caught Spade Cooley's late show at the hotel's Lariat Room, then saw Chrissie Virginia Renfro, weaving – 'maybe on hop'– walk into her building.

Grabber – Bud sat still, worked it up.

Grab Lynette Ellen Kendrick, DOD L.A. County last week. Grab an unrelated snitch – Lamar Hinton stooling everything in sight. Grabs: Dwight Gilette – Kathy Janeway's ex-pimp – supplied whores for Spade Cooley's parties. Spade was an opium smoker, a 'degenerate dope fiend.' Spade was in L.A., playing the El Rancho Klub on the Strip – a mile from Lynette Kendrick's pad.

355

First glitch: Spade couldn't have a jacket, no way to check his blood type – he rode in Sheriff Biscailuz' volunteer posse – P.R. stuff – nobody with a yellow sheet allowed.

Keep grabbing, check the M.E.'s report, 'Bloodstream Contents.' Page 2, a scorcher – 'undigested foodstuffs, semen, a heavily narcotizing amount of food-dispersed opium further verified by tar residue in teeth.'

Bud threw his arms up – like he could reach through the roof and haul down the moon. He banged the ceiling, came back to earth thinking – this was not a solo job, he was hiding out from Exley, Dudley just didn't care. He saw a phone, hit the ceiling, came down with a partner:

Ellis Loew – sex murders made him drool.

He grabbed the phone.

Chapter Fifty-six

Hilda Lefferts tapped a mugshot. 'There, that's Susan Nancy's beau. Will you take me home now?'

Bingo – a pudgy hardcase type, a real Duke Cathcart lookalike. Dean NMI Van Gelder, W.M., DOB 3/4/21. 5'8¾", 178 lbs., blue eyes, brown hair. One armed-robbery bounce – 6/42 – ten to twenty, released from Folsom 6/52, full minimum sentence topped – no parole. No further arrests – chalk it up to Bud White's theory – Van Gelder got it at the Nite Owl.

Hilda said, 'That's it – *Dean*. Susan Nancy called him "Dean," but he said, "No, get used to calling me "Duke." '

Jack said, 'You sure?'

'Yes, I'm sure. Six hours of looking at these awful pictures and you ask me if I'm sure? If I wanted to lie I would have pointed somebody out hours ago. *Please*, Officer. First you find a body under my house, next you subject me to these pictures. Now will you please take me home?'

Jack shook his head no. Work it: Who? to Van Gelder to Cathcart to the Nite Owl. One parlay made sense – the Englekling brothers to Cathcart to a brush with Mickey Cohen – in stir back in '53. He picked up the phone, dialed O.

'Operator.'

'Operator, this is a police emergency. I need to be put through to somebody in administration at McNeil Federal Penitentiary, Puget Sound, Washington.'

'I see. And your name?'

'Sergeant Vincennes, Los Angeles Police Department. Tell them I'm on a homicide investigation.'

'I see. Circuits to Washington State have been – '

'Shit. I'm at MAdison 60042. Will you – '

'I'll try your call now, sir.'

Jack hung up. Forty seconds by the wall clock – *bbring brinng*.

'Vincennes.'

'Deputy Warden Cahill at McNeil. This pertains to a homicide?'

Hilda Lefferts was pouting – Jack turned away from her. 'Yeah, and all I need's one answer. Got a pencil?'

'Of course.'

'Okay. I need to know if a white male named Dean Van Gelder, that's two separate words on the last name, visited an inmate at McNeil say from February through April 1953. All I need's a yes or no and the names of any inmates he visited.'

A sigh. 'All right, please hold. This may take a while.'

Jack held counting minutes – Cahill came back on at twelve plus. 'That's a positive. Dean Van Gelder, DOB 3/4/21, visited inmate David Goldman on three occasions: 3/27/53, 4/1/53 and 4/3/53. Goldman was at McNeil on tax charges. Perhaps you've heard – '

Work in Davey G. – Mickey Cohen's man. Work in Van Gelder's last visit – two weeks before the Nite Owl, the same time the Englekling brothers lubed Mickey – the meet where they spilled the smut plan. The prison man kept babbling – Jack hung up on him. The Nite Owl case started to shake.

Chapter Fifty-seven

Ed drove Lynn Bracken home, a last shot before having her arrested. She protested, then went along: her day of truth dope, counterdope and browbeating showed – she looked frazzled, exhausted. Call her smart, strong and chemically fortified; she gave up nothing but Pierce Patchett crumbs – however she managed it. Patchett knew a whitewash wouldn't wash; Lynn funneled out her call girl tale – and Patchett had to have lawyers waiting in case that crumb went to indictments. Reopening day one was pure insane: Dudley Smith up in Gaitsville while his hot dogs shook down Darktown; Vincennes' body under the house and his ID on Dean Van Gelder – Davey Goldman's McNeil visitor pre-Nite Owl. Bud White for a runner, then his *Whisper* leak breaking – he was a fool to trust him for a second. All of that he could take: he was a professional detective used to dealing with chaos.

But the Atherton case and his father circuiting in was something else. Now he felt suspended, one simple instinct running him: the Nite Owl had a life past any detective's volition – and the will to make its horror known whether he was there to probe evidence or not, whether he was capable of forming plans or just hanging on for the ride.

He had a plan to work Bracken and Patchett.

Lynn blew smoke rings out the window. 'Down two blocks and turn left. You can stop there, I'm right near the corner.'

Ed braked short. 'One last question. At the Bureau you implied that you knew Patchett and Sid Hudgens were planning to work an extortion racket.'

'I don't recall endorsing that statement.'

'You didn't dispute it.'

'I was tired and bored.'

'You endorsed it, implicitly. And it's in Jack Vincennes' deposition.'

'Then perhaps Vincennes lied about that part. He used to be quite a celebrity. Wouldn't you also call him quite a self-dramatist?'

An opening. 'Yes.'

'And do you think you can trust him?'

Fake chagrin oozing. 'I don't know. He's my weak point.'

'So there you are. Mr. Exley, are you going to arrest me?'

'I'm beginning to think it wouldn't do any good. What did White say when he told you to come in for questioning?'

'Just to come clean. Did you show him Vincennes' deposition?'

The truth – make her grateful. 'No.'

'I'm glad, because I'm sure it's full of lies. Why didn't you show it to him?'

'Because he's a limited detective, and the less he knows the better. He's also a protégé of a rival officer on the case, and I didn't want him passing information to him.'

'Are you speaking of Dudley Smith?'

'Yes. Do you know him?'

'No, but Bud speaks of him often. I think he's afraid of him, which means that Smith must be quite a man.'

'Dudley's brilliant and vicious to the core, but I'm better. And look, it's late.'

'Can I give you a drink?'

'Why? You spat in my face today.'

'Well, given the circumstances.'

Her smile made his smile easy. 'Given the circumstances, one drink.'

Lynn got out of the car. Ed watched her move: high heels, a shit day – but her feet hardly touched the ground. She led him to her building, unlocked the bottom door and hit a light.

Ed walked in. Exquisite – the fabrics, the art. Lynn

360

kicked off her shoes and poured brandies; Ed sat on a sofa – pure velvet.

Lynn joined him. Ed took his drink, sipped. Lynn warmed the glass with her hands. 'Do you know why I invited you in?'

'You're too intelligent to try to wrangle a deal, so I'll guess you're just curious about me.'

'Bud hates you more than he loves me or anyone else. I'm beginning to see why.'

'I don't really want your opinion.'

'I was leading up to a compliment.'

'Some other time, all right?'

'I'll change the subject then. How's Inez Soto handling the publicity? She's been all over the papers.'

'She's taking it poorly, and I don't want to talk about her.'

'It galls you that I know so much about you. You don't have information to compete.'

Move the wedge. 'I have Vincennes' deposition.'

'Which I suspect you doubt the truth of.'

Throw the change-up. 'You mentioned that Patchett financed some early Raymond Dieterling films. Can you elaborate on that?'

'Why? Because your father is associated with Dieterling? You see the disadvantages of being the son of a famous man?'

No hink, a deft touch with the knife. 'Just a policeman's question.'

Lynn shrugged. 'Pierce mentioned it to me in passing several years ago.'

The phone rang – Lynn ignored it. 'I can tell you don't want to talk about Jack Vincennes.'

'I can tell you do.'

'I haven't seen much in the news about him lately.'

'That's because he flushed everything he had down the toilet. *Badge of Honor*, his friendship with Miller Stanton, all of it. Sid Hudgens getting murdered didn't help, since *Hush-Hush* owed half its filth to Vincennes' shakedowns.'

Lynn sipped brandy. 'You don't like Jack.'

'No, but there's part of his deposition that I believe absolutely. Patchett has carbons of Sid Hudgens' private dirt files, including a carbon of a file on Vincennes himself. You can do yourself some good by acknowledging it.'

If she bit she'd start now.

'I can't acknowledge it, and the next time we speak I'll have a lawyer. But I can tell you that I think I know what such a file would contain.'

First wedge in place. 'And?'

'Well, I think the year was 1947. Vincennes got involved in a gunfight at the beach. He was under the influence of narcotics and shot and killed two innocent people, a husband and wife. My source has verification, including the testimony of an ambulance deputy and a notarized statement from the doctor who treated Jack for his wounds. My source has blood test results that show the drugs in his system and testimony from eyewitnesses who didn't come forth. Is that information you'd suppress to protect a brother officer, Captain?'

The Malibu Rendezvous: Trashcan's glory job. The phone rang – Lynn let it go. Ed said, 'Jesus Christ,' no need to fake.

'Yes. You know, when I read about Vincennes I always thought he had some very dark reasons for persecuting dope users, so I wasn't surprised when I found that out. And, Captain? If Pierce did have file carbons, I'm sure he would have destroyed them.'

Her last bit rang fake – Ed played a lie off it. 'I know Jack loves dope, it's been a rumor around the Bureau for years. And I know you're lying about the files and I know Vincennes would do anything to get his file back. You and Patchett shouldn't underestimate him.'

'The way you've underestimated Bud White?'

Her smile came on like a target – he thought for a second that he'd hit her. She laughed before he could; he leaned in and kissed her instead. Lynn pulled back, then kissed back; they rolled to the floor shedding clothes. The phone rang – Ed kicked it off the hook. Lynn pulled him inside her; they rolled, moved together, trashed furniture.

362

It ended as fast as it started – he could feel Lynn reaching to peak. Seconds apart for that, good enough, rest. His story laid out between sighs, like it was a burden too heavy to carry.

Rogue cop Jack Vincennes, on dope and too hot to handle. He'd do anything to get his file back, he had to get that file. Captain E. J. Exley had to use him for what he knew – but Vincennes was doped up, boozed up, going psycho on him –

Chapter Fifty-eight

Bud hit L.A. at dawn, off the midnight bus down from Frisco. His city looked strange, new – like everything else in his life.

He got a taxi and dozed; he kept snapping awake to Ellis Loew: 'It sounds like a great case, but multiple homicides are tricky and Spade Cooley is a well-known figure. I'll put a D.A.'s Bureau team on it and *you stay out of it for now*.' Cut to Lynn: calls, the phone off the hook, smothered. Strange, but like her – when she wanted to sleep she wanted to sleep.

He couldn't believe his life, it was just too goddamn amazing.

The cab dropped him off. He found a note on his door – 'Sergeant Duane W. Fisk' on the letterhead.

Sgt. White –
    Captain Exley wants to see you immediately (something pertaining to *Whisper* magazine and a body under a house). Report to I.A. immediately upon your return to Los Angeles.

Bud laughed, packed a bag: clothes, his paper stash – the hooker killings, the Nite Owl – Dudley's for the asking. He threw the note in the toilet, pissed on it.

He drove to Gardena, checked into the Victory: a room with clean sheets, a hot plate, no bloodstains on the walls. Fuck sleep – he fixed coffee, worked.

Everything he knew on Spade Cooley – half a longhand page.

Cooley was an Okie fiddler/singer, a skinny guy, maybe late forties. He had a couple of hit records, his TV show was big for a while. His bass player, Burt Arthur Perkins, a.k.a. 'Deuce,' did time on a chain gang for sodomy on dogs and was rumored to have a shitload of mob K.A.'s.

On the investigation:

Lamar Hinton said Spade smoked opium; Spade played the Lariat Room in Frisco – across from Chrissie Renfro's place of death. Chrissie died with 'O' in her system; Spade was currently playing the El Rancho Klub in L.A., close by Lynette Ellen Kendrick's apartment. Lamar Hinton said Dwight Gilette – Kathy Janeway's old pimp – supplied whores for Cooley's parties.

Circumstantial – but tight.

A phone wired to the wall – Bud grabbed it, called the County Coroner's Office.

'Medical Examinations, Jensen.'

'Sergeant White for Dr. Harris. I know he's busy, but tell him it's just one thing.'

'Hold, please,' click, click, click. 'Sergeant, what is it this time?'

'One thing off your autopsy report.'

'You're not even a county officer.'

'Stomach and bloodstream contents on Lynette Kendrick. Come on, huh?'

'That's easy, because Kendrick won our best stomach award last week. Are you ready? Frankfurters with sauerkraut, french fries, Coca-Cola, opium, sperm. Jesus, what a last supper.'

Bud hung up. Ellis Loew said stay out of it. Kathy Janeway said GO.

He drove to the Strip, put the M.O. together.

First the El Rancho Klub, closed, 'Spade Cooley and His Cowboy Rhythm Band Appearing Nitely.' A publicity still by the door: Spade, Deuce Perkins, three other cracker types. No heavily ringed fingers; a lead rubber-stamped at the bottom: 'Represented by Nat Penzler Associates, 653 North La Cienega, Los Angeles.'

Across the street: the Hot Dog Hut, kraut dogs and fries on the menu. Down the Strip by Crescent Heights:

a well-known prostie stroll. A mile south at Melrose and Sweetzer: Lynette Ellen Kendrick's apartment.

Easy:

Spade picked her up late, no witnesses. He had the food and the dope, suggested a cozy all-nighter, took Lynette home. They got high, chowed down – Spade beat her to death, raped her three times postmortem.

Bud hooked south to La Cienega. 653: a redwood A-frame, 'Nat Penzler Assoc.' by the mailbox. The door propped open; a girl inside making coffee.

Bud walked in. The girl said, 'Yes, can I help you?'

'The boss around?'

'Mr. Penzler's on the telephone. Can *I* help you?'

One connecting door – 'N.P.' brass-stamped. Bud pushed it open; an old man yelled, 'Hey! I'm on a call! What are you, a bill collector? Hey, Gail! Give this clown a magazine!'

Bud flashed his badge. The man hung up the phone, pushed back from his desk. Bud said, 'You're Nat Penzler?'

'Call me Natsky. Are you looking for representation? I could get you work playing thugs. You have that Neanderthal look currently in vogue.'

Let it go. 'You're Spade Cooley's agent, right?'

'Right. You want to join Spade's band? Spade's a money-maker, but my shvartze cleaning lady sings better than him, so maybe I can get you a spot, a bouncer gig at the El Rancho at least. Lots of trim there, boychik. A moose like you could get reamed, steamed and dry-cleaned.'

'You through, pops?'

Penzler flushed. 'Mr. Natsky to you, caveman.'

Bud shut the door. 'I need to see Cooley's booking records going back to '51. You want to do this nice or not?'

Penzler got up, blocked his filing cabinets. 'Showtime's over, Godzilla. I never divulge client information, even under threat of a subpoena. So amscray and come back for lunch sometime, say on the twelfth of never.'

Bud tore the phone cord from the wall; Penzler slid the top drawer open. 'No rough stuff, please, caveman! I do my best work with my face!'

Bud thumbed folders, hit 'Cooley, Donnell Clyde,' dumped it on the desk. A picture hit the blotter: Spade, four rings on ten fingers. Pink sheets, white sheets, then blue sheets – booking records clipped by year.

Penzler stood by muttering. Bud matched dates.

Jane Mildred Hamsher, 3/8/51, San Diego – Spade there at the El Cortez Sky Room. April '53, Kathy Janeway, the Cowboy Rhythm Band at Bido Lito's – South L.A. Sharon, Sally, Chrissie Virginia, Maria up to Lynette: Bakersfield, Needles, Arizona, Frisco, Seattle, back to L.A., shifting personnel listed on pay cards: Deuce Perkins playing bass most of the time, drum and sax guys coming and going, Spade Cooley *always* headlining, in those cities on those DODs.

Blue sheets dripping wet – his own sweat. 'Where's the band staying?'

Penzler: 'The Biltmore, and you didn't get it from Natsky.'

'That's good, 'cause this is Murder One and I wasn't here.'

'I am like the Sphinx, I swear to you. My God, Spade and his lowlife crew. My God, do you know what he grossed last year?'

He called the lead in to Ellis Loew; Loew hit the roof: 'I told you to stay out! I've got three *civilized* men on it, and I'll tell them what you've got, but you stay out and get back to the Nite Owl, *do you understand me?*'

He understood: Kathy Janeway kept saying GO.

The Biltmore.

He forced himself to drive there slow, park by the back entrance, politely ask the clerk where to find Mr. Cooley's party. The clerk said, 'The El Presidente Suite, floor nine'; he said, 'Thank you' so calm that everything went into slow motion and he thought for a second he was swimming.

The stairs were like swimming upstream – Little Kathy kept saying KILL HIM. The suite: double doors, gold-filigreed – eagles, American flags. He jiggled the knob, the doors opened.

High swank gone white trash – three crackers passed out on the floor. Booze empties, dumped ashtrays, no Spade.

Connecting doors – the one on the right featured noise. Bud kicked it in.

Deuce Perkins in bed watching cartoons. Bud pulled his gun. 'Where's Cooley?'

Perkins popped in a toothpick. 'On a drunk, which is where I'm goin'. You want to see him, come to the El Rancho tonight. Chances are he'll show up.'

'The fuck, he's the headliner.'

'Most times. But Spade's been erratic lately, so I been fillin' in. I sing good as him and I'm better lookin', so nobody seems to mind. Now, you want to get out of here and leave me alone with my entertainment?'

'Where's he drinking?'

'Put that gun away, junior. The worse you got him for's nonpayment of child support, and Spade always pays sooner or later.'

'Nix, this is Murder One, and I heard he likes opium.'

Perkins coughed out his toothpick. 'What'd you say?'

'Hookers. Spade like young girls?'

'He don't like to kill them, just play hide the tubesteak like you and me.'

'*Where is he?*'

'Man, I'm not no snitch.'

Backhanded pistol whips – Perkins yelped, spat teeth. The TV went loud; kids squealing for Kellogg's Cornflakes. Bud shot the screen out.

Deuce snitched: 'Check the "O" joints in Chinatown and please fuckin' leave me alone!'

Kathy said KILL HIM. Bud thought of his mother for the first time in years.

Chapter Fifty-nine

The doctor said, 'I told this to your Captain Exley, and I told him an interview with Mr. Goldman would most likely prove fruitless – the man is simply not lucid most of the time. However, since he insisted on sending you up here, I'll run through it again.'

Jack looked around. Camarillo was creepy: lots of geeks, geek artwork on the walls. 'Would you? The captain wants a statement from him.'

'Well, he'll be lucky to get one. Last July, Mr. Goldman and his confrere Mickey Cohen were attacked with knives and pipes at McNeil Island Prison. Unidentified assailants apparently, and Cohen was relatively unharmed while Mr. Goldman suffered serious brain damage. Both men were paroled late last year, and Mr. Goldman began to behave quite erratically. Late in December he was arrested for urinating in public in Beverly Hills, and the judge ordered him here for ninety days' observation. We've had him since Christmas and we've just recycled him in for another ninety. Frankly, we can't do a thing with him, and the only thing mysterious is that Mr. Cohen visited and offered to transfer Mr. Goldman to a private treatment facility at his own expense, but Mr. Goldman refused and acted terrified of him. Isn't that odd?'

'Maybe not. Where is he?'

'On the other side of that door. Be gentle with him, please. The man was a gangster, but he's just a sad human being now.'

Jack opened the door. A small padded room; Davey Goldman on a long padded bench. He needed a shave; he reeked of Lysol. Slack-jawed Davey scoping a *National Geographic*.

Jack sat beside him – Goldman moved away. Jack said,

'This place is the shits. You should've let Mickey spring you.'

Goldman picked his nose, ate it.

'Davey, you on the outs with Mickey?'

Goldman held out his magazine – naked negroes waving spears.

'Cute, and when they start showing white stuff I'll subscribe. Davey, you remember me? Jack Vincennes? I used to work LAPD Narco and we used to run into each other on the Strip.'

Goldman scratched his balls. He smiled, low voltage, nobody home.

'Is this an act? Come on, Davey. You and the Mick go way back. You know he'd take care of you.'

Goldman squashed an invisible bug. 'Not anymore.'

A gone man's voice – nobody could fake it that good. 'Say, Davey, whatever happened to Dean Van Gelder? You remember him, he used to visit you at McNeil.'

Goldman picked his nose, wiped it on his feet. Jack said, 'Dean Van Gelder. He visited you at McNeil in '53, right around the time these two guys Pete and Bax Englekling visited Mickey. Now you're afraid of Mickey, and Van Gelder clipped a guy named Duke Cathcart and got clipped himself during the world famous Nite Owl fucking Massacre. You got any brains left to talk about that?'

No lights blinked on.

'Come on, Davey. You tell me, you won't feel so sad. Talk to your Uncle Jack.'

'Dutchman! Dutch fuck! Mickey should know to hurt me but he don't. Hub rachmones, Meyer, hub rachmones, Meyer Harris Cohen te absolvo my sins.'

His mouth did the talking – the rest of the man came off dead. Jack parlayed: Van Gelder the Dutchman, Yiddish to Latin, something like betrayal. 'Come on, keep going. Confess to Father Jack and I'll make it allll better.'

Goldman picked his nose; Jack shoved him. 'Come on!'

'Dutchman blew it!'

????? – maybe – a jail bid on Duke Cathcart. 'Blew what, come on!'

Goldman, a gone monotone. 'Franchise boys got theirs three triggers blip blip blip. Fucking slowdown ain't no hoedown, Mickey thinks he'll get the fish but the Irish Cheshire got the fishy and Mickey gets the bones no gravy he is dead meat for the meow monster. Hub rachmones Meyer, I could trust you, not them, it's all on ice but not for us te absolvo . . .'

??????????? 'Who are these guys you're talking about?'

Goldman hummed a tune, off key, familiar. Jack caught the melody: 'Take the "A" Train.' 'Davey, *talk* to me.'

Davey sang. 'Bumpa – bump bump bump bump bump bump bump bump the cute train bump bump bump bump the cute train.'

?????????????????????? – worse, like his brain had padded walls. 'Davey, just talk.'

Geek talk: 'Bzz, bzz bzz talking bug to hear. Betty, Benny bug to listen, Barney bug. Hub rachmones Meyer my dear friend.'

????????? into just maybe something:

The Engleklings saw Cohen *in his cell*, pitched him on Duke Cathcart's smut scheme. Mickey swore he did not tell a soul. Goldman found out about it, decided to crash the racket, dispatched Dean Van Gelder to snuff Cathcart – or maybe buy in on the deal. ???????? – How – ?????? – DID HE HAVE A BUG PLANTED IN COHEN'S CELL?

'Davey, *tell me about the bug*.'

Goldman started humming 'In the Mood.'

The doctor opened the door. 'That's it, Officer. You've bothered this man long enough.'

Exley okayed it on the phone: a run to McNeil to check for evidence of bugging apparatus in Mickey Cohen's former cell. The Ventura County Airport was a few miles away – he was to fly to Puget Sound, take a cab to the pen. Bob Gallaudet would have a Prison's Bureau man there to run liaison – the McNeil administrators pampered

371

Cohen, probably took bribes for the service, might not cooperate without a push. Exley called the bug theory a long shot; he ranted that Bud White was missing – Fisk and Kleckner were out looking for him, the bastard was probably running from his *Whisper* piece and the body in San Berdoo – Fisk left him a note, mentioned the discovery. Parker said Dudley Smith was studying the Englekling case file and would report on it soon; Lynn Bracken was still holding back. Jack said, 'What do we do about that?' Exley said, 'The Dining Car at midnight. We'll discuss it.'

Scary Captain Ed closing ominous.

Jack drove to Ventura, caught his flight – Exley called ahead, vouchered his ticket. A stewardess handed out newspapers; he grabbed a *Times* and *Daily News* and read Nite Owl.

Dudley's boys were ripping up Darktown, hauling in known Negro offenders, looking for the *real* punks popping shotguns in Griffith Park. Pure bullshit: whoever planted the weapons in Ray Coates' car planted the matching shells in the park, feeding off location leads in the press – only pros would have the brains and the balls to do it. Mike Breuning and Dick Carlisle were running a command post at 77th Street Station – the entire squad and twenty extra men from Homicide detached to work the case. No way were crazed darkies guilty – it was starting to look like 1953 all over again. The *Daily News* showed photos: Central Avenue swarmed by placard-waving boogies, the house Exley bought Inez Soto. A dandy shot in the *Times* – Inez outside Ray Dieterling's place in Laguna, shielding her eyes from flashbulbs.

Jack kept reading.

The State Attorney General's Office issued a statement: Ellis Loew outfoxed them by planting a restraining order, but they were still interested in the case and would intercede when the order lapsed – unless the LAPD solved the Nite Owl mess to the satisfaction of the Los Angeles County Grand Jury within a suitable period of time. LAPD issued a press release – a detail-packed doozie on

Inez Soto's 1953 gang rape accompanied by a heartwarming rendition of how Captain Ed Exley helped her rebuild her life. Exley's old man got a treatment: the *Daily News* played up the completion of the Southern California freeway system and reported a late-breaking rumor – Big Preston was soon to announce his candidacy in the governor's race, a scant two and a half months before the Republican primary, the eleventh-hour announcement strategy a ploy to capitalize on upcoming freeway brouhaha. How would his son's bad press affect his chances?

Jack measured his own chances. He was back on with Karen because she saw he was trying; the best way to keep it going was to cash in his twenty, grab his pension, get out of L.A. The next two months would be a sprint dodging bullets: the reopening, what Patchett and Bracken had on him. Odds you couldn't figure – for a sprinter he was scared and tired – and starting to feel old. Exley had sprint moves in mind – late dinner meets weren't his style. Bracken and Patchett might deal his dirt in; Parker might quash it to protect the Department. But Karen would know, and what was left of the marriage would go down – because she could just barely take that she'd married a drunk and a bagman. 'Murderer' was one bullet they both couldn't dodge.

Three hours in the air; three hours pent up thinking. The plane touched down at Puget Sound; Jack caught a cab to McNeil.

Ugly: a gray monolith on a gray rock island. Gray walls, gray fog, barbed wire at the edge of gray water. Jack got out at the guard hut; the gatekeeper checked his ID, nodded. Steel gates slid back into stone.

Jack walked in. A wiry little man met him in the sallyport. 'Sergeant Vincennes? I'm Agent Goddard, Prison's Bureau.'

A good handshake. 'Did Exley tell you what it's about?'

'Bob Gallaudet did. You're on the Nite Owl and related conspiracy cases and you think Cohen's cell might have been bugged. We're looking for evidence to support that theory, which I don't think is so farfetched.'

'Why?'

They walked bucking wind – Goddard talked above it. 'Cohen got the royal treatment here, Goldman too. Privileges up the wazoo, unlimited visitors and not too much scrutiny on the stuff brought into their tier, so a bug could have been planted. Are you thinking Goldman crossed Mickey?'

'Something like that.'

'Well, could be. They had cells two doors apart, on a tier Mickey requested, because half the cells had ruined plumbing and you couldn't house inmates in them. You'll see, I've got the whole row vacated and closed off.'

Checkpoints, the blocks – six-story tiers linked by cat-walks. Upstairs to a corridor – eight empty cells. Goddard said, 'The penthouse. Quiet, underpopulated and a nice day room for the boys to play cards in. We have an informant who says Cohen got approval on the inmates placed up here. Can you feature the cheek of that?'

Jack said, 'Jesus, you're good. And fast.'

'Well, Exley and Gallaudet carry weight, and the powers that be here didn't have time to prepare. Now check the goodies I brought.'

On the day room table: crowbars, chisels, mallets, a long thin pole with a hook at the end. On a blanket: a tape recorder, a tangle of wires. Goddard said, 'First we tear this tier up. I admit it's a long shot, but I brought a recorder along in case we find tape.'

'I'd call that a maybe. Goldman and Cohen got paroled last fall, but they got bushwacked in July and Davey got his brains scrambled. I'm thinking if he was the one monitoring the tape then maybe he was too wet-brained to pull the machine.'

'Enough gabbing. Let's dig.'

They dug.

Goddard plumbed a line from the heat duct in Cohen's cell to the heat duct in Goldman's, marked a line on the ceilings of the two cells in between, started probing with a mallet and chisel. Jack pried a protection plate off the duct on Mickey's wall, banged around inside the chute with the hook device. Nothing but hollow tin walls, no wires just inside. Frustrating: it was the logical place to plant a microphone. Heat boomed out the duct; Jack changed his mind, Washington was cold, the heat would be on too much of the time, drowning out conversation. He checked the walls and ceiling for other conduits – nothing – then the area around the vent. Irregularly applied spackling dotted with pinholes right by the protector plate; he smashed his mallet until half the wall came down and a small Spackle-covered microphone dangling off a wire came loose. The wire jerked from his hand, straight back into the wall. Five seconds later Goddard stood there holding it – attached to a tape recorder covered with plastic. 'Halfway between the cells, a little hidey-hole right off the vent. Let's listen, huh?'

They fired it up in the day room. Goddard hooked up his machine, changed spools, pushed buttons – tape-recorded tape.

Static, a dog yipping, 'There, there, bubeleh' – Mickey Cohen's voice. Goddard said, 'They let him keep a dog in his cell. Only in America, huh?'

Cohen: 'Quit licking your schnitzel, little precious.' More yips, a long silence, a click-off sound. Goddard said, 'I was timing it. Voice-activated mike. Five minutes and it goes off automatically.'

Jack brushed plaster off his hands. 'How'd Goldman get in to change the tape?'

'He must have had some kind of hook thing, like that pole I gave you. The grate on his heat vent was loose, so we know somebody was poking around in there. Jesus, this thing has been in there how long? And Goldman had to have help, this is no one-man operation. Listen, here that click?'

Another click, a strange voice: 'For how much? I'll have that guard place the bet.' Cohen: 'A thousand on Basilio, that little guinea is mean. And take a run by the infirmary and see Davey, my God a goddamn turnip those goons turned him into, I swear I will live to see them in a vegetable puree.' Overlapping voices, mumbles, Mickey cooing, his dog yipping.

Nail the time: Goldman and Cohen had been attacked; Mickey laid down an early bet on the Robinson-Basilio fight last September, he was probably out by then – he got down before the odds dropped.

Click off, click on, forty-six minutes of Mickey and at least two other men playing cards, mumbling, flushing the toilet. The used tape almost gone; click off, click on, the fucking dog yowling.

Mickey: 'Six years and ten months here and to lose Davey's redoubtable brain right before I leave. Such tsurus to go home on. Mickey Junior, quit licking your putz, you faigeleh.'

A strange voice: 'Get him a bitch, and he won't have to.'

Cohen: 'My God to be so nimble and so hung, like Heifetz on the fiddle with his shlong that dog is, and hung like Johnny Stompanato to boot. And on the topic of boots, I read Hedda Hopper's column and see Johnny's putting the boots to Lana Turner, such a crush he's had for so long, she must have a cunt like chinchilla.'

The strange-voice man cracked up. Cohen: 'Enough already, you brownnoser, save some for Jack Benny. Johnny I need now, Johnny I can't locate 'cause he's playing bury the brisket with movie stars. My franchise guys keep getting clipped and I need Johnny to put an ear down for who, but that big dick dago cunt-bandit is nowhere! I want those cocksuckers clipped! I want those shitbirds who hurt Davey to cease residence on this earth!'

Mickey cough, cough, coughed. Strange Voice: 'How about Lee Vachss and Abe Teitlebaum. You could put them on it.'

Cohen: 'Such a shmendrik you are for a confidant, but you do play cribbage good. No, Abe has grown too soft to work muscle, too much grease noshed at his deli, such grease clogs the arteries that inspire mayhem, and Lee

Vachss loves death too much to be discerning. Lana, what a snatch she must have, like cashmere.'

The tape ran out. Goddard said, 'Mickey sure does have a verbal style, but what did all that have to do with the Nite Owl case?'

'How's "nothing" sound?'

Chapter Sixty

One wall of his den was now a graph: Nite Owl related case players connected by horizontal lines, vertical lines linking them to a large sheet of cardboard blocked off into information sections – events culled from Vincennes' deposition. Ed wrote margin notes; his father's call still hammered him: 'Edmund, I'm running for governor. Your recent notoriety may have hurt me, but put that aside. I don't want the Atherton case resurrected in print and tied to your various cases, and I don't want Ray Dieterling bothered. I want you to direct all your queries along those lines to me, and between the two of us we'll work things out.'

He agreed. It rankled. It made him feel like a child – like sleeping with Lynn Bracken made him feel whorish. And too many Dieterling names were popping up on the graph.

Ed crossed lines.

Sid Hudgens lined to the ink smut Vincennes found in '53; the smut lined to Pierce Patchett. Line to: Christine Bergeron, her son Daryl and Bobby Inge, smut posers who disappeared almost concurrent with the Nite Owl. Have Fisk and Kleckner initiate a new search for them; attempt to identify the other posers – one more time. Put the smut/Hudgens line to the Atherton case aside, former Inspector Preston Exley would make discreet inquiries when asked.

A theoretical line – Pierce Patchett to Duke Cathcart. Lynn Bracken denied it, a lie, Vincennes' deposition had Patchett pushing the smut Cathcart planned to distribute – *but who made it?* Hudgens to Patchett and Bracken: the dirtmonger was terrified that Vincennes was nosing around Fleur-de-Lis; Lynn told Jack that Patchett and Hudgens were going in on a gig together, she now denied it, another lie. He needed another graph just to chart lies – he didn't have a room big enough to hold it.

More lines:

Davey Goldman to Dean Van Gelder to Duke Cathcart and Susan Nancy Lefferts – incomprehensible until Vincennes reported back from McNeil Island, and Bud White, obviously hiding out, was questioned on what he might be suppressing. Vocational lines – Patchett, the Englekling brothers and their father possessed chemistry backgrounds; Patchett, a reputed heroin sniffer, had plastic surgery connections to Dr. Terry Lux, the owner of a booze/dope sanitarium. Dudley Smith's report to Parker stated that Pete and Bax Englekling were tortured to death with corrosive chemicals, no other details added. Conclusion: the link to decipher every interconnected line had to be Patchett – his whores, his smut posers, Patchett the conduit to the man who made the blood smut, killed Hudgens and formed the final line stretching back to 1934 and his own father's glory case.

Too many lines to ignore.

Patchett bankrolled early Dieterling films. Dieterling's son Billy and boyfriend Timmy Valburn used Fleur-de-Lis; Valburn was a Bobby Inge K.A. Billy worked on *Badge of Honor*, the first focus of the Hudgens homicide investigation. *Badge of Honor* co-star Miller Stanton was a Dieterling kid star around the same time that Wee Willie Wennerholm was murdered – by Loren Atherton? Slash lines – Atherton to the smut to Hudgens; lines of coincidence too convenient not to cut at family loyalty – seventeen years post-Atherton, Preston Exley builds Dream-a-Dreamland.

Governor Exley. Chief of Detectives Exley.

Ed thought of Lynn, tasted her, shuddered. A quick jump to Inez – a new line to utilize.

He drove to Laguna Beach.

The press, swarming: perched by their cars, playing cards on Ray Dieterling's lawn. Ed pulled around the block, walked up, sprinted.

They saw him, chased him. He made the door, slammed the knocker. The door opened – straight into Inez.

She slammed it, bolted it. Ed walked into the living room – Dream-a-Dreamland smiled all around him.

Gimcracks, porcelain statues: Moochie, Danny, Scooter. Wall photos: Dieterling and crippled children. Canceled checks encased in plastic – six figures to fight kids' diseases.

'See, I've got company.'

Ed turned to face her. 'Thanks for letting me in.'

'They've been treating you worse than me, so I figured I owed you.'

She looked pale. 'Thanks. And you know it'll pass, just like last time.'

'Maybe. You look lousy, Exley.'

'People keep telling me that.'

'Then maybe it's true. Look, if you want to stay and talk awhile, fine, but please don't talk about Bud or all this *mierda* that's going on.'

'I wasn't planning on it, but small talk was never our forte.'

She walked up. Ed embraced her; she grabbed his arms and pushed herself away. Ed tried a smile. 'I saw some gray hairs. When you're my age you'll probably be as gray as I am. How's that for small talk?'

'Small, and I can do better. Preston's running for governor, unless his notorious son ruins his chances. I'm going to be his campaign coordinator.'

'Governor Dad. Did he say I'd ruin his chances?'

'No, because he'd never say bad things about you. Just try to do what you can not to hurt him.'

Reporters outside – Ed heard them laughing. 'I don't want Father to be hurt either. And you can help me prevent it.'

'How?'

'A favor. A favor between you and me, nobody else to know.'

'What? Explain it.'

380

'It's very complicated, and it involves Ray Dieterling. Do you know the name "Pierce Patchett"?'

Inez shook her head. 'No, who is he?'

'He's an investor of sorts, that's all I can tell you. I need you to use your access at Dream-a-Dreamland to check his financial connections to Dieterling. Check back to the late '20s, very quietly. Will you do that for me?'

'Exley, this sounds like police business. And what does it have to do with your father?'

Recoiling: doubting the man who formed him. 'Father might be in some tax trouble. I need you to check Dieterling's financial records for mention of him.'

'Bad trouble?'

'Yes.'

'Check back to '50 or so? When they began planning for Dream-a-Dreamland?'

'No, go back to 1932. I know you've seen the books at Dieterling Productions, and I know you can do it.'

'With explanations to follow?'

More recoil. 'On Election Day. Come on, Inez. You love him almost as much as I do.'

'All right. For your father.'

'No other reason?'

'All right, for what you've done for me and the friends you gave me. And if that sounds cruel, I'm sorry.'

A Moochie Mouse clock struck ten. Ed said, 'I should go, I've got a meeting in L.A.'

'Go out the back way. I think I still hear the vultures.'

The recoil got squared driving back.

Call it standard elimination procedure:

If his father really did know Ray Dieterling during the time of the Atherton case, he had a valid reason for not revealing it, he was probably embarrassed at plumbing business deals with a man he once rubbed shoulders with in the process of a hellish murder investigation. Preston Exley believed that policemen striking friendships with influential civilians was inimical to the concept of impartial absolute justice, and if he fell short of his own standards

381

it was understandable that he would not want the fact known.

Squared with love and respect.

Ed made the Dining Car early; the maître d' said his guest was waiting. He walked back to his favorite booth – a private nook behind the bar. Vincennes was there, holding a tape spool.

Ed sat down. 'That's tape off a bug?'

Vincennes slid the spool over. 'Yeah, filled with Mickey C. running off at the mouth on stuff that has nothing to do with the Nite Owl. Too bad, but I think we can put Davey down as a traitor to Mickey, and I think he must have heard the Engleklings offer Mick the Cathcart deal. He liked the sound of it and sent Van Gelder after Duke. And that's as far as I can take it.'

The man looked shot. 'Good work, Jack. Really, I mean it.'

'Thanks, and that first name bit just went over large.'

Ed picked up a menu, emptied his pockets underneath it. 'It's midnight and I'm all out of subtlety.'

'You're working up to something. What'd you get out of Bracken?'

'Nothing but lies. And you're right, Sergeant. The McNeil end is dead for now.'

'So?'

'So tomorrow I'm hitting Patchett. I'm sealing I.A. off from Dudley and his men and bringing in Terry Lux, Chester Yorkin and every Patchett flunky that Fisk and Kleckner can find.'

'Yeah, but what about Bracken and Patchett?'

Ed saw Lynn naked. 'Bracken tried to buy out of your deposition. She snitched you on that escapade in Malibu, and I played her back on it.'

Trash slammed his head down on two clenched fists. Ed said, 'I told her you'd do anything to get the file back. I told her you still love dope and you're in hock to some bookies. You're up for a trial board and you want to crash Patchett's rackets.'

Vincennes raised his head – pale, knuckle-gouged. 'So tell me you'll square what's in the file.'

Ed picked up his menu. Underneath: heroin, Benzedrine, a switchblade, a 9mm automatic. 'You're going to shake Patchett down. He snorts heroin, so you offer him some. If you want some stuff to get your own juice up, you've got it. You're going after him to get your file back and to find out who made the blood smut and killed Hudgens. I'm working on a script, and you'll have it by tomorrow night. You're going to scare the shit out of Patchett and you're going to do whatever it takes to get what we both want. I know you can do it, so don't make me threaten you.'

Vincennes smiled. He almost hit the chord – the old big-time Big V. 'Suppose it goes bad?'

'Then kill him.'

Chapter Sixty-one

Opium fumes banged his head; chink backtalk banged it worse: 'Spade not here, my place have police sanction, I pay I pay!' Uncle Ace Kwan sent him to Fat Dewey Shin, who sent him to a string of dens on Alameda – Spade was there, but Spade was gone, 'I pay! I pay!', try Uncle Minh, Uncle Chin, Uncle Chan. The Chinatown runaround, it took him hours to figure it out, a shuffle from enemy to enemy. Uncle Danny Tao pulled a shotgun; he took it away from him, blackjacked him, still couldn't force a snitch. Spade was there, Spade was gone – and if he took one more whiff of 'O' he knew he'd curl up and die or start shooting. The punch line: he was shaking Chinatown for a man named Cooley.

Chinatown dead for now.

Bud called the D.A.'s Bureau, gave the squad whip his Perkins/Cooley leads; the man yawned along, signed off bored. Out to the Strip; the Cowboy Rhythm Band on stage, no Spade, nobody had seen him in a couple of days. Hillbilly clubs, local bars, night spots – no sightings of Donnell Clyde Cooley. 1:00 fucking A.M., no place to go but Lynn's – 'Where *were* you?' and a bed.

Rain came on – a downpour. Bud counted taillights to stay awake: red dots, hypnotizing. He made Nottingham Drive near gone – dizzy, numb in the limbs.

Lynn on her porch, watching the rain. Bud ran up; she held her arms out. He slipped, steadied himself with her body.

She stepped back. Bud said, 'I was worried. I kept calling you last night before things got crazy.'

'Crazy how?'

'The morning, it's too long a story for now. How did it – '

Lynn touched his lips. 'I told them things about Pierce

that you already know, and I've been getting misty with the rain and thinking about telling them more.'

'More what?'

'I'm thinking that it's over with Pierce. In the morning, sweetie. Both our stories for breakfast.'

Bud leaned on the porch rail. Lightning lit up the street – and dry tears on Lynn's face. 'Honey, what is it? Is it Exley? Did he hardnose you?'

'It's Exley, but not what you're thinking. And I know why you hate him so much.'

'What do you mean?'

'That he's just the opposite of all the good things you are. He's more like I am.'

'I don't get it.'

'Well, it's a credibility he has for being so calculating. I started out hating him because you do, then he made me realize some things about Pierce just by being who he is. He told me some things he didn't have to, and my own reactions surprised me.'

More lightning – Lynn looked god-awful sad. Bud said, 'For instance?'

'For instance Jack Vincennes is going crazy and has some kind of vendetta against Pierce. And I don't care half as much as I should.'

'How did you get so friendly with Exley?'

Lynn laughed. '*In vino veritas*. You know, sweetie, you're thirty-nine years old and I keep waiting for you to get exhausted being who you are.'

'I'm exhausted tonight.'

'That's not what I meant.'

Bud turned on the porch light. 'You gonna tell me what happened with you and Exley?'

'We just talked.'

Her makeup was tear streaked – it was the first time he'd seen her not beautiful. 'So tell me about it.'

'In the morning.'

'No, now.'

'Honey, I'm as tired as you are.'

Her little half smile did it. 'You slept with him.'

385

Lynn looked away. Bud hit her – once, twice, three times. Lynn faced straight into the blows. Bud stopped when he saw he couldn't break her.

Chapter Sixty-two

IAD – packed.

Chester Yorkin, the Fleur-de-Lis delivery man, stashed in booth #1; in 2 and 3: Paula Brown and Lorraine Malvasi, Patchett whores – Ava Gardner, Rita Hayworth. Lamar Hinton, Bobby Inge, Christine Bergeron and son could not be located; ditto the smut posers – Fisk and Kleckner failed to make them from extensive mugbook prowls. In booth 4: Sharon Kostenza, real name Mary Alice Mertz, a plum off Vincennes' deposition – the woman who once bailed Bobby Inge out of jail and paid a surety bond for Chris Bergeron. In booth 5: Dr. Terry Lux, his attorney – the great Jerry Geisler.

Ray Pinker standing by with counterdope – so far none of the new fish looked drugged.

Two officers guarding the squadroom – private interrogations – strict I.A. autonomy.

Kleckner and Fisk grilling Mertz and pseudo Ava – armed with deposition copies, smut photos, a case summary. Yorkin, Lux and phony Rita cooling their heels.

Ed worked in his office; draft three of Vincennes' script. A thought nagged him: if Lynn Bracken reported to Patchett in full, he would have yanked his people before the police could bring them in – the way Inge, Bergeron and son disappeared immediately pre-Nite Owl. Two possibles on that – she was playing an angle or their rutting had her confused and she was stalling to figure the upshot. Most likely the former – the woman cut her last confused breath at birth.

He could still taste her.

Ed drew lines on paper. Inez to check Dieterling connections to Patchett and his father – that thought still made him wince. Two I.A. men out looking for White – apprehend the bastard and break him. Billy Dieterling

387

and Timmy Valburn to be questioned – kid gloves, they
had prestige, juice. A line to the Hudgens kill and the
Hudgens/Patchett 'gig' – Vincennes' deposition stated that
Hudgens' *Badge of Honor* files were missing at the time
of his death, anomalous, the show was a Hudgens fixation.
The *Badge of Honor* people were alibied for the murder –
but another reading of the case file was in order.

Half his maze of cases read extortion.

Line to an outside issue – Dudley Smith, going crazy
for a quick Darktown collar. Line to a rumor: Thad Green
was going to take over the U.S. Border Patrol come May.
A theoretical line: Parker would choose his new chief of
detectives solely on the basis of the Nite Owl case – him
or Smith. Dudley might send White back to break his
autonomy; criss cross all lines to keep *his* case sealed.

Kleckner walked in. 'Sir, the Mertz woman won't cooperate. All she'll say is that she lives under that Sharon
Kostenza alias and that she makes bail for Patchett's
people when they get arrested for outside charges.
Nobody's *ever* been arrested working for him, we know
that. She says she can't ID the people in the photos and
she's mum on that extortion angle you told me to play
up. She deadpanned the Nite Owl – and I believe her.'

'Release her, I want her to go to Patchett and panic
him. What did Duane get off Ava Gardner?'

Kleckner passed him a sheet of paper. 'Lots. Here's
the high points, and he's got the actual interview on tape.'

'Good. You go soften up Yorkin for me. Bring him a
beer and baby sit him.'

Kleckner walked out smiling. Ed read Fisk's memo.

Witness Paula Brown 3/25/58
   1. Witness revealed names of numerous P.P. call
girl/male prostitute customers (specifics to follow in
separate memo & on tape)
   2. Could not ID people in photos (seems truthful
on this)
   3. Extortion hook got her talking
   a. P.P. gave his girls/male prostitutes bonuses to

get their customers to reveal intimate details of their lives

    b. P.P. makes his prosts quit at 30 (apparent bee in his bonnet)

    c. On in-home prostitution assignments, P.P. had prosts leave doors/windows open so men with cameras could take compromising photos. Prosts also made wax impressions of locks on certain rich custs doors

    d. P.P. had famous (T. Lux obviously) plastic surgeon cut male/female prosts to look like movie stars and thus make more $

    e. Male prosts extorted $ from married homosexual custs & split take with P.P.

    f. Bored by Nite Owl quests (obviously has no guilty knowledge)

Astounding audacious perversion.

Ed hit sweatbox row, checked the mirrors. Fisk and phony Ava talking; Kleckner and Yorkin drinking beer. Terry Lux reading a magazine, Jerry Geisler fuming. Lorraine Malvasi alone in a cloud of smoke. Astounding audacious perversion – the woman had Rita Hayworth's face down to the bone, up to the hairdo from *Gilda*.

He opened the door. Rita/Lorraine stood up, sat down, lit a cigarette. Ed handed her Fisk's memo. 'Please read this, Miss Malvasi.'

She read, chewing lipstick. 'So?'

'So do you confirm that or not?'

'So I'm entitled to a lawyer.'

'Not for seventy-two hours.'

'You can't hold me here that long.'

'Caaant' – a bad New York accent. 'Not here, but we can hold you at the Woman's Jail.'

Lorraine bit at a nail, drew blood. 'You caan't.'

'Sure I can. Sharon Kostenza's in custody, so she can't make bail for you. Pierce Patchett is under surveillance and your friend Ava just spilled what you read there. She talked first, and all I want you to do is fill in some blanks.'

A little sob. 'I caan't.'

'Why not?'

'Pierce has been too nice to – '

Cut her off. 'Pierce is finished. Lynn Bracken turned state's on him. She's in protective custody, and I can go to her for the answers or save myself the trouble and ask you.'

'I caaan't.'

'You can and you will.'

'No, I caaan't.'

'You'd better, because you're an accessory to eleven felonies in Paula Brown's statement alone. Are you afraid of the dykes at the jail?'

No answer.

'You should be, but the matrons are worse. Big husky bull daggers with nightsticks. You know what they do with those – '

'All right all right all right! All right I'll tell you!'

Ed took out a notepad, wrote 'Chrono.' Lorraine: 'It's not Pierce's fault. This guy made him do it.'

'What guy?'

'I don't know. Really, for real, I don't know.'

'Chrono' underlined. 'When did you start working for Patchett?'

'When I was twenty-one.'

'Give me the year.'

'1951.'

'And he had Terry Lux perform surgery on you?'

'Yes! To make me more beautiful!'

'Easy now, please. Now a second ago you said that a guy – '

'I don't know who the guy is! I caan't tell you what I don't know!'

'Sssh, please. Now, you confirmed Paula Brown's statement and you said that a "guy," *whose identity you don't know*, coerced Patchett into the extortion plans detailed in that statement. Is that correct?'

Lorraine put out her cigarette, lit another one. 'Yes. Extortion is like blackmail, right, so yes.'

'When, Lorraine? Do you know *when* "this guy" approached Patchett?'

She counted on her fingers. 'Five years ago, May.'

'Chrono' hard underlined. 'That's May of 1953?'

'Yeah, 'cause my father died that month. Pierce called us kids in and said we had to do it, he didn't want to, but this guy had him by the you-know-whats. He didn't say the guy's name and I don't think none of the other kids know it either.'

'Chrono' one month post-Nite Owl. 'Think fast, Lorraine. The Nite Owl massacre. Remember that?'

'What? Some people got shot, right?'

'Never mind. What else did Patchett tell you when he called you in?'

'Nothing.'

'*Nothing* else on Patchett and extortion? Remember, I'm not asking you if you did any of this. I'm not asking you to incriminate yourself.'

'Well, maybe three months or so before that I heard Veronica – I mean Lynn – and Pierce talking. He said him and that scandal mag man who got killed later were gonna run this squeeze thing where Pierce would tell him about our clients' secret little . . . you know, fetishes, and the man would threaten the clients with being in *Hush-Hush*. You know, pay money or be in the scandal mag.'

Extortion theory validated. An instinct: on some level Lynn was playing straight, she hadn't told Patchett to prepare – he never would have let these people come in. 'Lorraine, did Sergeant Kleckner show you some pornographic pictures?'

A nod. 'I told him and I'll tell you. I don't know any of the people and those pictures gave me the creeps.'

Ed walked out. Duane Fisk in the hallway. 'Good work, sir. When you got her on that "this guy" bit, I went back and ran it by Ava. She confirmed it and confirmed that no ID.'

Ed nodded. 'Tell her that Rita and Yorkin have been booked, then release her. I want her to go back to Patchett. How's Kleckner doing with Yorkin?'

Fisk shook his head. 'That boy's a hardcase. He's prac-
tically daring Don to make him talk. Hey, where's Bud
White now that we need him?'

'Amusing, but don't keep it up. And right now I want
you to take Lux and Geisler to lunch. Lux is here voluntarily, so be nice. Tell Geisler that this is a multiple
homicide major conspiracy case, and tell him Lux gets
full collateral immunity for his cooperation and a signed
promise of no courtroom testimony. Tell him it's already
in writing, and if he wants verification to call Ellis Loew.'

Fisk nodded, walked down to booth 5. Ed checked the
#1 look-in.

Chester Yorkin wising off at the mirror: making faces,
flipping the bird. Skinny, a pompadour flopped over his
eyes oozing grease. Welts on his arms – maybe old needle
marks.

Ed opened the door. Yorkin said, 'Hey, I know you, I
read about you.'

Tracks confirmed – scar tissue on the welts. 'I've been
in the news.'

Giggle, giggle. 'This is an old one, *kemo sabe*. Something like you saying, "I never hit suspects 'cause that's
the cop lowered to the level of the criminal." You wanta
hear my answer? I never snitch 'cause cops are all cocksuckers who get their cookies off making guys talk.'

'You through?' – Bud White's stock line.

'No. Your father takes it up the ass from Moochie
Mouse.'

Scared, but he did it – an elbow to the windpipe. Yorkin
gasped; Ed got behind him, cuffed him, shoved him to
the floor.

Scared, but steady hands: look, Dad, no fear.

Yorkin backed into a corner.

Scared, another Bad Bud move: a chair, a roundhouse
swing, the chair smashed to the wall just above the suspect's head. Yorkin tried to squirm away; Ed kicked him
back to his corner. Slow now: don't let your voice break,
don't let your eyes go soft behind your glasses. '*Everything*. I want to know about the smut and the other shit

392

you push through Fleur-de-Lis. *Everything*. You start with those tracks on your arms and why a smart man like Patchett trusts a junkie like you. And you know one thing right now – Patchett is finished and I'm the only one who can cut you a deal. *Do you understand me?*'

Yorkin bobbed his head yes yes yes. 'Test pilot. I flew for him! Test pilot!'

Ed unlocked his cuffs. 'Say that again.'

Yorkin rubbed his neck. 'Guinea pig.'

'What?'

'I let him test horse on me. Here and there, a little at a time.'

'Start over. Slowly.'

Yorkin coughed. 'Pierce got this heroin stolen off this Cohen–Jack Dragna deal years ago. This guy Buzz Meeks left some with these guys Pete and Bax Englekling, just a sample, and they gave it to their father, who was some kind of chemistry hotshot. He taught Pierce in college, and he laid the shit off to him and died, a heart attack or something. This other guy, I don't know his name so don't ask me, he killed Meeks or something like that. He got the rest of the shit, like eighteen pounds' worth. Pierce has been developing compounds with the stuff for years. He wants to make the cheapest and the safest and the best. I just . . . I just take some test pops.'

Astounding lines crossing. 'You were making deliveries for Fleur-de-Lis five years ago, right?'

'Right, yeah, sure.'

'You and Lamar Hinton.'

'I ain't seen Lamar in years, you can't pin Lamar's shit on me!'

Ed grabbed the spare chair, brandished it. 'I don't want to. Give me an answer on this, and if I like it I'll owe you a solid. It's a test and you're a test pilot, so you should do well. Who shot at Jack Vincennes outside the Hollywood drop back in '53?'

Yorkin cringed. 'Me. Pierce told me to clip him. I shouldn't of done it by the drop. I fucked up and Pierce got pissed.'

Patchett nailed: attempted murder on a police officer. 'What did he do to you for that?'

'He tested me bad. He gave me all these bad compounds he said he had to eliminate. He made me take these bad fucking flights.'

'So you hate him for it.'

'Man, Pierce ain't like regular people. I hate him, but I dig him too.'

Ed pushed the chair away. 'Do you remember the Nite Owl shootings?'

'Sure, years ago. What's that got to do – '

'Never mind, and here's the important thing. If you fill this in for me, I'll give you a written immunity statement and put you up in protective custody until Patchett's down. Smut, Chester. You remember those orgy books Fleur-de-Lis was running five years ago?'

Yorkin bobbed his head yes.

'The ink blood on the pictures, do you remember that?'

Yorkin smiled – snitching eager now. 'I know that story good. Pierce is going down for real?'

Ten hours from the script. 'Maybe tonight.'

'Then fuck him for all those bad flights.'

'Chester, just tell me slowly.'

Yorkin stood up, worked the kinks from his legs. 'You know what's a bitch about Pierce? He'd say all these things around me when I was on a flight, like I was harmless 'cause I couldn't remember nothing he said.'

Ed got out his notebook. 'Try to tell it in order.'

Yorkin rubbed his throat, coughed. 'Okay, Pierce had this old string of girls that he let go, this was around when we were moving them picture books. Some guy, I don't know his name, he talked some of the girls and their johns into posing for them pictures. He made books out of them and went to Pierce to get money to move the books wide, you know, he promised Pierce a cut. Pierce, he liked the idea, but he didn't want to expose his girls or their johns. He bought a bunch of the books off the guy to move through Fleur-de-Lis, you know, just a close distribution

394

he called it, like a test market, he figured he could keep track of the stuff that way.'

Old lines crossing: the close distribution wasn't that close, Ad Vice retrieved throwaway copies – Vincennes to the case. 'Keep going, Chester.'

'Well, the guy who made the stuff, somehow he weaseled some info on the Englekling brothers out of Pierce, how they had this printing press place and was always bent for money. He found himself a front man, and the front man, he approached the brothers. You know, a plan to make the shit bulk and move it.'

The front man: Duke Cathcart. Zigzag lines from Cohen to the brothers, the brothers to Patchett, back on a sideswipe: Mickey at McNeil Island – then Goldman and Van Gelder. *Line the heroin to the pornography.* 'Chester, how do you know all this?'

Yorkin laughed. 'I'd be on a mainline flight and Pierce, he'd be on safe old white horse up the nose. He'd just jaw at me like I some kind of dog you talk to.'

'So Patchett and the smut are dead, right? All he's interested in is pushing the heroin.'

'Nix. That guy who brought Pierce the eighteen pounds years ago? Well, he's got a hard-on for the smut. He's got lists of all these rich perverts and all these contacts in South America. Him and Pierce, they sat on the original pictures for years, then they had some new books made up who-knows-where. They got the shit in a warehouse someplace, I don't know where, just waiting to go. I think Pierce was waiting for some kind of heat to die down.'

No new lines crossed. A phrase sunk in: *profit motive.* Pornography by itself was chancy; twenty pounds of heroin *developed* meant millions. Yorkin said, 'One more 'case you get antsy on my deal. Pierce has got him a booby-trapped safe by his house. He's got money, dope, all kinds of stuff stashed there.'

Ed kept thinking MONEY.

Yorkin: 'Hey, talk to me! You want the new drop address? 8819 Linden, Long Beach. Exley, talk to me!'

'Steak in your cell, Chester. You've earned it.'

Fresh lines – Ed pulled Fisk's and Kleckner's summaries, added the Yorkin/Malvasi revelations.

Heroin and pornography lined. 'The Guy' who made the smut books as Sid Hudgens' killer, his front man Duke Cathcart – killed by Dean Van Gelder, ordered killed or merely approached by Davey Goldman – who learned of the smut proposal via the bug in Mickey Cohen's cell. Cohen omnipresent – his stolen heroin ended up with both the Engleklings and 'The Man' who brought Patchett the eighteen pounds of 'H' for development, 'The Man' who also loved pornography and convinced Patchett to manufacture new books from the 1953 prototypes. An instinct: Cohen was Mr. Patsy going back eight years, in and out of jail, a focal point who never dealt his own hand into the welter of cases. A line to a conclusion: the Nite Owl killings were semiprofessional at least, an attempt to take over the heroin and pornography rackets of Pierce Patchett. Cathcart, attempting to push the smut on his own, was the focus of the killings. Did he misrepresent his importance to the wrong people, or did the shooters deliberately take out Van Gelder, knowing or not knowing he was a Cathcart impersonator? Lines to organized crime intrigue, semipro at least, with all mob lines dead or incapacitated: Franz Englekling and sons – dead, Davy Goldman a vegetable, Mickey Cohen befuddled by the action going on around him. A question line: who clipped Pete and Bax Englekling? The terror line: Loren Atherton, 1934. How could it be?

Fisk rapped on the door. 'Sir, I brought Lux and Geisler back.'

'And?'

'Geisler gave me a prepared statement.'

'Read it.'

Fisk pulled out a sheet. ' "Pertaining to my relationship with Pierce Morehouse Parchett, I, Terence Lux, M.D., do offer the following notarized statement. To wit: my relationship with Pierce Patchett is professional: i.e., I have performed extensive plastic surgery on a number of male and female acquaintances of his, perfecting already existing resemblances to exact resemblances of several notable actors and actresses. Unsubstantiated rumors hold that Patchett employs these young people for purposes of prostitution, but I have no conclusive evidence that this is true. Duly sworn," et cetera.'

Ed said, 'Not good enough. Duane, you take Yorkin and Rita Hayworth across the street and book them. Aiding and Abetting, and leave the arrest dates blank. Allow them one phone call each, then go down to Long Beach and seize 8819 Linden. That's a Fleur-de-Lis drop, and I'm sure Patchett's cleaned it out, but do it anyway. If you find the place virgin, bust it up and leave the door open.'

Fisk swallowed. 'Uh, sir? Bust it up? And no booking date on our suspects?'

'Bust it up. Make a statement. And don't question my orders.'

Fisk said, 'Uh, yes, sir.' Ed closed the door, buzzed Kleckner. 'Don, send Dr. Lux and Mr. Geisler in.'

'Yes, sir,' loud on the intercom. Whispered: 'They're pissed, Captain. Thought you should know.'

Ed opened the door. Geisler and Lux walked up – brusque.

No handshakes. Geisler said, 'Frankly, that lunch didn't begin to cover the hourly rate I'm going to have to charge Dr. Lux. I think it's reprehensible that he came here voluntarily and was kept waiting so long.'

Ed smiled. 'I apologize. I accept the formal statement you offered and I have no real questions for Dr. Lux. I have just one favor to ask and a large one to grant in return. And send me your bill, Mr. Geisler. You know I can afford it.'

'I know your father can. Continue, please. You're holding my interest so far.'

Ed to Lux. 'Doctor, I know who you know and you know who I know. And I know you deal in legal morphine cures. Help me with something and I'll pledge my friendship.'

Lux cleaned his nails with a scalpel. 'The *Daily News* says you're obsolescent.'

'They're mistaken. Pierce Patchett and heroin, Doctor. I'll settle for rumors and I won't ask for your sources.'

Geisler and Lux went into a huddle – a step out of the door, whispers. Lux broke it off. 'I've heard Pierce is connected to some very bad men who want to control the heroin trade in Los Angeles. He's quite the chemist, you know, and he's been developing a special blend for years. Hormones, antipsychotic strains, quite a brew. I've heard it puts regular heroin to shame and I heard it's ready to be manufactured and sold. One in my column, Captain. Jerry, take the man at his word and send him my bill.'

Semipro, pro – his new lines all spelled HEROIN. Ed called Bob Gallaudet, left a message with his secretary: Nite Owl maybe breaking – call me. A picture on his desk hooked him: Inez and his father at Arrowhead. He called Lynn Bracken.

'Hello?'

'Lynn, it's Exley.'

'God, hello.'

'You didn't go to Patchett, did you?'

'Did you think I would? Were you setting me up to?'

Ed laid the picture face down. 'I want you to get out of L.A. for a week or so. I have a place at Lake Arrowhead, you can stay there. Leave this afternoon.'

'Is Pierce . . . '

'I'll tell you later.'

'Will you come up?'

Ed checked the Vincennes script. 'As soon as I set something up. Have you seen White?'

'He came and went, and I don't know where he is. Is he all right?'

'Yes. No, shit, I don't know. Meet me at Fernando's on the lake. It's right by my place. Say six?'

'I'll be there.'

'I figured you'd take some convincing.'

'I've already convinced myself of lots of things. Leaving town just makes it easier.'

'*Why*, Lynn?'

'The party was over, I guess. Do you think keeping your mouth shut's a heroic act?'

Chapter Sixty-three

Bud woke up at the Victory. Dusk out the window – he'd slept through half a night and a day. He rubbed his eyes; Spade Cooley locked right back on him. He smelled cigarette smoke, saw Dudley sitting by the door.

'Bad dreams, lad? You were thrashing a bit.'

Nightmare: Inez trashed by the press, his fault – what he did to nail Exley.

'Lad, in repose you reminded me of my daughters. And you know I care for you no less.'

He'd sweated the sheets through. 'What's with the job? What's next?'

'Next you listen. I've long been involved in containing hard crime so that myself and a few colleagues might someday enjoy a profit dispensation, and that day will soon be arriving. As a colleague, you will share handsomely. Grand means will be in our hands, lad. Imagine the means to keep the nigger filth sedated and extrapolate from there. One obstreperous Italian you've dealt with in the past is involved, and I think you can be particularly useful in keeping him in line.'

Bud stretched, cracked his knuckles. 'I meant the reopening. Talk straight, okay?'

'Edmund Jennings Exley is as straight as I can be. He's trying to prove bad things against Lynn, lad. Salt on all the old wounds he's given you.'

Live wires buzzing. 'You knew about us. I should've known.'

'There is precious little I don't know, and nothing I would not do for you. Coward Exley has touched the only two women you've loved, lad. Think of grand ways to hurt him.'

Chapter Sixty-four

They made love straight off – Ed knew they'd have to talk if they didn't, Lynn seemed to sense the same thing. The cabin was musty, the bed unmade – stale from last time with Inez. Ed kept the lights on: the more he saw, the less he'd think. It helped him through the act; counting Lynn's freckles kept him from peaking. Slow on the act, both of them, making up for their tumble off the couch. Lynn had bruises; Ed knew they came from Bud White. For a tightrope act they were gentle; their long embrace after felt like payback for their lies. When they started talking they'd never stop. Ed wondered who'd say 'Bud White' first.

Lynn said it. Bud was the fulcrum that convinced her to lie to Patchett: the police investigation was a joke, they were grasping at straws. White knew of Patchett's milder doings, she was afraid he'd get in trouble if Pierce fought back. Pierce might try to buy his friendship, he thought everyone had a price tag, he didn't know her Wendell couldn't be bought. Bud got her thinking; the more she thought the more she hurt; a certain police captain kissing a certain ex-whore at the only moment she would have let him just added to the party's over, Pierce made me but he's bad deep down, if I let him go then maybe I'll get back some of the good things he's killed in me. Ed winced through the words, knew he couldn't return her candor – now Jack Vincennes was going in barefoot, he'd counted on Lynn to push Patchett to panic, past Fisk taking a fire axe to the drop, past his people grilled and arrested. Lynn met his silence with words – excerpts from her diary, a show-and-tell for fugitive lovers her pronouncement. Funny, sad – old tricks derided, a monologue on carhop hookers that almost had him laughing. Lynn on Inez and Bud White – he loved her here and there and mostly at a distance because her rage was worse than his, drained him, a night here and there was all he could take. No jealousy – so his own jealousy jumped up, almost forced him to shout questions: heroin and extortion, astounding audacious perversion, just how much do you know? The gift she gave him wouldn't let him; soft hands on his chest made him throw out a parity in candor before he started interrogating or lying just to have something to say.

He went straight to his family, spiraled past to present. Mama's boy Eddie, golden boy Thomas, the jig he danced when his brother stopped six bullets. Being a policeman/patrician from a long line of Scotland Yard detectives. Inez, four men killed out of weakness; Dudley Smith going crazy to find a suitable scapegoat that Ellis Loew and Chief Parker just might accept as a panacea. A head-long rush to the great Preston Exley in all his intractable glory and how ink-embossed pornography lined to a dead scandalmonger, vivisected children and his father and Raymond Dieterling twenty-four years ago. A rush until there was nothing left to say and Lynn kissed his lips shut and he fell asleep touching her bruises.

Chapter Sixty-five

Rogue cop Big V – give Exley credit for good casting. He synced his approach call to the drop raid – Patchett said, 'Yes, I'll talk to you. Eleven tonight, and come alone.'

He wore a tape wire hooked across a bulletproof vest.

He carried a bag of heroin, a switchblade, a 9mm automatic. Exley's Benzedrine down the toilet, grief he didn't need.

He walked up, rang the bell – stage fright all the way.

Patchett opened the door. Pinned-back eyes like Exley predicted – a nose junkie.

Jack, per the script: 'Hello, Pierce' – all contempt.

Patchett shut the door. Jack threw the dope in his face. It hit him, fell to the floor.

Ad lib time. 'Just a peace offering. Not up to that shit you tested on Yorkin anyway. Did you know my brother-in-law's the city D.A.? He's a bonus you get if you make a deal with me.'

Patchett: 'Where did you get that?' Calm, the stuff up his nose wouldn't let him show fear.

Jack pulled out the knife, scratched his neck with the blade. He felt blood, licked it off a finger – Academy Award psycho. 'I shook down some niggers. You know all about that, right? *Hush-Hush* Magazine used to write me up. You and Sid Hudgens go way back, so you should know.'

No fear. 'You made trouble for me five years ago. I still have that file carbon on you, and I think it's fair to say that you broke your part of our bargain. I'm assuming you've shown your superiors your deposition.'

Knife bit: the tip of the blade in one palm, a little push to retract it. More blood, a key Exley line. 'I'm way past you in the information department. I know about the heroin you got from the Cohen-Dragna deal and what you've been doing with it. I know about the smut you were pushing in '53, and I know all about those extortion shakedowns with your whores. And all I want is my file and some information. You give me that and I'll put the fritz to everything Captain Exley has.'

'What information?'

The script, verbatim. 'I made a deal with Hudgens. The deal was my file destroyed and ten grand in cash in exchange for some juicy dirt I had on the LAPD high brass. I knew Sid was going to work a shakedown scheme with you, and I'd already backed down on Fleur-de-Lis – you know that's true. Sid got killed before I could pick up the money and the file, and I think the killer got both of them. I need that money, 'cause I'm getting shitcanned off the Department before I can collect my pension, and I want the fucker who robbed me dead. You didn't *make* that smut back in '53, but whoever did killed Sid and robbed me. Give me the name and I'm yours.'

Patchett smiled. Jack smiled – one last push before the pistol-whipping. 'Pierce, the Nite Owl was smut and heroin – yours. Do you want to swing for that?'

Patchett pulled out a piece, shot him three times. Silencer thwaps – the slugs shattered the tape gizmo, bounced off his vest.

Three more shots – two in the vest, one wide.

Jack crashed into a table, came up aiming. A jammed slide, Patchett on him, two misfire clicks right up close. Patchett in his face, the knife out, a blind stab, a scream – the blade catching.

Patchett's left hand nailed to the table. Another scream, his right hand arcing – a hypo in it. The needle mainline close, stab, zooooom somewhere nice. Shots rifle loud, 'No, Abe, no, Lee, no!' Flames, smoke, rolling away from the grief, so he could live to love the needle again, maybe see the funny man with his hand shivved to the table.

Chapter Sixty-six

The clock in his head was way off, his watch had quit working – he wasn't sure if it was Wednesday or Thursday. His Nite Owl 'disclosure' ate up a whole evening – Dudley was so far ahead of him he never even took notes. The man left him at midnight, pumped up with bold language, no date for the strongarm cop's ball. Dud's date was Exley: clear the Nite Owl and ruin his career, seconds for Bad Bud White: 'Think of grand ways to hurt him.' Murder was all he could think of – a fair trade for Lynn; killing an LAPD captain was the springs in his clock all snapping – one more span of skewed time and he'd do it. Some point early A.M. Kathy Janeway hit him up – Kathy the way she looked then. She found him a date for the wee small hours – the man who killed her.

And Spade Cooley stood him up.

He went by the Biltmore, talked to the Cowboy Rhythm Band – Spade was still gone, Deuce Perkins was off on his own toot. The D.A.'s Bureau night clerk gave him the brush – were they even on the case? Another tear through Chinatown, a run by his apartment – a couple of I.A. hard-ons parked out front. A wolfed meal at a burger stand, dawn creeping up, a pile of *Heralds* that told him it was Friday. A Nite Owl headline: jigs crying police brutality, Chief Parker promising justice.

He felt tired one second, keyed up the next. He tried to set his watch to the radio; the hands stuck; he threw a hundred-dollar Gruen out the window. Tired, he saw Kathy; keyed up, he saw Exley and Lynn. He drove to Nottingham Drive to check cars.

No white Packard – and Lynn always parked the same place.

Bud walked around the building – no sign of Exley's blue Plymouth. A neighbor woman bringing in milk. She said, 'Good morning. You're Miss Bracken's friend, aren't you?'

The old snoop – Lynn said she peeped bedrooms. 'That's right.'

'Well, as you can see, she's not here.'

'Yeah, and you don't know where she is.'

'Well . . .'

'Well what? You seen her with a man? Tall, glasses?'

'No, I haven't. And mind your tone, young man. Well what, indeed.'

Bud badged her. '*Well what*, lady? You were gonna tell me something.'

'Until you got cheeky, I was going to tell you where Miss Bracken went. I heard her talking to the manager last night. She was asking for directions.'

'*Where to?*'

'Lake Arrowhead, and I would have told you before you got cheeky.'

Exley's place, Inez told him about it, a cabin flying flags: American, state, LAPD. Bud drove to Arrowhead, cruised by the lake, found it: banners cutting wind, no blue Plymouth. Lynn's Packard in the driveway.

A brodie to the porch; a leap up the steps. Bud punched in a window, unlatched the door. No response to the noise – just a musty front room done up hunting lodge provincial.

He walked into the bedroom. Sweat stink, lipstick blots on the bed. He kicked the feathers out of the pillows, dumped the mattress, saw a leather binder underneath. Lynn's 'Scarlet Letters' for sure – she'd been talking up her diary for years.

Bud grabbed it, got ready to rip – down the spine like his old phone book trick. The smell made him stop – if he didn't look, he was a coward.

Flip to the last page. Lynn's handwriting, bold black ink, the gold pen he'd bought her.

March 26, 1958

More on E.E. He just drove off and I could tell he was chagrined by all the things he told me last night. He looked vulnerable in the A.M. light, stumbling to the bathroom without his glasses. I pity Pierce his misfortune in encountering such an essentially frightened and unyielding man. E.E. makes love like my Wendell, like he never wants it to end, because when it ends he will have to return to what he is. He is perhaps the only man I have ever met who is as compromised as I am, who is so smart, circumspect and cautious that you can always see his wheels turning and thus wish you could always talk in the dark so that face value would be less complex. He is so smart and pragmatic that he makes W.W. appear childish and thus less heroic than he really is. And considering his dilemma, my betrayal of Pierce's friendship and patronage seem frankly callow. This man has been so obsessively beholden to his father for so long that the crux of it must influence every step he takes, yet he is still taking steps, which amazes me. E.E. didn't delve too far into specifics, but the basic thrust is that some of the more artful pornographic books that Pierce was selling five years ago have diagrams that match the mutilations on Sid Hudgens' body and the wounds on the victims of a murderer named Loren Atherton, who was apprehended by Preston Exley in the 1930s. P.E. is soon to announce his candidacy for governor and E.E. now considers that his father solved the Atherton case incorrectly and inferred that he suspects P.E. of establishing business relations with Raymond Dieterling at the time of that case (one of Atherton's victims was a Dieterling child star). Another strange crux: E.E., my *très* smart pragmatist, considers his father such a moral exemplar and paragon of efficacy that he is terrified of accepting normal incompetence and rational business self-interest as within the bounds of acceptable human behavior. He is afraid that solving his 'Nite Owl related' cases will reveal P.E.'s fallibility to the world and destroy his gubernatorial chances, and he is obviously even more afraid of having to accept his father as a mortal, especially difficult since he has never accepted himself as one. But he will go ahead with his cases, deep down he seems quite determined. As much as I love him, in the same situation my Wendell would just shoot everyone involved, then look for somebody a bit more intelligent to sort out the bodies, like that urbane Irishman Dudley Smith he always mentions. More on this and related matters after a walk, breakfast and three strong cups of coffee.

Now he ripped – down the spine, across the grain, leather and paper shredded to bits.

The phone, IAD direct. Buzz, buzz, 'Internal Affairs, Kleckner.'

'It's White. Put Exley on.'

'White, you're in troub – ' A new voice on the line. 'This is Exley. White, where are you?'

'Arrowhead. I just read Lynn's diary and got the whole story on your old man, Atherton and Dieterling. *The whole fucking story*. I'm running a suspect down, and when I find him it's your daddy on the six o'clock news.'

'I'll make a deal with you. Just listen.'

'Never.'

Back to L.A., the old Spade routine: Chinatown, the Strip, the Biltmore, his third circuit since time went haywire. The chinks were starting to look like the Cowboy Rhythm Band, the El Rancho guys were growing slant eyes. Every known haunt triple-checked, three times everything – except for a single hit on his agent.

Bud drove to Nat Penzler Associates. The connecting door was open – Mr. Natsky was eating a sandwich. He took a bite, said, 'Oh shit.'

'Spade's been ditching out on his gig. He must be costing you money.'

Penzler eased a hand behind his desk. 'Caveman, if you knew the grief my clients cause me.'

'You don't sound so concerned.'

'Bad pennies always turn up.'

'Do you know where he is?'

Penzler brought his hand up. 'My guess is on the planet Pluto, hanging out with his pal Jack Daniels.'

'What were you doing with your hand?'

'Scratching my balls. You want the job? It pays five yards a week, but you have to kick back ten percent to your agent.'

'Where is he?'

'He is somewhere in the vicinity of nowhere I know. Check with me next week and write when you get brains.'

'Like that, huh?'

'Caveman, if I knew would I withhold from a bruiser like you?'

Bud kicked him out of his chair. Penzler hit the floor; the chair spun, tipped. Bud reached under the desk, pulled out a bundle wrapped with string. A foot on top, a jerk on the knot – clean black cowboy shirts.

Penzler stood up. 'Lincoln Heights. The basement at Sammy Ling's, and you didn't get it from Natsky.'

Ling's Chow Mein: a dive on Broadway up from Chinatown. Parking spaces in back; a rear entrance to the kitchen. No outside basement access, steam shooting from an underground vent. Bud circled the place, heard voices out the vent. Make the trapdoor in the kitchen.

He found a two-by-four in the lot, went in the back way. Two slants frying meat, an old geek skinning a duck. A fix on the trapdoor, easy: lift the pallet by the oven.

They spotted him. The young chinks jabbered; Papa-san waved them quiet. Bud held his shield out.

The old man rubbed fingers. 'I pay! I pay I pay! You go!'

'Spade Cooley, Papa. You go downstairs and tell him Natsky brought the laundry. Chop-chop.'

'Spade pay! You leave alone! I pay! I pay!'

The kids circled. Papa-san waved his cleaver.

'You go now! Go now! I pay!'

Bud fixed a line on the floor. Papa stepped over it.

Bud swung his stick – pops caught it waist-high. He crashed into the stove, his face hit a burner, his hair caught fire. The kids charged; Bud got their legs in one shot. They hit the floor tangled up – Bud smashed in their ribs. Pops doused his head in the sink, charged with his face scorched black.

A roundhouse to the knees – Papa went down glued to that cleaver. Bud stepped on his hand, cracked the fingers – Papa let go screaming. Bud dragged him to the oven, kicked the pallet loose. Yank the trapdoor, drag the old man downstairs.

Fumes: opium, steam. Bud kicked Papa-san quiet. Through the fumes: dope suckers on mattresses.

Bud kicked through them. All chinks – they grumbled, swatted, sucked back to dreamland, Smoke: in his face, up his nose, breathing hard so he took it down his lungs. Steam like a beacon: a sweat room at the back.

He kicked over to the door. Throught a mist: naked Spade Cooley, three naked girls. Giggles, arms and legs cockeyed – an orgy on a slippery tile bench. Spade so tangled up in women that you couldn't shoot him clean.

Bud flipped a wall switch. The steam died, the mist fizzled. Spade looked over. Bud took his gun out.

KILL HIM.

Cooley moved first: a shield, two girls pressed tight. Bud moved in – yanking arms, legs, nails raking his face. The girls slipped, stumbled, tumbled out the door. Spade said, 'Jesus, Mary and Joseph.'

Smoke inside him, brewing up his very own dreamland. Last rites, stretch the moment. 'Kathy Janeway, Jane Mildred Hamsher, Lynette Ellen Kendrick, Sharon – '

Cooley yelled, 'GODDAMN YOU IT'S PERKINS!'

The moment snapped – Bud saw his gun half-triggered. Colors swirled around him; Cooley talked rapid fire. 'I saw Deuce with that last girlie, that Kendrick. I know'd he liked to hurt hooers and when that last girlie turned

410

up dead on the TV I asked him 'bout it. Deuce, he like to scared me to death, so's I took off on this here toot. Mister, you gotta believe me.'

Color flashes: Deuce Perkins, plain vicious. One color blinking – turquoise, Spade's hands. 'Those rings, where'd you get them?'

Cooley pulled a towel over his lap. 'Deuce, he makes them. He brings a hobby kit with him on the road. He's been crackin' all these vague-type jokes for years, how they protects his hands for his intimate-type work, and now I know what he means.'

'Opium. Can he get it?'

'That cracker shitbird steals my shit! Mister, you gotta believe me!'

Starting to. 'My killing dates put you in the right place to do the jobs. Just *you*. Your booking records show different goddamn guys traveling with you, so how do you – '

'Deuce, he's been my road manager since '49, he *always* travels with me. Mister, you gotta believe me!'

'*Where is he?*'

'I don't know!'

'Girlfriends, buddies, other perverts. *Give.*'

'That miserable sumbitch got no friends I know of 'cept that wop shitbird Johnny Stompanato. Mister, you gotta believe – '

'I believe you. You believe I'll kill you if you scare him away from me?'

'Praise Jesus, I believe.'

Bud walked into the smoke. The chinks were still on the nod, Papa was just barely breathing.

R&I on Perkins:

No California beefs, clean on his Alabama parole – he'd spent '44–'46 on a chain gang for animal sodomy. Transient musician, no known address listed. K.A. confirmation on Johnny Stompanato – ditto Lee Vachss and Abe Teitlebaum – mob punks all. Bud hung up, remembered a talk with Jack Vincennes – he'd rousted Deuce

411

at a *Badge of Honor* party – Johnny, Teitlebaum and Vachss were there with him.

Kid gloves: Johnny used to be his snitch, Johnny hated him, feared him.

Bud called the DMV, got Stomp's phone number – ten rings, no answer. Two more no-answers: the Cowboy Rhythm Band at the Biltmore, the El Rancho. Kikey Teitlebaum's deli next – Kikey and Johnny were tight.

A run out Pico, shaking off fumes. A keen edge settling in: get Perkins alone, kill him. Then Exley.

Bud parked, looked in the window. A slow afternoon, pay dirt – Johnny Stomp, Kikey T. at a table.

He walked in. They spotted him, whispered. Years since he'd seen them – Abe was fatter, Stomp still guinea slick.

Kikey waved. Bud grabbed a chair, carried it over. Stomp said, 'Wendell White. How's tricks, *paesano*?'

'Tricky. How's tricks with Lana Turner?'

'Trickier. Who told you?'

'Mickey C.'

Teitlebaum laughed. 'Must have a hole like the Third Street Tunnel. Johnny's leaving for Acapulco with her tonight, and me, I shack with Sadie five-fingers. White, what brings you here? I ain't seen you since Dick Stens used to work for me.'

'I'm looking for Deuce Perkins.'

Johnny tap-tapped the table. 'So talk to Spade Cooley.'

'Spade don't know where he is.'

'So why ask me? Mickey tell you Deuce and me are close?'

No ritual question: what do you want him for? And fat-mouth Kikey too quiet. 'Spade said you and him were acquaintances.'

'Acquaintances is right. We go back, *paesano*, so I'll tell you I haven't seen Deuce in years.'

Change-up pitch. 'You ain't my *paesano*, you wop cock-sucker.'

Johnny smiled, maybe relieved, their old cop-snitch game one more time. A look at Kikey – the fat man

412

working on spooked. 'Abe, you're tight with Perkins, right?'

'Nix. Deuce is too meshugeneh for me. He's just a guy to say hi to once in a blue fucking moon.'

A lie – Perkins' rap sheet said different. 'So maybe I'm confused. I know you guys are tight with Lee Vachss, and I heard him and Deuce are tight.'

Kikey laughed – too stagy. 'What a yuck. Johnny, I think Wendell here is really confused.'

Stomp said, 'Oil and water, those two. Tight? What a howl.'

Standing up for Vachss for no reason. 'You guys are the howl. I figured you'd ask me what the grief was right off.'

Kikey pushed his plate aside. 'It occur to you we just don't care?'

'Yeah, but you guys love to shmooz and milk the grapevine.'

'So shmooz.'

A rumor: Kikey beat a guy to death for calling him a yid. 'I'll shmooz, it's a nice day and I got nothing better to do than hobnob with a greasy wop and a fat yid.'

Abe ho-ho-ho'd, cuffed his arm oh-you-kid. 'You're a pisser. So what do you want Deuce for?'

Bud cuffed him back hard – 'None of your fucking business, Jewboy' – throw a change-up to Johnny. 'What are you doing now that Mickey's out?'

Tap, tap, tap – a pinky ring on a bottle of Schlitz. 'Nothing you'd be interested in. I got things contained, so don't you worry. What are *you* doing?'

'I'm on the Nite Owl reopening.'

Johnny tap-tapped too hard – his bottle almost tipped. Kikey, working on pale. 'You don't think Deuce Perkins . . . '

Stompanato: 'Come on, Abe. Deuce for the Nite Owl, what a howl.'

Bud said, 'I gotta piss,' walked to the bathroom. He closed the door, counted to ten, opened it a crack. The shitbirds spieling full blast – Abe wiping his face with a napkin. Let the pieces fit in.

413

Hink: Deuce for the Nite Owl.

Jack V. spotted Vachss, Stomp, Kikey and Perkins at a party – maybe a year pre-Nite Owl.

A Mobster Squad roust, a snitch off Joe Sifakis: *three-man* trigger gangs clipping Cohen franchise hoods, maverick hoods. The Victory Motel buzzing hard.

Bud grabbed the piece, dropped it, grabbed it.

'Contain.'

Dudley's favorite big word – 'containment.'

His motel pitch: 'containing,' 'profit dispensation,' 'obstreperous Italian you've dealt with in the past' – Johnny Stomp an old snitch who hated him. Dud hot for his 'full disclosure'; the Lamar Hinton roust – a shakedown for Nite Owl information, Dot Rothstein there, Kikey Teitlebaum's cousin –

Bud washed his face, walked back calm. Stomp said, 'Have a good one?'

'Yeah, and you're right. I want Deuce for some old warrants, but I got a hunch on the Nite Owl.'

Calm Johnny: 'Oh, yeah?'

Calm Kikey: 'Some new shvoogies, right? All I know's what I read in the papers.'

Bud: 'Maybe, but if it wasn't some new niggers, then that purple car by the Nite Owl was a plant. Take care, guys. If you see Deuce, tell him to call me at the Bureau.'

Calm Johnny tap-tap-tapped.

Calm Kikey coughed, popped sweat.

Calm Bud, not so calm: out to the car, around the corner to a pay phone. The P.C. Bell police number, one long fucking wait.

'Uh, yes, who's requesting?'

'Sergeant White, LAPD. It's a trace job.'

'For when, Sergeant?'

'*For now*. It's a homicide priority, private lines and pay phones at a restaurant. *It's now*.'

'One second, please.'

Transfer click-click-clicks – a new woman. 'Sergeant, what exactly do you need?'

No Calm Bud. 'Abe's Noshery at Pico and Veteran. All

calls out on all phones for the next fifteen goddamn minutes. Lady, don't hump me on this.'

'We can't initiate actual traces, Officer.'

'Just who the calls are to, goddamn it.'

'Well, if it *is* a homicide priority. What is your number now?'

Bud read off the phone. 'GRanite 48112.'

Harumph. 'Fifteen minutes then. And next time allow us more operating leeway.'

Bud hung up – Dudley Dudley Dudley Dudley Dudley – hard time cut off by *brrrinnngg*. He grabbed the phone, fumbled it, cradled it. 'Yeah?'

'Two calls. One to DUnkirk 32758 – a Miss Dot Rothstein holds that number. The second to AXminster 46811, the residence of a Mr. Dudley L. Smith.'

Bud dropped the receiver. The clerk babbled from someplace safe and calm that he'd never see again – no Lynn, no safety in a badge.

Captain Dudley Liam Smith for the Nite Owl.

Chapter Sixty-seven

Jack Vincennes confessed.

He confessed to knocking up a girl at the St. Anatole's Orphan Home, to killing Mr. and Mrs. Harold J. Scoggins. He confessed to tank-jobbing Bill McPherson with a hot little nigger girl, to planting dope on Charlie Parker, to shaking down hopheads for *Hush-Hush* Magazine. He tried to jerk out of bed and raise his hands to form the Stations of the Cross. He babbled something like hub rachmones, Mickey, and bump bump bump bump the cute train. He confessed to beating up junkies, to running bag for Ellis Loew. He begged his wife to forgive him for fucking whores who looked like women in dirty picture books. He confessed that he loved dope and was unfit to love Jesus.

Karen Vincennes stood by weeping: she couldn't listen, she had to listen. Ed tried to shoo her out – she wouldn't let him. He called the Bureau from outside Arrowhead; Fisk gave him the word: Pierce Patchett shot and killed last night, his mansion torched, burned to the ground. Fireman had discovered Vincennes in the backyard – smoke inhalation, rips in his bulletproof vest. They got him to Central Receiving, a doctor took a blood sample. The results: Trashcan on a test flight, a heroin/antipsychotic drug compound. He'd live, he'd be fine – when the OD in his system flushed out.

A nurse swabbed Vincennes' face; Karen fretted Kleenex. Ed checked Fisk's memo: 'Inez Soto called. No info on R.D. $ dealings. R.D. suspicious of queries??? – she was cryptic – D.W.'

Ed crumpled it, tossed it. Vincennes went in barefoot – while he was shacked with Lynn. Somebody killed Patchett, left them both to burn.

Burned like Exley father and son – Bud White holding the torch.

He couldn't look at Karen.

'Captain, I've got something.'

Fisk in the hallway. Ed walked over, led him away from the door. 'What is it?'

'Nort Layman completed the autopsy. Patchett's cause of death was five .30–30 slugs fired from two different rifles. Ray Pinker ran ballistics tests and came up with a match to an old Riverside County bulletin. May of '55, unsolved with no leads, I checked. Two men gunned down outside a tavern. It looked like a gangland job.'

All coming down to the heroin. 'That's all you've got?'

'No. Bud White tore up a dope den in Chinatown and beat three Chinamen half to death. He came in asking questions, badged them and went crazy. One of them ID'd his personnel photo. Thad Green called I.A. on it, and I caught the squeal. Pickup order, sir? I know you want him and Chief Green said it's your call.'

Ed almost laughed. 'No, no pickup order.'

'Sir?'

'I said no, so cut it off there. And you and Kleckner do this for me. Contact Miller Stanton, Max Peltz, Timmy Valburn and Billy Dieterling. Have them come to my office tonight at 8:00 for questioning. Tell them *I'm* the investigating officer, and if they want no publicity, then bring no lawyers. And get me Homicide's file on the old Loren Atherton case. Seal it, Sergeant. I don't want you to look at it.'

'Sir . . .'

Ed turned away. Karen in the doorway, dry-eyed. 'Do you think Jack did those things?'

'Yes.'

'He mustn't know that I know. Will you promise not to tell him?'

Ed nodded, looked in the room. The Big V begged for communion.

Chapter Sixty-eight

A file room at the main DMV – boxes stacked shoulder-high. A confirmation search – a riff on Johnny and Kikey's last hink. Riff in, out, back, around – he was so high he could think it through and prowl registration records at the same time.

Make Stomp, Teitlebaum and Lee Vachss for the Nite Owl triggers; make them the shooter gang bumping upstart mobsters and Cohen franchise holders. Deuce Perkins was part of the gang – the others didn't know he beat hookers to death – they'd consider it amateur shit, wouldn't tolerate it. Dudley was the leader – he couldn't be anything else. All his job offer stuff was a try at recruiting him; the Lamar Hinton roust was Dud frosting out loose ends on the Patchett side of things – make Patchett and Smith some kind of K.A.'s, make Hinton dead, Breuning and Carlisle part of the gang. 'Contain,' 'Contained,' 'Containment,' 'Profit Dispensation.' Call it Dudley trying to control the L.A. rackets – and pin the Nite Owl on a new bunch of jigs.

Bud tore through boxes: auto registrations, early April '53. Schoolboy thinking: he figured the car by the Nite Owl was a plant; the shotguns in Coates' car, the shells in Griffith Park, both plants – the killers followed the case, got lucky on the Merc, found some boogies to take the heat. Wrong – LAPD conspirators were in on the job. They read crime reports, got hipped to some joyriding spooks firing shotguns – lay the onus on them – they figured the arresting officers would kill them, case closed.

So they got themselves a car that matched the crime report description. They made sure it was spotted near the Nite Owl. They wouldn't steal a car – cops wouldn't risk a late night roust. They didn't buy a purple car – they bought a different colored one and painted it.

Bud kept working. No logic to the file mess: Mercs, Chevies, Caddies, L.A., Sacramento, Frisco, whoever registered the car would've used a phony name. One luck-out: the registers' race, DOB and physical stats listed on cards attached to the initial purchase carbons. Facts to eliminate against, like he learned in school: '48–'50 Mercs, Southern California purchasers, stats that matched to Dudley, Stomp, Vachss, Teitlebaum, Perkins, Carlisle and Breuning. Hours of digging, a pile inches thick – then a strange one that felt warm.

1948 primer-gray Merc coupe, purchased April 10, 1953. Register: Margaret Louise March, W.F., DOB 7/23/18, brown and brown, 5'9", 215 lbs. Register's address: 1804 East Oxford, Los Angeles. Phone number: NOrmandie 32758.

Warm to scalding – Fat Dot Rothstein's specs. Oxford ran north-south – not east-west. The call to Dot from the Noshery – DU-32758 – the dumb dyke tacked her own number onto a different exchange.

And bought herself some purple paint.

Bud whooped, punched the air, kicked boxes. Two cases made in one day – if anyone believed him. All dressed up and no one to kill. Circumstantial Dudley evidence – no hard proof. Dudley too well placed to fall, nobody who cared like he did.

Except Exley.

Chapter Sixty-nine

A stakeout on the house he grew up in. He couldn't go in and question his father; he couldn't ask for his help. He couldn't tell the man he confided secrets to a woman – and gave a brutal enemy the means to patricide. He brought the Atherton file with him – there was nothing in it he didn't already know, the man who made the smut and killed Sid Hudgens was intrinsic to the Atherton murders, maybe the killer himself – truths Preston Exley would dispute out of pride. He couldn't go in; he couldn't stop thinking. He counted memories instead.

His father bought the house for his mother; it was really just a sop to his pride – the Exleys flee the middle class grandly. They never had Christmas lights on the lawn – Preston Exley said it was lowlife. Thomas fell off balconies – and had the style not to cry. His father threw him a 'back from the war' party – only the mayor, the City Council and LAPD men who could further his career were invited.

Art De Spain walked to his car, looking frail, one arm bandaged. Ed watched him drive off, his father's man, his Dutch uncle. Memory: Art said he wasn't cut out to be a detective.

The house loomed big and cold. Ed drove back to the hospital.

Trash was up, giving Fisk a statement. Ed watched from the doorway.

'. . . and I was playing off Exley's script. I don't remember exactly what I said, but Patchett pulled out a gun and shot me. That shit piece Exley gave me jammed, and Patchett slammed me with a hypo. Then I heard shots and "No, Abe, no, Lee, no." And now you know as much as I do.'

From the hall, loud: 'Abe Teitlebaum, Johnny Stompanato and Lee Vachss. They did the Nite Owl. Throw
in Deuce Perkins as part of the gang and get ready to shit
when I tell you who else I got.'

Ed smelled his sweat, his breath. White pushed him
inside – firm, not too rough. 'Put our stuff aside for a
minute. Did you hear what I said?'

The names registered: gang muscle, a not-bad line to
HEROIN. White looked insane – disheveled, a zealot.
Fisk said, 'Sir, do you want me to . . . '

Ed moved his shoulders – White dropped his hands
right on cue. 'Two minutes, *Captain*.'

Scared – *be a captain*. 'Duane, go get yourself some
coffee. White, get my interest before I ream you for the
Chinamen.'

Fisk walked out. Ed said, 'Jack, you stay. White, you
keep my interest.'

White closed the door. Disheveled: soiled clothes, ink-
smudged hands. 'Good I heard the radio on you, Trashcan. I didn't know you were here, I mighta tried to do it
all myself.'

Vincennes, on the bed looking queasy. 'Do *what*? Abe,
Lee. You make Teitlebaum and Vachss for Patchett, spell
it out.'

Ed: 'You look Crim 101, White. Make like you're writing an occurrence chronology.'

White smiled – pure kamikaze. 'I been tracking a string
of hooker killings for years. It started with this girl Kathy
Janeway. She got snuffed back in '53, right around the
Nite Owl. She was Duke Cathcart's girlfriend.'

Ed nodded. 'I know that story. I.A. ran a personal on
you when you passed the sergeant's exam.'

'Oh, yeah? What you don't know is that a few years
ago my case broke. I thought my killer was Spade Cooley
– his band was in all the hooker snuff cities on the DODs.
I was wrong. Cooley ratted off the real killer – Burt Arthur
Perkins.'

Vincennes spoke up. 'I buy Deuce as a woman killer.
He's wrong to the core.'

421

White said, 'You should know, 'cause Cooley said he was pals with Johnny Stompanato, and back around '52 you told me you rousted him hanging out with Johnny Stomp, Kikey T. and Lee Vachss. Cooley told me Johnny and Deuce were tight, so I went looking for Johnny.'

Ed said, 'All right, so you went to Stompanato.'

White lit a cigarette. 'Nix. Now I tell you that Dudley Smith has been using me for strongarm jobs on the Mobster Squad going back years. You know how he talks? "Containment," that's one of his favorite words. Contain crime, contain this, contain that. He's been beating around the bush about offering me outside work, and the other night he said I could be useful keeping the "obstreperous Italian" that's afraid of me in line. Johnny Stomp's afraid of me – he used to snitch for me and I used to muscle him good. You know how Dud's this so-called gangland peacemaker? Well, the other night him, Carlisle and Breuning worked over this guy Lamar Hinton at the Victory, supposedly a Mobster Squad job. Bullshit – all Dudley asked him about was Nite Owl stuff – smut, Pierce Patchett.'

Ed, bug-eyed: this can't be coming. 'So you went to Stompanato looking for Perkins.'

'Right. I go to Kikey's deli, and Johnny's there with Kikey. I ask Johnny about Deuce, and Johnny's all hinked. Kikey's hinked worse and they both lie and say Deuce is just some bumfuck acquaintance. They deny that Deuce is tight with Lee Vachss, when I know goddamn otherwise. Johnny uses the word 'containment,' which is not a Johnny-type word. Hink all over these guys, and I drop that I'm on the Nite Owl reopening and they almost shit, Deuce for the Nite Owl, ho, ho. I leave, go to a pay phone and have P.C. Bell put a fifteen-minute trace on all calls out of the deli. Two calls – one to Dot Rothstein, Dudley's good pal and Kikey's cousin, one to Dudley's house.'

Vincennes said, 'Holy fucking shit.' Ed jerked a hand to his gun – wrong – White was a cop. 'Give me corroboration.'

White flicked his smoke out the window. 'Crim 101. The niggers didn't do it, so Dud and his gang planted a car by the Nite Owl. I went to the DMV and checked April '53 registrations, Caucasians this time. Dot Rothstein bought a '48 Merc, primer gray, on April 10. A phony name, a phony address, but the stupid bitch used the real digits on her own phone number.'

Vincennes looked shell-shocked. Ed reeled in a line so he wouldn't scream DUDLEY. 'Right before the Nite Owl I was working late at Hollywood Station. Spade Cooley was playing a retirement party downstairs, and I saw Burt Perkins roaming the halls. Try this theory: Mal Lunceford, ex-LAPD patrolman. Call him the forgotten Nite Owl victim, and remember he worked Hollywood Division for most of his time on the Department. Now, did one of the shooters have a grudge against Lunceford? Was Perkins removing records of it that night at the station? Did the conspirators know that Lunceford was a Nite Owl regular and plan their Cathcart or Cathcart-impersonator hit so that they could clip him too?'

White answered. 'Dudley put me on the Lunceford background check, probably because he thought I'd fuck it up. I checked for old Lunceford F.I.'s and couldn't find a goddamn one. I buy that theory.'

DUDLEY past screaming – Ed held it down. Vincennes: 'Fisk told me about Patchett, how he got the Cohen-Dragna summit heroin, how him and this unnamed bad guy who's obviously Dudley were getting ready to push it. Now, I know for a fact that Dud bodyguarded that deal, and there was this rumor floating around years ago – that Dud led this posse that killed this guy Buzz Meeks who heisted the summit. Fisk said that Patchett got most of the white horse that got clouted, some from the Englekling brothers and their father, some from this bad guy who's obviously Dudley. Okay, so what I'm thinking is – could Lunceford have been in on the posse? Was *that* when Dudley got the dope?'

White shook his head – new stuff for him. 'You fill me in on that, because I got a lead that ties in. Dud was talking up his containment shit, and he said something about keeping the niggers sedated, which sounds like heroin to me.'

Ed said, 'Call that done for now. Jack, run with the Goldman-Van Gelder angle. Put it together with our new leads.'

Trash stood up, steadied himself on the bed rail. 'Okay, let's say Davey G. was in with Dudley, Stompanato, Kikey, Vachss and Dot. How any of them could trust a psycho like Deuce I don't know, but fuck it. Anyway, they're all conspiring against Mickey C. White, you don't know this, but Goldman had a bug in Mickey's cell at McNeil. I'm betting Dudley and his friends were in with Davey from the beginning, but fuck it, however it happened, Davey heard the Englekling brothers approach Mickey with Duke Cathcart's smut deal.'

Ed raised a hand. 'Chester Yorkin said that the man who brought Patchett the bulk of the heroin – let's assume it's Dudley – had a hard-on for smut and quote "contacts in South America and pervert mailing lists." I always wondered about the profit on pornography, and now Dudley's connection makes it seem more feasible.'

Vincennes said, 'Let me keep going. Dud worked with the OSS in Paraguay after the war and he ran Ad Vice back in '39 or so, so I know he's got those contacts, but sit on that. Right now we've got Goldman going to Smith and Stompanato with the word on the smut plan. Everybody, especially Dud, likes the idea, and they decide to crash the racket. On his own, a double cross, I don't know, Davey sends Dean Van Gelder, his prison visitor, to talk to Cathcart. Van Gelder decides to crash Duke's prostie racket and the smut gig on his own. He'd been seen by Davey face-to-face, but the outside prison men had never seen him. He figured he looked like Cathcart, so he could impersonate Cathcart and cut his own deal. By the time the impersonation was found out he'd be too far in good with the outside men for Davey to care what he'd done. So Van Gelder moved to San Berdoo to be close to the Englekling brothers. He fell in with Sue

Lefferts and snuffed Duke. He knew the names of at least one of the outside men, called them at a pay phone from the Lefferts' house and asked for a meet. He went in tough and suggested a public place, he figured Sue could sit nearby and he'd be safe. One of the outside guys put Lunceford together with the Nite Owl and said let's meet there. Dud or one of his guys approached Patchett right *before* the Nite Owl and told him to get his loose ends tidied. Patchett didn't know exactly what was gonna happen, but he had Chris Bergeron and her kid and Bobby Inge blow town just as I was starting in on the smut gig for Ad Vice.'

An air-cooled room – Ed felt every word boost the temperature. 'Let me throw out a chronology, starting right after Van Gelder as Cathcart contacts the outside men. Now, we know Dudley loves pornography, we know he's been sitting on eighteen pounds of 'H' since the Cohen-Dragna deal. Try this theory: he breaks into Cathcart's apartment and finds something that leads him to Patchett, something that includes mention of his chemistry background and his connections to old Dr. Englekling. He goes to Patchett, they strike a deal – develop the heroin, push the smut. He's astounded that Patchett's thinking along the same lines, that he's already got some of the horse from Doc Englekling. Now Dudley wants Cathcart killed, Mal Lunceford silenced for whatever reason – and he wants Patchett terrified. He's a policeman, and he's read about those Negroes discharging shotguns in Griffith Park. He sets up the meet at the Nite Owl, knowing Lunceford will be there, and Jack's right – he was ambiguous, but he told Patchett to get rid of his loose ends. Moving ahead, the investigation goes wider than Dudley thinks it will – because the Negroes don't get killed during their arrest, and they don't confess. He puts White on the Cathcart background check, and he probably *didn't* know that Perkins killed the Janeway girl, but he wanted White steered away from getting involved on general principles – he wanted him to steer clear of possible Cathcart-Nite Owl connections.

All eyes on Bud White. The zealot: 'Okay, Dudley put me on the Cathcart check because he thought I'd screw up. But I checked out Duke's pad and saw that it was print-wiped, and I figured that somebody had tried on his clothes. The Dudley guys wiped the place, but they didn't touch the phone books, and I could tell that the San Berdoo printshop listings had been looked over. Now, I got a theory. When I was on the Carthcart check, I met Kathy Janeway at this motel out in the valley. Two days later she's raped and killed. When I left the motel I thought I was being tailed, but then I forgot about it. I think the tail was Deuce Perkins. I think Dud put a tail on Cathcart's K.A.'s, just to keep tabs on the investi- gation, which explains how he's always known so much about all this stuff that I've always kept secret. So Deuce, who's a rape-o shitbird psycho, sees Kathy and goes for her. Maybe Dudley knew he killed her, maybe he didn't. Either way he fucking pays.'

Vincennes lit a cigarette, coughed. 'We've got no evi- dence, but I've got some more stuff to tie in. One, Doc Layman took five .30–30 slugs out of Patchett, and he said they match this gang unsolved in Riverside County. When Davey Goldman was babbling away up in Cama- rillo, he said something about three triggers. He babbled some other stuff that keeps running through my head, but it doesn't make any sense. Exley, did you listen to that tape I found at McNeil?'

Ed nodded. 'You're right. Nothing salient at all, just a passing mention of some gang hits.

White: 'There's been a bunch of mob unsolveds. I know, 'cause a suspect spilled some tangent stuff on them on a Mobster Squad roust. Always three triggers, Cohen franchise holders and upstart hoods clipped. Easy money: Stompanato, Vachss and Teitlebaum keeping things copa- cetic for Mickey C.'s parole. They wanted to keep things chilled for their containment gig and they figured when Mickey got out they'd test the wind and either clip him or use him. My bet's on clip. They had Cohen and Goldman bushwhacked in prison – a pure cross on Davey. Mickey's house got bombed and Mickey lived to tell. They'll clip him before too long and they'll contain real good, 'cause Dud's Mr. Mobster Squad and he's got Parker's fucking – what's the word? mandate? – to keep out-of-town muscle out. Do you fucking believe it?'

Trash laughed. 'Grand, lad, grand. And all the hits were paving the way for Dud to push Patchett's heroin. He got the command on the reopening so he could find some new patsies, and he's set to push the horse. He's got the smut stashed, and he didn't warn Patchett about the investigation because he was already planning to kill him. He didn't touch Lynn Bracken, because he figured Patchett kept her in the dark on all his worst stuff. He let her come in for questioning because he figured she'd stall Exley's part of the investigation.'

Lynn Bracken.

Ed winced, moved toward the door. 'And we still don't know who made the smut and killed Hudgens. Or the Englekling brothers, which doesn't look like a pro job. White, you went up to Gaitsville with Dudley, and he submitted a soft-pedal report on – '

'It was another psycho job. Heroin lying around, and the killer just left it. He tortured the brothers with chemicals and burned up a bunch of smut negatives with acid solutions. The lab tech said he thought the killer was trying to ID the people in the pictures. The chemistry stuff made me think Patchett, but then I thought he must've already known who the picture people were. I don't really think their heroin ties to our heroin, the brothers were dope peddlers on and off for years. Chemists and dope peddlers, and if Patchett wanted their dope, he would've stolen it. I think the brothers got killed by somebody, I don't know, outside the center of this mess.'

Trash sighed. *'There's no evidence.* Patchett and the whole Englekling family are dead, and Dud probably killed Lamar Hinton. You got nothing at the Fleur-de-Lis drop and White's little grandstand with Stompanato and Teitlebaum means that now Dudley's been alerted and he's taking care of *his* loose ends. I don't think we've got much of a case.'

Ed thought it through. 'Chester Yorkin told me Patchett had a booby-trapped safe outside his house. The house is being guarded now, the West L.A. squad has a team on it. In a day or so, I'll go lift the guards. There might be something in that safe that nails Dudley.'

White said, 'So right now, what? No evidence, and Stompanato's leaving for Acapulco today with Lana Turner. What now?'

Ed opened the door – Fisk was outside drinking coffee. 'Duane, get back in touch with Valburn, Stanton, Billy Dieterling and Peltz. Change the meeting to the downtown Statler at 8:00. Call the hotel and set up three suites and call Bob Gallaudet and tell him to call me here – tell him it's urgent.'

Fisk went for a phone. Vincennes said, 'You're hitting the Hudgens end.'

Ed turned away from White. '*Think.* Dudley's a policeman. We need evidence, and we may get it tonight.'

'I'll take Stanton. We used to be friends.'

Line it – a Dieterling kid star, Preston Exley. 'No . . . I mean are you up to it?'

'It's my case too, Captain. I've come this far, and I went up against Patchett for you and damn near got killed.'

Weigh the risk. 'All right, you take Stanton.'

Trash rubbed his face – pale, stubbled. 'Did I . . . I mean when Karen was here and I was unconscious . . . did I . . . '

'She doesn't know anything you don't want her to. Now go home, I want to talk to White.'

Vincennes walked out – ten years older in a day. White said, 'The Hudgens end is bullshit. It's all Dudley now.'

'No. First we buy some time.'

'Protecting Daddy? Jesus, and I thought I was dumb on women.'

'*Just think.* Think what Dudley is and what taking him down means. Think, and I'll make you a deal.'

'I told you *never.*'

'You'll like this one. You keep quiet about my father and the Atherton case and I'll let you have Dudley and Perkins.'

White laughed. 'The collars? I got them anyway.'

'No. I'll let you kill them.'

Chapter Seventy

Exley's rule rankled: no hitting, Billy and Timmy were too upscale to take muscle. Hotel good guy/bad guy rankled – they should be muscling Dudley at the Victory. Bob Gallaudet took Max Peltz; Trashcan was grilling Miller Stanton. Gallaudet got briefed by Exley – everything but the Atherton angle. He thought he could prosecute Dudley Smith, Exley didn't tell him Dud and Deuce Perkins were paid for. Fucking Exley wouldn't let him out of his sight – he took him through every piece of the case step by step, like they were partners who could trust each other. The case all put together was amazing, Exley had an amazing fucking brain – but he was stupid if he didn't know one thing: after Dudley and Deuce, Preston E. was next. Easy: Dick Stens wouldn't have it otherwise.

Bud watched – a crack in the bathroom doorway.

The queers sat side by side; Mr. Good Guy pussyfooted. Yes, they bought Fleur-de-Lis dope; yes, they knew Pierce Patchett 'socially.' Yes, Pierce snorted 'H,' we heard rumors he sold pornographic books – but *we* never indulged in such things. Kid gloves: the fruits thought the Patchett snuff was why they got the royal hotel treatment. Captain Exley would never be nasty – Preston Exley was running for governor, Ray Dieterling throwing hot financial backup.

Exley, loud. 'Gentlemen, there's an old homicide that might tie in to the Patchett killing.'

Bud walked in. Exley said, 'This is Sergeant White. He has a few questions for you, then I think we can wrap it up.'

Timmy Valburn sighed. 'Well, I'm not surprised. Miller Stanton and Max Peltz are down the hall, and the last time the police questioned all of us was when that awful man Sid Hudgens was killed. So *I'm* not surprised.'

Bud pulled a chair up. 'Why'd you say "awful"? You kill him?'

'Oh, Sergeant *really*. Do I look like the killer type to you?'

'Yeah, you do. Guy who makes his living playing a mouse has gotta be capable of anything.'

'Sergeant, *really*.'

'Besides, *you* weren't called in on the Hudgens job. Billy tell you about it? A little pillow talk, maybe?'

Billy Dieterling to Exley. 'Captain, I don't like this man's tone.'

Exley said, 'Sergeant, keep it clean.'

Bud laughed. 'That's the pot calling the kettle black, but screw it. You guys alibied each other for Hudgens, now it's five years later and you alibi each other up for Patchett. Hinky to me. My take on fruits is that they can't stick to the same bed for five minutes, let alone five years.'

Valburn: 'You're an animal.'

Bud pulled out a file sheet. 'Alibis on the Hudgens case. You and Billy in bed together, Max Peltz porking some teenage quiff. Miller Stanton at a party where your queer buddy Brett Chase also happens to be. So far, we got a real all-American crew on *Badge of Honor*. David Mertens the set man, he's at home with his male nurse, so maybe he's fruit, too. What I want – '

Exley, on cue: 'Sergeant, watch your language and get to the point.'

Valburn seethed; Billy D. faked boredom. But something in the last spiel nudged him – his eyes went from good guy to bad guy. 'The point is that Sid Hudgens had a boner for *Badge of Honor* at the time he was killed. Patchett gets killed five years later, and him and Hudgens were partners. These homos here, they're both tied to *Badge of Honor* and they kicked loose with intimate details on Patchett's rackets. Captain, if it walks, talks and quacks like a duck, then it's a duck – not a mouse.'

Valburn said, 'Quack, quack, idiot. Captain, will you tell this man who he's dealing with?'

Exley, stern. 'Sergeant, these gentlemen aren't suspects. They're voluntary interviewees.'

'Well, shit, sir, I don't see no difference.'

Exley, exasperated. 'Gentleman, to end this once and for all, please tell the sergeant. Did either of you even *know* Sid Hudgens personally?'

Two 'No' head shakes. Bud flew – Exley poetry. 'If it squeaks like a mouse and swishes, it's a queer mouse. Captain, *think*. These guys bought dope off Fleur-de-Lis, and they admitted they knew Patchett sniffed horse and pushed pornography. They've got the lowdown on Patchett's rackets, but they claim they didn't know Patchett and Hudgens were partners. I say we take them through Patchett's little enterprises and see what they do know.'

Exley raised his hands – fake helpless. 'A few more specific questions then, gentlemen. Again, anything illegal that you admit to will be overlooked – and will not go outside this room. Do you understand, Sergeant?'

Fucking brilliant: build them up to who made the blood smut. Trash said Timmy was spooked by the stuff – he showed it to him in '53. Credit Exley with balls – the closer they got to the smut the closer they got to his old man and Atherton. 'Okay, sir.'

Timmy and Billy shared a look: nice people strafed by low class. Exley flashed it over. 'And, Sergeant – I'll ask the questions.'

'Yes, sir. You guys tell the truth. I'll know if you're lying.'

Exley sighed. 'Just a few questions. First, did you know that Patchett procured call girls for business associates?'

Two 'Yes' nods. Bud said, 'He ran boys, too. You guys ever buy any outside stuff?'

Exley: 'Not another word, Sergeant.'

Timmy slid closer to Billy. 'I won't dignify that last question with an answer.'

Bud winked. 'You're cute. I ever wind up in stir, I hope you're in my cell.'

Billy mimed spitting on the floor. Exley rolled his eyes – God save us from this heathen. 'Moving along. Were you aware that Patchett employed a plastic surgeon to surgically alter his prostitutes to resemble movie stars?'

Timmy said, 'Yes', Billy said, 'Yes.' Exley smiled like that was everyday stuff. 'Were you also aware that those prostitutes, both male and female, engaged in other criminal pursuits at Patchett's direction?'

Build them up to 'extortion,' the Patchett/Hudgens partnership. Exley told him the story: Lorraine/Rita said 'This Guy' made Patchett squeeze his 'clients,' right when Pierce was set to go partners with Hudgens – *right after the Nite Owl killings.* A brainstorm coming – maybe a connector back to Dudley. 'Answer the captain, shitbirds.'

Billy said, 'Ed, make him stop. Really, this has gone far enough.'

Bud laughed. '*Ed?* Oops, I forgot, boss. Your daddy's pals with his daddy.'

Exley riled for real – flushed, trembling. 'White, shut your mouth.'

The fruits loved it – smiles, titters. Exley said, 'Gentlemen, please answer the question.'

Timmy shrugged. 'Be specific. What other "criminal pursuits"?'

'Specifically blackmail.'

Two legs brushing twitched apart – Bud caught it plain. Exley touched his necktie – GO FULL.

Brainstorm: Johnny Stomp as 'This Guy.' Johnny Stomp an old shake artist, no visible means of support. Crim 101 – Lorraine Malvasi said the squeezes went down May '53 – Dudley's gang had already teamed up with Patchett. 'Yeah, *blackmail.* Married johns and pervs and queers are prone to it. It's like an occupational hazard. Ever get squeezed by one of your playmates?'

Now Billy rolled his eyes. 'We don't frequent prostitutes. Male or female.'

Bud pulled his chair closer. 'Well, your sweetie pie here was a known associate of a known fruit hustler named Bobby Inge. If it quacks like a duck, it's a duck. So quack, quack, and kick loose with who put the arm on you.'

Exley, stern. 'Gentlemen, do you know the names of any specific Patchett prostitutes?'

Billy came on butch. 'He's a storm trooper, and we don't have to answer his questions.'

'The fuck. You crawl around in sewers, you gotta meet some rats. Ever hear of a cute little twist named Daryl Bergeron? Ever get a yen for a woman and go for his mother? Daryl did – Trashcan Jack Vincennes has got a smut book with pictures of them fucking on roller skates. You're floating in a sewer on a Popsicle stick you fucking queer bastards, so – '

Valburn: 'Ed, make him stop!'

Exley: 'Sergeant, enough!'

Bud, dizzy, like a man inside his head was feeding him lines. 'The hell you say. These geeks are all over Patchett's schemes. One of them's a TV star, one of them's got a famous daddy. Two faggots with plenty of money just fucking ripe to be squeezed. That don't play smart to you?'

Exley – KEEP STILL – a finger to his collar. 'Sergeant White has a point, although I apologize for his way of expressing it. Gentlemen, just for the record. Have either of you any knowledge of extortion schemes involving Pierce Patchett and/or his prostitutes?'

Timmy Valburn said, 'No.'

Billy Dieterling said, 'No.'

Bud got ready to whisper.

Exley leaned forward. 'Have either of you ever been threatened with blackmail?'

Two more nos – two queers sweating up a nice cool room. Bud whispered, 'Johnny Stompanato.'

The fags froze. Bud said, '*Badge of Honor* dirt. Is that what he wanted?'

Valburn started to speak – Billy shushed him. Exley: SLOW.

The dizzy head man said NO. 'Did he have dirt on your father? The great fucking Raymond Dieterling?'

Exley shot the cut-off sign. The dizzy man showed his face: Dick Stens sucking gas. '*Dirt*. Wee Willie Wennerholm, Loren Atherton and the kiddie murders. *Your father*.'

Billy trembled, pointed to Exley. '*His* father!'

Four-way stares – cut off by Valburn sobbing. Billy helped him up, embraced him. Exley said, 'Get out. Now. You're free to go.'

He looked sad more than mad or scared.

Billy walked Timmy out. Bud walked to the window. Exley walked over, talked to a hand mike. 'Duane, Valburn and Dieterling are on their way. You and Don tail them.'

Bud scoped him – a little taller, half his bulk. Something made him say, 'I shouldn't have done that.'

Exley looked out the window. 'It'll be over soon. All of it.'

Bud looked down. Fisk and Kleckner stood by the door; the queers hit the sidewalk running. The I.A. men chased – a bus held them back. The bus zoomed by – no Billy and Timmy. Fisk and Kleckner stood in the street looking stupid.

Exley started laughing.

Something made Bud laugh.

Chapter Seventy-one

They rehashed old times; Stanton drank room service bubbly. Jack laid out his pitch: Patchett/Hudgens, smut, heroin, the Nite Owl. He could tell Miller knew something; he could tell he wanted to spill it.

Old touches: how he taught Miller to play a cop; how he took Miller down to Central Avenue to get laid and wound up rousting Art Pepper. Gallaudet poked his head in, said Max Peltz was clean – Max stories ate up another hour. Miller got misty – '58 would be the show's last season. Too bad they lost touch with each other, but the Big V was acting too crazy, a pariah in the Industry. White and Exley arguing next door – Jack cut to it.

'Miller, is there something you're dying to tell me?'

'I don't know, Jack. It's old rebop.'

'This mess *goes* back. You know Patchett, don't you?'

'How'd you know that?'

'Educated guess. And the captain's file said Patchett bankrolled some old Dieterling films.'

Stanton checked his glass – empty. 'Okay, I know Patchett from way back. It's some story, but I don't see how it applies to what you're interested in.'

Jack heard the side door scrape carpet. 'All I know is that you've been dying to tell me ever since I said the word "Patchett." '

'Damn, I don't feel like a cop around you. I feel like a fat actor about to lose his series.'

Jack looked away – cut the man slack. Stanton said, 'You know I was the chubby kid in Dieterling's serials way back when. Willie Wennerholm, Wee Willie, he was the big star. I used to see Patchett at the studio school, and I knew he was some kind of Dieterling business partner, because our tutor had a crush on him and told all the kids who he was.'

436

'And?'

'And Wee Willie was kidnapped from the school and chopped up by Dr. Frankenstein. You were the case, it was famous. The police picked up this guy Loren Atherton. They said he killed Willie and all these other children. Jack, this is the hard part.'

'So tell it fast.'

Very fast. 'Mr. Dieterling and Patchett came to me. They gave me tranquilizers and told me I had to come along with this older boy and visit a police station. I was fourteen, the older boy was maybe seventeen. Patchett and Mr. Dieterling coached me, and we went to the station. We talked to Preston Exley, he was a detective back then. We told him just what Patchett and Mr. Dieterling told us to – that we'd seen Atherton prowling around the studio school. We identified Atherton and Exley believed us.'

An actor's pause. Jack said, 'Goddammit, *and?*'

Slower. 'I never saw the older boy again, and I can't even remember his name. Atherton was convicted and executed, and I wasn't asked to testify at his trial. It got to be '39, right in there. I was still in the Dieterling stable, but I was a boy ingenue. Mr. Dieterling had this little studio contingent go out to the opening of the Arroyo Seco Freeway, just a publicity appearance. Preston Exley, he was a big-shot contractor now, and he cut the ribbon. I heard Mr. Dieterling, Patchett and Terry Lux, you know him, talking.'

Pins and needles. 'Miller, come on.'

'I'll never forget what they said, Jack. Patchett told Lux, "I've got the chemicals to keep him from hurting anybody and you plasticked him." Lux said, "And I'll get him a keeper." Mr. Dieterling, I'll never forget the way his voice sounded. He said, "And I gave Preston Exley a scapegoat he believes in beyond Loren Atherton. And I think the man owes me too much now to hurt me."'

Jack touched himself – he thought he'd stopped breathing. Breathing behind him – strained. Eyes on Exley and White in the doorway – up close to each other frozen.

Chapter Seventy-two

Now all his lines crossed in ink.

Red ink mutilations. An inkwell spilling blood. Cartoon characters on a marquee with Raymond Dieterling, Preston Exley, an all-star criminal cast. Ink colors: red, green for bribe money. Black for mourning – the dead supporting players. White and Vincennes knew, they'd probably tell Gallaudet – he kicked them out of the hotel knowing it. He could warn his father or not warn his father and the end would be the same. He could keep going or sit in this room and watch his life explode on television.

Long hours down – he couldn't reach for the phone. He turned on the TV, saw his father at a freeway ceremony, stuck his gun in his mouth while the man mouthed platitudes. The trigger half back – fade to a commercial. He emptied four rounds, spun the cylinder, put the barrel to his head. He squeezed the trigger twice, empty chambers, he couldn't believe what he'd done. He threw his piece out the window – a wino grabbed it off the sidewalk, shot up the sky. He laughed, sobbed, punched himself out on the furniture.

More hours down doing nothing.

The phone rang – Ed flailed for it blind. 'Uh . . . yes?'

'Captain, you there? It's Vincennes.'

'I'm here. What is it?'

'I'm at the Bureau with White. We just caught a squeal and grabbed it. 2206 North New Hampshire, Billy Dieterling's house. Billy and an unknown male dead. Fisk rolled on it already. Cap, *are you there*?'

No no no – yes. 'I'm going . . . I'll be there.'

'Will do. And by the way, White and I didn't tell Gallaudet what Stanton said. Thought you should know that.'

'Thank you, Sergeant.'

'Thank White. He's the one you had to worry about.'

Fisk met him there – a mock Tudor lit by headlights – black-and-whites, crime lab cars on the lawn.

Ed ran up; Fisk spoke shorthand. 'Neighbor woman heard screams, waited half an hour and called. She saw a man run out, get into Billy Dieterling's car and take off. He hit a tree down the block, got out and ran. I took a statement. White, male, early forties, average build. Sir, brace yourself.'

Flashbulb pops inside. Ed said, '*Seal it here*. No Homicide, no station cops. No press, and I don't want Dieterling's father to find out. Have Kleckner seal the car and go get me Timmy Valburn. *Find him. Now.*'

'Sir, they blew our tail. I feel bad about this, like it's our fault.'

'It doesn't matter, just do what I told you.'

Fisk ran to his car; Ed walked in, looked.

Billy Dieterling on a white couch soaked red. A knife in his throat; two knives in his stomach. His scalp on the floor, stuck to the carpet with an icepick. A few feet away: a fortyish white man – disemboweled, eviscerated, knives in his cheeks, two kitchen forks in his eyes. Drug capsules soaking in floor blood.

No artful desecrations – his man was past it now.

Ed walked into the kitchen. Patchett to Lux '39: 'I've got the chemicals to keep him from hurting anybody, and you plasticked him.' Cupboards dumped; forks and spoons on the floor. Ray Dieterling '39: 'A scapegoat he believes in.' Bloody footprints in and out – his man made trips for more adornment. Lux: 'I'll get him a keeper.' A scalp section in the sink. 'Preston Exley, he was a big-shot contractor now.' A bloody handprint on the wall, a psycho passion job for Crim 101's all-time list.

Ed squinted at the print – ridges and whirls showed plainly. Psycho oblivion: his man pressed his hand there to leave an imprimatur.

Back to the living room. Trashcan Jack in the middle

of a half dozen lab techs. Bad flashbulb glare, no Bud White.

Trash said, 'The other man's Jerry Marsalas. He's a male nurse, and he's sort of the keeper of this guy on the *Badge of Honor* crew. David Mertens, the set designer. Very quiet, he's got epilepsy or something like that.'

'Plastic surgery scars?'

'Graft scars all over his neck and back. I saw him with his shirt off once.'

Tech swarming now – Ed led Vincennes out to the porch. Cool air, bright bright headlights. Trash said, 'Mertens is the right age to be that older kid Stanton was talking about. Lux cut him, so Miller wouldn't have recognized him on the set. All the grafts on his back, he could have been cut lots of times. Jesus, the look on your face. You're taking it all the way?'

'I don't know. I want one more day to see what we can get on Dudley.'

'And see if White tries to shank you. He could have told Gallaudet the whole story, but he didn't.'

'White's as crazy as anybody in this thing.'

Trash laughed. 'Yeah, like you. Boss, if you and Gallaudet want this mess to go to due process, you'd better lock that boy up. He's out to kill Dudley and Deuce, and believe me he'll do it.'

Ed laughed. 'I told him he could.'

'You'd *let him* do – '

Cut him off. 'Jack, do this. Stake Mertens' place and see if you can find White, then – '

'He's chasing down Perkins, how do I – '

'Just try to find him. And with or without him, meet me at Mickey Cohen's house tomorrow at nine. We're going to brace him on Dudley.'

Vincennes looked around. 'I don't see anybody from Homicide here.'

'You and Fisk caught it, so Homicide doesn't know. I can keep it I.A.-sealed for twenty-four hours or so. It's ours until the press gets it.'

'No APB on Mertens?'

'I'll call out half of I.A. He's a drooling psychotic. We'll get him.'

'Suppose I find him. You don't want him talking old times, not with your father part of it.'

'Take him alive. I want to talk to him.'

Vincennes said, 'For crazy, White's got nothing on you.'

Ed sealed it.

He called Chief Parker, told him he had an I.A.-related double homicide and was keeping the victims' identities secret. He woke up five I.A. men, filled them in on David Mertens, sent them out to canvass for him. He made the neighbor lady who called in the squeal take a sedative, go to bed, promise she wouldn't spill the name 'Billy Dieterling' to the press. The press arrived – he mollified them with John Doe IDs, sent them packing. He walked to the end of the block and examined the car – Kleckner watchdogging it – a Packard Caribbean with the front wheels up on the curb, the fender nosed into a tree. The driver's seat, dash and shift lever – bloody; perfect bloody handprints on the outside of the windshield. Kleckner stripped the license plates; Ed told him to drive the car home, stash it, team up with the searchers. Courtesy calls from a pay phone: the watch commander at Rampart Station, the duty M.E. at the City Morgue. A lie: Parker wanted a twenty-four-hour blanket on the killings – no statements to the press, no autopsy reports circulated. 3:40 A.M., no Homicide brass at the scene – Parker carte-blanched him.

Sealed.

Ed walked back to the house. Quiet – no newsmen, no rubberneckers. Tape outlines – no bodies. Techs dusting, bagging evidence. Fisk in the kitchen doorway – looking nervous. 'Sir, I've got Valburn. Inez Soto's with him. I went down to Laguna on a hunch. You told me Miss Soto knew him.'

'What did Valburn tell you?'

'Nothing. He said he'd only talk to you. I broke it to

442

him, and he cried himself out on the ride up. He said he's ready to make a statement.'

Inez walked out. Grief all over her, her nails chewed bloody. 'I blame you for this. I blame you for pushing Billy to it.'

'I don't know what you mean, but I'm sorry.'

'You had me spy on Raymond. Now you did this.'

Ed stepped toward her. She slapped him, hit him. 'Leave us all alone!'

Fisk grabbed her, eased her outside. Gentle – soft hands, a low voice. Ed walked down the hall looking in rooms.

Valburn in the den, taking pictures off the wall. Bright eyes glazed over, a too-bright voice. 'If I keep doing things I'll be fine.'

A group shot came down. 'I need a full statement.'

'Oh, you'll get one.'

'Mertens killed Hudgens, Billy and Marsalas, plus Wee Willie and those other children. I need the why. Timmy, look at me.'

Timmy plucked a framed photo. 'We were together since 1949. We had our little indiscretions, but we always stayed together and loved each other. Don't give me a speech about getting his killer, Ed. I just couldn't bear it. I'll tell you what you want to know, but try not to be déclassé.'

'Timmy – '

Valburn threw the frame at the wall. 'David Mertens, goddamn you!'

Glass shattered. The picture landed face up: Raymond Dieterling holding an inkwell. 'Start with the pornography. Jack Vincennes talked to you about it five years ago, and he thought you were holding back.'

'Is this another third degree?'

'Don't make it one.'

Timmy squared a stack of frames. 'Jerry Marsalas made David create that strange . . . filth. Jerry was a very bad man. He'd been David's companion for years, and he regulated the drugs that kept him . . . relatively normal.

443

Sometimes he'd escalate and de-escalate his dosages and get David to do commercial art piecework, just so he could keep the money. Raymond paid Jerry to look after David. He got David the job at *Badge of Honor* so that Billy could look after him, too – Billy ran the camera crew since the show first went on.'

Ed said, 'Don't get ahead of yourself. Where did Marsalas and Mertens find the posers?'

Timmy hugged his pictures. 'Fleur-de-Lis. Marsalas had used the service for years. He'd buy call girls when he was flush, and he knew lots of Pierce's old string of girls and lots of . . . sexually adventurous people that the girls told him about. He found out that a lot of Fleur-de-Lis customers had a bent for specialty smut, and he talked some of Pierce's old girls into letting him voyeur their sex parties. Jerry took pictures, David took pictures, and Jerry escalated David's drug intake and made him do pasteup work. The ink blood was all David's idea. Jerry hired some studio art director to make finished books out of the pictures and took them to Pierce. Do you follow? I don't know what *you* know.'

Ed got out his notebook. 'Miller Stanton told us some background things. Patchett and Dieterling were partners at the time of the Atherton killings, and you know I make Mertens for them. Just keep going. If I need something clarified, I'll tell you.'

Timmy said, 'All right then. If you don't know it, the ink pictures were similar to the woundings on the Atherton victims. Pierce didn't know it when he saw the books, I guess only policemen saw the evidence photos. He also didn't know that David Mertens was the Wennerholm killer's new identity, so when Marsalas hatched this plan to sell the books and went to Pierce for financing, he just thought it was dirty books that compromised his prostitutes and their customers. He turned Marsalas down on his offer, but he did buy some of the books to sell through Fleur-de-Lis. Then Marsalas went to this man Duke Cathcart, and he went to these people the Engle-

444

kling brothers. Ed, your Mr. Fisk hinted that all this has to do with the Nite Owl case, but I don't – '

'I'll tell you later. You're talking about early '53, and I'm following you so far. Just keep telling it in order.'

Timmy laid his pictures down. 'Then Patchett went to Sid Hudgens. He and Hudgens were going to be partners in some extortion thing that I don't know anything about, and Pierce told Hudgens about Marsalas and his smut. He'd had Marsalas checked out, and he knew he was a regular on the *Badge of Honor* set, which interested Hudgens, because he had always wanted to do an exposé on the show for *Hush-Hush*. Pierce gave Hudgens a few of the books he'd held back from Fleur-de-Lis, and Hudgens approached Marsalas. He demanded information on the show's stars and threatened Jerry with exposure of his smut dealings if he didn't cooperate. Jerry gave him some tame stuff on Max Peltz, and a little while later it appeared in print. Then Hudgens was murdered, and of course it was Jerry who put David up to it. He lowered his drug dosage and drove him insane. David reverted to his old . . . to the way he killed the children. Marsalas did it because he was afraid Hudgens would keep trying to extort him. He went with David, and he stole Hudgens' *Badge of Honor* files from his house, including an incomplete file Hudgens had on him and David. I don't think he knew that Pierce already had carbons of the files he and Hudgens were going to use for their blackmail thing, or that Pierce knew the bank where Hudgens kept his original files stashed.'

Three key questions coming up; more corroboration first. 'Timmy, when Vincennes questioned you five years ago, you acted suspiciously. Did you know back then that Mertens made the smut?'

'Yes, but I didn't know who David *was*. All I knew was that Billy kept an eye on him, so I kept quiet to Jack.'

Question number one. 'How do you know all this? Everything you've told me.'

Timmy's eyes glazed fresh. 'I found out tonight. After the hotel, Billy wanted that awful policeman's hints about

445

Johnny Stompanato explained. Billy's known most of the story for years, but he wanted to know the rest. We went to Raymond's house in Laguna. Raymond knew about the more recent things from Pierce, and he told Billy the whole story. I just listened.'

'And Inez was there.'

'Yes, she heard it all. She blames you, sweetie. Pandora's box and all that.'

She knew, his father probably knew. Full disclosure as good as public. 'So Patchett supplied the dope that's kept Mertens docile all these years.'

'Yes, he's quite physiologically ill. He gets brain inflammations periodically, and that's when he's most dangerous.'

'And Dieterling got him the job with *Badge of Honor* so Billy could look after him.'

'Yes. After the Hudgens killing Raymond read about the mutilations and thought they sounded like the ones from the old child murders. He contacted Patchett, who he knew was friendly with Hudgens. Raymond revealed David's identity to Pierce, and Pierce became terrified. Raymond was afraid to take David away from Jerry, and he's been paying Jerry extraordinary money to keep David drugged up.'

Key question two. 'You've been waiting for this one, Timmy. Why has Ray Dieterling gone to all this trouble for David?'

Timmy turned a picture around – Billy, a lump-faced man. 'David is Raymond's illegitimate son. He's Billy's half brother, and look at him. Terry Lux has cut him so often that he's so ugly next to my sweet Billy that you almost can't look.'

Moving on grief – Ed cut in before he snapped. 'What happened tonight?'

'Tonight Raymond filled Billy in on everything going back to Sid Hudgens – he didn't know any of it. Billy made me stay with Inez at Laguna. He told me he was going to snatch David from Jerry's house and wean him off the drugs. He must have tried it, and Marsalas must

446

have retaliated. I saw those pills on the floor . . . and oh God David must have just gone insane. He couldn't understand who was good and who was bad and just . . . '

Three. 'At the hotel you reacted to Johnny Stompanato. Why?'

'Stompanato's been blackmailing Pierce's customers for years. He caught me with another man and got part of the Mertens story out of me. Not much, just that Raymond paid for David's upkeep. It . . . it was before I knew very much. Stompanato's been preparing a dossier to bleed Raymond dry. He's been threatening Billy with notes, but I don't think he knows who David is. Billy was trying to convince his father to have him killed.'

Sun broke through a window – it caught Timmy when his tears broke through. He held Billy's picture, a hand over David's face.

Chapter Seventy-three

An I.A. goon relieved him at 7:00 – pissed that he was sleeping, slumped in the doorway with his gun out. The house stayed virgin – no blood-crazed David Mertens showed up. The I.A. guy said Mertens was still at large; Captain Exley's orders: meet him and Bud White at Mickey Cohen's place at 9:00. Jack rolled to a pay phone, played a hunch.

A call to the Bureau – Dudley Smith on 'emergency family leave.' Breuning and Carlisle working 'out of state' – the squad lieutenant at 77th the temporary Nite Owl boss. A buzz to the Main Woman's Jail: Deputy Dot Rothstein on 'emergency family leave.' The hunch: they had nothing but theories, Dudley's loose ends were getting snipped.

Jack drove home, shaking off a dream: Davey Goldman's wet-brain ramblings. Make the 'Dutchman' Dean Van Gelder, the 'Irish Cheshire' Dudley. 'Franchise boys got theirs three triggers blip blip blip' – call that the shooters – Stompanato, Vachss, Teitlebaum – taking out hoods. 'Bump bump bump bump bump bump bump cute train' – ??????? Crazy – maybe Patchett's dope was still working some voodoo.

Karen's car was gone. Jack walked in, saw a layout on the coffee table: airplane tickets, a note.

J. –

    Hawaii, and note the date. May 15, the day you become an official pensioner. Ten days and nights to get reacquainted. Dinner tonight. I made reservations at Perino's, and if you're still working call me so I can cancel.

                xxxxx K.

P.S. I know you're wondering, so I'll tell you. When you were at the hospital you talked in your sleep. Jack, I know the worst I can possibly know and I don't care. We never have to discuss it. Capt. Exley heard you and I don't think he cares either. (He's not as bad as you said he was.)

Many X's
K.

Jack tried to cry – no go. He shaved, showered, put on slacks and his best sports jacket – over a Hawaiian shirt. He drove to Brentwood thinking everything around him looked new.

Exley on the sidewalk, holding a tape recorder. Bud White on the porch – I.A. must have found him. Jack made it a threesome.

White walked over. Exley said, 'I just spoke to Gallaudet. He said without hard evidence we can't go to Loew. Mertens and Perkins are still out there, and Stompanato's in Mexico with Lana Turner. If Mickey doesn't give us anything good, then I'm going directly to Parker. Full disclosure on Dudley.'

From the doorway: 'Are you coming in or aren't you? You want to give me grief, give me indoor grief.'

Mickey Cohen in a robe and Jew beanie. 'Last call to give grief! Are you coming?'

They walked up. Cohen closed the door, pointed to a small gold coffin. 'My late canine heir, Mickey Cohen, Jr. Distract me from my real grief, you goyisher cop fucks. The service is today at Mount Sinai. I bribed the rabbi to give my beloved a human sendoff. The shmendriks at the mortuary think they're burying a midget. Talk to me.'

Exley talked. 'We came to tell you who's been killing your franchise people.'

'What "franchise people"? Continue in this vein and I shall have to stand on the Fifth Amendment. And what is that tape doohickey you're holding?'

'Johnny Stompanato, Lee Vachss and Abe Teitlebaum.

449

They're part of a gang, and they got the heroin you lost at your meeting with Jack Dragna back in '50. They've been killing your franchise people, and they tried to have you and Davey Goldman killed at McNeil. They bombed your house and didn't get you, but sooner or later they will.'

Cohen laughed outright. 'Granted, those old pals have been vacant from my life and are not amenable to rejoining me. But they do not have the intelligence to fuck with the Mickster and succeed.'

White: 'Davey Goldman was working with them. They crossed him when they tried to clip you two at McNeil.'

Mickey Cohen, livid. 'No! Never in six thousand millenniums would Davey do that to me! Never! Sedition in the same league as Communism you are talking!'

Jack said, 'We got proof. Davey had your cell bugged. That's how word on the Englekling brothers and who knows what else got out.'

'Lies! Combine Davey with the others and you still do not have the voltage to fuck with me!'

Exley futzed with the recorder – tape spun. Whirr, whirr, 'My God to be so nimble and so hung, like Heifetz on the fiddle with his shlong that dog is, and hung like – '

Cohen hit the roof. 'No! No! No man on earth is capable of shtupping me like that!'

Exley pushed buttons. Start – 'Lana, what a snatch she must have' – stop, start – a card game, a toilet flushing. Mickey kicked the coffin. 'All right! I believe you!'

Jack: 'Now you know why Davey wouldn't let you put him in a rest home.'

Cohen wiped his face with his beanie. 'Not even Hitler is capable of such things. Who could be so brainy and so ruthless?'

White said, 'Dudley Smith.'

'Oh, Jesus Christ. Him I could believe. No . . . tell me in full view of my late beloved you are joking.'

'An LAPD captain? This is for real, Mick.'

'No, this I don't believe. Give me proof, give me evidence.'

Exley said, 'Mickey, you give *us* some.'

Cohen sat down on the coffin. 'I think I know who tried to clip me and Davey in the pen. Coleman Stein, George Magdaleno and Sal Bonventre. They're en route to San Quentin, a pickup chain from other jails. When they land, you could talk to them, ask them who put out the bid on me and Davey. I was going to clip them, but I couldn't get a good rate, such gonifs these jailhouse killers are.'

Exley packed up his tape kit. 'Thanks. When the bus gets in, we'll be there.'

Cohen moaned. White said, 'Kleckner left me a memo. Kikey and Lee Vachss are supposed to be meeting at the deli this morning. I say we brace them.'

Exley said, 'Let's do it.'

Chapter Seventy-four

Abe's Noshery: the tables full, Kikey T. at the cash register. White pressed up to the window. 'Lee Vachss at a table on the right.' Ed put a hand on his holster – empty – his suicide play. Trashcan opened the door.

Chimes. Kikey glanced over, reached under the register. Ed saw Vachss make heat, make like he was smoothing his trousers. Metal flashing waist-high.

People ate, talked. Waitresses circulated. Trash walked toward the register; White eyeballed Vachss. Metal flashed: under the table coming up.

Ed pulled White to the floor.

Kikey and Vincennes drew down.

Crossfire – six shots – the window went out, Kikey hit a stack of canned goods. Screams, panic runs, blind shots – Vachss firing wild toward the door. An old man went down coughing blood; White stood up shooting, a moving target – Vachss weaving back toward the kitchen. A spare on White's waistband – Ed stumbled up, grabbed it.

Two triggers on Vachss. Ed fired – Vachss spun around grabbing his shoulder. White fired wide; Vachss tripped, crawled, stood up – his gun to a waitress' head.

White walked toward him. Vincennes circled left; Ed circled right. Vachss blew the woman's brains out point-blank.

White fired. Vincennes fired. Ed fired. No hits – the woman's body took their shots. Vachss inched backward. White ran up; Vachss wiped brains off his face. White emptied his gun – all head shots.

Screams, a stampede to the door, a man bucking glass shards out the window. Ed ran to the counter, bolted it.

Kikey on the floor, blood gouting from chest wounds. Ed got right up in his face. 'Give me Dudley. Give me Dudley for the Nite Owl.'

Sirens loud. Ed cupped an ear, bent down.

'Grand. Begorra, lad.'

Down closer. 'Who took out the Nite Owl?'

Blood gurgles. 'Me. Lee. Johnny Stomp. Deuce drove.'

Abe, give me Dudley.

'Grand, lad.'

Sirens brutal loud. Shouts, footsteps. 'The Nite Owl. *Why?*'

Kikey coughed blood. 'Dope. Picture books. Cathcart had go. Lunceford on posse what got dope and hung out Nite Owl. F.I.'s on Stomp so Deucey stole. Man said scare Patchett. Two birds one stone Duke and Mal. Mal wanted money 'cause he knew man on posse.'

'Give me Dudley. Say Dudley Smith was your partner.'

Vincennes squatted down. The restaurant boomed: millions of voices. Blood on the counter – Ed thought of David Mertens. A flash – the Dieterling studio school – a mile from Billy D.'s house. 'Abe, he can't hurt you now.'

Kikey started choking.

'Abe – '

'Can too hurt can too.'

Fading – Trash slammed his chest. 'You fuck, give us something!'

Kikey mumbled, pulled a gold star off his neck. 'Mitzvah. Johnny wants jail guys out. Q train. Dot got guns.'

Vincennes, looking crazed. 'It's a train, not a bus. It's a crash-out. Davey G. knew about it, he was rambling. Exley, the cute train, the *Q train*. Cohen said the guys from the jail bid are on it.'

Ed grabbed at it, caught it. 'YOU CALL.'

Trash ran out. Ed stood up, breathed chaos: cops, shattered glass, an ambulance backed through the window loading bodies. Bud White shouting orders, a little girl in a blood-spattered dress eating a doughnut.

Trash came back – more crazed. 'The train left L.A. ten minutes ago. Thirty-two inmates in one car, and the phone on board's out. I called Kleckner and told him to find Dot Rothstein. This was a set-up, Captain. Kleckner never left White that memo – this had to be Dudley.'

Ed shut his eyes.

'Exley – '

'All right, you and White go to the train. I'll call the Sheriff's and Highway Patrol and have them set up a diversion.'

White walked over, winked at Ed. He said, 'Thanks for the push,' stepped on Kikey T.'s face until he quit breathing.

Chapter Seventy-five

A motorcycle escort met them, shot them out the Pomona Freeway. Half the stretch elevated: you could see the California Central tracks, a single train running north – a freight carrier, inmate cargo in the third car – barred windows, steel-reinforced doors. Surface streets outside Fontana – up to hills abutting the tracks – and a small standing army.

Nine prowl cars, sixteen men with gas masks and riot pumps. Sharpshooters in the hills, two machinegunners, three guys with smoke grenades. At the edge of the curve: a big buck deer on the tracks.

A deputy handed them shotguns, gas masks. 'Your pal Kleckner called the command post, said that Rothstein woman was DOA at her apartment. She either hanged herself or somebody hanged her. Either way, we gotta assume she got the guns on. There's four guards and six crewmen on board that train. We stand ready with smoke and call for the password – every prison chain's got one. We hear the okay, we call a warning and wait. No okay, we go in.'

A train whistle blew. Somebody yelled, 'Now!'

The sharpshooters ducked down. The gas men hugged the ground. The fire team ran behind a pine row – Bud found a tree up close. Jack took a spot beside him.

The train made the curve – brakes caught, sparks on the tracks. The engine car stopped – nose up to the obstruction.

Megaphone: 'Sheriff's! Identify yourself with the password!'

Silence – ten seconds' worth. Bud eyeballed the engine car window – blue denim flashed.

'Sheriff's! Identify yourself with the password!'

Silence – then a fake bird call.

The gas men hit the windows – grenades broke glass, slipped between the bars. Tommygunners charged car 3 – full clips took down the door.

Smoke, screams.

Somebody yelled, 'Now!'

Smoke out the door – men in khaki running through it. A sharpshooter picked one off; somebody yelled, 'No, they're ours!'

Cops swarmed the car – masks on, shotguns up. Jack grabbed Bud. 'They're not in that one!'

Bud ran, hit the car 4 platform. Open the door – a dead guard just inside, inmates running helter-skelter.

Bud fired, pumped, fired – three went down, one aimed a handgun. Bud pumped, fired, missed – a crate beside the man exploded. Jack jumped on the platform – the inmate squeezed a shot. Jack caught it in the face, spun, hit the tracks.

The shooter ran. Bud pumped, hit empty. He dropped his shotgun, pulled his .38 – one, two, three, four, five, six shots – hits in the back, he was killing a dead man. Noise outside the car – convicts on the tracks by Trashcan's body. Deputies behind them firing close – buckshot and blood, black/red air.

A smoke bomb exploded – Bud ran into #5 gagging. Gunfire: white guys in denim shooting colored guys in denim, guards in khaki shooting both of them. He jumped the train, ran for the trees.

Bodies on the tracks.

Convicts picked off sitting duck-style.

Bud hit the pines, hit his car, gunned it over the tracks dragging the axles. Into a gully, fishtailing down, tires sliding on gravel. A tall man standing by a car. Bud saw who he was, aimed straight for him.

The man ran. Bud sideswiped the car, skidded to a stop. He got out – groggy, bloody from a crack on the dash. Deuce Perkins walked up shooting.

Bud caught one in the leg, one in the side. Two misses, a hit in the shoulder. Another miss – Perkins dropped the gun, pulled a knife. Bud saw rings on his fingers.

Deuce stabbed. Bud felt his chest rip, tried to make fists, couldn't. Deuce lowered his face, smirked – Bud kneed him in the balls and bit his nose off. Perkins shrieked; Bud bit into his arm, threw his weight down.

They tumbled. Perkins made animal noises. Bud thrashed his head, felt the arm rip out of its socket.

Deuce dropped the knife. Bud picked it up – blinded by rings that killed women. He dropped the knife, beat Perkins to death with his own two wounded hands.

Chapter Seventy-six

The Patchett estate in ruins – two acres of soot, debris. Shingles on the lawn, a scorched palm tree in the pool. The house itself rubble – collapsed stucco, soaked ashes. Find a booby-trapped safe inside a six-trillion-square-inch perimeter.

Ed kicked through the rubble. David Mertens hovered – he had to be *there*, it was just too right.

The floor collapsed into the foundation blocks – timber to be cleared away. Wood heaps, mounds of sodden fabric – no telltale metal glints. A ten-man/one-week job, a tech for the booby trap. Around to the yard.

A cement back porch – a slab with fried furniture. Solid cement – no cracks, no grooves, no obvious access to a safe hole. The pool house another rubble heap.

Wood three feet high – too much work if Mertens was *there*. Circuit the pool – burned chairs, a diving platform. A handgrenade pin floating in the water.

Ed kicked the floating palm tree. Porcelain chips in the fronds; a piece of shrapnel embedded in the trunk. Down prone, squinting: capsules in the water, black squares that looked like detonator caps. The shallow end steps exploded plaster – metal grids showing, more pills. Check the lawn – extra-scorched grass running from the pool to the house.

Access to the safe. Grenade and dynamite safeguards. Flames shooting to the terminus, defusing the booby trap – just maybe.

Ed jumped in the water, tore at the plaster – pills and bubbles broke to the surface. Two-handed rips – plaster, water, bubbles, a swinging metal door. Pill eruptions, folders under plastic, plastic over cash and white powder. Loads and loads and loads – then nothing but a deep black hole. Sopping-wet runs to his car – the sun beat down – he was almost dry when he got the stash loaded. One last trip in case HE was THERE: pills scooped from the deep end.

The car heater warmed him up. He drove to the Dieterling school, bolted the fence.

Quiet – Saturday – no classes. A typical playground – basketball hoops, softball diamonds. Moochie Mouse on everything – backboards to base markers.

Ed walked to the south fence perimeter – the closest route from Billy Dieterling's house. Gristled skin on chain links – handholds up and over. Dark dots on faded asphalt – blood, an easy trail.

Across the playground, down steps to a boiler room door. Blood on the knob, a light on inside. He took out Bud White's spare, walked in.

David Mertens shivering in a corner. A hot room – the man sweating up bloody clothes. He showed his teeth, twisted his mouth into a screech. Ed threw the pills at him.

He grabbed them, gagged them down. Ed aimed at his mouth, couldn't pull the trigger. Mertens stared at him. Something strange happened with time – it left them alone. Mertens fell asleep, his lips curled over his gums. Ed looked at his face, tried for some outrage. He still couldn't kill him.

Time came back: the wrong way. Trials, sanity hearings, Preston Exley reviled for letting this monster go free. Time hard on the trigger – he still couldn't do it.

Ed picked the man up, carried him out to his car.

Pacific Sanitarium – Malibu Canyon. Ed told the gate guard to send down Dr. Lux – Captain Exley wanted to pay back his favor.

The guard pointed him to a space. Ed parked, ripped off Mertens' shirt. Brutal – the man was one huge scar.

Lux headed over. Ed pulled out two bags of powder, two stacks of thousand-dollar bills. He placed them on the hood, rolled down the rear windows.

459

Lux walked up, checked the back seat. 'I know that work. That's Douglas Dieterling.'

'Just like that?'

Lux tapped the powder. 'The late Pierce Patchett's? Let's not be outraged, Captain. The last I heard you were no Cub Scout. And what is it that you wish?'

'That man taken care of on a locked ward for the rest of his life.'

'I find that acceptable. Is this compassion or the desire to spare our future governor's reputation?'

'I don't know.'

'Not a typical Exley answer. Enjoy the grounds, Captain. I'll have my orderlies clean up here.'

Ed walked to a terrace, looked at the ocean. Sun, waves – maybe some sharks out feeding. A radio snapped on behind him. ' . . . so for more on that thwarted prison train break. A Highway Patrol spokesman told reporters that the death toll now stands at twenty-eight inmates, seven guards and crew members. Four deputy sheriffs were injured and Sergeant John Vincennes, celebrated Los Angeles policeman and the former technical advisor to the *Badge of Honor* TV show, was shot and killed. Sergeant Vincennes' partner, LAPD Sergeant Wendell White, is in critical condition at Fontana General Hospital. White pursued and killed the crash-out's pickup man, identified as Burt Arthur "Deuce" Perkins, a nightclub entertainer with underworld connections. A team of doctors are now striving to save the valiant officer's life, although he is not expected to live. Captain George Rachlis of the California Highway Patrol calls this tragedy – '

The ocean blurred through his tears. White winked and said, 'Thanks for the push.' Ed turned around. The monster, the dope, the money – gone.

Chapter Seventy-seven

The pool stash: twenty-one pounds of heroin, $871,400, carbons of Sid Hudgens' dirt files. Included: blackmail photos, records of Pierce Patchett's criminal enterprises. The name 'Dudley Smith' did not appear – nor did the names of John Stompanato, Burt Arthur Perkins, Abe Teitlebaum, Lee Vachss, Dot Rothstein, Sergeant Mike Breuning, Officer Dick Carlisle. Coleman Stein, Sal Bonventre, George Magdaleno – killed in the crash-out. Davey Goldman reinterviewed at Camarillo State Hospital – he could not give a coherent statement. The Los Angeles County Coroner's Office ruled Dot Rothstein's death a suicide. David Mertens stayed in locked-ward custody at Pacific Sanitarium. Relatives of the three innocent citizens killed at Abe's Noshery brought suit against the LAPD for reckless endangerment. The crash-out received national news coverage, was labeled the 'Blue Denim Massacre.' Surviving inmates told sheriff's detectives that squabbling among the armed prisoners resulted in guns changing hands – soon every inmate on the train was free. Racial tensions flared up, aborting the crash-out before the authorities arrived.

Jack Vincennes was posthumously awarded the LAPD's Medal of Valor. No LAPD men were invited to the funeral – the widow refused an audience with Captain Ed Exley.

Bud White refused to die. He remained in intensive care at Fontana General Hospital. He survived massive shock, neurological trauma, the loss of over half the blood in his body. Lynn Bracken stayed with him. He could not speak, but responded to questions with nods. Chief Parker presented him with his Medal of Valor. White freed an arm from a traction sling, threw the medal in his face.

Ten days passed.

A warehouse in San Pedro burned to the ground –
remnants of pornographic books were discovered. Detectives labeled the fire 'professional arson,' reported no
leads. The building was owned by Pierce Patchett. Chester
Yorkin and Lorraine Malvasi were reinterrogated. They
offered no salient information, were released from custody.

Ed Exley burned the heroin, kept the files and the
money. His final Nite Owl report omitted mention of
Dudley Smith and the fact that David Mertens, now the
object of an all-points bulletin for his murders of Sid
Hudgens, Billy Dieterling and Jerry Marsalas, was also
the 1934 slayer of Wee Willie Wennerholm and five other
children. Preston Exley's name was not spoken in any
context.

Chief Parker held a press conference. He announced
that the Nite Owl case had been solved – correctly this
time. The gunmen were Burt Arthur 'Deuce' Perkins,
Lee Vachss, Abraham 'Kikey' Teitlebaum – their motive
to kill Dean Van Gelder, an ex-convict masquerading as
the incorrectly identified Delbert 'Duke' Cathcart. The
shootings were conceived as a terror tactic, an attempt to
take over the vice kingdom of Pierce Morehouse Patchett,
a recent murder victim himself. The State Attorney General's Office reviewed Captain Ed Exley's 114-page case
summary and announced that it was satisfied. Ed Exley
again received credit for breaking the Nite Owl murder
case. He was promoted to inspector in a televised ceremony.

The next day Preston Exley announced that he would
seek the Republican Party's gubernatorial nomination. He
shot to the front of a hastily conducted poll.

Johnny Stompanato returned from Acapulco, moved
into Lana Turner's house in Beverly Hills. He remained
there, never venturing outside, the object of a constant
surveillance supervised by Sergeants Duane Fisk and Don
Kleckner. Chief Parker and Ed Exley referred to him as
their Nite Owl 'Addendum' – the living perpetrator to
feed the public now that they were temporarily mollified

with dead killers. When Stompanato left Beverly Hills for Los Angeles City proper, he would be arrested. Parker wanted a clean front-page arrest just over the city line – he was willing to wait for it.

The Nite Owl case and the murders of Billy Dieterling and Jerry Marsalas remained news. They were never speculatively connected. Timmy Valburn refused to comment. Raymond Dieterling issued a press release expressing grief over the loss of his son. He closed down Dream-a-Dreamland for a one-month period of mourning. He remained in seclusion at his house in Laguna Beach, attended to by his friend and aide Inez Soto.

Sergeant Mike Breuning and Officer Dick Carlisle remained on emergency leave.

Captain Dudley Smith remained front stage center throughout the post-reopening round of press conferences and LAPD/D.A.'s Office meetings. He served as toast-master at Thad Green's surprise party honoring Inspector Ed Exley. He did not appear in any way flustered knowing that Johnny Stompanato remained at large, was under twenty-four-hour surveillance and thus immune to assassination. He did not seem to care that Stompanato would be arrested in the near future.

Preston Exley, Raymond Dieterling and Inez Soto did not contact Ed Exley to congratulate him on his promotion and reversal of bad press.

Ed knew they knew. He assumed Dudley knew. Vincennes dead, White fighting to live. Only he and Bob Gallaudet knew – and Gallaudet knew nothing pertaining to his father and the Atherton case.

Ed wanted to kill Dudley outright.

Gallaudet said, kill yourself instead, that's what you'd be doing.

They decided to wait it out, do it right.

Bud White made the wait unbearable.

He had tubes in his arms, splints on his fingers. His chest held three hundred stitches. Bullets had shattered bones, ripped arteries. He had a plate in his head. Lynn Bracken tended to him – she could not meet Ed's eyes.

White could not talk – being able to talk in the future was doubtful. His eyes were eloquent: Dudley. Your father. What are you going to do about it? He kept trying to make the V-for-victory sign. Three visits, Ed finally got it: the Victory Motel, Mobster Squad HQ.

He went there. He found detailed notes on White's prostitute-killing investigation. The notes were a limited man reaching for the stars, pulling most of them down. Limits exceeded through a brilliantly persistent rage. Absolute justice – anonymous, no rank and glory. A single line on the Englekling brothers that told him their killer still walked free. Room 11 at the Victory Motel – Wendell 'Bud' White seen for the first time.

Ed knew why he sent him there – and followed up.

A phone company check, one interview – all it took. Confirmation, an epigraph to build on it: Absolute Justice. The TV news said Ray Dieterling walked through Dream-a-Dreamland every day – easing his grief in a deserted fantasy kingdom. He'd give Bud White a full day of his justice.

Good Friday, 1958. The A.M. news showed Preston Exley entering St. James Episcopal Church. Ed drove to City Hall, walked up to Ellis Loew's office.

Still early – no receptionist. Loew at his desk, reading. Ed rapped on the door.

Loew glanced up. 'Inspector Ed. Have a chair.'

'I'll stand.'

'Oh? Is this business?'

'Of sorts. Last month Bud White called you from San Francisco and told you Spade Cooley was a sex killer. You said you'd put a D.A.'s Bureau team on it, and you didn't. Cooley has donated in excess of fifteen thousand dollars to your slush fund. You called the Biltmore Hotel from your place in Newport and talked to a member of Cooley's band. You told him to warn Spade and the rest of the guys that a crazy cop was going to come around and cause trouble. White braced Deuce Perkins, the real killer. Perkins sent him after Spade, he probably thought he'd kill

464

him and save him from the rap. Perkins was warned by you and went into hiding. He stayed out long enough to turn White into a vegetable.'

Loew, calm. 'You can't prove any of that. And since when are you so concerned about White?'

Ed laid a folder on his desk. 'Sid Hudgens had a file on you. Contribution shakedowns, felony indictments you dismissed for money. He's got the McPherson tank job documented, and Pierce Patchett had a photograph of you sucking a male prostitute's dick. Resign from office or it all goes public.'

Loew – sheet white. 'I'll take you with me.'

'Do it. I'd enjoy the ride.'

He saw it from the freeway: Rocketland and Paul's World juxtaposed – a spaceship growing out of a mountain, a big empty parking lot. He took surface streets to the gate, showed the guard his shield. The man nodded, swung the fence open.

Two figures strolled the Grand Promenade. Ed parked, walked up to them. Dream-a-Dreamland stood hear-a-pin-drop silent.

Inez saw him – a pivot, a hand on Dieterling's arm. They whispered; Inez walked off.

Dieterling turned. 'Inspector.'

'Mr. Dieterling.'

'It's Ray. And I'm tempted to say what took you so long.'

'You knew I'd be coming?'

'Yes. Your father disagreed and went on with his plans, but I knew better. And I'm grateful for the chance to tell it here.'

Paul's World across from them – fake snow near blinding. Dieterling said, 'Your father, Pierce and I were dreamers. Pierce's dreams were twisted, mine were kind and good. Your father's dreams were ruthless – as I suspect yours are. You should know that before you judge me.'

Ed leaned against a rail, settled in. Dieterling spoke to his mountain.

1920.

His first wife, Margaret, died in an automobile accident – she bore his son Paul. 1924 – his second wife, Janice, gave birth to son Billy. While married to Margaret, he had an affair with a disturbed woman named Faye Borchard. She gave him son Douglas in 1917. He gave her money to keep the boy's existence secret – he was a rising young filmmaker, wished a life free of complications, was willing to pay for it. Only he and Faye knew the facts of Douglas' parentage. Douglas knew Ray Dieterling as a kindly friend.

Douglas grew up with his mother; Dieterling visited frequently, a two-family life: wife Margaret dead, sons Paul and Billy ensconced with himself and wife Janice – a sad woman who went on to divorce him.

Faye Borchard drank laudanum. She made Douglas watch pornographic cartoons that Raymond made for money, part of a Pierce Patchett scheme – cash to finance their legitimate dealings. The films were erotic, horrific – they featured flying monsters that raped and killed. The concept was Patchett's – he put his narcotic fantasies on paper, handed Ray Dieterling an inkwell. Douglas became obsessed with flight and its sexual possibilities.

Dieterling loved his son Douglas – despite his rages and fits of strange behavior. He despised his son Paul – who was petty, tyrannical, stupid. Douglas and Paul greatly resembled each other.

Ray Dieterling grew famous; Douglas Borchard grew wild. He lived with Faye, watched his father's cartoon nightmares – birds plucking children out of schoolyards – Patchett fantasies painted on film. He grew into his teens stealing, torturing animals, hiding out in skid row strip shows. He met Loren Atherton on the row – that evil man found an accomplice.

Atherton's obsession was dismemberment; Douglas' obsession was flight. They shared an interest in photography, were sexually aroused by children. They spawned the idea of creating children to their own specifications.

They began killing and building hybrid children, photo-

466

graphing their works in progress. Douglas killed birds to provide wings for their creations. They needed a beautiful face; Douglas suggested Wee Willie Wennerholm's – it would be a kindly nod to kindly 'Uncle Ray' – whose early work he found so exciting. They snatched Wee Willie, butchered him.

The newspapers called the child killer 'Dr. Frankenstein' – it was assumed there was only one assailant. Inspector Preston Exley commanded the police investigation. He learned of Loren Atherton, a paroled child molester. He arrested Atherton, discovered his storage garage abattoir, his collection of photographs. Atherton confessed to the crimes, said that they were his work solely, did not implicate Douglas and stated his desire to die as the King of Death. The press lauded Inspector Exley, echoed his appeal: citizens with information on Atherton were asked to come forth as witnesses.

Ray Dieterling visited Douglas. Alone in his room, he discovered a trunk full of slaughtered birds, a child's fingers packed in dry ice. He *knew* immediately.

And felt responsible – his quick-buck obscenities had created a monster. He confronted Douglas, learned that he might have been seen at the school near the time Wee Willie was kidnapped.

Protective measures:

A psychiatrist bribed to silence diagnosed Douglas: a psychotic personality, his disorder compounded by chemical brain imbalances. Remedy: the proper drugs applied for life to keep him docile. Ray Dieterling was friends with Pierce Patchett – a chemist who dabbled in such drugs. Pierce for inner protection – Pierce's friend Terry Lux for the outer.

Lux cut Douglas a whole new face. Atherton's lawyer stalled the trial. Preston Exley kept looking for witnesses – a well-publicized search. Ray Dieterling treaded panic – then formed a bold plan.

He fed drugs to Douglas and young Miller Stanton. He coached them to say they saw Loren Atherton, *alone*, kidnap Wee Willie Wennerholm – they were afraid to come forth until now – afraid Dr. Frankenstein would get them. The boys told Preston Exley their story; he believed them; they identified the monster. Atherton did not recognize his surgically altered friend.

Two years passed. Loren Atherton was tried, convicted, executed. Terry Lux cut Douglas again – destroying his resemblance to the witness boy. Douglas lived in Pierce Patchett sedation, a room at a private hospital – guarded by male nurses. Ray Dieterling became even more successful. Then Preston Exley knocked on his door.

His news: a young girl, older now, had come forth. She had seen Dieterling's son Paul with Loren Atherton – at the school the day Wee Willie was kidnapped.

Dieterling knew it was really Douglas – his resemblance to Paul was that strong. He offered Exley a large amount of money to desist. Exley took the money – then attempted to return it. He said, 'Justice. I want to arrest the boy.'

Dieterling saw his empire ruined. He saw the petty and mindless Paul exonerated. He saw Douglas somehow captured – destroyed for the grief his art had spawned. He insisted that Exley keep the money – Exley did not protest. He asked him if there was no other way.

Exley asked him if Paul was guilty.

Raymond Dieterling said, 'Yes.'

Preston Exley said, 'Execution.'

Raymond Dieterling agreed.

He took Paul camping in the Sierra Nevada. Preston Exley was waiting. They dosed the boy's food; Exley shot him in his sleep and buried him. The world thought Paul was lost in an avalanche – the world believed the lie. Dieterling thought he would hate the man. The price of justice on his face told him he was just another victim. They shared a bond now. Preston Exley gave up police work to build buildings with Dieterling seed money. When Thomas Exley was killed, Ray Dieterling was the first one he called. Together they built from the weight of their dead.

Dieterling ended it. 'And all of this is my rather pathetic happy ending.'

Mountains, rockets, rivers – they all seemed to smile. 'My father never knew about Douglas? He really thought Paul was guilty?'

'Yes. Will you forgive me? In your father's name.'

Ed took out a clasp. Gold oak-leafs – Preston Exley's inspector's insignia. A hand-me-down – Thomas got it first. 'No. I'm going to submit a report to the county grand jury requesting that you be indicted for the murder of your son.'

'A week to get my affairs in order? Where could I run to, someone as famous as I am.'

Ed said, 'Yes,' walked to his car.

The freeway model gone – replaced by campaign posters. Art De Spain unpacking leaflets, no arm bandage – a textbook bullet scar. 'Hello, Eddie.'

'Where's Father?'

'He'll be back soon. And congratulations on inspector. I should have called you, but things have been hectic around here.'

'Father hasn't called me either. You're all pretending everything's fine.'

'Eddie . . .'

A bulge on Art's left hip – he still carried a piece. 'I just spoke to Ray Dieterling.'

'We didn't think you would.'

'Give me your gun, Art.'

De Spain handed it over butt first. Silencer threads, S&W.38s.

'Why?'

'Eddie . . .'

Ed dumped the shells. 'Dieterling told me everything. And you were Father's exec back then.'

The man looked proud. 'You know my M.O., Sunny Jim. It was for Preston. I've always been his loyal adjutant.'

'And you knew about Paul Dieterling.'

De Spain took his gun back. 'Yes, and I've known for years that he wasn't the real killer. I got a tip back in '48 or so. It placed the kid somewhere else at the time of the Wennerholm snatch. I didn't know if Ray gave Paul over legitimately or not, and I couldn't break Preston's heart by telling him he killed an innocent boy. I couldn't upset his friendship with Ray – it just would have hurt him too much. You know how the Atherton case has always driven me. I've always had to know who killed those kids.'

'And you never found out.'

De Spain shook his head. 'No.'

Ed said, 'Get to the Englekling brothers.'

Art picked up a poster: Preston backdropped by building grids. 'I was visiting the Bureau. I know it was '53, right in there. I saw these pictures on the Ad Vice board. Nice-looking kids, like a stag-shot daisy chain. The design reminded me of the pictures Loren Atherton took, and I knew that just Preston and I and a few other officers had seen them. I tried to track down the pictures and didn't get anywhere. A while later I heard how the Englekling brothers gave that smut testimony for the Nite Owl investigation, but you didn't follow up on it. I figured they were a lead, but I couldn't find them. Late last year I got a tip that they were working at this printshop up near Frisco. I went up to talk to them. All I wanted was to find out who made that smut.'

White's notes: God-awful torture. 'Just to talk to them? I *know* what happened there.'

Awful pride glaring. 'They took it for a shakedown. It went bad. They had some old smut negatives, and I tried to get them to ID the people. They had some heroin and some antipsychotic drugs. They said they knew a sugar daddy who was going to push some horse blend that would set the world on fire, but they could do better. They laughed at me, called me "pops." I got this notion that they had to know who made that smut. I don't know . . . I know I went crazy. I think I thought they killed all those children. I think I thought they'd hurt Preston somehow. Eddie, they *laughed* at me. I figured they were dope pushers, I figured next to Preston they were nothing. And this old man took them both out.'

He'd fretted the poster to shreds. 'You killed two men for nothing.'

'Not for nothing. For Preston. And I beg you not to tell him.'

'Just another victim' – maybe the victim that justice lets slide.

'Eddie, he can't know. And he can't know that Paul Dieterling was innocent. Eddie, please.'

Ed pushed him aside, walked through the house. His mother's tapestries made him think of Lynn. His old room made him think of Bud and Jack. The house felt filthy – bad money bought and paid for. He walked downstairs, saw his father in the doorway.

'Edmund?'

'I'm arresting you for the murder of Paul Dieterling. I'll be by in a few days to take you in.'

The man did not budge an inch. 'Paul Dieterling was a psychopathic killer who richly deserved the punishment I gave him.'

'He was innocent. And it's Murder One either way.'

Not one flicker of remorse. Unbudging, unyielding, unflinching, intractable rectitude. 'Edmund, you're quite disturbed at this moment.'

Ed walked past him. His goodbye: 'Goddamn you for the bad things you made me.'

Downtown to the Dining Car: a bright place full of nice people. Gallaudet at the bar, sipping a martini. 'Bad news on Dudley. You don't want to hear this.'

'It can't be any worse than some other things I've heard today.'

'Yeah? Well, Dudley's scot-free. Lana Turner's daughter just knifed Johnny Stompanato. D.O. fucking A. Fisk was staked out across the street and saw the meat wagon and the Beverly Hills P.D. take Johnny away. No Dudley witness, no Dudley evidence. Grand, lad.'

Ed grabbed the martini, killed it. 'Fuck Dudley sideways. I've got a shitload of Patchett's money for a bank-roll, and I'll burn down that Irish cocksucker if it's the last fucking thing I ever do. *Lad*.'

Gallaudet laughed. 'May I make an observation, Inspector?'

'Sure.'

'You sound more like Bud White every day.'

CALENDAR

APRIL 1958

EXTRACT: L.A. *Times*, April 12:

GRAND JURY REVIEWS NITE OWL EVIDENCE; DECLARES CASE CLOSED

Almost five years to the day after the crime, the City and County of Los Angeles bid official farewell to the Southland's 'Crime of the Century,' the infamous Nite Owl murder case.

On April 16, 1953, three gunmen entered the Nite Owl Coffee Shop on Hollywood Boulevard and shot-gunned three employees and three patrons to death. Robbery was the assumed motive, and suspicion soon fell on three Negro youths, who were arrested on suspicion of the crime. The three: Raymond Coates, Tyrone Jones and Leroy Fontaine, escaped from jail and were killed resisting arrest. The three allegedly confessed to District Attorney Ellis Loew prior to their escape, and the case was assumed to have been solved.

Four years and ten months later, a San Quentin inmate, Otis John Shortell, came forward with infor-mation that led many to believe that the three youths were innocent of the Nite Owl killings. Shortell said that he was in the presence of Coates, Jones and Fontaine while they were engaged in the gang rape of a young woman, at the exact time of the coffee

472

shop slaughter. Shortell's testimony, verified by lie detector tests, created a public clamor to reopen the case.

The clamor was fanned by the February 25 murders of Peter and Baxter Englekling. The brothers, convicted narcotics traffickers, were material witnesses to the 1953 Nite Owl investigation and asserted at that time that the killings originated from a web of intrigue involving pornography. The Englekling killings remain unsolved. In the words of Marin County Sheriff's Lieutenant Eugene Hatcher, 'No leads at all. But we're still trying.'

The Nite Owl case was reopened, and an involved pornography link was revealed. On March 27, wealthy investor Pierce Morehouse Patchett was shot and killed at his Brentwood home, and two days later police shot and killed Abraham Teitlebaum, 49, and Lee Peter Vachss, 44, his assumed slayers. Later that day the infamous 'Blue Denim Massacre' occurred. Among the criminal dead: Burt Arthur 'Deuce' Perkins, a nightclub singer with underworld ties. Teitlebaum, Vachss and Perkins were assumed to be the Nite Owl killers. LAPD Captain Dudley Smith elaborated.

'The Nite Owl killings derived from a grandly realized scheme to distribute heinous and soul-destroying pornographic filth. Teitlebaum, Vachss and Perkins were attempting to kill Nite Owl patron Delbert "Duke" Cathcart, an independent smut merchant, and take over Pierce Patchett's smut racket in the process. Alas, it was really one Dean Van Gelder, a criminal impersonating Cathcart, who was there in Cathcart's place. The Nite Owl murder case will go down as a testimony to the cruel caprices of fate, and I am glad that it has finally been resolved.'

Then Captain, now Inspector Edmund Exley, credited with solving the Nite Owl reopening case, said that it has finally been resolved, despite rumors that a fourth conspirator died abruptly, just as he was about to be arrested. 'That's nonsense,' Exley said. 'I gave the county grand jury a detailed brief on the case and testified extensively myself. They accepted my findings. It's over.'

At some great cost. LAPD Chief of Detectives Thad Green, soon to retire and assume command of the U.S. Border Patrol, said, 'For sheer expense and the number of accumulated investigatory man-hours, the Nite Owl case has no equal. It was a once-in-a-lifetime case and the price for clearing it was very, very high.'

EXTRACT: L.A. *Mirror-News*, April 15:

LOEW RESIGNATION A SHOCKER; LEGAL CROWD BUZZES

Speculation in Southland legal circles rages: why did Los Angeles District Attorney Ellis Loew resign from office yesterday and scotch a brilliant political career? Loew, 49, announced his resignation at his regular weekly press conference, citing nervous exhaustion and a desire to return to private practice. Aides close to the man described the abrupt retirement as stupefyingly atypical. The D.A.'s Office is stunned: Ellis Loew appeared happy, fit and in perfect health.

Chief Criminal Prosecutor Robert Gallaudet told this reporter: 'Look, I'm stunned, and I don't stun easily. What's Ellis' underlying motive? I don't know, ask him. And when the City Council appoints an interim D.A., I hope it's me.'

After the shock waves subsided, plaudits rolled in. LAPD Chief William H. Parker described Loew as a 'vigorous and fair-minded foe of criminals,' and Parker's aide, Captain Dudley Smith, said, 'We'll miss Ellis. He was a grand friend of justice.' Governor Knight and Mayor Norris Poulson sent Loew telegrams asking him to reconsider his decision. Loew himself could not be reached for comment.

EXTRACT: L.A. *Herald-Express*, April 19:

DREAM-A-DREAMLAND SUICIDES: GRIEF, BEWILDERMENT CONTINUE

They were found together at Dream-a-Dreamland, temporarily closed to mourn the death of a great man's son. Preston Exley, 64, former Los Angeles policeman, master builder and neophyte politician; Inez Soto, 28, publicity director at the world's most celebrated amusement complex and a key witness in the awful Nite Owl murder case. And Raymond Dieterling, 66, the father of modern animation, the genius who virtually created the cartoon art form, the man who built Dream-a-Dreamland as a tribute to a child tragically lost. The world at large and Los Angeles in particular have expressed great grief and bewilderment.

They were found last week, together, on Dream-a-Dreamland's Grand Promenade. There were no notes, but County Coroner Frederic Newbarr quickly ruled out foul play and established the deaths as suicides. The means: all three had ingested fatal quantities of a rare antipsychotic drug. Expressions of grief greeted the news – President Eisenhower, Governor Knight and Senator William Knowland were among those who offered condolences to the loved ones of the three. Exley and Dieterling left fortunes: the building magnate willed his construction kingdom to his longtime aide Arthur De Spain and his $17-million financial estate to his son Edmund, a Los Angeles police officer. Dieterling left his more than vast holdings to a legal trust, with instructions to disperse the funds and future Dream-a-Dreamland profits among various children's charities. With the legalities taken care of and public shock and bereavement hardly abating, speculation into the motives for the suicides began to rage.

Miss Soto was romantically linked to Preston Exley's son Edmund and had been despondent over recent publicity pertaining to her involvement in the Nite Owl case. Raymond Dieterling was distraught over the recent murder of his son William. Preston Exley, however, had recently celebrated his greatest triumph, the completion of the Southern California mass freeway system, and had just announced his candidacy in the governor's race. A poll conducted shortly before his death showed him gaining and favored to win the Republican nomination. There seems to be no logical motive for the man to take his own life. Those closest to Preston Exley – Arthur De Spain and son Edmund – have refused comment.

Letters of sympathy and floral tributes flood Dream-a-Dreamland and Preston Exley's Hancock Park home. Flags fly at half mast throughout the State of California. Hollywood grieves the loss of a moviemaking colossus. The single word 'Why?' rests on millions of lips.

Preston Exley and Ray Dieterling were giants. Inez Soto was a spunky hard-luck girl who became their trusted aide and close friend. Before their deaths, all three added codicils to their wills, stating that they wished to be buried at sea together. Yesterday they were, summarily, with no religious service and no guests in attendance. The Dream-a-Dreamland security chief handled the arrangements and would not disclose the location where the bodies were laid to rest. The word 'Why?' still rests on millions of lips.

Mayor Norris Poulson doesn't know why. But he does offer a fitting eulogy. 'Very simply, these two men symbolized the fulfillment of a vision – Los Angeles as a place of enchantment and high-quality everyday life. More than anyone else, Raymond Dieterling and Preston Exley personified the grand and good dreams that have built this city.'

476

Part Five

After You've Gone

Chapter Seventy-eight

Ed in his dress blue uniform.

Parker smiled, pinned gold stars to his shoulders. 'Deputy Chief Edmund Exley. Chief of Detectives, Los Angeles Police Department.'

Applause, flashbulbs. Ed shook Parker's hand, checked the crowd. Politicos, Thad Green, Dudley Smith. Lynn at the back of the room.

More applause, a handshake line. Mayor Poulson, Gallaudet, Dudley.

'Lad, you have performed so grandly. I look forward to serving under you.'

'Thank you, Captain. I'm sure we'll have a grand time together.'

Dudley winked.

The City Council filed by; Parker led the crowd to refreshments. Lynn stayed in the doorway.

Ed walked over. Lynn said, 'I can't believe it. I'm giving up a hotshot with seventeen million dollars for a cripple with a pension. Arizona, love. The air's good for pensioners and I know where everything is.'

She'd aged the past month – beautiful to handsome. 'When?'

'Right now, before I back down.'

'Open your purse.'

'What?'

'Just do it.'

Lynn opened her purse – Ed dropped in a plastic bundle. 'Spend it fast, it's bad money.'

'How much?'

'Enough to buy Arizona. Where's White?'

'At the car.'

'I'll walk you.'

They skirted the party, took side stairs down. Lynn's

479

Packard in the watch commander's space, a summons stuck to the windshield. Ed tore it up, checked the back seat.

Bud White. Braces on his legs, his head shaved and sutured. No splints on his hands – they looked strong. A wired-up mouth that made him look goofy.

Lynn stood a few feet away. White tried to smile, grimaced. Ed said, 'I swear to you I'll get Dudley. I swear to you I'll do it.'

White grabbed his hands, squeezed until they both winced. Ed said, 'Thanks for the push.'

A smile, a laugh – Bud forced them through wires. Ed touched his face. 'You were my redemption.'

Party noise upstairs – Dudley Smith laughing. Lynn said, 'We should go now.'

'Was I ever in the running?'

'Some men get the world, some men get ex-hookers and a trip to Arizona. You're in with the former, but my God I don't envy you the blood on your conscience.'

Ed kissed her cheek. Lynn got in the car, rolled up the windows. Bud pressed his hands to the glass.

Ed touched his side, palms half the man's size. The car moved – Ed ran with it, hands against hands. A turn into traffic, a goodbye toot on the horn.

Gold stars. Alone with his dead.